# Fires Of Desire

The horses nickered quietly in acknowledgment of their presence as Adam carried Emma under the tree. He lowered her onto the blanket, but he did not release her. Instead he held her against him with one hand on her waist.

"Adam." The word escaped her lips like a sigh.

"I want you so much, Emma." He pulled her to him and slid both hands inside the web of her hair, cradling her head. "Let me make you a woman."

She wanted to be strong, to dispel this weakness that he had cast over her. But it was a weakness she craved . . . a delicious, engulfing weakness. Yet she knew she had to fight him as she had fought all men who had tried to control her. "I already am a woman, Adam. I'm strong and—"

He drew her head back and gazed into her eyes. "Then let me make you my wife."

\* \* \*

# The Burning Plains

## CATHERINE PALMER

PAGEANT BOOKS

PAGEANT BOOKS
225 Park Avenue South
New York, New York 10003

Copyright © 1988 by Catherine Palmer

Cover artwork by Sharon Spiak

Printed in the U.S.A.

First Pageant Books printing: December, 1988

10 9 8 7 6 5 4 3 2 1

*For Libby, my sister and my friend.*

*For Tim, whose love and labor
helped make this possible.*

*For my parents, who gave me Africa.*

Grateful acknowledgment is given to the sources listed below for permission to reprint the following material:

"The Cowboy" words and music by John A. Lomax and Alan Lomax, copyright © 1938, 1966 by Ludlow Music, Inc., New York. Used by permission.

"The Cowboy's Life" collected by John A. Lomax and Alan Lomax, copyright © 1938, 1966 by Ludlow Music, Inc., New York. Used by permission.

"The Cowboy's Dance Song," "The Cowboy's Meditation," "The Cowman's Prayer," "The Disheartened Ranger," "The Jolly Cowboy," "A Man Named Hods," "Panhandle Cob," "The Range Riders," "Red River Valley," "Rounded Up In Glory," "Rye Whiskey," "The Santa Fe Trail," "Silver Jack," "Speaking Of Cowboy's Home," "Young Champions" collected, adapted, and arranged by John A. Lomax and Alan Lomax, copyright © 1938, 1966 by Ludlow Music, Inc., New York. Used by permission.

"Red River Shore" collected and adapted by John A. Lomax and Alan Lomax, copyright © 1934, 1962 by Ludlow Music, Inc., New York. Used by permission.

"Hell In Texas," "Sweet Betsy From Pike" collected, adapted, and arranged by John A. Lomax and Alan Lomax, copyright © 1934, 1962 by Ludlow Music, Inc., New York. Used by Permission.

Expressions from Cowboy Slang by "Frosty" Potter, copyright © 1986 by Edgar G. Potter. Used by permission of Golden West Publishers.

The Burning Plains

# Chapter One

✦ ✦ ✦ ✦

*Come all you old cow-punchers, a story I will tell,*
*And if you'll all be quiet, I sure will sing it well;*
*And if you boys don't like it, you sure can go to hell.*

—"A Man Named Hods"

*Yet waft me from the harbor-mouth,*
*Wild wind! I seek a warmer sky,*
*And I will see before I die*
*The palms and temples of the South.*

—Alfred, Lord Tennyson
"Saint Agnes' Eve"

*June 1898: Mombasa Harbor*
*British Protectorate of East Africa*

"OH, EMMA—WHAT shall I do?" Priscilla Pickworth lifted her tear-rimmed blue eyes to her sister's face. Sniffling, she raised her white lace handkerchief and dabbed at her cheeks.

Emma sighed inwardly as she looked at her sis-

1

ter. "You will do as you've always done, Cissy. You will put on your brightest smile and bid him farewell as if he didn't mean a thing in the world to you." Stepping back from the open trunk, Emma tossed a pink ostrich-plumed hat onto the bed. "This one will simply have to do, Cissy. We haven't time to look for the white one. Father is already waiting on deck."

"Oh, but Emma, you don't understand. Rolf is different! I do love him—truly!"

Emma buckled the trunk shut and picked up her own lavender hat. How many times had she helped her sister get over a broken heart? She pursed her lips for a moment, then said firmly, "I know you love him. But Cissy, honestly—you've loved them all. You insisted you loved that awful what's-his-name who tried to take you off to Sussex. And you loved that banker fellow who was going to carry you away to France if Father hadn't broken it up and locked you in your room for three days."

"Emma, Rolf isn't like those other men." Cissy sniffled again and ran her delicate fingers through the ostrich plumes. "Rolf is good and kind. He *loves* me, Emma. We want to be *married*."

With another sigh, Emma crossed the floor of the steamship cabin and knelt at her sister's feet. "Cissy dear, you must face the facts. Look at the situation from a practical point of view. Rolf is a soldier. He has no money at all. He's leaving the ship in less than an hour for his post along the border. And Cissy—he's not even English!"

At this Cissy burst into renewed sobs. "Oh, Emma, I know it's hopeless! We'll get off this ship so Father can survey his beloved railway—and I'll never see Rolf again!"

Emma took her sister into her arms. "There, there. It's not so bad." Emma reflected for a moment upon that morning—was it only three weeks ago?—when she and Cissy had been promenading. They had turned a corner and come upon the cluster of young German soldiers. She smiled, remembering the awkward introductions . . . the men gazing in awe of Cissy, as men always did . . . and Cissy's hat blowing, as if on cue, into the arms of the most handsome of all the soldiers. Emma had gone off on her own then—preferring the ocean breeze and the rolling waves to empty chatter. She remembered climbing to the highest deck and standing alone beneath a brilliant azure sky. She had stared out across the empty ocean as if she might catch a glimpse of her future.

The meetings between Rolf and Cissy had all been secret, though of course Emma had known. It was her responsibility to keep Cissy in hand. Fully aware that she was the practical one, Emma had attempted to dissuade her sister from the fruitless course. But perhaps it had been the sea air . . . or the glorious sunshine. . . . At any rate, Emma found her own hours easily consumed with preparations for the two months of adventure awaiting her in the British Protectorate of East Africa.

Books, geographical society pamphlets, maps . . . as she scanned them, she could hardly wait to see the magical land unfold before her. The strange animals seemed to beckon her—lions, giraffes, antelopes, elephants. She tried to envision the snow-capped mountain called Kilimanjaro—and that other, Kenya Mountain, the mist-enshrouded home of the African spirit-god. More important still, this land held hidden promises. Perhaps here she would be able to realize her dream to find a mission hospital where she could practice nursing and escape her father.

"It's lovely for you, Emma!" Cissy said petulantly, breaking into her sister's thoughts. "This is just your sort of thing—savages and wild animals! But where does that leave me? You'll never get married—and Father won't let me marry until you do!"

Emma bit at her lower lip as she straightened her ruffled cuffs. She wished for the thousandth time that Cissy would follow the example she set and take hold of her own life. "Listen, Cissy—you know Father dotes on you. He'll let you marry soon enough, I know he will."

"But I won't have Rolf!"

"But you will have *someone*. Someone who will love you. . . . You'll have children and a happy home—and everything you've dreamed of for such a long time. I just know you will."

"I want to marry Rolf." Cissy wadded her handkerchief into a tiny ball and set her jaw stubbornly.

It was a look Emma knew well enough. With a grin, she gave her sister a hug and set the pink hat on Cissy's head. "There now. Dry your eyes and put on your smile. We really must leave soon. Father's probably getting impatient."

Rising, Emma shook out the folds of her lavender silk skirt and stepped to the mirror on the wall beside the door. Cissy shuffled to her side, and together they adjusted and pinned their hats to the rolls of hair coiled upon their heads. Emma watched Cissy dab at her soft blue eyes, twin sapphires set in porcelain, and pinch her cheeks to bring out the roses. It was easy to see why men were so mad for Cissy, Emma thought. Her sister's hair shone like the sun, and she had curves in all the right places.

Cissy smiled at her reflection, a flash of pearl-white teeth between pink lips. "When I get my inheritance," she said, "I shall have servants with me wherever I go. And then I shall never be without the proper hat for each dress."

Emma watched her sister fussing with the plumes. Did Rolf know Cissy would inherit half of their father's money? she wondered. She would have half, too—if she married a man of her father's choosing. The very thought threw cold water on the embers of hope burning in her breast.

For a moment Emma gazed frankly at her own reflection, then she turned from the mirror to pull on her gloves. Her olive-green eyes were an advantage, she knew, but her hair waved so wildly, and it was that awful wheat color. She ran a hand across her tight corset. How she despised it for conforming her tall, willowy body into the rigidly proper shape! Within its torture, her slender torso and narrow hips were contorted into a wasp-waist that curved out into full hips—looking much as Cissy's did naturally. Her legs were also too long, her neck too thin, and her back too straight for the popular fashions.

What did she care for fashion? Given a choice, she would have preferred diving into the pond with the stableboys at the country estate, or perching atop the haycart, perhaps even learning to ride a horse. She would have loved to wade barefoot in the streams or picnic on an island, given a choice. But then—she never had been given a choice.

Picking up a lavender parasol from beside the

trunk, Emma wandered from the mirror toward the window on the other side of the cabin to wait for Cissy to finish her toilet. From the tiny porthole above her bed she had gazed out at the turquoise Indian Ocean for weeks, all the while longing for a sight of the protectorate. Finally, just that morning, they had made port. This raw, untamed territory on the east coast of Africa held her dream on its burning plains. And she was determined to fulfill her destiny.

"Emma, do you think I *should* wear this pink dress today?" Cissy asked, interrupting her thoughts. "Perhaps Rolf will think it too gay and will not believe how sad I am to lose him."

"No, it's lovely," Emma said absently as she lifted her skirts and placed one knee across her bed to move closer to the porthole. Pushing back the gauze curtain with one hand, she leaned up to the round window.

Through the film of salt on the glass, she gazed at the busy harbor of Mombasa. An array of small wooden craft bustling with Arab traders surrounded the steamship. From one of the upper decks, a long plank held bale after bale, crate after crate of goods brought up from the hold of the ship. Crewmen scurried about, rolling and edging the cargo onto the pier.

Mangy dogs and scrawny children chased one another through the throng of sailors and native dockworkers on the pier. Stray chickens, blind in their quest for spilled grain or seed, bobbed across the footpaths and were kicked aside to flutter and squawk in the dust. She observed groups of stuffy Englishmen—no doubt new colonists to the Protectorate of British East Africa—standing stiffly among the scampering natives, who wore little more than a cloth tied about the waist or shoulder. The Englishmen ran fingers around their stiff white collars and lifted their top hats to let in a gust of fresh air. Carrying umbrellas against the fierce afternoon sun, they spoke animatedly with one another, and Emma imagined they were sharing their dreams of riches and bounty in the new land.

Suddenly her eyes were drawn to a frenzied movement near the cargo plank. A huge wooden crate had broken loose from its ropes and was careening down the long slope toward the pier. Gasping, she watched in frozen breathlessness as the African dockworkers attempted to slow the runaway box, which gained momentum every second. Shouts echoed across the water as men fled for their lives before the hurtling crate.

"Oh, no!" Emma cried as the box slammed into two men, knocking them into the water. With the impact, the huge crate began to break apart—jagged, splintered boards seesawing this way and that. As it careened the final few feet toward the pier, Emma spotted a tiny child—oblivious to the commotion all around him—spinning a tin hoop directly into its path.

"No—stop!" Helpless, Emma pressed her clammy palms on the cool glass as she watched the scene before her. The ragged boy's brown eyes suddenly darted up, and his face reflected his terror. His dark sparrow legs froze, rooted to the dusty pier. Just as the splintered box flew off the gangway two paces from the child, a huge black horse thundered through the circle of horrified onlookers and a dark figure swept the child into the air. The crate tumbled onto the pier and split into a thousand fragments—bolts of fabric, boxes of tea, chairs, iron barrels—but the horse, rider, and child were safe. For an instant, Emma glimpsed a black-hatted man cradling the frightened boy in his arms.

Then the crowd swarmed around the scene, and Emma bolted from the window toward the cabin door. Her heart in her throat, she could barely choke out the words, "Cissy, come quickly! People have been hurt—"

"Emma, what—?"Cissy grabbed her parasol and hurried into the hallway after her sister. "Emma, what has happened?"

"A box broke loose and men are in the water and a child—" Emma lifted her skirts and sped up the stairs from the first-class cabins in the ship's hold and out onto the deck. The certain knowledge that she was needed propelled her legs toward the gangplank. Bright sunshine broke over her, and she sucked in a great gulp of fresh sea air. Brushing past the row of Englishmen lining the ship's guardrail, she dashed down the long ramp.

One of the men who had fallen into the water lay on the pier. Pushing her way through the circle of agitated onlookers, Emma ran to the unconscious man and knelt at his side. Her mind hastily reviewed the lessons she had learned under the tutelage of her beloved Miss Nightingale. Her long fingers performing by rote, she quickly but thoroughly checked his vital signs.

"He's breathing," she whispered. Stripping off her lavender kid gloves, she slid back the man's eyelids and peered into his dark eyes."He's had a blow on the head. Shock. We must warm him." Her hands traveled swiftly across his skull and pressed for signs of fracture, but she found none. Nodding with satisfaction, she ran her fingers down his ebony limbs as she checked for distortion and bleeding.

Peering intently at his face, she took in the swelling behind his ear. Yes, a blow to the head. "This man is in shock! We must—"

Just then two deeply tanned arms slid beneath the man and lifted him from the ground. Emma watched as the wounded dockworker was supported against the broad expanse of a leather-vested chest. "Let's get him out of the sun," a deep voice said decisively.

Emma's gaze darted up. Eyes the color of a rain-washed sky looked down at her from a face that might have been carved from oak. Though young, it had been worn into striking planes and hollows by the wind. The sun had burned it to a buckskin brown. A shock of black hair fell across the wide forehead and brushed the dark brows.

Realizing at once he was the man she had seen on the dark horse, Emma tore her eyes from his and nodded. "Yes, he should be in the shade. But don't let him cool down too rapidly."

The tall man turned from her, and the crowd parted as he made his way to a grove of palm trees. Emma stared after him in frank admiration. Clad as no man she had ever known, the stranger wore trousers of a blue that might have been indigo once but had long since faded into a soft, light color. They molded to his long legs and tight hips as if to become a part of him. His feet were shod in thick brown leather boots—not the sort of soft leather spats and buttoned footgear her father wore, but boots with odd chunky heels and squared-off toes and shiny silver spurs that spun when he walked.

Her eyes traced back up his lean thighs to the tawny leather vest over the man's white shirt. It was a clean white shirt—brilliant in the afternoon sun—but it didn't do the things a shirt was meant to do. It had somehow lost its stiffness, the collar hanging loosely at his strong brown neck and the sleeves rolled to his elbows. But the oddest thing of all was his hat. Not a derby, a top hat, or even a straw hat, this was made of jet-black felt, and it bore a wide, curling brim with a black leather band. The crown rose above the stranger's head, then dipped into a valley at the center.

Emma swallowed hard as she watched him gently place the semiconscious man in a patch of cool white sand, then rise and stride to his horse. He slid a woolen blanket from behind the black saddle and stalked back to the injured man.

"Emma, come quickly!" Cissy's voice jerked Emma's attention away from the dark figure carefully wrapping the wounded man in his blanket. "They've brought the other one out of the water, and he's bleeding. No one will touch him!"

Whirling, Emma followed her sister through the jostling crowd to the second African, who lay among the debris of the shattered crate. His body, clothed only in a fabric of native weave tied at the shoulder, glistened with harbor water. He was fully awake, but he was bleeding from a long slash across his arm.

"Cissy, we must bind the cut tightly," Emma announced, kneeling beside the moaning man. She glanced up to find her sister's normally rosy cheeks pale, her eyes wide with shock. Knowing she would be no help, Emma turned back to the man and heaved his trembling shoulders into her lap.

"Now, now. You'll be all right, my dear man," she said quietly, remembering how comforting words can be to the injured. "I know you cannot understand what I'm telling you, but you must not struggle against me so. Here now, let me have that arm. That's right. Oh, dear, you *have* got a nasty gash. If only I had some suturing thread, I believe I could put that just right. But for now we must wrap it tightly and stop the bleeding."

Observing the sea of dark faces surrounding her, Emma sighed in frustration. The crowd was paralyzed, and no one moved an inch. "Honestly," she muttered. Quickly lifting the hem of her lavender skirt, she grasped her muslin petticoat and tore off a wide swath. Then she expertly gripped the arm and wrapped the muslin around and around until at last she tied the ends into a neat knot.

"You must keep that clean—" She stopped and looked up again. Cissy had vanished, and the rows of faces gaped at her blankly. "Does anyone here speak English?"

"I'll talk to him for you, ma'am." The oddly dressed stranger shouldered his way into the clearing and knelt in the dust beside her. "To touch a dead man is against these folks' religion," he told her. "They're all afraid these men are going to die."

"But that's nonsense! Can you talk to him?"

"If he speaks Swahili."

"But you're an American, aren't you? You speak . . . oddly." Emma looked up into the brilliant blue eyes and felt her stomach flutter as the man's mouth curved into a slow grin.

"Texas. But I've lived here enough years to get by in the language."

"Well, please tell him he's to go home and wash that laceration in clean water as soon as the bleeding's had a chance to stop. And he must keep it wrapped in clean cloths—*clean* ones, mind you. He really should have stitches."

The stranger listened intently, then turned his

eyes from hers. *"Bwana,"* he addressed the wide-eyed patient, *"memsahib wambie kwenda nyumbani na asafishe kidonda hiki katika maji safi. Ufungue katika kitambaa safi sana."*

Emma blinked at the string of incomprehensible syllables. "What did you tell him?"

"What you said—but he won't do it, ma'am. He'll visit the *mganga*—the witch doctor—and get some homemade remedies. He'll be all right."

"The witch doctor! But that's dreadful—"

"Emmaline Ann Pickworth!" a deep voice rumbled as a tight hand closed around Emma's arm and jerked her to her feet. The wounded man's head bounced from her lap to the hard ground, and he cried aloud and rolled himself into a ball. "What do you think you are doing?"

Turning quickly, Emma confronted the hard gray eyes of her father. "I was just bandaging this man's arm, Father. He's been injured and—"

"Emma, look at yourself," Godfrey Pickworth commanded.

Emma bent her head to survey her lavender silk skirt, now spotted with bright blood and dusted with brown. Her stuffed straw bustle had shifted from its proper place and now hung half-askew behind one hip. A coil of wheaten hair had slipped from beneath her velvet hat and lay curled across her breast. Quickly shifting her bustle back into place and tucking her hair up into her hat, Emma focused back on her father's red face.

"You were saying, Father?" Emma knew she had no choice but to play the demure daughter, though a surge of familiar anger boiled up inside her.

The bulging gray eyes closed for a moment, and

Emma saw a tracery of thin red veins running across them. Then the eyes flicked open, and her father's portly chest rose in an unhappy sigh. "Emmaline, please attempt to comport yourself in the manner in which you were brought up." Without waiting for her response, he continued, "Emmaline, I should like you to meet the assistant engineer of the railway—Mr. Nicholas Bond. Mr. Bond, my elder daughter, Emmaline."

A tall man sporting a red-gold mustache stepped around her father and extended a white-gloved hand. "Delighted to meet you, Miss Pickworth."

Emma knitted her bare fingers for a moment, then thrust out her hand. "Charmed, I'm sure. Do forgive me—I believe I've lost my gloves."

"Not at all." His lips brushed the back of her hand. Raising his sandy-red head, he smiled, but the gesture could not mask the calculating look Emma saw in the depths of his light brown eyes. "I'm dreadfully sorry you've had such a rude introduction to the protectorate. We're not always this boorish."

Emma turned her eyes to the injured man again. He was sitting up now, picking at the tight muslin bandage. The dark stranger beside him stood and removed his black hat. He looked at Nicholas as if expecting an introduction, but Bond's brown eyes froze and his hands remained stiffly at his sides.

Shrugging, the tall stranger thrust out his hand. "I'm Adam King, ma'am. I don't believe we've been introduced."

Emma placed her hand in the large warm grasp. This time she carefully studied the sky-blue eyes. "Emmaline Pickworth. Thank you for your assistance. . . ."

"Any time." He held her hand gently yet firmly. "You're a nurse."

"No, she is *not* a nurse," Emma's father broke in. "And who, sir, are you?"

"Sir," Nicholas Bond interrupted, "this man is not worthy of your acquaintance. He's a trouble-maker for the protectorate and does not belong on Queen Victoria's lands."

"As bad as that, are you?" Mr. Pickworth surveyed Adam. "Then perhaps I should learn more about such an adversary."

"Adam King. Rancher." Adam held out his bare hand to the heavily jowled man standing before him.

"Godfrey Pickworth." Hesitantly, he shook the extended hand. "Member of the queen's Parliament and director of the British Railway. Adam King . . . your name sounds familiar to me. Have you a business in transportation? Railway, perhaps, or shipping?"

Nicholas's eyes darkened. "I can assure you, sir," he snapped, "this man is involved in nothing so honorable as transportation. His closest associates are uneducated farmworkers and savages of the lowest form."

Cold anger briefly transformed the tall man's features, but he did not reply. The moment left a feeling of dread in the pit of Emma's stomach as the railman turned away with an imperious nod.

"And now, if you will excuse us, Mr. King, we must make our way back to the ship and see that the Pickworths' baggage is sent directly to government quarters. Miss Pickworth will be wanting to ready herself for tonight's dance in honor of her father—and I should be delighted to escort her. Miss Pickworth?"

Taken aback by Nicholas's cutting remarks about the American, Emma nonetheless turned to him and put on a smile. "Why, that's very kind, Mr. Bond. I had no idea there was to be a dance."

"It's not every day the protectorate is graced with such charming company as you and your sister." With that he crooked his elbow for her to take.

Silently dreading the scene that she knew would come later with her father, Emma slipped her hand around the firm muscle of the engineer's arm, lifted her skirt above the dust, and started to walk away with the man. Then she paused beside the Texan, and Nicholas had no choice but to do the same. "Mr. King," she said quietly. The dark rancher looked at her appraisingly. "Again—thank you for your assistance."

He nodded.

"And Mr. King—" Emma pulled Nicholas back again. "Will the two men be all right?"

Adam's eyes pierced hers. "I'm sure they will, Miss Pickworth."

"And the child—the one you lifted onto your horse?" For some reason, she wanted him to know she had seen him save the boy.

One corner of his mouth tipped up. "He's with his mother."

Emma dipped a little curtsy and tilted her head. "Good day, Mr. King." Without meeting his disturbing gaze again, she turned and allowed herself to be led up the gangway and back onto the ship.

Nicholas joined Godfrey Pickworth among the myriad trunks and hatboxes emerging from below deck. Emma walked to where her sister stood along the railing. Cissy clutched her hankie tightly in one fist and gripped the railing with the other.

"What is it, Cissy?" Emma murmured.

"Rolf." Cissy stared sadly at the contingent of German soldiers marching down the pier to begin their coastal journey toward the border post. Emma could see the broad-shouldered Rolf, his back ramrod straight and his eyes steadily forward. As the soldiers turned inland, he glanced back for an instant, and his gaze locked on Cissy. Then he marched around a corner and was gone. Cissy stifled a sob. "It's so hard, Emma," she said softly. "You just can't understand."

I don't suppose I can, Emma mused, placing her hand over Cissy's. But then, I don't care a fig about men. At the thought, her eyes wandered over her sister's shoulder to the pier below. Amid the dispersing crowd, the tall rancher stood watching her. One hand still clutched his hat, and he had hooked the thumb of the other through his belt loop. His weight rested on one leg, the other casually bent forward at the knee, while his broad shoulders slanted in an easy slouch. He looked so comfortable with himself, she thought, so at home in his body. She had never been allowed to feel so at ease with herself. Corsets and laces and crinolines. What would he be like alone, away from the throng? Hadn't the warmth of his hand on hers made her shiver, hadn't it conveyed a promise of—

"Cissy . . ." Emma forced herself back to the present and drew her eyes away. Nicholas was marching toward them, obviously wanting an introduction. Emma spoke up, trying to divert attention from the color she felt rising in her cheeks. "Cissy, please meet Mr. Nicholas Bond—assistant engineer of the Uganda Railway. Mr. Bond, my sister, Priscilla Pickworth."

"Delighted to meet you, Miss Pickworth." Nicholas smiled and swept off his top hat as his lips fell on Cissy's hand. But Emma barely heard him ask Cissy to help him identify her baggage in the nearby assortment.

"Who is that odd-looking chap on the pier, Emma?" Cissy asked as she turned to go. "The one in the strange hat?"

"His name is Adam King," Emma whispered, her eyes scanning the scene below until she located the dark rancher. "He's an American."

Adam was speaking with a fat crewman from the ship, possibly the steward or the purser. Suddenly his hand darted out—the index finger punctuating words Emma could not hear with regular jabs at the man's chest.

Her eyes fastened on the tall man, Emma watched as he pushed the crewman backward step by step with his prodding finger. He was obviously furious, and she wondered what the purser had done to anger him so. The American looked so different now—all his dark strength surged upward into black fury. Emma gripped the iron rail, unconscious of her heart beating in heightened rhythm with the angry advance of the rancher. Just as the purser backed into a low wooden box and could go no farther, Adam stopped, obviously on the verge of throwing the hefty crewman into the harbor. From behind his back the fat man suddenly whisked out a long white envelope and thrust it into the rancher's face.

Emma's green eyes narrowed in her effort to see. The American ripped the envelope out of the man's hand. The purser stumbled away, scampering up the gangway like the hare who has just barely eluded the fox.

Emma watched as the rancher tore open the envelope and pulled out a white sheet of paper. Flipping it open, he lowered his head, devouring the contents. Emma craned forward, anticipating the reaction. Suddenly lifting his head, he raised his eyes to the sky.

For a moment the man stood frozen—a great tower of energy and power, barely leashed by rigid muscles. Then, as if a cord had been severed, the bonds broke and he whipped back into life. Ripping the letter in two, he hurled it to the ground and spun on his spurred heel. Striding across the pier, he grabbed his horse's reins and leapt into the saddle. The horse rose into the air for a split second, then turned and galloped away across the harbor and out of sight.

"Oh, look," Cissy said, pointing at the fluttering sheets of the torn letter as she rejoined Emma at the rail. "That American has dropped his letter. . . . I shall go and fetch it—"

"No, Cissy!" Emma caught her sister's arm. "It's not our business."

"Honestly, Emma—haven't you the least bit of curiosity? After all, it's not every day one sees a cowboy!"

"A cowboy?" Emma's forehead furrowed. "Yes, I suppose that is what you might call him. . . ."

"Well, he's *American*, isn't he? What else could he be but a cowboy? And with that horse and those boots and spurs . . ."

Emma watched the dust settling along the path the horse had trod. A cowboy . . . a type of man she had only heard stories about—chasing Indians and leading wagon trains across the prairies and driving huge herds of longhorn cattle down trails with names like Santa Fe and Chisholm . . .

"Emma, are you all right?"

Cissy's light voice broke into Emma's reverie and her head jerked up. "Oh—yes, of course."

The two women started across the deck, and Emma glanced over at her father and the railroad executive. Suddenly the two British men looked faded, Nicholas just a younger and more animated version of her father.

Nicholas was striding toward them, his top hat a burnished black in the late sunlight. He held his shoulders straight and his chin up. Nothing about him echoed the casual slouch of the cowboy rancher. With a careful smile, he escorted the sisters down the gangway behind their father.

"Your trunks are safely stowed," he announced, clapping his white-gloved hands to summon a trolley down the pier. As the strapping young native men pulled the two-seated trolley to a halt, he turned to the women. "May I assist the Misses Pickworth?"

Cissy dipped her head in polite acknowledgment and held out her hand. As Nicholas and her father lifted Cissy up the squeaky stair into the covered trolley, a flutter of white caught Emma's eye. Turning, she saw one half of Adam King's letter tumbling toward her in the gentle breeze. Unable to resist, she snatched it up.

Roses the color of blood and wine bloomed in a tangle of green vines across the top of the paper. The scent of floral perfume, heady and evocative, clung to the letter as Emma lifted it and brushed it fully open.

"My darling," it began. The words swam out in flowing blue ink. "How I've longed to be in your arms! How I've missed you—" The torn paper stopped the words. Emma looked up, but the men were busy tucking Cissy's skirts into the trolley.

She read on, "As you know, I had planned to arrive in January, but unfortunately—" Another stop. Emma scanned. ". . . the governor's inauguration on the twenty-fifth, and I do wish you could . . . such a long trip, but I know it will be worth it to see you . . . I know how lonely you've been and how much you want someone to . . . and so after a great deal of careful deliberation as well as numerous conversations with . . ."

"Emmaline!"

Her father's voice froze Emma's eyes on the last words: "I remain forever, your faithful wife—" The torn paper cut through her like a knife.

Dropping the letter, Emma saw the breeze catch it and whip it across the pier, then whisk it high into the air and send it fluttering lazily into the turquoise sea.

"Emmaline!"

Her father's voice left no room for longing.

## Chapter Two

❖ ❖ ❖ ❖

*You can't expect a cowboy to agitate his shanks*
*In etiquettish manner in aristocratic ranks,*
*When he's always been accustomed to shake the heel and toe*
*At the rattling rancher dances where much etiquette don't go.*

*—"The Cowboy's Dance Song"*

*I . . . am beginning to opine*
*Those girls are only half-divine*
*Whose waists yon wicked boys entwine*
*In giddy waltz.*
*I fear that arm above that shoulder,*
*I wish them wiser, graver, older,*
*Sedater, and no harm if colder,*
*And panting less.*

—Walter Savage Landor
"On Lucretia Borgia's Hair"

EMMA ADJUSTED HER bustle on the narrow trolley seat as Nicholas sat down beside her. She would have preferred to sit by Cissy, but the layers of crinolines lining their skirts prevented that possibility. As a result, she was forced to ride back to back with her sister in the trolley car. The space was cramped, and Emma found herself leaning awkwardly against Nicholas as the trolley jerked to life.

The air smelled of the sea, and Emma lifted her face into the sunshine and breathed in the salty freshness. The turquoise waters of the ocean mirrored the sky; long, rippling clouds paralleled an endless white-sand beach. And between shore and sky the seagulls fluttered, calling raucously above the crash of the waves and the shouts of the dockworkers.

"The town is on an island," Nicholas explained over the rattle of the trolley. "Actually the coastal strip belongs to the sultan of Zanzibar, and we English control the inland area to Lake Victoria. As you know, we've had a bit of trouble with the Germans over who controls the Uganda territory."

Godfrey leaned over the back of the seat, his arm pressing against Emma's back. "That's why it is imperative that we arrive at the lake with our railway before they get there with theirs."

The younger man nodded. "I agree. My dream is to see the protectorate become a full-fledged colony of the Crown!"

Only half listening, Emma shifted from her perch on the edge of the leather seat and gazed out across the landscape. Whitewashed huts with thatched roofs squatted in the shade of graceful palm trees. Chickens and dogs and goats wandered across the road, oblivious to the trolley. The day smelled thick with salt and fish and seawater, and Emma felt a trickle of perspiration run between her breasts and slide into the depths of her corset.

She had so longed for this moment—had dreamed of the day she would see this land of hope. Lying awake at night on board the steamship, she had tried mentally to fill the countryside with people and vegetation and animals. What would it be like—this vast continent that needed her medical knowledge so desperately, this land where she planned to escape her father and cast her fate? But now—here, at last—she could barely concentrate on any of it.

Rather than the white-rimmed waters and the fishing boats, her eyes saw a dark man rising into the sky on a gleaming black stallion. Her ears heard not the sounds of laughing children and clattering trolley wheels, but a deep voice with a strange, lazy accent like a long slow river winding to the sea. Her ungloved hands felt the touch of another hand worn and callused—yet warm and honest. Even the strong sea scent faded beneath an overwhelming memory of leather and dusty felt and denim.

She wondered what her aunt Prudence would

have thought of Adam King. Emma smiled, knowing at once that her beloved mentor would find the man just as entrancing as she did. Her thoughts slipped back in time to Aunt Prue's big old house in London where she had spent the years after her mother's death. Before their mother's calamitous visit to the continent, the family had spent many happier years at their rambling country estate. But after she died, their father's business and his failing health had forced Emma and Cissy to the city.

Aunt Prue, with her adventuring heart and rebellious schemes, had proven the only solace for Emma's mourning. With her mother gone, Emma had felt such responsibility for Cissy—and the circumstances of their mother's death had changed their father so much. . . .

Emma pulled her thoughts from her father and remembered the secret plans and victories she had shared with Aunt Prue. She smiled at the memory of her years of clandestine nursing training at St. Thomas's. Despite her father's rigidly confining determination that she marry the man of his choice and settle quickly into her place in society, she had completed her studies.

"And how is the railway progressing, Mr. Bond?" Godfrey's deep voice broke into Emma's thoughts, but she could not bring herself to look at her father.

"Quite well, despite a few setbacks. Did the association receive my correspondence about the workers from India?"

"Indeed. Superb idea, we thought."

"Yes, it has worked out nicely. One hasn't a hope of employing the natives. They're far too unpredictable." Nicholas hesitated a moment. "Did you receive the letter about the lions?"

"Lions? No, what about them?"

Emma tilted her head back toward Cissy to see if the men's conversation was disturbing her. Her sister's eyes had glazed with tears again. Emma knew she was mourning the loss of Rolf and probably had not even heard about the lions. Cissy held her pink handkerchief to the corner of one blue eye, but a glistening rivulet trickled from the other.

"Well, we have had a bit of trouble with lions, sir . . . farther north—in the Tsavo area . . ." Nicholas glanced at Cissy. "Perhaps we should discuss this later."

Emma turned her attention to Nicholas. She could not afford to dwell on the dark rancher and his absent wife. After all, she would probably never see him again. And wasn't it just as well? She had to think of her future—and the immediate present—what was all this about lions? The railman's classic profile, clear and white against the black trolley hood, revealed a subtle tension.

"Do speak frankly, Mr. Bond," Emma said. She and Cissy were quite familiar with railway business. Since their mother's death, Emma had reluctantly hosted many of their father's associates in their home.

Nicholas tipped his head in polite acknowledgment, but Emma saw his fingers tighten on the brim of his top hat as it lay in his lap. "Well . . . it appears that two lions have taken to . . . raiding the workers' camps."

"Raiding?" Cissy's voice was high-pitched, strained. Her eyes—suddenly attentive—darted back and forth from Emma to Nicholas. "Whatever can you mean, Mr. Bond?"

Nicholas cleared his throat. His face was rigid

but flushed, his eyes alive as they watched Cissy. "The lions have become . . . man-eaters."

Cissy quickly averted her head. Emma touched the foreman's arm to catch his attention. "Mr. Bond, are you telling us that lions have been killing . . . and eating . . . the railworkers?"

"Perhaps we should discuss this later, Mr. Bond," Godfrey cut in. "My daughters are accustomed to railway talk, but this is a bit different."

"Yes, I quite agree." A thin line of perspiration trickled from Nicholas Bond's blond sideburn over the elegant ridge of his cheekbone. "The situation is righting itself even as we speak. Lieutenant Colonel Patterson, the supervising engineer for the railway, has taken the problem head on. There is nothing to fear, I assure you."

Godfrey ran a hand across his heavy jowls. "Have you need for additional forces—or munitions? We can telegraph for the funds from England if the need arises."

"No, no." Nicholas shook his head firmly. "Everything is under control."

Emma heard her father let out a quick sigh, but she could feel the tension in Nicholas's shoulder against hers. Looking out the window again, she saw that the trolley had taken them into the narrow, cobblestone streets of Mombasa. The flat-roofed two-story houses, row upon row of them sandwiched together, sagged and hung upon one another as if weary of standing in the blazing heat. Their iron-and-wooden balconies thrust out over the street. Wooden doors, heavily carved in fantastic geometric shapes and studded with brass, stood open to reveal sun-filled courtyards.

"This is the main section of town," Nicholas

said, his voice stronger now as he regained his confidence. "There are parts of it devoted primarily to shopping. One can find the most luxurious wares brought in from the Far East on the dhows—those small ships you saw in the harbor—that sail the monsoon winds. Mombasa is an Arab town mostly, though the Portuguese have had quite an influence. Ah, here we are. . . ."

The trolley rolled up to an iron gate and stopped. As the gate swung open, the four passengers descended to the street. Emma caught her breath as they started slowly down a long, palm-lined driveway. It was a tropical paradise. The grounds of the British compound were a sea of lush green grass dotted with fragrant islands of orange and blue bird of paradise, deep purple bougainvillea, fuchsia hibiscus, and dark philodendron.

The two men deposited their hats with white-gloved servants and walked ahead into the shadows of the wide verandah.

"Emma," Cissy whispered urgently, catching her sister's arm. "Do you think there's danger here? From lions and—"

"No, Cissy," Emma interrupted, looking into her sister's wide blue eyes. "There's a huge fence all around. Just look! We're quite safe."

"Gracious, I feel so at odds with everything here. It's so dreadfully hot, and all that talk about the man-eating lions. Oh, Emma—I want to go back to England. I'm not suited for this sort of thing."

Emma squeezed her sister's hand and led her up the stairs into the cool depths of the verandah. "Perhaps you are and you just don't know it yet."

"Emmaline, Priscilla—do come here."

Godfrey stood beside a handsome man and

woman. Emma thought the woman did not look much older than herself, and her brilliant smile was instantly warming. An elegantly tailored tea dress and white gloves identified her instantly as a lady, but her face bore a ruddy glow from long hours in the sun. Clearly older, but equally lively looking, her husband also was dressed for tea. His refined face with its aquiline nose was a study in classic comeliness.

"I should like very much to make introductions." Godfrey swept out a hand. "Lord and Lady Delamere, may I present my elder—and regrettably unkempt—daughter, Emmaline Pickworth, and her sister, Priscilla Pickworth? Emmaline and Priscilla, meet Hugh Cholmondeley, third Baron Delamere of Vale Royal in Cheshire, and his wife, Lady Delamere."

"Such formality!" Lady Delamere laughed, and her eyes lit up with a twinkle. "I'm Florence, and everyone in the protectorate calls my husband 'D.' You must do the same, of course!"

Her husband chuckled. "You'll soon learn one can't be terribly proper here—though we try to keep up a good show."

"You have a lovely home," Emma said politely.

"Oh, this is not our home!" Florence's mouth turned up at the corners in an infectious grin. "Sir Charles Eliot—Her Majesty's commissioner in East Africa—normally lives here. You've just missed him, as he's gone on leave. Hugh and I live up country at Njoro. We're farming a large tract. You must plan a visit. Now I'm certain you both are exhausted from your long journey. Shall I have tea sent to your rooms?"

"Yes, thank you. I must apologize for my appearance." Emma looked ruefully at her blood-spattered gown and dusty hem. "I was called upon to attend some injured men—"

"Emmaline is always finding something awkward with which to fill her time," Godfrey interrupted with a snort. "I shall look forward to seeing you both at dinner. Good day, Emmaline . . . Priscilla."

Knowing she had been dismissed after dutifully playing out her ornamental role, Emma sighed as she watched her father walk into the house with Lord Delamere. Nicholas started after them, then stopped suddenly and turned back.

"Miss Pickworth," he said, his light brown eyes on Emma, "remember, I look forward to escorting you this evening. I shall meet you in the parlor after dinner."

Emma dipped her head. "As you wish, Mr. Bond."

With a knowing smile, Florence Delamere led the young women into the house behind Nicholas. The inside was sumptuously furnished with heavy oak tables and chintz-covered settees. Emma thought she might as well be in England for all the lace antimacassars, embroidered firescreens, and porcelain figurines scattered through the dimly lit rooms. The only things that reminded her she was in Africa were the rhinoceros horn coat rack beside the front door and the zebra skin on the hall floor. An intricately woven Persian carpet graced the floor at the foot of the stairs. Emma wondered as she ascended to the guest quarters if it had come by Arab dhow.

Left alone at last in their suite, Emma and Cissy hurried to the long sofa and fell into the soft cushions. Cissy stretched out her legs and leaned her golden head against the wall. "I'm ready for a bath—are you?"

"Nothing could be better," Emma agreed. Then she frowned, her eyes darkening momentarily. "Yes . . . it could be better. But a bath will have to do."

With a warm bath and a refreshing cup of tea to rejuvenate her, Emma set her sights on the evening at hand. As Cissy laced the corset over her sister's chemise and fastened a ruffled crinoline in its proper place, Emma silently worked out her strategy. She would not allow this evening to go to waste. Nicholas Bond had lived in the protectorate long enough to know the ins and outs of the country—and she would get him to tell her everything she wanted to know about the locations of hospital missions, their need for nurses, living quarters, access to medicines, and all the other questions that clamored to be asked. Once they were answered, she could map out a detailed plan—and the sooner she set that plan into motion, the less time her father would have to think up other options for her future.

When the sisters were dressed at last, they descended the stairs to dinner. Cissy floated in a cloud of blue silk and feathers. Her hair, artfully arranged around an artificial bluebird, gleamed a brilliant gold. Emma felt as awkward as she always did beside her glowing sister. Though her green gown was trimmed in the softest of pink roses that cascaded from her silk-sashed waist to the floor, she knew she could never compare with the dainty treasure at her side. And though her sleeveless shoulders were equally creamy and her waist as tiny, she would never look as fairylike as Cissy. Shrugging inwardly, she knew it did not matter—neither men nor fashion were the objects of her dreams.

Cissy placed a gloved hand on Emma's arm and leaned to her ear. "Do I look all right?"

Emma smiled. "You will turn all the men's heads."

But Cissy's face did not brighten. "I miss Rolf. I miss him dreadfully."

Stifling the resigned sigh that threatened to escape at the hundredth mention of Cissy's German soldier, Emma directed her sister's attention to the opposite side of the room, where their father stood. "Listen, you must not mention Rolf to Father, Cissy. You know how he feels about that sort of thing."

Cissy nodded glumly. The dinner bell rang, and the young women made their way to the dining room. It might have been an evening at Aunt Prue's house in London for all Emma could tell. Course followed course across the long, white-clothed table. There were finger bowls and crystal goblets filled with excellent wines. The men and women attending wore the latest fashions and behaved as though they had just arrived from a visit with Queen Victoria. Even the conversation revolved around the empire.

When dinner was over, Emma rose with the others and, with a grateful sigh, strode out of the dining room. Though the other guests wandered toward the sound of waltz music coming from the ballroom, Emma marched purposefully toward the parlor.

"Good evening, Mr. Bond." She stepped into the center of the room, her eyes on the tall, black-suited figure standing beside the desk. Nicholas turned, and for an instant Emma thought she had been mistaken—and that she was looking at the stern form of her father. Something in the way he set his shoulders and peered out from beneath his brow evoked the dark, uncompromising side of Godfrey Pickworth. But he quickly swept his top hat from his head and smiled at her with a bow.

"Good evening, Miss Pickworth. You look ravishing." The darkness gone, his eyes sparkled as he hurried to her side and lifted her gloved hand to his lips. "I'm delighted to be your escort this evening."

"Shall we, then?"

As they drifted into the ballroom, they saw that Lord Delamere had ascended the platform to stand before the military band. He was addressing the hushed crowd.

"Mr. Godfrey Pickworth is the finest example of our proud heritage, our noble empire," he was saying. His voice carried that slightly nasal quality of the well-bred Englishman. "A self-made man, a man not afraid of the challenge of adventure. He is a man who believes—as do we all—in the supremacy of our beloved isle and her God-given directive to rule the earth! It is with the greatest pleasure that I give you the honored guest of our evening, the humble servant of Her Majesty's Parliament and director of Her Majesty's Railway—Godfrey Pickworth!"

Emma clapped with the others as her father climbed to the platform beside Lord Delamere. She knew she should be proud of her father, but as he stood there—lauding England and his part in her glories—she saw nothing but a hollow man. For all his wealth and power, Godfrey Pickworth was a bitter and selfish person who wanted only to conform the world and the lives of those around him to his exacting expectations. He had done that to her mother, and—

"Your father is the sort of man who has made England what she is today," Nicholas murmured, startling Emma as he took her into his arms and whirled her onto the dance floor. She had not heard her father stop speaking nor the music start, and she stumbled a little as she strove to match her step with Nicholas's.

The corners of his glossy blond mustache turned up as he smiled. He had fine white teeth, and his breath smelled of mint. Conscious of his hand around her waist, Emma averted her gaze from his eyes. He wore a finely tailored black suit with a tailcoat and white gloves. His vest of red brocade silk had been carefully embroidered in black, and his stiff white collar stood fashionably high.

"You were very brave this afternoon at the harbor, Miss Pickworth," he whispered, his mouth close to her ear. "I don't wonder that your father was concerned. This is not England—you must be careful."

Emma swallowed, seeing her chance. "I assist others as the need for my skills arises, Mr. Bond. You see, I have studied nursing under the tutelage of Miss Florence Nightingale of St. Thomas's Hospital."

The briefest flicker of a frown crossed his face. "Nursing. A rather unusual pastime for a woman of your standing, is it not, Miss Pickworth?"

"Nursing is not a pastime with me. It is my vocation, Mr. Bond."

Nicholas lifted his eyebrows. "Strong words for a strong belief. I like that in a woman."

Emma glanced up to his face. Although he

seemed to have spoken seriously, she felt no conviction behind the words themselves. Then his concentration focused on a disturbance in the hall. She took the opportunity to study his fine nose and well-shaped lips. His face might have been carved from marble if not for those searching eyes. "Mr. Bond, can you tell me whether there are any mission-sponsored hospitals in the protectorate? I was wondering if I might—"

"Excuse me." He stopped dancing and turned toward the door, his eyes suddenly hard.

Unnerved, Emma followed his gaze across the room. The music broke off in awkward discord as the dancers ceased moving and all attention turned to the hallway. Voices, arguing, growing louder, suddenly filled the ballroom. In came a group of angry men surrounding a figure who rose head and shoulders above them.

Emma caught her breath as she saw the American Adam King. His blue eyes quickly surveyed the crowd and locked upon her. He took off his black hat and started across the room, but instantly the commotion began again.

"What is the meaning of this?" Lord Delamere's nasal voice rose over the hubbub.

"My lord, this man insists on entering the consulate without invitation," one the servants explained apologetically to Lord Delamere.

"Mr. King." Lord Delamere blinked in confusion. "I had no idea you were in Mombasa."

Adam gathered the servant's collar in his large brown hand and lifted the astonished man out of his path. "I'm in Mombasa. Mind if I join you?"

"Not at all, sir. Do come in," Lord Delamere said warmly. "I'll stand you a whiskey when I've had another dance." He turned back to the band and signaled it to begin playing again. "Carry on, carry on!"

As the music started up, the dancers slowly drew their eyes away from the tall rancher and swung back into the waltz. But Nicholas hovered rigidly clutching Emma's elbow as he eyed Adam making his way toward them through the swirling skirts.

"Good evening, Miss Pickworth . . . Bond." The American's blue eyes did not waver from Emma's, though she found it hard to meet them.

"Good evening, Mr. King." She held out her hand, and this time he lifted it to his lips. His thick hair, glossy in the lamplight, shone a blue black.

"What do you want, King?" Nicholas's voice was harsh.

"I came to return these." Adam reached into the back pocket of his black trousers and pulled out Emma's lavender gloves.

Emma's green eyes shot to his face. "My goodness—I thought I would never see those gloves again. Thank you so much, Mr. King. It was very kind of you."

"Yes, thank you, Mr. King. Now if you'll excuse us, Miss Pickworth and I—"

"Oh, Mr. Bond, perhaps I should reserve *this* dance for Mr. King . . ." The words tumbled suddenly from her mouth. "In thanks for returning my gloves. . . ."

Nicholas stared at her as if she had said something untoward. He opened his mouth to protest, then thought better of it. "Of course, Miss Pickworth," he muttered stiffly. "I shall attend your father until the next dance."

As he backed away Emma looked up at Adam, who wore an amused expression. "Perhaps I spoke out of turn, Mr. King. I normally am not so bold."

"Aren't you? You were pretty bold this afternoon on the pier." His mouth curved into a warm smile. He had liked that about her right away—how she had taken over without stopping to think of the consequences. A woman needed courage in this country.

"Thank you. I have been trained as a nurse, you see."

He searched the olive eyes, wanting to be certain before he set his plan in motion. "But your father said—"

"My father disapproves. Nevertheless, I have undertaken a rigorous course in nursing at Miss Nightingale's school in St. Thomas's Hospital."

"Well, I don't know who Miss Nightingale is, but I'm sure she has a fine school." He stood before her, making no move to dance. "Does your father know about—"

The music stopped and Adam's sentence with it. His eyes lifted to the bowing couples. Clutching her lavender gloves, Emma peered around Adam's broad shoulder to see Nicholas striding across the room toward them. She looked back at Adam. The strains of the Blue Danube waltz swelled into the tense air.

"Mr. Bond is coming to escort me. Thank you once again for returning my gloves—"

Nicholas arrived and slipped his arm beneath Emma's. But as he began to lead her away, Adam's hand shot to the railman's chest and stopped him cold. "Whoa there, buckaroo. I do believe I'm owed a dance with this young la—"

"Mr. King," Nicholas interrupted in a voice of steel, "let us get two things perfectly straight. Number one—I am not a 'buckaroo.' And number two—Miss Pickworth offered you the last dance. I am here to retrieve her now. If you will excuse us . . ."

"No, I won't excuse you, Bond." Adam took a looming step toward the shorter man. "But I will thank you to let go of the lady until I've had my dance."

Nicholas's eyes suddenly blazed into flame. "And I will thank you to hold your tongue. I am Miss Pickworth's escort. Have you no manners at all?"

"Don't talk to me about manners, Bond." Adam fought with himself to keep his mouth shut. He knew there were things a man shouldn't reveal in the presence of a lady, but he was not one of these sissified British gentlemen, and he wasn't about to leave until he got what he'd come for. The silence hung tensely between them until he spoke again. "I have manners. I know that I was invited to dance by this young woman, and it would be damned rude of me not to give her a whirl. And if you intend to interfere, I'll have to move you out of the way."

"Is that a threat?" Nicholas smiled coldly. "Because if it is—"

"Gentlemen, please." Emma carefully stepped away from the railman. "Mr. Bond, I'm afraid I did promise; I shall join you in a moment. Mr. King, shall we . . .?"

Emma held out her arms in the proper position, but Adam made no move toward her. His eyes darted back and forth between her and the railman as he ran his hat brim between his hands. For a moment, Emma thought the Englishman's sneer would be shattered by a crashing blow from the American's huge fist. But just as she had started to step backward, Adam stuffed his hat onto the back of his head, swept her into his arms, and spun her out onto the floor.

"Mr. King!" Emma's eyes flew open as Adam whirled her around and around the room, barely avoiding collisions with the sedate waltzers, who stared at them in alarm. An unfamiliar surge of excitement coursed through Emma at the realization that the American had come back into her life . . . had sought her out . . . was holding her, even now, in his strong, warm arms. His deep blue gaze was hotter than his breath on her cheek, and the scent of his skin played havoc with her thundering heart. Emma's feet barely touched the floor as the music swelled through the room. Letting go of Adam's shoulder, she clutched the spray of pink roses in her hair for fear of losing it. But it made no difference that her arms did not hold him—for one of his hands wrapped firmly around her waist, and the other wove through her fingers.

"I'm not much of a high-toned dancer, to tell you the truth, ma'am," Adam said beneath the music, spinning Emma toward the band so swiftly that her dress billowed up around her calves. The fact was, he felt damned foolish cantering around among these society folks when the most experience he'd ever had was doing the two-step half-drunk at a Texas barn dance. But he was determined to talk to this woman, and he wasn't about to be cowed by some fancy dance.

Emma caught a glimpse of Cissy gawking at her in astonishment. "Well, this is a bit—" She caught her breath as he flung her away from him, then whipped her back against his chest in a crushing hold. "A bit different!"

He threw back his head in a hearty laugh, then looked down at her with shining eyes. It wasn't half-bad, after all, this dancing business. She was soft and yielding in his arms, and her long neck arched backward as he spun her around and around. Her high, full breasts were pressed tight against his chest, rising up from the low-cut gown so smooth and creamy that it was all he could do to keep his eyes from them.

"I guess if I knew how to dance fancy, I'd do it." He made himself keep to the subject. "This is the way we dance in Texas. The band just needs a fiddle or two and a swig of rye whiskey under their belts—and then they'd cook this tune up right."

"I do believe this is the way Mr. Strauss intended it played."

"Sort of dull, don't you think?" Adam nodded at the glowering Nicholas as they passed him in a mad whirl.

Emma gave up on her hair and tossed her head back, letting the curls pull out and tumble down her back. Catching his shoulder once again, she felt the muscle ripple beneath his white linen shirt. His black tie fluttered at his neck, and his hair bounced loosely around his head, falling over his ears and cascading down his forehead. He was all movement, all action and rhythm—nothing like the stiff men who held her so primly, as though she were made of porcelain. And as they danced, she felt her body loosen and sway against his, melting into his easy whirl.

As the music slowed, Adam guided her toward the wide French doors that opened onto the long verandah. "Mind if we walk for a couple of minutes, Miss Pickworth?" Before she could answer, he eased her out onto the dimly lit walkway. The last strains of the waltz faded away. "I want to talk to you about something."

Emma glanced back into the crowd and caught sight of Nicholas searching for her. "I really should go back in. . . ." Then she looked up at the dark figure towering over her and knew she would go with him. It was more than curiosity—she knew she would be with him . . . alone. "Yes, we can walk for a moment."

As Adam cocked his elbow and she slipped her hand around the hard muscle of his arm, she wondered at herself. Hadn't Nicholas said this man was untrustworthy? And hadn't she seen him use force twice this very day—once against the purser on the pier and once against the servant? And he was married . . . *married.* Somewhere his wife waited for him, wanting and missing and loving him. Emma let her hand drop to her side.

"What is it you want to discuss with me, Mr. King?"

He hooked his thumb through the belt loop of his black trousers as he walked. The fabric strained against his long thighs, pulling tight with every step. She could see his boots beneath the hems of his trousers and wondered if he had ridden his horse to the consulate.

Away from the stuffy, perfumed air of the ballroom, she suddenly caught the scent of his black leather vest and closed her eyes against an almost overwhelming urge to—to what? She had never felt so odd, so off balance . . . and she stopped walking as if to focus herself.

"Miss Pickworth?" His voice was low. He caught her arm, suddenly realizing how long it had been since he'd been with a woman like this . . . "You all right?"

"I think I'm out of breath—the dancing . . ."

"Want to sit down? There are some chairs at the other end of the—"

"No, no—I'm fine now." Emma took her hand away again. "You wanted to speak with me?"

"Yes, I do." He straightened up and moved away slightly, dismissing the momentary discomfort she'd given him. He couldn't let himself think about the fact that she was beautiful and brave . . . and completely a woman. Emma Pickworth could be useful to him, that was all, and he might as well lay the cards on the table. "I want to know more about your nursing skills."

Emma tilted her head in surprise. "My nursing?"

"Yes. How much practical experience have you had?"

"Not enough." She sighed. "I have longed for practical experience in nursing, Mr. King. Though Miss Nightingale's philosophy does not encourage nurses to learn too much pure medicine, I have always longed to know as much as any doctor. But as to practical experience—" She stopped suddenly. "Why do you wish to know about my nursing?"

Adam started forward again, almost as if he were stalking some imaginary beast, and Emma was forced to keep up. "Can you do surgical kinds of things—like sewing people up and setting bones?"

"I've watched them done. But I have neither the tools nor the skills to do them myself. Mr. King, why are you asking me these questions?"

He couldn't tell her everything, but she was too smart to keep completely in the dark. He'd just lead her around to what he wanted to get out of her. "I understand that doctors have found ways to make people unconscious these days. Know anything about that?"

"Anesthesia. I've seen it used in operations. Why?"

"Do you know much about drugs? Medicines?"

"Morphia, quinine, cocaine, laudanum—I've dispensed them all. But I certainly haven't the right to prescribe—"

"But you *do* know what they're used for. You know what can help pain—constant pain."

"We normally use morphia. Cocaine injected into the spine can be of great benefit, of course. And laudanum . . . though once taken, it can become addictive later. But—"

"Miss Pickworth?" Nicholas Bond's voice rang out down the long verandah and startled Emma into silence. The red-haired railman posed outlined in the light from the ballroom. His top hat sat high on his head, and his long coattails—the only part of him that moved—fluttered in the night breeze.

Emma glanced up at Adam and noted that his brows had lowered to hood his blue eyes. She licked her lips, not wanting the confrontation. "Yes, Mr. Bond?"

"Your father is quite concerned for your safety, Miss Pickworth."

"The lady's fine, Bond." Adam stepped into the squares of yellow light that fell on the verandah beside the nearest French doors.

"Miss Pickworth?"

"Oh, yes, I'm perfectly safe, Mr. Bond." She knew it was time to leave the rancher and return to the ballroom. All etiquette told her she had been wrong to walk with him unaccompanied in the first place. But why was he so curious about her nursing? She could not deny that it felt wonderful to talk about the subject she had been ordered never to mention, not even to Cissy. "Mr. King and I were just discussing his unusual dancing style. Were we not, Mr. King?"

Confusion clouded Adam's eyes for an instant. Then he picked up on her lead. "Yes, we were talking about my dancing—and Miss Pickworth has offered to teach me a step or two of that high-society English jig you folks do. You won't mind if we make a circle or two, will you, *buckaroo?*"

Nicholas frowned, his thin lips tightening into a grim line. "Miss Pickworth, I—"

"Dear Mr. Bond, it does seem the proper thing to do, under the circumstances." Emma was surprised at her own words. "I . . . I think it would not show the English to good advantage if we let this American chap continue his ignorance of the waltz."

Nicholas flipped back his coattails and thrust his fists to his hips. He started to speak, paused, then turned abruptly and left. Emma's eyebrows raised slightly. How odd that he should become so angry over a dance.

"Come, Mr. King—one dance and you shall know all I have to show you." She crossed to the French doors, and Adam pushed them open. Laying her lavender gloves on a side table, she gave a little curtsy and held out her arms.

Adam took her into his arms. "Shall we dance?"

Emma did not move. She gazed into the blue eyes and watched them looking back at her. They had gone dark now, with black rims that matched the lashes framing them. His hand held her against him as it tightened and pulled her closer. Even through her heavy corset, she sensed its strength. Without taking his eyes from hers, he spread her slender fingers and slipped his between them so that she felt the blood stop.

The music barely filtered through her ears, though she knew it was there—for as he drifted her out onto the floor, Emma's sense of the world around her seemed to vanish. All she heard was the heavy throb of her heartbeat and the quiet jingle of Adam's spurs as his boot heels tapped the wooden floor. She was aware of her skirt, floating behind her on its stiff crinolines—meant to keep the dancers apart, but failing tonight. His chest crushed against her breasts as he held her close—too close for this dance . . . and yet she could not stop him, could not make herself say the proper words, the polite things, the gracious empty syllables.

"Emma . . ." The word floated from his lips in his strange, beguiling accent. His breath felt warm against her ear. Her mind told her to pull back from him, warned her—he was treacherous, he was foreign, he was married . . . Yet he lifted her feet from the floor, and her cheek fell against his vest; the scent of leather and the plains filled her nostrils . . . and her mind reeled away with all its doubts and warnings.

Her eyes met his again, and they were as they had been once before. Open and blue, deep pools in which she thought she might drown. "Mr. King," she whispered, trying to prevent herself from falling into them.

"Call me Adam." He slowed their movement, then stopped, still holding her close in his arms, trying to make sense of things. Somehow—against every last shred of sense and determina-

tion he possessed—he'd let this strange, willful
woman affect him . . . and all he could do was
stare down at her, wanting her. Her flushed
cheeks and shining emerald eyes and elegant
nose . . . her full rosy lips, barely parted and
tilted slightly upward . . . He lowered his head,
and his lips gently met hers.

Soft as they covered Emma's mouth, Adam's lips
belied the hard outlines of his face. Emma felt as
though he were drinking her—draining her self-re-
straint and sapping her every reserve of manners
and morals. And then it was over.

The music stopped, and the dancers whirled into
bows and curtsies and polite applause. She knew
he was staring down at her, for she could feel his
eyes burning her already hot cheeks.

"Emma." He lifted her chin with a finger, and
she raised her eyes to his. "Thank you."

Wanting to speak, she found that the words refused to form on her tongue. She glanced out into
the crowd as the music started up again. Cissy
stood in one corner surrounded by a bevy of attentive men. Emma looked back and found Nicholas
at her side, grasping her elbow.

"Miss Pickworth—your face is ashen. Are you
well?"

Emma's eyes flew to Adam, and she saw the
corner of his mouth turn up in the hint of a grin.
"Yes, Mr. Bond. I'm quite well, thank you."

Nicholas coldly surveyed the rancher. "You may
leave now, Mr. King. And I advise you to keep
your ill-mannered attentions from Miss Pickworth
from now on."

"Don't talk to me about manners, Bond."
Adam's eyes flashed with an anger that twisted
Emma's stomach into a hard knot. "And don't pre-

sume to tell me how to act—unless you're willing to stand up and take your medicine."

"Another threat? Perhaps I shall be forced to speak with Lord Delamere and Commissioner Eliot about the sorts of traitors scratching out a living on the queen's protectorate."

"You can talk all you want. I'm not budging from my ranch—not for you, or for Delamere or Eliot or for the queen herself. Excuse me, Miss Pickworth. I have some business to take care of."

Adam doffed his black hat and strode through the whirling dancers toward the verandah, his heavy footsteps echoing across the floor.

"I must apologize, Miss Pickworth. You can see the man has no respect for our queen or our empire!" Nicholas's neck was red above his white collar. "He is a treacherous troublemaker. I do beg of you to keep yourself under guard if you chance to meet Adam King again. His forward behavior with you was inexcusable."

Emma brushed her hand over her forehead. "Mr. Bond, I'm feeling rather tired suddenly. Do you mind if we sit?"

"Not at all." He guided her carefully across the room to the sofa beside a set of French doors. But as she sat down, she saw Cissy flying across the room, her eyes shining brilliantly.

"Oh, Emma—may I speak with you for just a moment? Do you mind dreadfully, Mr. Bond?"

Emma glanced at the young railman. Though he tried to maintain his equilibrium, irritation showed clearly on his face. Emma spoke up softly. "I'll only be a moment, Mr. Bond. And then we shall dance the rest of the evening."

"Of course, Miss Pickworth." He rose and helped Emma to her feet.

Cissy slipped her hand around her sister's arm and propelled her across the room.

"Emma, what has gotten into you!" Cissy's voice was a shrill whisper. "You let that man—that *cowboy*—kiss you right in the middle of the dance floor! Father is livid. Honestly, Emma, what *were* you thinking of?"

"I don't know, Cissy. I don't know how it happened. One moment we were dancing, and then the next . . ."

"You're meant to be dancing with Mr. Bond! He's your escort."

"Adam said I should teach him to dance . . . fancy. High-toned dancing, he called it." Emma slowed and pulled her sister toward the doors. "He was asking me about my nursing, and then . . ."

"Adam? You call him Adam?"

But Emma did not hear her sister's words. She was staring at the gloves on the side table beside the door. Lifting her eyes to the glass door, she looked out into the moonlit night. A movement caught her attention, and she focused on the long gravel drive lined with flowering trees. Down its silvery path galloped a dark shadow of a horse. As the rider spurred his mount through the gate and turned onto the street, Emma gingerly lifted her gloves from the table.

# Chapter Three

✦✦✦✦✦

*Such is the fortune of all womenkind,*
*They are always controlled, they are always made mind;*
*Controlled by their parents until they become wives,*
*And slaves of their husbands the rest of their lives.*

—"Red River Shore"

*Let's contend no more, Love,*
*Strive nor weep;*
*All be as before, Love—*
*Only sleep!*

*What so wild as words are?*
*I and thou*
*In debate, as birds are,*
*Hawk on bough!*

—Robert Browning
"A Woman's Last Word"

"EMMALINE!"

Whirling from the ballroom window, Emma faced her father. His mouth was rimmed in white, and his nostrils flared dangerously. "Yes, Father?" She heard the tremble in her voice.

"Come with me, Emmaline."

Emma glanced at Cissy. Her sister's eyes were wide. With a quick squeeze on the hand, Cissy nudged Emma toward their father. Godfrey turned on his heel and stalked across the ballroom toward the hall doors. Following, Emma swallowed at the fear of what was to come—the scene father and daughter had so often played out. But knowing what to expect did nothing to calm the thundering of her heart. She ventured a

47

look at Nicholas. He had risen from the sofa, his eyes veiled in curiosity.

"Father, what is it?" Emma called after the departing figure, though she knew her offense before he even spoke the words. He thrust open the parlor doors and marched to the long windows.

"Emmaline, sit down."

"Yes, Father." She settled on the edge of a long, overstuffed couch and spread her skirts demurely over her petticoats. Godfrey posed in front of a heavily curtained window and placed the tips of his fingers on the back of an armchair. Emma could see that they were stiff with tension.

"Emmaline, did my eyes deceive me in the ballroom?"

Emma studied her knotted fingers. "What did you see, Father?"

"I believe I saw you kissing that American."

"He kissed me. Honestly—I had no idea he was going to do it. And if I had—" She stopped speaking, her eyes on her father. Was he angry enough to strike her? Sudden defiance burst uncontrollably from her breast. "Why must I defend myself? You've always demanded that I marry—and the sooner the better. Why should it matter to you where I place my attentions?"

Godfrey's eyes blazed. "Yes, I want you to marry. I expect you to marry, as every decent woman marries! But I plan for your husband to be at least somewhat suitable, Emmaline. Now take Nicholas Bond—"

"No, *you* take Nicholas Bond!" Emma jumped to her feet, throwing caution to the wind. "I don't want him. I don't want him or any of the other puppets you've chosen for me. I don't want Adam

King, for that matter. I don' t want anyone. I want to be a nurse—and I shall be one!"

"Emmaline! Control yourself." Godfrey stormed around the armchair toward her, then caught himself and stopped. He lowered his voice. "I'm quite certain our words can be heard in the hall."

Emma backed away from his harshness. She had spoken out of turn—her mother would have been horrified. A picture of her mother's face, white and drawn with tension as her daughter and husband argued, flashed through Emma's mind. Godfrey glared at her now, his eyes narrowed and angry.

"Sit down, Emmaline."

She set her shoulders. "Father, I am twenty-two years old. Please speak to me as an adult."

"I would speak to you as an adult, *if* you would behave as one. But you insist on carrying forth with your immature behaviors—as you did just now on the ballroom floor. And you insist on acting as though only your feelings mattered in your future."

"What else does matter?"

"The right and proper thing to do! Emmaline, you are a woman of potentially immense wealth."

Emma sighed. She had heard it all before, so often she could almost recite his words with him.

"You must see to it that the inheritance I have prepared for you is not squandered! You must marry the correct sort of man—one who is responsible and business-minded."

"You wish you could take every damned tuppence with you when you die!" Her words couldn't be stopped. She couldn't hold it in any longer. "You can't take your money with you, but you intend to make certain it's never wasted. I'm nothing more than a bank to you! If I marry the 'right' man, your money will grow and grow—and that's all you care about. How I feel doesn't matter, or what I want to do—or even if I'm happy with my future . . . it's only to assure that *your* precious holdings continue to grow and your name—"

"Emmaline!" Godfrey exploded, his voice quivering with rage. He stalked toward her as he spoke. "You are my daughter. You will control your tongue and not speak to me in that tone. You will obey me! You will marry, or you will never have a farthing of my wealth—and you will marry the man I select!"

"I shall not!" Emma took a step backward, astonished at the words she heard coming out of her mouth. "I don't care if I never see tuppence from you again! I don't want to get married and be a slave the rest of my life. I want to do what I'm meant to do! And you cannot stop me!"

"I can stop you, and I shall stop you!" Her father loomed before her now, his veins bulging and one hand gripping his chest over his heart.

Emma trembled as she faced him. "You cannot stop me!"

As her words registered, his hand shot out and caught her sharply across the cheek in a stinging blow. Her head jerked backward, and she saw the ceiling spin around and grow dark for an instant. Then she was on the floor, clutching her burning face.

Her father stepped forward and placed his foot on her skirt, crushing the soft pink roses. "I control you, Emmaline Pickworth," he said evenly. "I tell you what to do, and you do it. And I am telling you now that you will marry the man I select, and you will not have anything more to do with nursing or any other hotheaded scheme. Look at your mother's wickedness! I shall not allow you to disgrace me as she did. Do you understand?"

"Yes, Father." Her head felt as if it had burst, and she licked at the blood on her lip.

"Your behavior tonight was despicable and will not be tolerated again. You embarrassed me, Emmaline. I shall not allow you to behave in such a manner!"

Emma closed her eyes. She had tried to do as he asked. Her efforts to obey had gone as far as restraining her sister to prevent their father's ire. Cissy had no idea how often Emma had blocked the advances of potential suitors. And yet when Cissy did fall in love . . . and she often did . . . her father lightly reproved her, then hugged and pampered her. Emma bore the brunt of—no, it was not Cissy's fault that their father loved her more.

"Priscilla is your younger sister—your charge. You must set a worthy example for her." Godfrey spoke the old familiar words, and Emma listened to them again. "I expect you to take care of her and protect her. I cannot be both mother and father to my daughters! Is that perfectly clear?"

"Yes, Father."

"Then rise and go to your room. I shall inform Mr. Bond you were not feeling well."

Struggling to her feet, Emma pulled her dress from beneath her father's foot. At the door, she picked up the lavender gloves and held them beneath her nose.

"Miss Pickworth?" Nicholas Bond emerged from the shadows beside the stairwell as Emma carefully shut the parlor door behind her.

She did not pause to look at him. "Excuse me, sir. I am not well." She pulled the gloves away and saw that they were spotted with blood.

"Miss Pickworth—will you not return to the dance?"

She was halfway up the stairs. "Not tonight. I'm sorry."

"May I assist you in any way?"

"No, nothing can be done." She hurried down the hall out of his sight. As she burst into the room, she slammed the door behind her and ran to the window. Throwing back the curtain, she pressed her cheek against the cool glass and let the tears flow.

He was right, of course! She could never escape him—she must do as he said. Always. She would never be a nurse, never put into practice all the exciting things she had learned at St. Thomas's. She would marry some man her father chose—a proper man, as her mother had done—and live in a fine house in London during the season and spend the rest of the time at an estate in the country.

She would have children and maids and guests by the score. And she would do all the things she had been brought up to do. She would receive visitors in the parlor and go to kettledrums with Cissy and drink tea and bouillon and eat little sandwiches and cakes—just as they always did. She would play tennis and croquet and go yachting and bicycling. And everything would be just the same.

"Emma!" The door swung open, and Cissy's voice filled the room with an urgent cry.

Emma drew away from the window and focused

on her sister across the darkened room. "I'm here, Cissy—what is it?"

"It's Father! He's having one of his spells—you must come!"

For an instant Emma hesitated. He didn't want her to be a nurse. She could refuse to go to him now. She could let him suffer—maybe even . . .

"Where is he?"

"In the parlor. Mr. Bond found him collapsed on the floor!"

"Did you try the smelling salts?" She headed across the room to her sister's side.

"No!" Cissy sounded nearly hysterical. "Oh, Emma, you know how useless I am in a panic."

"It's all right, Cissy." Emma lifted her skirts and ran down the stairs.

The parlor was crowded with guests as Emma pushed her way toward the sofa where her father lay. He was being tended by Lady Delamere and Nicholas, who had placed a wet cloth on his pallid forehead.

"Please clear the room, Mr. Bond," Emma ordered as she knelt on the carpet at her father's side. She saw at once that his round stomach rose and fell evenly. Flipping back his coat pocket, she removed the bottle of salts and held it under his nose. Instantly his eyes fluttered open and he began coughing.

"It's Emmaline, Father." She murmured softly, as her mother always had. "You've had another attack, but all is well now. You must rest."

He caught her arm. "Emmaline, is Cissy . . . ?"

"Yes, Father." Emma knew the question that always formed itself upon his lips after an attack. "Cissy is fine. You've given her a bit of a fright.

Everyone is fine. I shall instruct the servants to attend you, but you must not move for a time. Please rest."

Rising, she spoke with Lady Delamere for a moment, then slipped out of the room.

Cissy ran on light feet to her sister's side. "Emma, did something happen in the parlor? Did you have another fight?"

Emma turned to her sister and looked into her eyes. Cissy gasped. "Oh, Emma! He's hit you again, hasn't he? Why can't you just be quiet, why must you always make him so angry?"

Cissy's eyes brimmed, and Emma put her arm around her sister's shoulder. "He seems to provoke me deliberately. I know it's wrong of me, but I cannot keep quiet."

They walked into their suite, and Cissy turned up the gas lamp so that the room was bathed in a golden glow. She turned toward her sister. "Come with me, Emma."

Emma allowed herself to be led to the mirror. When she gazed into it, she saw two figures gazing back at her. One was just as she had been when they'd left the room once before—prim and soft in a powder-blue dress, golden hair coiled around a bright bird, eyes shining.

But the other figure Emma barely recognized. Her hair, no longer curled and pinned to the top of her head, hung wild about her shoulders from her dancing with Adam. A pink stain from her father's hand marred her cheek, and her eyelid had begun to turn a light blue. One nostril was lightly rimmed with blood. Her fingertips flew to her cheek. What had people thought in the parlor below?

"Who am I?" she whispered.

"You're my sister—and I love you. Do as he says, Emma. Please don't let him hurt you again . . . please."

Emma folded her frail sister into her arms. "I love you, too, Cissy."

A loud thumping, thundering sound woke Emma from a deep and tortured dream. Sitting up instantly, she blinked in confusion at her surroundings.

"Emma, do come and look!" Cissy was fluttering before the window in her long silken nightgown.

Clutching her aching temple, Emma slid from her bed and padded across the room. "What is that noise?"

"Just look!" Cissy clapped her hands with glee as Emma peered out the window onto the tin roof of the level below. A handful of monkeys danced and cavorted across it—thin, spidery monkeys with gray fur and funny black faces. Emma had to smile, but as she did her lip cracked painfully.

Cissy's brow furrowed. "Are you all right? You look as though you've been to battle."

"I have been to battle." She absently watched the monkeys and licked the salty blood from her lip. "We shall have our fill of wild creatures, you know. The train leaves at eight—what time is it?"

"Six-thirty. The servants brought breakfast, but I didn't want to disturb you. It's on the table."

Emma turned into the room, but her sister's next words brought her head around quickly.

"Emma, look! It's the cowboy."

The shiny black horse she had seen yesterday

cantered down the long drive. Adam tipped his hat to the window, a lopsided grin lighting the features of his handsome face. Emma shrank back, her hand over her bruised cheek.

"He saw you, Emma! Oh, isn't he odd—and wonderful at the same time?" Cissy held the curtain before her face and let her eyes peep out from behind it. "Just look at that strange coat. It's all leather of some sort. And his boots—aren't they rough?"

Emma could not resist peering over Cissy's shoulder. Adam slid easily from his horse and looped the reins over the branch of a flowering tree. A gentle breeze blew a bright red cotton scarf at his brown neck and lifted the back of his coat into a split.

"He's wearing those blue trousers again, isn't he?" Emma whispered. "They suit him. And I do like that hat—though it certainly isn't what one would wear in London."

"Do you think he's coming to see you?" Cissy mused aloud.

"Don't be ridiculous!" Emma pulled back from the window and started to the breakfast table, her heart fluttering despite her outward calm. "He has business with Lord Delamere, I suppose. They seemed to know one another."

"I think he likes you." Cissy eased herself into the gilt chair across from her sister and picked up a slice of cold toast. "From the way he kissed you last night, I would say—"

"He's married, Cissy." Emma swallowed a lump of the dry bread. "He has a wife—in America."

"Oh." Cissy's voice was low.

"Do pass the tea." Emma blinked back the tears

that inexplicably had filled her eyes. She snatched up a knife and buttered the tasteless toast, then set it down untouched. "I'm not going to get married, Cissy. Not ever."

Cissy's eyes clouded. "I'm not, either. Not unless it's to Rolf."

Emma half listened to Cissy, whose words, as usual, focused on herself. Sounds in the hallway beneath them were of greater interest at the moment. She wondered if Adam were now inside and what he had come for. What was his wife like? What was her name? . . .

"I miss Rolf so much that my insides ache with it," Cissy was saying. "Every moment I'm thinking about him, Emma. He's probably at his post by now, defending the borders against the enemy—the British!"

Emma took Cissy's thin white hand in hers. The kaiser had been causing no end of trouble for the queen, she knew. He was half the reason her father and his associates were so keen on building this railway. And, of course, the British Empire needed the ivory.

"Oh, Emma," Cissy cried, "do you hate the kaiser because he wants to stop the empire? I don't! I don't care about him at all. Rolf is a German, and he's nothing like that. He's good and kind, and he loves me."

"I'm sorry, Cissy. But you must forget him. They were three glorious weeks but you have your whole life ahead."

A knock on the door prevented a response. Emma rose and hurried across the room. A servant waited just outside the door, his hands holding a silver tray bearing a pen, a bottle of ink, and a scrap of folded white paper. She read the words written in a bold black hand: "Miss Emma Pickworth."

Glancing back at Cissy, she swept the note from the tray and opened it with suddenly trembling fingers. Her eye fell at once on the large letters at the bottom of the note: "Adam King."

Quickly, before she could think, she read the note. "Emma, please come down. I need to talk to you about the subject we were discussing last night. Adam King."

Emma noticed that the man who stood in the doorway respectfully kept his eyes from her face. She knew she could not see Adam. The constant conflict with her father had taken its toll on everyone. To preserve a fragile peace, it would be best to obey him. But Adam wanted to talk to her—it was about her nursing. . . . And she would be in his presence again. She would look into his eyes and memorize their color. Perhaps he would touch her hand. Or they might walk in the gardens together. Maybe he would take her in his arms as he had the night before—

Emma stopped her thoughts. She must write a note back and say she wasn't well. Or she could send Cissy down to him—no, her father wouldn't like that, either. She would write a note. With a sigh, Emma picked up the pen and paper on which Adam had written. Dipping the pen into the ink, she paused for a moment before writing.

"Dear Mr. King, I cannot speak with you again. Please forgive me. Emma Pickworth."

Quickly she folded the letter and placed it on the tray. The servant nodded in acknowledgment and headed down the hall toward the stairs that led to the first floor.

"Was it from the cowboy?" Cissy flew to Emma's side. "What did he want? What did you write?"

"He wanted to speak with me. I wrote that I couldn't go." Emma moved to the washstand as she spoke and surveyed her face with dismay. Her eyelid had turned a light blue green, and her cheek bore a pink bruise. She poured cold water into the basin and plunged her face into it. Why should she obey her father? Look what he had done to her! And hadn't she told him he could not keep her from nursing? But he had had his way, as always— she had refused to see the rancher who might have told her about a mission where she could go to work.

Angry with herself, she set her shoulders and marched to the open trunk. Yanking out a dun-colored traveling skirt and a white blouse, she tossed them onto the bed. Cissy helped Emma into her corset, then began the arduous process of lacing.

"You're going to see him, aren't you?"

"No, Cissy. I am not. Though I should, you know. Father has no right to tell me what I may and may not do."

"Well, he is our father."

"Yes, but I'm a grown woman. I can make up my own mind now."

Cissy struggled with the laces, and Emma sucked in her breath. As soon as the binding garment was on, she tossed her silk vest over her head and pulled her tangled waves of hair through it. She had just stepped into her drawers when a sharp *ping!* sounded at the window.

"Whatever can that be—one of the monkeys?" Cissy ran across the room and drew back the curtain. "Oh, my goodness, Emma! It's your cowboy—he's . . . he's—"

Emma threw her robe over her shoulders and followed her sister to the window. Adam stood below, whirling a long circling rope over his head. His hat was thrown back on his head, and his tanned face was lit with the golden light of early morning. Suddenly he released the rope, and both girls drew back as it flew through the air, landed on the tin roof, and slipped into a tight knot around the projecting drainpipe.

"Emma—dear God in heaven—he's climbing up here!" Cissy squeaked in horror and flew toward the sitting room of the suite as fast as her legs would carry her.

Watching the rope pull taut and the drainpipe strain downward as if it might pull loose at any moment, Emma clutched the curtain with white-knuckled fingers. If her father saw Adam climbing up to the window, he would have him tossed in jail in an instant. How dare he approach her when she had made it clear she could not see him? And why was her heart beating so wildly at the thought of being in his presence again?

The black hat bobbed over the edge of the roof, followed by Adam's bronzed face. In a trice he hauled himself onto the tin roof and sauntered across with his spurs jingling behind him and the gun in his hip holster glinting in the sun.

"Hello, Emma." He took off his hat and leaned against the white window frame.

Emma backed away, still hidden by the sheer curtain. "Mr. King, I told you I could not speak with you! And it's most improper to—"

"I needed to talk to you. Can I come in?"

"No, you cannot come in! Don't be ridiculous—I'm still in my nightclothes."

"That doesn't bother me." His blue eyes sparkled the color of the African sky and flicked lightly over her deshabille. She looked good . . . very good. The sheer fabric barely concealed the creamy curve of her breasts above her corset. She looked even better than he had thought she might—and he had thought about her a lot. He flashed a grin and hooked his thumb through the loop of his trousers, which pulled them more tightly against his lean legs. "Can we talk for a minute?"

"No, we cannot talk at all! Let yourself down by that . . . that rope thing, and—"

"My lasso?" He held up the thick white rope and began coiling it into a large circle. Emma was acting half-scared of him this morning—not at all the bold young woman he had met yesterday. Well, he couldn't let that concern him. Last night after he left her, he'd made up his mind to keep strictly to business with Emma Pickworth. One kiss and he'd felt things getting a little tangled. No, he couldn't let that happen. He smiled lightly at her. "Well, I aim to leave when the time comes, but first there are a few things I need to say."

"Hurry up, then. If my father finds you here—"

Adam laughed. "With all due respect, Emma, do you think I'm that concerned what your father thinks?"

The thought that any man would stand up to her father was new, and Emma found herself smiling despite her fears. "What do you want from me?"

"I need a nurse."

Emma blinked in surprise. "A nurse? Are you ill?"

"Not for me." His face grew serious, the blue eyes suddenly dark. "I have a friend—at my ranch. I need help—"

Suddenly remembering the letter she had read the day before, Emma wondered who this "friend" could be. A woman? Surely not a native. Or could that be the sort of evil Nicholas had been referring to?

"What sort of illness does your friend have?" Emma let the curtain drop a little. "Can you describe the symptoms?"

Adam gazed out across the tops of the palms. How could he tell her without arousing her suspicions and scaring her off? "It's not an illness. It's more like . . ." He turned back to Emma, but when his eyes fell on her face he suddenly reached through the open window and jerked the curtain out of her hands. "What happened to you? Who did this?"

Emma's hand flew to her cheek and eye. She tried to back away, but he caught her arm and pulled her toward him, lowering her hand. "It's nothing, nothing! Please let me go!"

As she struggled to free herself, she saw one booted foot reach over the windowsill and the other follow. And then he had gathered her into his arms and was brushing back the hair from her eye as he said softly, "Emma, Emma . . . who did this to you?"

His deep voice lulled her anguish and she grew still, though she held herself rigid against him. He circled her waist with one arm around the thin robe and lifted his fingers to stroke her eyelid, her swollen cheek. Frowning, he stared at the pink stain on her cheek and her puffy blue eyelid. No wonder she had shied like a scared colt. She hadn't wanted him to know. Damn . . . and now here he was holding her in his arms.

She closed her eyes and drifted in the warmth of his sun-heated skin and the scent of fresh air he had brought with him through the window. Her back loosened beneath his lightly caressing fingertips and the smell of his skin—tobacco and leather and dust. His lips came down to brush against her own—then suddenly he stiffened.

"Bond! He did this to you, didn't he?" Adam's voice hardened in anger, and Emma's eyes flew open. "I swear to you, I'll kill him—"

"No! No, it wasn't Nicholas Bond." She backed out of his embrace. "He never touched me. Please . . . please, Adam, just go away now."

"Emma, take this—" Without stopping to consider, he pulled his gun from the holster and thrust it into her hands. "This country's wild—full of animals and people who don't give a damn about anything but themselves. Survival of the fittest, you know. You need protection. Use this if you have to." He squeezed her hands around the pistol for emphasis. "Now you listen up—"

"No, I won't listen to you! I have nothing to say to you." Emma held the gun awkwardly, as if it were a dead thing. "Please just go! The train leaves at eight, and I have to dress—and you have no place here in my bedroom. . . ." She set the weapon on the window sill, glad to be rid of it.

"Emma, slow down." Adam caught her wrists and pulled her back to him. He'd never been a man to think things over. He just did what he knew felt right. And here she was, trembling against him. "I want you to come with me—I need your help. And I'll take care of you."

"I don't need taking care of! I don't need protecting. It's the last thing I want from you. I have my own plans—"

"Emma!" Cissy's voice sliced through her words, and Emma whirled toward the open door of the sitting room. Her sister stood there frozen, eyes wide.

"What is it, Cissy?"

"Emma, go with him!" Cissy darted across the floor on tiptoe. "Go with him, Emma! It's your chance to get away—to be a nurse, as you've always wanted. You'll be safe at last—and you can do what you want!"

Emma stared at her sister; it was unlike her to be so bold. Cissy had stopped halfway across the floor. Her robe billowed to her feet. Her mouth was open—a china doll's thin red lips. Her frail white arms were held wide, the delicate fingers spread with pleading. Emma whirled to Adam. He was leaning forward, one hand cocked on his belt, the other holding his hat.

"Come on, Emma." His eyes flashed with such intensity that she thought they might burst into blue flame. "Come with me."

Emma turned back to her sister. "Go on, Emma!" Cissy urged. "I shan't tell Father where you've gone. I'll say I woke to find you missing. He'll never find you."

Cissy poised before her, fragile as an angel. She looked as if she might break at any moment. And Emma knew she might without her sister for a stronghold. Emma saw her mother at that moment—the golden hair spread across the white pillow, the wide blue eyes gazing up out of the deathly white face. *Take care of Cissy, Emma,* her mother's words whispered to her. *Take care of your little sister. She needs you.*

A loud banging at the door startled Emma from her vision.

"Emmaline!"

Cissy gasped. "It's Father! Emma, go at once!"

Emma spun back to Adam, then to Cissy—then back to Adam again. "No, I can't go with you, Adam!"

"Emmaline, Priscilla—open this door at once."

"Adam, get out of here!" Emma hurled herself into him, pushing uselessly toward the window. "Please, please!"

"Emma, I'm staying here." And suddenly he saw it all clearly. "He did it, didn't he? He's the one who beat you. I'll make him pay for what he—"

"No! No, you can't fight him. Don't you see—I must stay with Cissy. And it will only be worse for us if he finds you here!"

Adam hesitated for an instant, his eyes locked on Emma's face. Her green eyes filled with fear, and her determination not to go with him blocked his impulse to sweep her up and carry her off. He had to leave her alone to face her father. Before he could change his mind, he vaulted through the window and was gone. Cissy scampered to the door and opened it.

"Emmaline!" Godfrey strode into the room, snapping an order to the man behind him. "Wait in the hall, Bond. I may need your help."

As the door was slamming shut, Emma glanced around her father to see the younger man brandishing a revolver menacingly.

"Where is he?" Godfrey demanded, his voice hard. "Where's King?"

"Adam King?" Emma struggled to feign surprise. She stepped back toward the curtains, and her fingers fell on the heavy gun behind her, but she did not pick it up. "Whatever makes you think we would know where Mr. King is?"

"Honestly!" Cissy put on her best pout. "Father, we were just in the middle of our breakfast and dressing for the train. What on earth are you doing in our room? Emma's just barely had time to slip that robe over her combinations!"

"Priscilla, do not lie to me." Godfrey stalked across the room and flung open the wardrobe. "Adam King was here—at the consulate! We know that. And the gardener saw him standing outside your window."

"He did call to us," Cissy said breathlessly. "He wanted to speak with Emma. But she refused to speak to him. And he rode away on his black horse."

Godfrey glowered at Emma. Unconscious of her action, she brushed a hand over her swollen eye. "Emmaline, if I find you have been lying to me, you will not see the end of my anger." Her father stomped across the bedroom and flashed a derringer he had pulled from his coat pocket. "If you're in here, King, I shall see you dead before I rest."

"He's not here!" Cissy drew her robe around her neck in self-righteous rage. "Father, we are not in the habit of telling lies."

Emma turned away, suppressing a smile at Cissy's favorite expression. Perhaps her sister did not need as much caring for as she believed.

As their father stormed out of the room and slammed the door behind him, both girls turned to the window. The driveway was empty, only a faint cloud of dust in a thin trail above it.

"You should have gone with him, Emma." Cissy's arm stole around her sister's shoulder.

Emma closed her eyes and breathed a sigh of

relief. As she inhaled, she drank in the morning—the fresh air and the lingering scent of tobacco and leather and dust.

# Chapter Four

✦ ✦ ✦ ✦

*He sets up drinks when he hasn't a cent;*
*He'll fight like hell with any young gent.*
*When he makes love, he goes it hell-bent,*
*Oh, he's some lover, this cowboy.*

—"The Cowboy"

*When filled with tears that cannot fall,*
*I brim with sorrow drowning song.*

—Alfred, Lord Tennyson
"In Memoriam A.H.H. XIX"

EMMA LEANED HER head against the side of the railcar window and gazed out at the placid blue ocean. The train had pulled out of the station not long before and now chugged across the three-quarter-mile Salisbury Bridge. Cissy sat on the seat across from Emma, a French novel lying unattended in her lap as she stared down at her hands. No doubt her sister was dwelling on Rolf, Emma thought. Cissy's pale eyelids betrayed the tears she had shed the night before in Emma's arms.

The train rolled onto the mainland from Mombasa island, and Emma, tensing suddenly with anticipation, drew her eyes away from her sister. At last—the protectorate in all its raw majesty. She watched the train's twelve-mile-an-hour pace leave the palm trees and mango and banana groves behind and replace them with huge gray baobabs, lush green acacias, and thick underbrush. Emma's olive-green eyes reflected the verdant terrain as she searched for signs of wild game, her own vol-

ume of poetry lying unread at her side. Though her
gaze was fixed on the landscape, she could not
keep from hearing the urgent conversation coming
from the berth behind her.

"Patterson had only been at Tsavo two or three
days when the first coolie was dragged off." Nicholas whispered loudly above the rattle of the car.
"That's been two months ago, sir. Since that time
the killings have escalated. Patterson's been after
the lions nearly every night, but so far they've
eluded him."

"And how many lions are there?" Godfrey
sounded tense.

"Two. That's for certain—only two. One would
think we could bag them, but they are so clever.
And of course the workers' camps are spread out
along the rail line so far that the lions have quite a
feeding ground, so to speak."

"Has Patterson tried poison?"

Nicholas hesitated a moment. "I'm afraid the
lions have acquired a taste for human flesh, sir.
They much prefer a live coolie to a poisoned dead
donkey."

"Can the workers not build fences?"

"They've built large hedges of thorns around the
tents, but unfortunately the lions are able to jump
over or go through anything so far erected. These
two lions are incredibly large and crafty, sir. The
coolies call them *shaitani*—devils."

A small knot of fear twisted in the pit of Emma's
stomach at the talk of lions. She had not known the
viciousness of beasts firsthand—but human cru-
elty was more than familiar. She shifted the heavy
white pith helmet in her lap. Adam's gun lay in the
cloth chatelaine bag beside her. Somehow it comforted her . . . not so much for the protection it

offered, but for the memories it stirred of the towering man who had held her so tenderly.

But knowing her path probably would never cross with Adam King's again on this sprawling continent, Emma forced her thoughts away from him and onto the situation at hand. Where would she and Cissy sleep? she wondered. How would they be kept safe from the marauding beasts Nicholas had spoken of? She had never fired a weapon in her life, and she could not imagine defending herself against a hungry lion. The thought of meeting a lion face to face intrigued her, however, even as it frightened her. She had always loved and respected animals. Part of her reason for coming to the protectorate so willingly had been her desire to see the magnificent creatures she had visited only in zoos, where they were kept behind awful iron bars and heavy fencing.

Willing her concentration away from the conversation behind her, Emma stood and grasped the handles of the glass window.

"What are you doing, Emma?" Cissy sat forward, and her novel slid to the floor.

"I need some fresh air." Emma heaved on the handles and slid the heavy window upward. A gust of clean, cool wind blew into the stuffy car and tugged a lock of hair from Emma's chignon. Golden in the late morning sunlight, the wisp danced about her chin as she propped her hands on the sill and leaned out the window.

There! Beneath an enormous baobab tree in the far distance stood a great red-gray elephant. With tiny eyes it squinted at the train, then lifted its long wrinkled trunk, testing the air for scents of the strange clattering iron beast. Emma closed her eyes and sucked in a deep breath of morning air, but the aroma that filled her nostrils made her stop in mid-breath. It was not the fragrance of lush grass and sunburned earth, but a smell she knew all too well. The thick, pungent-sweet tobacco aroma instantly brought to mind a leather vest, a wild whirling dance, a stolen kiss.

Leaning farther out, Emma turned to the cars ahead. Two spurred boots, one crossed casually over the other, protruded from the distant window. Emma's fingers tightened on the sill, and she pulled in her head.

"What is it?" Cissy stood up.

Emma hesitated a moment, then stuck her head out again to make sure she had seen correctly. There they were again—two leather boots with square heels and toes, and silver spurs spinning lazily in the breeze.

Cissy gently pushed her sister to one side and peered out. In an instant she was back in the railcar and pulling Emma onto the berth beside her. "It's the cowboy!" she whispered urgently. Her eyes were wide, animated again. "He's followed you onto the train, Emma. You must go and speak with him."

Emma's gold-tipped lashes fluttered down for a moment. Then she looked up into her sister's face. "Cissy, you know I can't speak with him. Think what will happen if I'm caught."

Cissy's eyes darted to her sister's blue-tinged lid and livid cheek. "But he needs you; he told you that. And he'd protect you, Emma. I know he would. He's that sort of man. Like Rolf."

Emma looked out the window at the tangle of shrubbery brushing past. Adam King was that sort of man—at least she thought so. But why should she trust someone she knew so little about? His

behavior had proven him nothing but a rough
cad—shoving the purser about, kissing her in
public—and yet something about him . . . Her
mind went back to her first view of him. He had
been no more than a dark form on a black horse,
yet he had cradled the child so gently.

"If I get a chance, I shall go to him," Emma said
with quiet determination. "Though I'm quite certain he did not get on the train because of me. He
didn't even know I was going to be—"

"But he did! I heard you tell him we were leaving
on the eight o'clock train. He knew you'd be here,
Emma—he's waiting for you. He saw what Father
did." Cissy craned her neck over the back of the
berth and saw her father listening attentively to
Nicholas. Then she slid back down and tucked her
arm through her sister's. "The cowboy would
never cause you harm," she whispered. "He cares
for you."

"Honestly, Cissy. Where do you come up with
these ideas?"

"I know men." The corners of Cissy's mouth
turned up like rose petals unfolding. "I know men,
and I can easily see that the cowboy has taken a
strong fancy to you."

"Oh, Cissy." Emma half-angrily shoved the wisp
of hair back into her chignon. First of all, Cissy
knew nothing at all about Adam King—even less
than she herself knew. And second, the man was
married. His wife was somewhere in America getting ready for a governor's inauguration—and
waiting for him to join her. If Adam wanted to talk
with Emma at all, it was only because he knew she
was a nurse, and for some reason he seemed to
need one quite badly. She glanced sideways at

Cissy. How like her love-stricken sister to go setting her up with a man!

Her cheeks flushed, Emma leaned back on the leather seat and shut her eyes. What an utterly ridiculous idea! To think that Adam fancied her, to imagine that there could be any chance . . . Emma tightened her closed lids against the unbidden memory of his finger beneath her chin and his lips against hers. She could almost feel the graze of his rough cheek, almost smell the scent of his tobacco—

Rising suddenly, she grabbed the iron handles and slammed the window shut against the drift of blue-gray smoke.

Lunch came and went—steaming cream soup with lobster soufflé, not at all in keeping with the sweltering heat inside the railcar and the increasing herds of game outside. Nicholas chose to settle himself beside Emma after lunch and expound on his dreams for the railway. Though she tried to concentrate, Emma found her attention drawn to the changing landscape outside the window.

Over the Rabai Hills, the train descended to the wide expanse of the Taru Desert. This wilderness, so different from the wooded lands nearer the coast, was dotted with thin scrub and stunted trees. Layers of fine red dust carpeted everything, even working its way into the train so that Cissy rose again and again to shake out her thin white linen skirt.

Late in the afternoon, the train stopped at a station labeled in proud black letters, "Voi." One of

the major stops along the line, Voi had a crisp
whitewashed station building and several stone
houses. Nicholas deboarded with Godfrey, leaving
the two young women alone in the silent car. Cissy
locked eyes with Emma for a moment, then rose to
peer out the window.

"He's there, on the platform." Cissy's voice
held a note of low eagerness. "He's with a lot of
other men—railworkers, I imagine. They all look
a bit sloshed. But not him. He's walking down
the platform toward us. He's . . . he's looking
this way—"

Cissy drew back from the window. Her fingertips over her mouth, she looked at her sister. Emma
stared back. Then she carefully slid across the seat
and allowed her eyes to fall on the tall figure. Adam
stood with his shoulder against the blue wooden
post of the station. The thumb of one hand hung
through his belt loop, the other hand held the stub
of a thin brown cigar. A revolver rested in the
holster along his thigh. His eyes, shadowed beneath the wide brim of his black hat, were fastened
on her window.

An odd curling sensation slid through Emma's
stomach as she looked at him. He lifted his hand
from his belt loop and casually pushed back the
brim of his hat with one tanned finger. Then,
slowly, he brought the hand down and crooked
the finger at her.

Emma looked away. "He wants me to come outside, Cissy. Father will see me there." But she
knew he wanted to talk about nursing, and maybe
he could help her.

"He wants you, Emma! Oh, if he were Rolf, I'd
go at once. I wouldn't hesitate a second!"

Emma lifted her eyes. Her father stood a few

paces away, talking animatedly with Nicholas and
the stationmaster. "I can't." She shook her head at
Adam.

His shoulders rose and fell. Then he turned his
gaze to the car where he had been. Staring boldly
at Emma again, he carefully positioned his hand
in front of the wide silver buckle on his belt. One
finger jabbed repeatedly in the direction of the
car.

Emma slid back against the leather seat and tried
to think. Adam wanted her to go to his railcar. But
how could she? Her father would see—he'd know
at once. The train whistle blew, and Emma tilted
her head to the window. Adam was striding back
across the platform, his spurs spinning silver white
in the afternoon sun. The stub of the brown cheroot lying on the wooden platform sent a curl of
smoke into the air.

"Did you not wish to stretch your legs, Miss
Pickworth?" Nicholas resumed his place beside her
with a comfortable smile. His light brown eyes
twinkled with a warm light. "We still have over
thirty miles until we reach Tsavo station."

Emma returned his smile as the train jerked to
life and began its swaying rhythm down the dark
track. "No, thank you, Mr. Bond. How far have we
come to Voi?"

"A little more than one hundred miles. I expect
it will be dark before we arrive. The sun sets
promptly at six on the equator, you know."

Emma turned to the window. The flat, dry terrain had begun to change back to thick woods.
When the tea arrived, Nicholas allowed Emma to
pour him a cup, and as he sipped, he crossed his
legs.

"Has your father told you about our plans for the

inland station—Nairobi?" His voice was light, informative.

Cissy smiled at him. "Do tell us, Mr. Bond."

Emma tried to focus on the fine features of the railman's cleanly shaven face. He kept the sandwich crumbs from clinging to his blond mustache by regularly brushing it with a white napkin.

"Nairobi is to be the headquarters of the railway administration. The site is on a bare high plain, three hundred and twenty-seven miles from Mombasa." Nicholas's voice lilted as he spoke. "We'll build roads and bridges, houses and workshops, turntables and a station. We must lay in a water supply and a hundred other things."

"Will there be shops?" Cissy asked.

"I hope so. Perhaps a regular bazaar, like the one in Mombasa. With all the new colonists coming in from England, I can see it as a real town someday. And when the protectorate becomes a colony . . ."

Emma's eyes wandered to the pink-tipped foliage and the golden clouds lining the horizon. The sun hung above it, a giant orange ball. Sounds of gentle snoring drifted over the back of the seat. Her father's snoring. . . .

"Will you excuse me?" she said suddenly, rising to her feet and nearly upsetting the tea tray. "I believe I shall take a walk after all."

She glanced down to find Cissy looking at her knowingly, but she lifted her head and slid past Nicholas out into the aisle between the rows of seats.

"Miss Pickworth, shall I accompany you?" Nicholas leapt to her side. "The train's swaying can be decidedly treacherous."

"No, thank you, Mr. Bond. Please carry on with

your tale of . . . of what was the town you've planned?"

"Nairobi!" Cissy interjected, pulling Nicholas back onto the seat. "Yes, do carry on with your plans for Nairobi. Jolly clever ideas you've cooked up, Mr. Bond. Do continue."

Emma gave Cissy a grateful smile and hurried down the aisle before Nicholas could change his mind. She glanced back once before the door, but all she could see was Cissy's bobbing ostrich plumes and her father's top hat. Quietly pushing open the door to the outside, she stepped onto the shaking platform. A firm grip on the iron rail helped her balance as she worked her crinolined skirt across the swaying platform to the door of the next car. Blinking in the soot-filled air, she opened the door and stepped inside.

Far more shabbily outfitted, this car was filled with goods. Boxes and crates cluttered the seats and partially blocked the aisle, making her path difficult. There were bales of cloth and chests carved from camphorwood, along with folded cots, rickety chairs, and rough-hewn tables. The colonists' possessions. It would not be easy to live in this land, she realized as she reached the far end, turned the door handle and stepped outside onto the next platform. It would require a certain hardiness—a fortitude.

Steadying herself against the iron railing, she tugged open the door to the next car, but the sight that met her eyes made her step back outside to the dusky evening. She widened her stance on the shaking platform, cracked the door, and peered into the car. Filled with gray smoke, it was a jumble of sprawling limbs, broken bottles, top hats lying askew on the floor, button boots, umbrellas, and morning coats. Men of every description lay about moaning or sleeping. Others sat in groups, tossing playing cards onto tables amid shouts and cheers and hearty laughter. Over all, the smell of thick, stale smoke and liquor filled the car—and a strange plinking music drifted through the rattle.

"Sky is his ceiling, grass is his bed," a deep voice sang quietly. "Saddle is the pillow for the cowboy's head. . . ."

Emma, hidden behind the door, searched through the pall for the singer. At last she spotted him, perched on the high back of a berth. Adam looked out the window, his expression distant as if he were seeing something from another time. A large, yellow wooden guitar rested on one thigh, and he strummed the instrument now and then, humming along with the chords.

"Way out West where the antelope roam, and the coyotes howl round the cowboy's home . . ." he sang, his voice melodic. "Where the miner digs for the golden veins, and the cowboy rides o'er the silent plains; where the prairies are covered with chaparral frail, and the valleys are checkered with the cattle trails; where the eagles scream and the catamounts squall, the cowboy's home is the best of all. . . ."

"I say, cowboy!" One of the men lifted a glass of ale into the air beside Adam. "Have a drink and see if you can find something a bit more lively in that box of yours."

The men chuckled as Adam took the tankard and swilled a long draft. "Yes, Mr. King," another man called out. "Don't you cowboy chaps play any spirited songs on those guitars?"

Adam looked down and smiled. Then suddenly

he jumped onto the seat and let out a whoop. "Wake up, snakes, and bite a biscuit!" His fingers set into his guitar.

"I'll eat when I'm hungry, I'll drink when I'm dry; if the hard times don't kill me, I'll live till I die!"

The men began to clap and stomp their feet to the lively tune. Even some of the travelers lying on the floor lifted their heads. Adam leapt out into the aisle and danced a high-toed jig among the men as he sang. "Rye whisky, rye whisky, rye whisky, I cry. If you don't give me rye whisky, I surely will die! I'll tune up my fiddle, and I'll rosin my bow, and make myself welcome wherever I go. Beefsteak when I'm hungry, red liquor when I'm dry, greenbacks when I'm hard up, and religion when I die!"

"Rye whisky, rye whisky, rye whisky, I cry—" The men linked arms and rose to sing, swaying with the rhythm of the train. "If you don't give me rye whisky, I surely will die!"

Adam hopped onto a berth not far from the door behind which Emma peered at the strange, dream-like scene. "I'll buy my own whisky, I'll make my own stew; If I get drunk, madam, it's nothing to you. Rye whisky, rye whisky—"

He whirled, and his eye fell on the door. His words stopped suddenly as he saw Emma standing just behind it, but the raucous singing of the other men more than covered his absent voice. "Emma." His mouth formed the word, and he quickly covered the space between them.

Emma stepped back onto the outside platform, positioning her feet carefully on the heaving floor as Adam shut the door behind him.

"I'm glad you came," he said over the roar of the track clattering by beneath. He had brought his guitar, and the tiny space allowed barely enough room for them to stand.

The setting sun filtered through the sooty air, and Emma sensed the raw, animal strength of the man who stood before her. He had rolled his plaid sleeves to the elbow, and the red triangle scarf hung loose around his neck. "Shall we go into the baggage car?" She motioned behind her.

Adam did not speak. As Emma looked at him, she thought he might take her in his arms again—might hold her as he had done before. Her breath shortened as she looked into his indigo eyes. He stepped forward, and his thigh brushed against her leg. But he reached out across her shoulder, his hand grazing the soft fabric of her blouse, and pushed open the door behind her.

Color creeping into her cheeks as she thought of how boldly she had wanted his touch, Emma stepped from the platform into the baggage car. Adam set his guitar on a wooden chest and turned to her. His hands circled her waist, and before she knew it, he had lifted her gently onto a crate and eased his large frame up beside her.

"Where's your father?" he asked quietly.

Emma looked to the door at the far end of the car. "Asleep."

Adam slid back and hooked one heel over the edge of the box. He fastened upon her green eyes and saw their shining determination. Her stubbornness had beaten out her fear. He liked that in her. But he knew he had to get to his point. There wasn't much time if he wanted to keep her father out of range. "Listen, ma'am—Emma. You don't mind if I call you that, do you?"

Emma adjusted her skirt and turned so she could face him. He had cocked one arm around his knee. "It is quite irregular, you know. Men usually address me as Miss Pickworth."

One side of Adam's mouth turned up. "Are you always so proper, Emma? Don't you ever loosen up?"

Emma's back stiffened. She found herself doubting for the first time all the careful instruction in etiquette her mother had imparted. "I am always as proper as I can be, Mr. King. I was taught to be polite and courteous at all times. Especially to gentlemen who are my briefest acquaintances."

"I see." Adam shook his head, trying to suppress a chuckle. "Well, Miss Pickworth, I want to talk to you about two things. I only had one thing this morning when I went to the consulate, but now I have two."

Emma's fingers covered her eye, and she turned away self-consciously. But Adam's hand closed quickly around her wrist to pull her back to him. Lowering her hand, he ran his fingers over her eyelids and down her cheek. She closed her eyes, her nostrils flaring at the burning sensation that raced through her stomach and down into her legs at his touch.

"Emma, listen to me."

She opened her eyes and let them roam his rugged face. Cupping the soft curve of her jaw in his palm, he stroked her cheek with his thumb. Damn the man who did this, Adam thought. And damn me for caring.

"This morning—I'd have stayed, Emma." His eyes blazed with a blue fire. "I'll put him in his place, if you just say the word. He'll never touch you again, I swear it!"

"No, you can't. You mustn't do anything!" Emma wondered briefly whether he was more interested in defending her honor or using his fists. The thought made her shudder. She knotted her fingers. She had to make him understand that her father was only handling her the way he thought best. "You see, I've always been so stubborn. I made up my mind long ago what I wanted to do, and my father disapproves. He's trying to control me, you see."

"By hitting you? Hell, what is it you want to do that's so awful?"

"I want to practice medicine." The words suddenly came out in a rush. "I've trained for years. And now I've come here—I've come to do it, to become a nurse. But I have to get away, to find a place . . . a mission hospital or something. Do you know of anything like that? Any missions or doctors or—"

"There's a camp hospital with the railway. They've even got a doctor or two. A Dr. McCulloch . . . and there's another one—Dr. Brock, I think. Maybe you could get them to let you help out while you're here."

"No, no. It can't be with the railway. It's got to be somewhere permanent, someplace where my father has no control. Are there mission hospitals?"

"Not near the railway. Farther into the interior, I think." Adam stopped for a moment and sat forward. He was getting caught up in her dream, and he had to separate himself. He had to see that she was all right, but keep his distance. . . . "That's what I need to talk to you about—I need a nurse for my friend. I want you to come to my ranch and help me out, Emma."

"But you know how difficult—"

"If you'll do it, I'll take you to the interior. I'll

find you a mission hospital where you can be a nurse." He had to convince her. If she didn't come with him now, it might be too late.

"If I go with you, my father will know where I've gone! I could never risk the time it would take to stop at your ranch, don't you see? I must go straight to the hospital and seek sanctuary. And then—after it's all over—I could go to your ranch and help your friend."

"No, it—" Adam looked away. He had kept himself from thinking too much about it, but now he had to make her understand. "I think my friend is dying."

"You must take your friend to the railway clinic, then! You said they have doctors."

"I can't do that. I've had trouble with the railway . . . with someone—"

"Miss Pickworth?" Nicholas's voice echoed hollowly through the gloomy railcar. Emma sat up quickly, her green eyes wide. Adam instinctively grabbed her hand, and his strong fingers felt comforting against hers.

"Down here, Bond," he called.

Nicholas swung around, squinting in the dusk. "King, is that you?" His voice grew low. "Is Miss Pickworth there?"

"Yes, Mr. Bond, I'm here. Mr. King and I were just speaking for a moment about the railway."

Nicholas picked his way down the crate-littered aisle as he spoke. "Your father is awake, Miss Pickworth. He has been asking for you."

"And he's not going to know what she's been doing, isn't that right, Bond?" Adam jumped down from the crate and lifted Emma to the floor. "If you're half as smart as a bunkhouse rat, you'll keep your mouth shut."

"Or?" Nicholas halted before Adam, his fists planted firmly at his waist.

"Let me tell you something, Bond." Adam leaned closer and his voice dropped. "I'm not going to interfere between the lady and her father. But I'll damn sure interfere with you if you don't watch your step."

"Don't you dare threaten me, King! You've seen what I can do when I'm crossed—and I'll not hesitate to give you your due."

"I've seen your honorable way of handling things, you yellow-bellied bastard—"

Nicholas's fist shot out and caught Adam beneath his jaw. The rancher's head snapped back, sending his black hat to the floor. Adam staggered backward, thrusting Emma to one side and crashing into the crate. As Emma tumbled against the chest, she hit the guitar with a hollow thud. But her eyes were on Nicholas, who had pulled his fist back for a second blow. As he swung forward, Adam blocked the blow with one arm while his other swung forward, his huge fist finding its mark in the railman's stomach.

Emma untangled her skirts from the guitar and scrambled to her feet as Nicholas doubled over. "Stop it! Stop it, Adam—Nicholas!"

But the Englishman straightened, his face a mask of fury in the dim light as he threw himself at Adam. Emma grabbed the guitar and swung it at Nicholas, but the railman ducked, and the instrument crashed into a barrel with a discordant, twanging crack. Adam seized the momentary distraction to step backward and hoist himself onto a crate.

"Let it go, Bond!" Adam shouted as Nicholas

came after him. "Leave the fight for a better time and place!"

"You'd like that, wouldn't you? You know I have you now—you know—"

Adam's boot kicked out and caught Nicholas in the chest, stopping the railman's rush. "I said—let it go, Bond."

"Mr. Bond, please!" Emma watched in horror as the two men stood frozen, anger emanating from their bodies. She knew none of them could afford her father's disapproval if he learned of the fracas. Nicholas had to maintain a professionalism because of his position with the railway. Adam—if he intended to go on living in the protectorate and if he needed the railway at all—would have to avoid offending the powerful Godfrey. And she had already enraged her father so much that she could almost anticipate the violence this latest rendezvous with Adam would bring. She grasped the railman's arm. "Please do as he says!"

Nicholas's hand shook with rage as he struggled to refrain from the fight. He shoved the boot from his chest. "This is not over, King. I can assure you—this is not over!"

"Of course it's not over." Adam's voice dripped with venom. "You're going to pay for what you did. One way or another, you're going to pay."

"And you'll pay for who you are, Adam King—for what you're doing right now!"

Emma stared aghast at the two silhouetted men. She had seen such rage before. She had seen the anger of men, and she hated it. Grasping her skirts in her hands, she pushed past Nicholas and made her way down the aisle. This was why she would have nothing to do with them! This was the very reason she could not bear to be bound to a husband—this anger, this rage, this hatred. She knew from experience that one day it would turn on her.

"Emma." The deep voice drew her, but she did not stop. "Emma, remember what I told you—"

"Like bloody hell she'll remember you!" Nicholas's voice faded into the darkness as Emma shut the door behind her.

The sun had set when the train pulled to a hissing halt. Nicholas had left the baggage car shortly after Emma and he had sat silently beside her father for the remainder of the trip. She knew it was not over. It could not be over until her father had sorted out the facts and dealt with her in his own fashion. As they rose to make their way out of the train her eyes begged Nicholas to be silent.

"Tsavo station," he said quietly. "The end of the line."

Emma stepped down from the train onto the lantern-lit platform. Carefully she placed her white pith helmet onto her head and shook out her khaki skirt. Cissy came to her side, her eyes questioning, but Emma held her tongue.

The platform was a bustle of activity as the colonists and railworkers poured out of the cars with their boxes, chests, crates, and other belongings. Indian coolies, working fast to earn an extra coin or two, streamed back and forth carrying loads of goods. For a moment Emma thought she would not see Adam again, but then she caught sight of his hat in the crowd. . . .

"Emmaline, Priscilla," Godfrey said, drawing their attention to him, "I should like you to meet the railway physician, Dr. McCulloch." The stocky doctor's strong handshake, lively hazel eyes, and warm smile encouraged Emma. She made a mental note to talk to him later. Perhaps he could help her. Feeling her spirits lighten at the prospect of a sympathetic spirit, she ventured a glance behind her and centered on Adam. He had led his black horse down from a car and was strapping on a leather saddlebag. The red glow from his thin cigar traced bright arcs in the night.

"We have deemed it safest for your daughters to stay the night in the train, sir," Nicholas Bond was saying. "There is a sleeping car not far down the line."

Emma listened distractedly as she watched Adam shove a long rifle into its leather scabbard on his saddle.

"That will be suitable, will it not, Emmaline? . . . Emmaline."

Emma's head jerked around to face her father. "Yes—yes, of course. We should feel quite safe in the sleeping car."

Nicholas favored Godfrey with a slight bow. "If you like, I shall escort your daughters to the car, Mr. Pickworth. It will be my pleasure and will give you the chance to speak with Dr. McCulloch about the lion problem."

"Thank you very much, young man." Godfrey began to walk away, but stopped. "Emmaline, I shall visit your quarters later this evening. We have some matters to discuss, have we not?"

"Have we, Father?"

Godfrey's gray eyes went hard and cold. "Good evening, Emmaline."

"Good evening, Father." Emma set her jaw and hurried after Cissy and Nicholas. The car was some distance ahead of the one they had been in, but the platform was nearly empty of travelers now. The black horse had vanished, and with it Adam. A strange feeling of emptiness descended over her as Emma followed Cissy into the car.

"It's rarely been used," Nicholas explained, holding a kerosene lantern before them as they shouldered their way down the narrow aisle beside the windows. He opened one of the doors and showed them into a tiny compartment with two narrow beds. Placing the lantern on a hook by the door, he stepped back. "When the rail is long enough, of course, there will be night journeys. We park this car on a side track to use for guests such as yourselves. Dinner will be brought to you within the hour."

Emma placed her chatelaine bag with the gun in it on the cot's rough gray blanket, then moved to the window. "Thank you, Mr. Bond. You are most kind."

"Miss Pickworth—Emmaline—may I speak with you in private for a moment?"

Emma glanced at Cissy. "You may say whatever it is you would like to say in front of my sister. I will only tell her everything you say anyway."

"I think perhaps you will not, Miss Pickworth. Please. . . ."

With a glance back at her sister, Emma followed him. As Cissy shut the door behind them, they were plunged into darkness in the aisle. Emma followed the inky form ahead of her for a few paces, then stopped as he did.

"May I call you Emmaline?" he asked quietly.

Emma leaned against the paneled wall beside her. She had always hated that name—her father had used it so many times in anger. Yet she could not continue formalities with the man. Her mind wandered to Adam's question: *Are you always so proper? . . .* "Yes, you may call me Emmaline if you like."

"Thank you." His voice was low, and she could feel his presence close by her. "Emmaline, I must apologize for this evening in the baggage car. My behavior was unforgivably, inexplicably rude."

"Inexplicably? I think not. I am quite certain you can explain to me what has happened between you and Mr. King to cause such hatred."

The tall form shifted. "I beg of you not to think me rude again, but that is something between Mr. King and myself. Something better left buried."

"Obviously it is not buried. Every time you are together it erupts into violence. And I think I have a right to know."

"All right, if you must know. Mr. King is an American."

"I'm well aware of that . . . Nicholas. I believe it is not a crime."

Nicholas cleared his throat. "In Adam King's case one cannot be certain. He clearly does not have the empire at heart. His only concern is for his own interests, his ranch and his workers. He will do anything—anything—to advance himself. The man has no scruples, Emmaline."

Emma folded her arms and tilted her head away, annoyed. She hadn't come out here to hear more half-truths and evasions. There was far more—something had happened, she knew it. "And where is Mr. King's ranch?"

"Not far from here. He's bought a great many acres along the projected railway line." Nicholas stopped speaking and stepped toward Emma. Taking one of her hands in his, he drew her away from the wall. "Emmaline, you must understand . . . I—"

Emma felt his hands slip around her shoulders. "Mr. Bond," she said quickly, "does Mr. King have a person who is ill on his property?"

His long fingers stiffened suddenly, digging into her soft flesh. "Why do you ask that?"

"He mentioned that someone was ill. I wondered if you knew who it might be."

There was a long silence. Nicholas lowered his hands and shifted toward the window. Emma saw the starlight fall on his profile, silhouetting his strong nose and hard lips. His eyes glinted in the darkness. And, though the night was cool, a thin trickle of sweat ran from his sideburn. Brushing it away, he turned to face her.

"Mr. King is thought be a slaver," he said quietly. Half of his face shone a pale silver, the other half had disappeared into blackness. "There is still a great market for slaves, you see. The Orient. The Arabic states. And there is an active slave trade from the African interior."

"But the queen—" Emma hesitated, a hard lump in her throat blocking the words.

"Queen Victoria is opposed to slavery. And the United States has abolished it. But Mr. King is from one of the southern states—Texas, I believe. His heart is fettered to the money slaves can bring.

I would imagine, Emmaline, that the person he spoke of is a slave. He keeps them on his own property and transports them regularly from the Uganda territory. This sick one might be a favorite—a woman, perhaps. . . ."

"But he's—" Emma bit off the word before she spoke it. *He's married.* What difference would that make to a man who bought and sold human flesh? A female slave, a concubine. And his wife was still in America, after all. Why not? It all made sense.

"Emmaline, I tried to warn you. The man is treacherous. You cannot believe anything he tells you." Nicholas placed his hand around Emma's waist and drew her close to him. "I beg of you to stay away from him. . . . Emmaline—I wish to make clear my fondness and growing affection for you. You cannot be unaware of my devotion. . . ."

Emma lifted her eyes to the face above her. "Nicholas, your attentions have not escaped my notice, it is true. But the fact is—"

"Say no more." His eyes had turned the color of brass. "I am aware of your interest in pursuing a career. Perhaps you have had unpleasant experiences with men. But allow me to prove other men false, Emmaline. In me, you will find a man loyal and kind, generous and loving. You have two months here in the protectorate. Will you not give me opportunity to prove myself to you?"

Emma listened to the words of avowal she had heard from other men's mouths. Two months of Nicholas Bond's pursuit . . . two months of his persistent courting . . . the thought of it was enough to turn her dreams of freedom to dust. She stepped out of his arms. "Surely you can find another woman more willing. And as you have just stated, I intend

to practice nursing. That, and not marriage, is my
life's goal. Now if you will excuse me—"

"Wait!" He caught her hand. "There is one other
thing. A guard will be posted outside your window
tonight. But do not venture out of the railcar no
matter what the circumstance. The lions are not to
be taken lightly."

He lifted Emma's face to the moonlight and
pressed his lips to her mouth. The kiss was hard
and possessive, as though he wanted to seal her to
him. Emma stiffened, an unexplained sense of
panic rising in her throat at the touch of his lips.
When he drew away, his eyes wore a dark pleasure. "Good evening, Emmaline."

"Good night, Nicholas."

Emma stood back, her mouth dry and her hands
knotted, as he brushed past her to make his way
out of the train. When the door clanged shut behind him, she closed her eyes and leaned back
against the paneled wall.

*A slaver.* Adam sold human beings into bondage.
But why should she care? Why should her eyes
burn now with unshed tears and her throat con-
strict against a lump that would not diminish?
Brushing her cheek with the heel of her hand, she
straightened her shoulders and walked back to her
compartment.

"Cissy?" Emma knocked softly and pushed the
door open. Cissy was craning through the open
window, her soft white nightgown ruffling in the
cool breeze.

"Cissy, what are you doing?" Flying across the
room, Emma pushed her sister onto her bed and
slammed the window shut. "Have you forgotten
about the lions?"

Cissy's face had stiffened into a mask of pale

shock. Her bright blue eyes blinked twice, and she lifted her hands to her mouth.

Alarmed, Emma knelt at her sister's feet. "Cissy, what's wrong? What's happened? You look as if—"

"I heard him," Cissy whispered. "I heard him, Emma."

"Heard who?"

"Rolf." Cissy turned back to the window. "He was calling my name."

# Chapter Five
**✦ ✦ ✦ ✦ ✦**

*But when you get married, boys, you are done with this life,*
*You have sold your sweet comfort for to gain you a wife;*
*Your wife she will scold you, and the children will cry,*
*It will make those fair faces look withered and dry . . .*

*I have one more request to make, boys, before we part:*
*Never place your affection on a charming sweetheart;*
*She is dancing before you your affections to gain;*
*Just turn your back on her with scorn and disdain.*

—"The Range Riders"

*I . . . felt my blood*
*Glow with the glow that slowly crimsoned all*
*Thy presence and thy portals, while I lay,*
*Mouth, forehead, eyelids, growing dewy-warm*
*With kisses balmier than half-opening buds*
*Of April, and could hear the lips that kissed*
*Whispering I knew not what of wild and sweet.*

—Alfred, Lord Tennyson
"Tithonus"

"ROLF?"

"I know it sounds mad, Emma!" Cissy rose to the window again. "But it was his voice. He was calling me—Cissy, Cissy . . ."

"That's impossible. By now Rolf is at his post on the border, miles and miles from here." Emma tried to grasp her sister's wrist to pull her from the window, but Cissy jerked away and lifted the sash.

"Just be quiet and let me listen." Cissy leaned out through the open window, her eyes wide as she stared into the blackness, her golden hair fluttering in the breeze. Emma sat rooted to the bed, powerless to dispel her sister's foolish imaginings. Cissy rested her palms on the sill and thrust her head farther out into the night. Then, suddenly, she jerked back inside.

"There! Just listen, Emma. Rolf is calling me! He's out there somewhere calling me!"

Startled from the bed, Emma leapt to Cissy's side and listened. She could hear nothing but a wild cacophony of night noises. Crickets, strange birds, and humming, buzzing insects competed with one another in a symphony of discord. Drawn to the light of the kerosene lamp, myriad flitting moths and pebble-sized beetles whizzed through the window, smacking into walls and soft skin in their eagerness to gain the light. The lone African guard manned his station some distance away, his rifle resting against his shoulder. When a heavy round scarab sped into Emma's hair, she jumped back from the window in disgust.

"Cissy, do be sensible!" She tried once more to pull her sister from her post. "Let's shut the window. The cabin will be filled with insects in a minute, and we shan't get a moment's sleep—"

"Shh! There he is again."

Against her will, Emma poked her head back through the open window. This time she heard a distinctive sound—not the sound of a name, but a low, stomach-deep grunting. Swallowing against the dry lump in her throat, she listened again. Yes, there was something outside. A growling. A quiet, sniffing, searching grumble. An animal muttering. Grass swishing, parting. Emma reached for her chatelaine bag.

And then she heard it. "Cissy . . . Cissy . . . Cissy!" Or was it the wind? Was it the grass whisking aside beneath a lion's tawny underbelly? "Cissy . . . Cissy . . ."

Without warning, Cissy jerked upright and threw her arms around her sister for an instant. Then, before Emma could react, she tore out of the cabin. "Rolf! Rolf, I'm coming!"

"No, Cissy!" Emma screamed. Struggling to free the gun from her bag, she grabbed up her skirt, yanked the lamp from the wall, and followed her sister down the dark hallway. "Cissy, stop! The lion—it's the lion! Oh, dear God . . . Cissy!"

Just ahead of her, Emma heard the iron railcar door clang open and shut. Throwing herself against it, she fumbled with the latch. Tears scalded her cheeks as she tucked the gun under her arm and struggled to unclasp the latch. "Cissy, please stop! It's not Rolf!"

The heavy door swung open at last, and Emma stumbled down the darkened stairs. An earsplitting roar suddenly shattered the night, and close on its heels came the sound of anguished screams.

Emma froze, the lantern held high in her hand. Before her on the grass stood an enormous, shaggy beast, its powerful jaws clamped around the throat of the railway guard. The man lay limp, his long legs and arms hanging askew on the ground like a rag doll's as the lion eyed Emma.

Silence hung thick in the air as Emma and the lion stared at one another. Then, very slowly, she lifted her gun, pointed it at the creature's head, and squeezed the trigger. But as the gun exploded in a blinding flash, the lion bolted into the night, carrying the guard with it.

"What's happening? What's going on here?"

The area around the railcar erupted with running figures—Godfrey in his bathrobe, Dr. McCulloch with a rifle at his shoulder and lantern in hand, Nicholas with pistol drawn.

"Emmaline, where's Cissy?" Godfrey ran up to his daughter and shook her roughly.

Emma sagged, her face as white as the rising moon. "She ran off—the lion . . ."

Godfrey clutched at his chest, heaving in dismay. "The lion?"

"Look!" Dr. McCulloch shouted. "A lion's attacked here! There's blood all over the grass. Miss Pickworth, did you see what happened?"

"Emmaline," Nicholas shouted, dashing to Emma's side, "what happened? Did you fire that shot? Where's the guard?"

Emma pushed away from him and her father and ran across to the blood-soaked ground. All her healing skills, all her knowledge, could not save the guard now. As she knelt in the bloody grass, horror stiffening her legs, she heard a distant shout.

"What's going on here?" Adam King called loudly through the night. "I heard a shot."

Emma looked up to see the tall man ride into the dimly lit area, his silver pistol drawn from its holster. He was followed by someone she had never seen before, a short, barrel-chested young man with a shock of bright yellow hair. He rode a smaller, chestnut horse. Dismounting, Adam hurried to Emma and knelt in the grass before her.

"Emma, are you all right?" His voice was almost a whisper. "Where's your sister?"

Drawn to Adam's deep eyes, Emma saw his concern. But everything was happening so fast—so fast she could barely think.

The yellow-haired young man crouched beside Adam King. "You okay, ma'am?" He had the same slow tongue as his companion. "We heard more noise than hell emigratin' on cartwheels. You been tanglin' with li—"

An air-splitting roar stopped his words. Emma stiffened. Clutching the pistol tightly in her cold white fingers, she rose to her feet.

"Cissy . . ." The words formed on Emma's lips, but the sound never reached her ears. She had to find Cissy! Somewhere out there, her sister was wandering—alone . . . unarmed. And one of the two man-eaters had not yet made a kill. Her green eyes flashing in the lamplight, Emma frantically searched the darkness. She had to find Cissy. . . .

A second roar sundered the night. Emma sprang to her feet and ran toward the void, lamp in one hand, pistol in the other. Shouts followed her, cries of shock, but nothing registered in her mind. She had seen what the lion could do—and she could not allow that to happen to Cissy. Her sister was alive . . . she had to be!

As she sped into the shadows, the chestnut horse—frightened by the shouts—skittered before her. Without thinking, Emma set the lamp in the grass and caught the long leather reins with her gun hand. "Slow down, horse," she said, her tongue barely releasing the words. Shoving the pistol into her pocket, she threw her skirts above her knees and clambered onto the slick saddle.

"Hey! Hey, that's my horse!" The shout behind her sent the chestnut into a sideways leap, and Emma clung to the long mane for support as the horse cantered off into the brush. "Hey, Red! Aw, shucks. That damned horse ain't worth a pail of hot spit!"

"Emma!" Adam's voice sounded far away as Emma rode into the night breeze. "Emma, come back here! Soapy, where'd she go?"

"Emmaline! Emmaline!"

The black sky melted into a purple glow, and still Emma rode—calling her sister's name into the void. As the hours wore on, her mind began to wander. Once she fancied she was back in London, sitting beside Aunt Prudence in the parlor and discussing nursing. And then she imagined she heard a deep voice shouting out to her: "Emma, Emma." But visions of the guard's limp body and Cissy's white face and huge blue eyes drew her back to reality. Cissy had to be alive! And Emma had to find her!

She rode much of the night with eyes closed against thorny branches that tore at her sleeves and skirt. But as the sun peeked over the distant escarpment, its rays forced her eyes open and she lifted her head. Her vision awash in a sky streaked with triumphant oranges, pinks, and lavenders, Emma at last gave in to the fear and sorrow that had threatened to engulf her. She covered her eyes with her hands and sobbed. Cissy! Her beloved, beautiful Cissy—so childlike, so believing, so trusting. Even now, her sister's unblemished, untouched body might be lying torn to shreds, desecrated by the jaws of a killer lion.

Rolling with the amble of the horse, Emma sighed and wiped at a grimy cheek. And now where was she? She had come all this way, had searched through the night, for nothing. All in vain. Peering across the tall grass, she surveyed her surroundings, and a tremor of shock ran through her. This was the African bush country— and here she was, all alone. Lost.

In the distance, a herd of lazy zebras meandered along, munching at their breakfast. They were oblivious to the creature who sat watching them in a tattered white shirt, wet suede button boots, and a khaki skirt that was damp to the knees from the long dew-laden grass.

Like a sandy sea dotted with galleons, rolling grasslands broken by thorn trees fell away on every side. To her right, Emma made out a low outcropping of rock rising from the grass. The zebras ambled toward it. Against the sunrise a thick grove of tall thorn trees—leafier and greener than those in the rest of the landscape—wound like a long green snake toward the horizon. Perhaps a river ran among them, Emma surmised.

Far to the south she could discern an enormous mountain jutting like a pall of purple smoke along the horizon. Westward stretched more vast grasslands. Every surface was dotted with wildlife, most of which Emma could not identify. She watched the herd of zebras melting into another herd, this one of shaggy grayish beasts.

Startled by a sudden squeaking noise, Emma whirled in the saddle to find a small odd-looking squirrel peering at her quizzically from its rocky perch. The gray creature had no tail, but it managed to sit upright very comfortably as it crunched a beetle and dropped the insect's iridescent blue shell onto the stone. The satisfied munching of the sharp-faced animal reminded Emma of her own hunger. And as the sun climbed in the cloudless sky, she grew hotter and hotter. It was a dry heat, but already she could feel a dampness gathering beneath her corset. If she waited here for rescue, she would surely die of thirst. But where was the Tsavo rail camp?

Pursing her lips in resignation, she decided to make her way to the grove of trees, for a river would mean people, and people meant civilization. At least in England they did. Emma shook her head as she thought of herself here in the heart of Africa, unable to start a fire, track game, hunt, or even defend herself. The useless gun hung in her pocket like a dead weight.

The tired chestnut mare walked slowly toward the grove of thorn trees, and Emma reached down to pat her damp neck. Riding horses had never been allowed on the country estate because Godfrey thought it unladylike. After hours of aimless wandering, Emma had learned to control the horse a little by pulling at the reins left or right as she had seen carriage drivers do. But generally the little red mare went her own way, and Emma could do no more than ride along.

Her legs ached from the chafing saddle, and every vertebra protested the unaccustomed pressure.

By the time the sun had climbed well above the horizon most of the animals had vanished. Unable to find adequate shade for herself, Emma rode onward. The grove of thorn trees still was miles away, and she began to wonder if she would be able to reach it that day. Her thirst grew unbearable as the hours wore on, and black spots darted and twinkled before her eyes in a dizzying dance. The mare began to falter and stumble.

All day they wandered slowly toward the goal, too tired to notice anything but the next step ahead. Emma's whole body begged her to stop and rest, but she was too frightened to consider it. Overhead, vultures began to circle, and she sensed their eager eyes watching her.

As she floated through the mists that gathered before her eyes, her mind began to wander back in time. She was walking with Cissy beside the Thames, watching the boaters ply the calm green waters. Now they were having tea with Aunt Prudence—Cissy in her bright pink organdy gown and laughing pink mouth. Then they were children again, running ring-o-roses around their mother's skirts as she walked beneath the huge oak trees at the country estate. And they were singing a little song. What was it? Lavender blue dilly dilly, lavender green—when you are king, dilly dilly, I shall be queen—

The words suddenly caught in Emma's dry throat and she willed her mind to focus on the scene ahead. The sun had dipped into shadows, casting odd pink images in the grass. Her mother's skirt dwindled into a large shady thorn tree beneath which lay a pride of lions feasting on a bloody carcass. Emma caught her breath and blinked several times at the unreality of it.

One of the lions sat up. Licking its gory jaws with satisfaction, it stared at her. A cub meandered to the kill and tore away a strip of flesh with its teeth. Four striped legs of a dead zebra lay askew on the ground like scattered toothpicks. The adult lion lifted its head and emitted an earsplitting roar that rumbled through Emma's body. Another yawned widely, baring its pink teeth and wet black gums.

As Emma watched, it seemed the zebra's tattered limbs metamorphosed into human legs and arms. The bloody head no longer bore stripes, but a thick mane of golden hair around a pale, blue-eyed face.

Screaming at the gruesome vision, Emma dug her heels into the mare and they plunged through the grass. One of the lions bounded to its feet and roared thunderously behind her. But Emma averted her eyes from the certain death at her back. She rode head down through the scraggly thornbrush, the mare tripping over roots in her headlong race.

They galloped until the horse's feet disappeared beneath her and Emma tumbled to the spiny grass. Her lungs filled with a heavy liquid that choked her parched throat. Knives thrust through her sides and ripped into her stomach. A deep cloudy blackness gathered before her eyes, a blackness she could not evade. And she was lifted up into a silent emptiness.

A throbbing heartbeat, a roaring in her ears, brought Emma to the threshold of consciousness. A black curtain of darkness hung before her eyes.

And there was a smell—a pungent smoky smell that caught at her stomach and twisted it into contortions of pain so that she turned over and retched into the dust.

But it was the touch of a bare human palm on her cheek that made her sit up screaming into the void. Fully awake now, Emma struggled to stand, clawing away the hands that clutched at her. A voice, urgent and gentle, echoed in her ears. Strong, sinewy arms thrust her to the ground. And still she struggled against them, unable to see, unable to think. Her eyes wide open, she at last began to distinguish shadows moving over her—human hands, a human face. And behind it, stars! Countless pinpricks of light sparkled in a wide band across the inky sky.

"Emma." The voice was one she knew. Deep. Quiet. Gentle. In the starlight, she made out a rough outline—a firm jaw, a strong nose, a tall hat . . .

"Adam."

"Yes, Emma. I'm here. I've been looking for you." The dark face turned in profile. "Some friends of mine found you here beside Soapy's horse. Even old Red's been worried about you, though she's only half-alive herself." Adam reached across Emma's body and stroked the horse's velvet nose.

Nearby, a small fire crackled comfortingly, and Emma let her head fall to one side so that she could see the dark shapes reclining about. She was reminded suddenly of her search, her frantic journey across the burning wilderness . . . and the reason for it—

"Cissy? Have you—"

"No, no one's found her, Emma. At least they

hadn't when I took off. But don't worry—they've sent out four big search parties. Everyone's looking for her."

Emma placed her fingers over her eyes and nodded. Cissy was not dead. Something in Emma's heart told her. Reassured her. Somewhere, somehow, Cissy was safe.

"I'm sorry, Emma." Adam slipped his hands beneath her back and gently lifted her into his lap. Her head rolled against his chest as he stroked her tangled hair, more relieved than he wanted to admit that she was going to be all right.

Emma wanted to tell him about Cissy, about the lion and the guard, but all she could seem to do was lie against him. Lulled by his gentle fingers, she closed her eyes and let the tension drain out of her. "Adam," she murmured, "we must bring Cissy back to Tsavo."

"Emma, Cissy's . . . gone." Adam caught her face and turned her to him. She looked up with hollow eyes, her face scratched by thorns and her lips swollen with thirst. It was going to be hard for her—he knew that—but she would finally accept what had happened. Her very survival in the bush had proven her determination and strength. But he had to be gentle. "Your sister may be dead. And I need to take you back to the railway. . . ."

"No, you don't understand." Emma shook her head. "Cissy's not dead. She's alive. She ran away after Rolf called her, and then the lion came."

"Emma, you saw the blood on the grass—"

"The guard—the lion killed the guard. I came out of the train after Cissy, and the lion was holding the man . . . in his mouth and . . ." Emma faltered. "The lion had him by the neck . . . the throat . . . and he was dead, you see."

Adam looked at her long and hard. What was she saying? Was she rambling with delirium? He forced her eyes to meet his again. "The guard—are you sure?"

"Yes, not Cissy. Cissy is alive somewhere, and she may even be with Rolf—"

"Rolf? Who's Rolf?"

"Her suitor. He's a German soldier. . . ."

Adam looked away. Damn, this was beginning to sound like real trouble.

"Cissy kept telling me she heard Rolf calling her," Emma said. "She insisted he was outside the railcar calling her name."

Adam's hands slowly slipped away from her face. "Did you hear him—Rolf, calling your sister?"

Emma looked down. "I'm not sure. I heard . . . something. It sounded like a man calling. But it might have been the wind. And Rolf should be on the border with his contingent."

Adam looked at Emma in silence, his mouth a still line. For a long time he watched her, then he raised his eyes to the stars.

"Emma." His voice was so low she could barely hear it. "There's something I have to tell you. But before I do, I want you to know that your sister might still be alive. It'd be rough in the wild, but she could have lasted a day. Especially if one of the tribes found her. You survived, didn't you?"

Emma nodded.

"Well . . . what I have to tell you is about your father." Adam squared his shoulders, knowing the information was only going to make everything that much harder. But a person had to know the truth sooner or later. "When you took off after your sister, your father went down. Collapsed. And then he . . . they took him into the railcar and called the doctors. But he was—"

"He's dead, isn't he," she said flatly. It was a statement of fact, not a question. "He saw the blood on the grass. He thought it was Cissy, didn't he? He thought the lion had killed her. And I didn't explain. And now he's dead."

"Hell no, it wasn't like that at all." Adam searched for the right words. He wanted her to know how it really had been with Godfrey before his death. He had called out for both his daughters . . . had wept for Emma. It was hard to find the words, but he had to make her see. "Your father was worried about you running off, Emma. He didn't want to lose you—"

"You're wrong." Emma shivered as a chill wind blew over her. "My father loved Cissy."

She struggled out of Adam's arms and stood alone in the darkness. Her father was dead. How many times had she thought she would welcome those words? And now—now what? Now she felt only cold and empty. She felt nothing.

A movement from the fire drew her attention. Emma glanced over and saw a group of men crouched, surveying her uncertainly. In the fire glow she made out their elaborately braided hair and dangling earlobes. The soft light gleamed on their ropy biceps and reflected from their white, evenly spaced teeth. A pungent odor of woodsmoke and sweat emanated from the men, who began to converse quietly in a rhythmic language.

The men shook their heads and grinned as she looked at them. Then one of them rose and nodded at Adam. Emma saw that the man wore only a flapping leather sheet tied at one shoulder. He carried a long silvery spear with a wide, leaf-shaped blade.

The rancher sat up and spoke several words to the warrior, who then held out a long, hollow gourd, presenting it to Emma with a smile.

Emma held the vessel gingerly before her. Adam removed the small leather cap from the end of it. "Take a drink, Emma. It's not water—I don't have any of that—but it'll do you good."

Hesitantly, Emma lifted the gourd to her lips. When the liquid ran into her mouth, a sour, nauseating smell rose from within it, dilating her nostrils. But overcome by her aching thirst, she forced herself to drink.

A warm, thick liquid tasting like curdled, salty milk filled her mouth. Suppressing a gag, she gulped and managed to swallow. Before she could sicken, she drank a long draft. Once it was down, her stomach began to unknot and grow warmer.

"Thank you." She pulled her handkerchief from her sleeve and carefully wiped her mouth. "What is it?"

Adam's grin lit up his somber features. For a lady who kept a hankie in her sleeve, she sure could surprise him sometimes. "The drink is a mixture of blood and milk."

Emma's face went pale, but she kept her voice steady and emotionless. "Milk and blood. I see. And who are these men—your slaves?"

Adam frowned. "Slaves? I don't have slaves. These men are warriors from the Masai tribe. This is Kiriswa." The warrior who had given her the gourd motioned to his comrades. They spoke earnestly for a moment, then Kiriswa turned and gestured at Adam.

The rancher nodded. "They want to take us to their village for the night. It's not far, they say." While he spoke, the men doused the campfire with dirt.

In the sudden total darkness, Emma rigidly knotted her fingers at her breast. But then a warm arm encircled her shoulders and another slid beneath her knees. Lifted into the air, she held her breath while Adam deposited her gently on his horse.

"Can you take a little more riding, Emma?" He slid up behind her even as he spoke, holding her sideways against his chest. She didn't say anything, but she let him cradle her as the horse began its rhythmic stride.

As they started on into the night, Adam found it rough keeping his attention focused on the ride. Emma had nestled into his shoulder, and her soft hair brushed his cheek. There was just something about the way she molded into him, her small hips resting on his lap and her fingers touching his arm. The rhythm of his horse's stride set the woman rolling slightly back and forth across his thighs . . . and he felt an unbidden heat swell through him.

He focused on the night. Hell, what man wouldn't start to hunger after a woman like Emma? But what he didn't want to admit was the other feeling—the growing certainty that she was more than just another woman with a tempting body . . . that he'd begun to care what happened to her. Snapping shut the thought like it was poison, Adam forced his concentration back on the trail.

Emma relaxed, feeling the deep vibrations that emanated from Adam's throat and chest as he began to sing a low melody. Gradually her eyes adjusted to the moonless night, and she made out the long line of tall, angular men walking forward silently before the horse. Adam's arms, supportive yet supple, allowed her body the freedom to sway with the horse. Her shoulder rested against his chest, and she sensed his warmth through the thin fabric of her cotton shirt. He had on the same plaid shirt and vest he had been wearing earlier—he must have been looking for her a full day without stopping.

Closing her eyes, Emma allowed her head to roll against his neck, and she drank in the soothing scent of his skin. How odd she felt. How strangely alone and yet not alone.

She thought of her father. She could not imagine him dead, did not know how to feel or what to think. Life had always been the same, and she had never imagined that it could be truly different. Why didn't she mourn him? Why couldn't she weep? Guilt at her own lack of sorrow crept into her breast.

And what of Cissy? Where was she now? Emma shivered, and Adam instantly drew his arms tighter around her shoulders. No, Cissy was alive. And Emma had to find her. She lifted her head and gazed at the firm chin of the rancher. She had to find Cissy, but she would need help doing it.

As the night wore on, Emma forced her numbed mind to focus on an infant plan. Lost in thought, she was surprised when the warriors suddenly broke into a sprint. She looked up to see the soft red glow of a fire in the distance—no doubt the destination of the natives' long journey afoot. Several of the men began a low chant, echoed and modified by the others. Emma felt warm and comforted by their tones, for it was a peaceful rather than warlike song. How strange it was that these men could be so expressive—they were savages after all.

As they drew near the firelight, Emma distinguished the outlines of low earthen mounds surrounded by a fence of dead thornbushes piled high. The trampled area inside the fence was deserted as the warriors marched single file through an opening in the fence. Emma blinked to adjust to the light of the fire burning in the center of a group of rounded stones.

Most of the men melted silently into the darkness, and Emma and Adam were left with Kiriswa. A moment later a gnarled old man sauntered into the clearing and yawned sleepily.

"*Entasupai*," he growled and spat into his hand.

Adam kicked a leg over his saddle horn and slid down, taking Emma with him. He placed her on her feet, braced her for a moment to be sure she could stand, then grasped the old man's hand warmly. "*Hepa*."

While Adam murmured in the strange tongue, the old man listened with bowed head. Then he looked up into Emma's eyes. For a long moment he was silent.

"Sendeyo," he said at last, slapping his hand across his chest.

Adam smiled. "His name is Sendeyo, Emma. He's the chief elder of the tribe."

Emma gave a little curtsy. "So pleased to meet you."

"He wants to know if you'd like to sleep in one of his wives' huts. Frankly, I'd recommend—"

"No!" Emma caught Adam's sleeve. "I can't sleep now—there's no time! It's about Cissy."

"What is it?" he asked gently.

Emma looked up at him. The starlight had silvered his shoulders, and the breeze tugged at the red scarf around his neck. Ignoring the two men standing in the darkness beside them, she took his hands in hers and held them tightly. "I have a business proposal to make to you—and you must listen carefully."

Adam's brow furrowed slightly. Business? What in hell was she wanting to talk about business for in the middle of the night? "Couldn't it wait until tomor—"

"No, now is the time. I don't want to wait another minute. Cissy's life is at stake!"

"Emma . . ." Adam looked at her in confusion.

Emma swallowed, then squared her shoulders resolutely. Every event had led to this moment—the loss of Cissy, the lions, Rolf, her father's death, and her need for Adam's strength—and now she must put her own doubts aside. She must state her plan.

"I want to make a proposal," she said evenly. "Strictly a business proposal, you understand—that we marry."

Adam's mouth dropped open. He stepped back and took off his hat. A strange sound came out of his mouth as he tried to speak. Flustered, he spun on his heel and took two long strides. He glanced back, a look of disbelief plastered on his face. Finally he managed to croak, "Marry?"

"Adam, please. Just listen. I need your help to find my sister. You see, I believe Cissy actually might have heard Rolf. To find out if he is missing from his post will mean a journey to the border. Then I must go into the bush to find them. You see, Cissy needs me. She hasn't a clue how to survive on her own. Or even with a man—a man she barely knows."

"Emma, what are you driving at? What does marrying me have to do with all this?"

"I need help. You know the protectorate, Adam! You know how to speak to these people and how to find your way about." Emma's green eyes blazed hotter than the fire. "And you need money for your ranch! I need money, too. But unless I'm married, I can never touch my inheritance. If you'll agree to the marriage, then I shall pay you the sum of ten thousand pounds. We'll take the train back to Mombasa and collect half of it from the bank on my father's name. And I can get the money I need to finance my search for Cissy. We shall take supplies and horses and tents. But I assure you after two months—whether we have found Cissy or not"—Emma looked away—"we shall dissolve the marriage, and I shall pay you the remainder of the sum."

Adam stared at her in silence, his blue eyes unblinking in the starlight. Emma knew he was thinking of his wife in America. But what difference could the wife make? This would be a temporary contract strictly for business reasons. No one would ever have to know about the marriage to Emma—only the bank in Mombasa. The whole venture was purely monetary, and he would be free of her in two months. And then she would be free, too . . . completely free. She would find a hospital and begin her nursing. Nothing could hold her back.

"Emma, I can't—"

"Yes, you can! Think of it—ten thousand pounds!" She could see Adam hesitating. She knew he was thinking of the money. That was her key . . . the money would win him over. "I know you're a struggling rancher. Nicholas Bond told me so himself. Think what you could do on your ranch with ten thousand pounds, Adam. And all you would have to do is help me find Cissy—just help me. . . ."

Adam looked down at the brim of his hat. For long minutes he studied it in silence, running it around and around through his palm. He straightened the leather band, then slid his hand back and forth through the crown's center valley. Hell, the woman was crazy after all, he thought. And he wasn't much better for even bothering to consider her half-cocked scheme. He'd be loco to haul this citified Englishwoman all over the countryside looking for her sister, who was probably dead by now anyway. From the looks of her, she couldn't even ride a horse. . . . But she *did* have guts—and he was ripe for a good challenge after all. If he could get out of Emma what he wanted . . .

Adam looked up. "I'll do it on one condition."

Emma caught her breath. "And what is that?"

"You come to my ranch and tend to my friend after our stop at the border. The ranch isn't far from here, and it won't take long, but—"

"No! How can I do that? If I stop even for a day, something dreadful might happen to Cissy. You can't ask that of me, Adam!"

Adam shrugged. "I'm not crazy about the idea anyway. Marriage isn't much my style."

Shucking his hat onto the back of his head, he gave her a long look, his eyes indigo in the firelight, his hair coal black. Then he turned and started for his horse.

"Wait!" Emma ran forward and caught his arm. "All right—I'll do it! I'll stop and take care of your friend. But only preliminary care! I won't stay long, Adam. How can I? You don't know Cissy as I do. If she *is* still alive, she'll be frantic. She doesn't know how to do anything for herself. She can't even do her hair or lace her corset or—"

"If she's out in the bush with some runaway German soldier, she's going to have a lot more to worry about than lacing her damned corset, Emma," he said evenly.

"I know! That's what I'm saying—can't you see? She's helpless, she's just a child. She won't survive long, even if she is with someone to protect her." Emma brushed a hot tear from her cheek.

"Okay." Adam caught her handkerchief hand and pulled her toward him. "Okay, I'll help you find your sister."

Emma met his eyes. "Thank you. We shall find a church at Mombasa and take care of the wedding so that you can have your money. I promise, you won't regret it."

"Now hold on!" Adam took a step backward as a suffocating lump rose in his chest. "You never said anything about a church. I'm not going to do this thing in front of some damned preacher!"

"Well, what do you suggest, then? It has to be witnessed—it has to be real in some sense of the word. The bank in England will probably require signed documents to release the money to me. We can't just get married out here in the middle of the bush with no one to see but some . . . some savages."

"Why not?"

"What?"

"Why not? They have marriages. They're not

savages, Emma, no matter what your queen tells you. They're people, with pride and honor and a culture just as good as yours. Better, probably. We'll get old Sendeyo here to do the honors."

Emma glanced at the two men who had stood watching the animated exchange in silence. Sendeyo smiled, and his two front teeth shone a dull pink in the firelight. "But how could that be legal?" Her voice came out a whisper.

"It's legal here in the protectorate, I'd think. You don't suppose the British government would have the nerve to declare all these marriages to be adulterous affairs, now, do you?"

Emma's eyes swung back to Adam's face. "Could they sign something? Can they write?"

"I imagine they can sign something with a mark. That's legal enough for me."

"All right. Ask Mr. Sendeyo."

One corner of Adam's mouth turned up. "I'll ask Mr. Sendeyo." He quickly spoke to the elder man, who listened with bowed head to the discourse. Sendeyo nodded occasionally in understanding, but Emma could see the younger man, Kiriswa, biting his lower lip as if stifling a laugh.

At last the old man began to intone, slowly and with graceful gestures of his gnarled hands. His voice, deep and musical, lilted over phrases almost as though he were singing. At last he stopped and leaned on his spear.

Adam turned to Emma. "He won't do it."

"What? Why not? What right has he—"

"He says it's not their way. He says we have to observe the proper waiting time. It's not even calving season. And you don't have a hut ready to go to, and there's no cow to slaughter for the feast. We aren't even betrothed."

"But that's preposterous! Surely they don't get betrothed—"

"Yes, they do. It's called the *esirata*—the picking of one girl from many."

Emma's eyes flicked to the old man. He was staring at the moon. "Tell him I shall pay him well when I get my money from Mombasa. I shall give him fifty pounds."

"Fifty pounds, huh? Why not fifty thousand? He wouldn't know what to do with one shilling, let alone fifty pounds. The Masai way of life is based on cows."

"Then I shall send him a cow. Ten cows."

Adam laughed. "Okay—he's not going to go for it, but I'll try again."

The conversation was rapid this time. Emma listened in vain, struggling to understand the strings of syllables. One day she would know this language, she determined. It would help her to fulfill the destiny that lay almost within her grasp. She would find Cissy, and then . . .

Adam straightened and turned to her. "He'll do it."

Emma beamed at the old man. "Thank you, sir. I assure you, you will not regret your decision. I shall see to it that you have as many cows as you like."

"He doesn't want any cows, Emma. He wants me to pay the bride-price."

"Bride-price?" Disappointment surged through Emma. The whole thing was becoming so complicated, so difficult. Did she have to go to such lengths to realize her dream?

"Payment for you. I've got to give something to pay for you. And since there aren't any parents around, I'm to give the bride-price to you."

Adam walked over to his horse and quickly surveyed the saddle, saddlebags, stirrups . . . and then he whisked a knife from his boot and cut a leather strap from one of the bags. It was one of four that held the bag closed with brass rings, and he slipped the ring from the leather.

"Here's the bride-price," he muttered, stepping back to Emma. "Give me your hand."

Emma searched his face, but he did not meet her eyes as he slid the brass ring over her knuckle and onto the finger of her left hand. She knew he was thinking of another finger and another ring. Perhaps a golden ring, on a beautiful, lily-white hand.

Sendeyo grunted and held aloft a knobbed stick. Emma watched as he slowly lowered the stick and spoke in a raspy voice.

"I'm to take care of you," Adam translated in a whisper. "I'm to give you many children and a hut and lots of cattle. You're to take care of the children and the cattle and the hut. I can't divorce you unless you're barren, you practice witchcraft, you become a thief, you desert me, you behave badly, or you refuse me conjugal rights." Adam raised his eyebrows briefly but his face was not smiling. "You can't divorce me unless I do one of the above or am cruel, treat you badly, get drunk, or am impotent."

Sendeyo dropped the stick to the ground with a thud and then fastened his piercing eyes on the couple before him. His next words were firm, uncompromising.

"As God has willed it, we're married," Adam said.

Emma licked her dry lips and looked down at her finger. The brass ring glinted in the firelight. "I see."

"I'll get him to sign something in the morning."

"Morning, but . . . ?"

"I'm not going back to the train tonight, Emma. The horses are too tired, and so are you."

"All right." Emma sighed in resignation as Adam thanked the two men and watched them melt away into the shadows.

"He says we can have the hut by the gate. It's empty right now."

Emma's eyes flew to Adam's face. "Oh, I don't think—"

"I'll be sleeping out in the grass beside the horses." He stepped closer and took her hands, suddenly not wanting to let her go. "Come with me, Emma."

Emma could feel his fingers burning against her skin. Her stomach curled into a warm, throbbing ache as he drew her toward him, holding her tightly against the full length of his hard body. She let her eyes explore his and saw the wanting there, the desire that mirrored her own. His mouth came down on hers, his lips drinking her in—slowly, hungrily. Powerful arms slid around her back, hands moved gently to her neck and into her hair, loosening the rolls of curls.

"I want you, Emma." He spoke huskily against her lips. Trembling against him, as though every nerve sang of her own desire, she raised her hands to his arms to push him away. But instead, her fingers slipped up to his shoulders, caressing the rounded muscle and molding against his chest. He dropped his mouth to her cheek, soft and petal smooth against his lips. When his kisses fell on her neck, she arched upward into him with a little moan.

Trails of fire singed her skin as his lips moved down her neck and his fingers eased open the row of round pearl buttons at her collar. Down and down his hands worked with gentle pressure as her blouse released its hold on her full breasts. His legs leaned taut against hers, and one hand held her waist, cupping her to his iron-hard stomach.

"Adam, I don't think—" She wanted to tell him this was not in the plan. It was all meant to be monetary . . . business . . . But then his mouth silenced her protest, finding her parted lips hungrily, penetrating and seeking her out as if to confirm his need for her—for the rest of her inner self.

The warmth, the sweet warmth of her skin, ignited his hand as he brushed it against her breast. He let his palm drop to the burgeoning rise of her blouse and felt the hardened, swollen point beneath the layers of filmy cloth. She wanted him. Sweeping back the offending blouse and silken chemise, he slid his hand over the stiff corset beneath her breasts, full and opalescent in the starlight. For a moment he gazed at her body, drinking in the beauty of the untouched rose flowering before him, and then—a fire sweeping uncontrolled through his loins—he lowered his lips to kiss their dusky tips.

Emma's head fell against his shoulders as he lifted and caressed her breasts until her veins pulsed with molten fire. Her fingers twined through his hair, and his hat fell to the ground unnoticed as he brushed aside the remaining fragments of her blouse. Sliding his hands around her slender waist he drew her closer and closer into him until she could no longer ignore the presence of his hard hunger against the folds of her skirts and layers of petticoats.

His lips seared a path up her neck, and his hands cupped her breasts. Emma let her fingers fall again to his chest. Her mind reeled with the ache in her body, with the awakened fire that surged through her. Fumbling with the buttons on his shirt, she could feel the mat of his hair beneath it, and she turned her eyes to her hands. The brass ring flashed—a gentle yellow glow upon a trembling finger—and Emma stepped back from Adam with a sudden gasp.

"Adam." The ring—it was brass. His life was pledged to another woman. His body belonged to someone else.

He raised his eyes to hers, questioning for an instant, then seizing her again. But when he drew her into him, she stiffened. "Emma, don't . . . stop what you feel—"

"Adam, please." Emma pulled back again and caught the fluttering edges of her blouse. Her eyes dropped to her finger. "It's not real, you know. The marriage. The ring. None of it."

He looked at her, his eyes indigo in the darkness. "I want you and you want me. That's real."

Emma bit her lower lip and shook her head. "Good night, Adam."

# Chapter Six

✦ ✦ ✦ ✦

*Every nerve just got a-dancing to the music of delight*
*As I hugged the little sagehen uncomfortably tight;*
*But she never made a bellow and the glances of her eyes*
*Seemed to thank me for the pleasure of a genuine surprise.*
*She snuggled up against me in a loving sort of way,*
*And I hugged her all the tighter for her trustifying play.*

—"The Cowboy's Dance Song"

> *Be a god and hold me*
> *With a charm!*
> *Be a man and fold me*
> *With thine arm!* .
>
> *Teach me, only teach, Love!*
> *As I ought*
> *I will speak thy speech, Love,*
> *Think thy thought—*
>
> *Meet, if thou require it,*
> *Both demands,*
> *Laying flesh and spirit*
> *In thy hands.*

—Robert Browning
"A Woman's Last Word"

EMMA TURNED FROM Adam and walked to her horse. She felt his eyes following her across the clearing, but she could not bring herself to look back. His burning kiss seemed to have drawn the moisture from her mouth, and she licked her parched lips. With shaking hands, she untied the rolled blanket from behind the saddle. She listened for the jingle of Adam's spurs but heard only the muted chirp of a cricket. Clutching the blanket against her breasts,

121

she could feel their hardened points against her
arms.

"Where do you plan to sleep?" Adam's voice
was just above a whisper.

Emma spun around. He stood silhouetted
against the fire, his long body towering into the
darkness and his face obscured in the shadow of
his hat.

"There." She pointed to the long dry grass just
outside the thorny fence. He would be sleeping out
there, too, not far from her. She told herself she
should sleep in the hut for safety, but the grass
would be soft . . . and he would be near.

He nodded and sauntered across the clearing,
his boots sending up puffs of powdery dust as he
led the horses away from the fire. "Still have my
gun?"

Emma felt for the heavy weight in her pocket.
Her fingers closed around the cold metal, but she
knew the weapon was all but useless in her un-
trained hands. Shivering with fear of the unknown,
she followed Adam out of the enclosure. He tied
the two horses to a thorn tree a short distance from
where she stood and then unsaddled them. Emma
made her way through the tall grass to the side of
a small bush, its leaves shining silver in the moonlight.

She spread her blanket over the grass and knelt
on it gingerly. Curling her legs beneath her, she
unpinned the rolls of hair Adam had not loosened
and put the pins in her pocket beside the gun. As
she worked, she watched him toss a thick layer of
blankets onto the grass and flip his hat onto the
pallet he had made.

The moon lit up his black hair, dusting it with a
shimmery powder. She longed to touch it—to feel

its silky smoothness beneath her fingers. He unknotted his red neckerchief and shoved it into his
back pocket. Emma thought of his ritual: the hat
tossed down, then the scarf unknotted and put in
the back pocket. What would it be like to watch
him night after night, she wondered, to know every movement of his hands and every detail of his
actions?

Without looking up, Adam shrugged out of his
leather vest and laid it beside his hat. Then he
flicked open the buttons of his shirt. Emma glanced
down at her hands, remembering their touch on
his shirt.

Uncomfortable at the strange ache deep inside
her, she drew her gaze away from him and
pulled her own blouse from the waist of her skirt.
She lifted the filmy fabric to unlace her corset,
then unbuttoned her boots and set them on the
blanket. When she looked up, he was sitting with
his naked back against the tree. In the moonlight
she could sense his eyes locked on her body, following her every action, just as she had followed
his.

Unable to bear his scrutiny, Emma lay down on
her blanket and rolled onto her back with her arms
beneath her head. Like a trail of spilled sugar, the
stars glittered across the African sky. Never had
she seen so many and such brilliant stars—nor a
sky so velvety and deep. She closed her eyes,
wanting the sleep that her body demanded, but
her mind refused to rest.

What had Adam done to make her feel so out of
control? The very image of him—every movement,
every expression—had etched itself within her. She
had let it happen despite everything she knew was
right. Nicholas had warned her about Adam. Or

had it just been jealousy? But Adam *was* rough and impetuous and . . . so different. He was married, too. Why did she keep forgetting that? And then there was Cissy! Finding her sister should be uppermost in Emma's mind.

Emma willfully blocked the image of Adam from her thoughts and concentrated on her sister. Somewhere out in this wilderness Cissy was hiding, afraid and probably alone. *If* she were still alive. Emma clasped her hands together at the thought and rolled onto her side.

Cissy was out here. . . . The cricket chorus rose in Emma's ears, and she focused for the first time on the intensity of the night sounds. This was no English countryside with the call of the nightingale and the low chuck of a squirrel. The whole dark continent seemed to have come to life. Insects buzzed over her head or fluttered past, their wings fanning the air above her ear. Strange deep grunts echoed like love calls across the plains, and slippery, swishing sounds slid through the grass beside her blanket.

Her heart rapidly increasing its pace with every new sound that erupted, Emma dug Adam's pistol from her pocket. Clutching it in both hands, one finger resting on the trigger, she lay with its cold barrel touching the tip of her nose. Did lions hunt in the dark? They were cats . . . they could see in the blackest of nights. A shriek of high-pitched laughter suddenly split the air, and Emma sat up in fright, brandishing the gun before her. As the laughter wound down into a low growl, she swallowed nervously against the dryness in her throat and lay down again. What could it have been . . . that inhuman hilarity?

An earsplitting roar sent her to her knees, the

gun barely controlled in her trembling fingers. Struggling to her feet amid the tangle of her skirts, she glanced at Adam. His starlit body lay prone beneath the thorn tree, his hat over his eyes and his booted feet propped casually one atop the other. In the deathly silence that followed the roar, Emma turned to the village enclosure with its strong thorn fence and rounded huts. Jerking her blanket into her arms, she tossed it over her shoulder and pointed the gun before her, daring anyone 'or anything to stop her as she started toward the village.

"Emma." The soft voice behind her startled her more than the animal sounds had, and she whirled, pulling the trigger of the gun. A blaze of fire shot from the barrel, and the deafening report sent her staggering backward.

"Emma! Confound it, woman."Adam materialized beside her in the darkness. He wrapped his arm around her waist and wrested the gun from her frozen fingers."Give me that thing. You're going to get me killed . . . or yourself, more likely."

"Oh, Adam, I'm sorry." Emma sagged into the strength of his arms, feeling foolish."I heard the roar and I thought of the lion . . . and the guard . . . and Cissy—"

Adam silenced her trembling lips with a soft kiss. "Why didn't you tell me you were afraid, Emma?"

"I'm not afraid, I just—" She stopped and laid her cheek on his bare chest. It was rock hard, and she closed her eyes, drinking in the scent of his skin even as she struggled to resist it. "I don't know those sounds, those grunting things and those growls—"

"Come with me." He turned her body toward his blanket, but she drew away from the warmth of his arms. She knew if she went with him, and if he kissed her again, she would lose herself. . . .

"No, I'll just go into the village. The hut will be safe enough I'm sure, and tomorrow—"

"The hut is full of fleas and lice, and tomorrow you'll be a lot more miserable than you are right now." Before she could protest, he bent down and swung her into his arms. "I'll teach you about the African night, and then you won't be afraid."

Emma rested her forehead in the cool curve of his neck as he walked through the grass to the tree. What if he wanted to . . . She thought of the words she had heard whispered among her friends in the cover of night when they rode together to parties or walked in their gardens. They had spoken of things between men and women—secret, hidden places men could touch and mysterious things they could do with their bodies. Some had heard these acts were awful . . . painful and frightening, difficult to bear. They said that men were forceful, brutal, red, and ugly to look at. Others believed them wonderful and exciting—sources of pleasure and perhaps even fun. But no one knew for certain . . . no one had been there and seen these things a man could do.

The horses nickered quietly in acknowledgment of their presence as Adam carried Emma under the tree. He lowered her to her feet on the blanket, but he did not release her. Instead he held her against him with one hand at her waist.

"The roar was a lion. They're prowling this time of night." He brushed his hand across her cheek to sweep away a strand of hair. "Stalking their prey. Mating."

Emma searched his face, but the darkness had obscured his features. All she knew was the stroke of his fingertips down her arms and across the planes of her shoulders, the press of his body against hers. "And that awful laughing sound?" Her voice was a low whisper.

"Hyenas. They're not as bad as most folks think." He ran one finger down the front of her open blouse. "Misunderstood—like a lot of people . . . getting by the best way they know how."

Trying to weigh the significance of Adam's words, Emma could think only of the burning need he had built inside her. Its glowing lava coursed through her, heightening every sense. His voice seemed to blur beneath the thunder of her heartbeat as he parted her blouse and traced rings of fire around the jutting peaks of her breasts. Then he lifted her up against him so that they pressed into his bare chest, skin against singeing skin.

"Adam." The word escaped her lips like a sigh.

"I want you so much, Emma." He pulled her into him and slid both hands inside the web of her hair, cradling her head. "Let me make you a woman."

She wanted to be strong, to dispel this weakness that he had cast over her. But it was a weakness she craved . . . a delicious, engulfing weakness. Yet she knew she had to fight him as she had fought all men who tried to control her. "I already am a woman, Adam. I'm strong and—"

He drew her head back and gazed into her eyes. "Then let me make you my wife."

She wanted to answer that he already had a wife. But his mouth found hers, and suddenly she knew that nothing mattered but this moment. There could be no weakness in taking what she ached to have. She looked into his eyes as their lips parted, and she knew. She wanted him.

Freed from her restraints, Emma reached out to Adam and drew his face to hers. "I've wanted to . . . touch you," she said softly. Tilting his chin to the moonlight, she ran her fingers over the planes of his cheeks and the ridge of his brow. His skin felt as she had dreamed it would, hard with the years of work in the wind and sun—yet smooth and young and supple.

He turned his head in her hands and kissed one palm. Her caresses had turned his body into a red-hot torch, and he struggled to control himself. "You are the most beautiful . . . beautiful woman, Emma."

Wanting her—needing her—with a force that surpassed any he had ever known, Adam eased the edges of her blouse and chemise from her shoulders and let them fall to the blanket. For a moment he could only gaze in wonder at the delicate beauty of her pale moonlit skin and soft shoulders. Then, knowing he wanted to draw out and savor every moment with her, he unclasped her skirt and slowly slid it over her petticoats. He let his hands follow its movement down her body until he was kneeling at her feet. Then he looked up at her. A groan escaped him as he wrapped his hands first around one silken thigh and then the other to draw her stockings down her legs.

Every touch of his fingers, every press of his lips against her bare skin, lit a fire upon her until she felt as though her whole body were aflame. The night air—with its soft, fragrant breeze that brought her breasts even more erect—only fanned the blaze. Adam rose and pulled Emma close against him, stroking his hands down her back and over the smooth curves of her naked hips and buttocks as if he were memorizing her.

Her mind was filled with him and nothing else—as though the whole world had slipped away. His hair smelled of grass, and she buried her face in its thickness, running her fingers through its waves. His mouth on hers was a tantalizing promise of the secrets she had heard whispered—but never spoken. Seeking, probing, tasting, teasing . . . making her want more of him, more than she had of him. His lips drew her in and in to him, even as every intimate part of her blossomed outward. Her breasts throbbed as if to burst from the touch of his tongue. A molten fire seemed to flow between her legs, pulsing with an insatiable hunger.

"Adam—" Her breath was so short she could barely speak the word. She had to tell him . . . had to make him see that she was dying for want of him. . . . "Adam, teach me. I need you—"

"Dear God, Emma." The words escaped his lips against her ear. Suddenly he felt helpless in her presence, unable to exert the power he had always held over those he wanted to control. "What are you doing to me?"

He stopped speaking as Emma fumbled for the buttons on his denim trousers. Though she had never experienced the ways of men and women, every sense told her that here—this hardened part of him that pressed against her so urgently—lay the satisfaction of her hunger. As she peeled back his trousers, her eyes fell upon the fullness of his naked body. But he did not allow a fear to rise in her. Instead he pulled her against him and slowly lowered their bodies to the blanket.

Holding her tightly, kissing her lips, Adam stroked down the length of her. She gasped in pleasure as his fingers slid into the moist silk between her legs and caressed her until her hips danced against his hand. Clutching at his back, she drew him closer and closer. Then, when she knew she could bear no more, he gently parted her thighs and slid inside her. As he broke through her maidenhead, she sucked in her breath at the sudden pain. Adam froze and drew upward in surprise.

He started to speak, but she pulled his mouth to hers. When he moved within her, the pain seemed to wash away beneath the ecstasy of his body on hers. Pleasure mounted with the rhythmic play of their tongues as she wrapped her legs around his. He regained control then, his desire to give her satisfaction outweighing his groaning need, and began a slow and rousing dance upon her. His lips found the curve of her neck, the inner shell of her ear, the dip of her temple. She drank in the smell of his skin and the taste of his mouth.

Knowing she had found what she had been seeking, she let him take her upward through plateaus of passion until at last she cried out and, with a shiver of undreamed-of pleasure, reached a pulsing peak. Digging her fingers into his back, she clung to him as the waves racked through her. And her shuddering body sent his over the brink in a wash of blinding pleasure. He whispered her name again and again as his flesh rode with hers across endless plains until they drifted to a breathless peace in each other's arms.

Many minutes passed before Emma could begin to see past the lights that had flashed across her eyes, blinding her to all but the man at her side. Her heartbeat slowly calmed, and she heard her breath grow quiet.

"I didn't know it would be like that," she said softly at last. She turned to him and realized that though she was lying on her back, he was on his side. His elbow was propped onto the blanket, and his head rested on the heel of his palm as he gazed down at her.

"It isn't like that." He held her eyes locked on his. "It isn't ever like that."

Emma marveled at the brilliant sky. The stars hung in the branches of the thorn tree, and the moon slid toward the horizon.

"Emma." He stroked his fingers down her arm, needing to understand this unfathomable woman. She turned her face to him. "You told me you already were a woman. I thought—"

"I am a woman. Not like that . . . but in every other way. And now, in all ways." She rolled onto her side facing him. "I'm not sorry."

"Damn." The whispered word escaped his lips as Adam glanced down at her breasts. Their rose-hued nipples seemed to call out to him wantonly, and he reached to touch her. But he caught himself, pulled his hand away, and forced his attention upward. It was no better . . . now her green eyes—her depthless olive eyes—seemed to be devouring his very soul.

"I wanted you . . . I wanted to—" He could hear his own voice stammering like a fool over the words he was trying to say. "But I didn't know I would . . . you would . . . Emma, you're so beautiful. You're like no other woman I've ever known." He sat up suddenly. "Damn! I'm getting tangled up here."

He shot to his feet and grabbed his trousers, but Emma reached up and caught his hand. "It's all right, it's all right, Adam," she said.

Pulling him down beside her, she took his shoulders and eased him back onto the blanket. As she stretched out along his body, she felt the tension in his muscles. She knew what he had meant about getting tangled up. It wasn't supposed to be this way. The words of promise they had spoken in the village had meant nothing to him. He hadn't planned to feel anything for her other than the pleasure of her body. She hadn't meant to, either. She had just wanted to know him—all of him. But now . . .

Tears welled in her eyes, and she looked through them at the fuzzy pinpricks of starlight. The moon had almost gone, and the sky was yellowing. How *could* Adam make her a part of his life? He already had promised himself to another woman. He belonged in her arms, not Emma's. Brushing a tear from her cheek before he could see, she braced herself. Adam could not give himself to her—and he didn't want to. This sudden knowledge slammed into her, and she steeled herself against it. Well, if he could give her nothing, she wanted nothing from him. After all, she had her plans. And Adam King did *not* fit in. She twisted the brass ring on her finger. It was all just business anyway.

"Adam, don't think twice about tonight." Emma sat up and drew her chemise over her shoulders. "It was lovely, of course, but we have to get on with these other matters. I must find Cissy. That comes above everything. And then I shall set about to find a mission hospital where I can work. That's what I really want—certainly not entanglements. I can't afford them any more than you can."

She slipped her skirt over her hips and buttoned it. Trying to still her trembling fingers, she wondered if she had made her words as forceful as she had intended. The last thing Adam must know was how she really felt. But how *did* she feel?

"Emma, listen to me." Adam caught her wrist and forced her to look at him. "What we shared here was—"

"Adam, please!" She couldn't bear to hear him end it more finally. He would try to ease it over, and it would only hurt worse. "We're business partners. We shall behave as if nothing has passed between us. I shall not expect anything from you other than what you agreed to do—help me to find my sister."

Adam's eyes were dark in the light of the brightening sky. Emma wanted to look away from his smoldering gaze, but she found herself locked to him. If she couldn't draw back, she would think of his lips on hers and his body pressed against her. She would think of the height of pleasure she had known in his arms, of the ways he had touched her, of the places they had been . . .

"Good night, Adam." The words choked out of her. "I really must sleep. It's almost dawn."

Curling into a ball against the ache in her heart, Emma closed her eyes. But sleep had not come when she heard Adam rise and dress. The horses stamped and snorted, and the first herd of cattle headed out of the village toward a day on the burning plains.

"Emma." Adam's voice drew her from her restless thoughts, and Emma raised herself onto one elbow on the blanket. He was crouching beside her, fully clothed, his gun at his side. "Sendeyo's senior wife wants you to come for breakfast in her hut."

Emma sat up and gazed at the man before her. He wore a look of fatigue, and she wondered if it was from the sleepless night—or from some carefully hidden emotion she sensed buried in the depths of his blue eyes. As she brushed the thick waves of her hair back from her neck, she heard his breath catch in his throat.

Eyeing him carefully—trying to read him—Emma uncurled her legs. "Are you going?"

"Where?"

"To breakfast . . ."

"Sure." Adam stood up suddenly and pulled out his neckerchief. "It won't be much, but we have a long day ahead of us. And I'm sure you could use some grub. I'll meet you inside the fence."

Emma nodded and watched him walk away, but when she rose she saw that he had turned his head. His eyes raked over her, then he looked away and strode into the village. Emma glanced down at herself and saw at once that her silken chemise had hidden nothing from his eyes—the creamy expanse of her round breasts rose fully over the low neckline, their rosy peaks barely masked by the sheer lacy fabric.

Snatching up her blouse, she pulled it on and quickly buttoned the long row up to the top of her neck. Across the grassy clearing beneath the bush where she had begun her night, she saw her corset and boots lying on the blanket. Carrying her stockings, she waded through the tall, spiny grass and tried not to think of Adam's hands slipping the soft fabric down her thighs. She pulled on the stockings and stuffed her feet into her boots, cursing the buttons that delayed her. Let the savages have the corset, she thought as she rolled up the blanket and carried it to the horses, leaving the torturous garment behind. She strapped her blanket behind the saddle and bent to pick up the pallet. At that moment her eye fell upon the stain of blood on the gray wool of Adam's blanket.

She gazed down at it for a moment, knowing it was all that remained—was all that *could* remain—of the night with Adam. She had given herself to him, and it was a bond between them that could never be broken. Yet she knew she would not use it to try to fetter him to her. Instead she would set him free—pretend it had been of no great consequence—though she knew in her heart that from that moment on, no man could touch her as Adam King had. No man would hold the place in her heart he held.

Kneeling, she folded the stained blanket and rolled it tightly. Setting her jaw, she shoved the blanket behind Adam's saddle and buckled it on. Then she lifted her skirts and ran through the dewy grass to the village.

Stepping to one side, Emma let a herd of scrawny goats file past. The naked child who scampered behind them stopped in astonishment at the sight of the tall, golden-haired white woman. The two eyed each other for a long moment, Emma taking in the boy's sparrow-thin legs, his protruding stomach, the flies crusting his eyes, and the blue-black haze in his stare. The child scanned Emma up and down, and she read his amusement at her impractical garments and wildly waving hair. A sudden cry from the village startled him, and he broke free of her gaze, running harum-scarum to catch up to his goats.

Emma watched the boy dart over a low hill, then

she strolled through the gate. Her attention fell
instantly upon Adam, whose eyes were riveted to
her every move.

"Maasai children herd the animals," he said quietly. "It's their tradition."

Emma approached him nonchalantly, trying to
keep her focus from his piercing blue eyes. "The
boy was so thin . . . and the flies. Is he well?"

"As well as a child can be with almost no water
and very little food. Even the flies have to get their
moisture where they can find it."

Looking back toward the path the child had
taken, she felt her heart go out to the little boy.
"Why don't they dig wells and grow gardens . . .
and wash? . . . It's all so primitive—"

The sentence caught in her throat as she became
aware of the flat-topped mud huts and the gathering crowd of curious villagers. The women wore
layer upon layer of bright beaded necklaces, and
their earrings hung from lobes stretched nearly to
their shoulders. The skin-clad men stood on one
leg and leaned against their spears, with long
wooden clubs resting in the crook between their
legs.

"They're nomads," Adam said, smiling at the
jostling onlookers. "They follow the green grass
and pray for rain. Doesn't do much good to dig a
well when there's no water under the ground. And
they don't like vegetables any more than a good
cowboy does—"

He stopped speaking when an ancient crone el-
bowed through the group and hobbled up to stand
before him. Rheumy eyes barely glittered through
narrow slits. Her two breasts hung like flat, empty
purses beneath the stack of necklaces piled to her
chin. She wore a leather skirt over her thin body,

and her bare feet were planted crooked and gnarled in the dust.

Adam took off his hat and dipped his head low, as though she might have been the queen. "*Takwenya*, Endebelai," he said.

The old woman smiled. "*Iko.*" She only had one tooth on top, and the scattered bottom ones looked as if they had not long to remain.

Adam took Emma's elbow and propelled her toward the woman. "This is Endebelai. She's Sendeyo's senior wife. Say '*Takwenya*' to her. It's a form of greeting."

"*Takwenya*, Endebelai." Emma curtsied.

"*Iko.*" The old woman smiled again, then cackled aloud—obviously amused at Emma's poorly spoken greeting. At her merriment, the crowd around them suddenly relaxed and surged forward, surrounding Emma. Their hands cautiously slipped out to brush against her skirt and fondle her hair. One little girl lifted her hem and peered in amazement at the layers of white frothy petticoats.

At first Emma froze, uncomfortable beneath the scrutiny and touch of the natives. The people smelled pungent—of woodsmoke, sweat, and things she could not identify. She held her breath for a moment, nearly suffocating in the crush. But as Adam reached out to rescue her from the ever-growing throng, she held up a hand to stop him.

Then, kneeling among the children, she touched their faces and ran her hands down their thin arms just as they had hers. Here was a little girl whose arm bore an angry, blistered burn. Emma stroked over the scarring skin, knowing the child would bear the ugly mark for the rest of her life. Here was a boy with a long festering black thorn embedded in his leg. . . . And this baby! The child's fly-rimmed eyes were infected. . . .

"Oh, Adam!" Emma rose from the sea of silent, now serious faces. Adam was looking at her, his eyes grim with understanding. She covered her mouth, trying to still her trembling lips. Then she let her hand fall to her side. "Have they no hospital?"

He shook his head. "They have a *laibon*. A witch doctor."

"But this baby will lose his sight before long! And the thorn in this child's leg is infected—it will become gangrenous . . . and he'll die! I must tend them. We must have water and . . . and—"

"Emma." Adam drew her against him. "Emma, the protectorate is filled with villages no different from this. You can't save them all. Try to understand . . . the people live with disease and death. They haven't learned to expect much more from life."

"But I must help them. You don't understand—"

"I *do* understand." He took her face in his hands and tilted her chin so that she was forced to look into his eyes. It was this about her that made her so hard to resist—this deep caring and the desire to change her world. And it was this that he was counting on when he got her to his ranch. "I *do* understand, Emma. I want you to help them . . . and you will. But first you have to find out what happened to your sister. The Masai will be waiting here for you when you come to them. They'll need you just as much as they do right now . . no more, no less."

Before Emma could respond, Endebelai grasped her arm firmly and pulled her toward one of the huts. The crone hobbled along, fumbling her way down the side of the mud wall. As they approached the tunnel-like doorway leading inside, Endebelai carefully ran her hands around the opening before entering in . . . and Emma realized the old woman was blind.

Bending from the waist, Endebelai slipped into the tunnel, drawing her guest along. A heavy pall of smoke flooded Emma's nostrils, forcing her to gasp for air. Unable to see anything, she bumped suddenly into the still form of Endebelai. The Maasai woman grasped her by the upper arms and thrust her into a sitting position against one wall of the chamber they had entered. Emma heard fumbling and muttering and at last saw a spark of light as Endebelai fanned the embers of her fire into flame.

Instantly the hovel filled with even more smoke. Coughing, Emma surveyed her surroundings. She could see no windows, although a small hole in the low ceiling allowed for ventilation of a sort. On the dirt floor lay several cowhides, and stacked in one recess was a collection of clay and gourd cooking utensils.

The dim light filtering in from the tunnel was suddenly snuffed, and Emma squinted to see Adam struggle into the hut. His body seemed enormous—all long legs and arms in the cramped hut filled with small goats, stray dogs, and people. Adam folded himself onto the floor beside her and set his hat on one knee.

"Pretty smoky," he said quietly. "Keeps the bugs down."

Startled, Emma glanced up to find him wearing his lopsided grin. But she quickly tucked her skirts around her legs all the same.

Endebelai groped into the recess for a pan, placed it on the fire, and poured milk into it from a small gourd. A beatific smile played on her lips as she stirred the contents with a wooden spoon. Adam began to converse with the old woman in the singsong language of the Maasai, and she answered him in soft, careful phrases.

Before long the milk started simmering, and Endebelai heaved the steaming pan from the fire with her bare hands to pour the milk into another gourd. Groping under some skins beside her, she extracted and unwrapped a grass-bound bundle. Emma recognized it as some sort of soft white cheese. Breaking off a large chunk, the old woman passed it along with the milk to her guests.

Emma tentatively bit into the bitter cheese and drank of the hot milk. Her stomach unknotted gratefully, and she began to relax.

"What have you been saying to her?" Emma took another sip. It was the oddest thing, how comfortable she felt here in the dark smoky hut. Endebelai, for all her quirks, was every bit as warm as any English mother—warmer than most. Her home felt like just that . . . a home.

"We've been talking about her son." Adam stretched out his long legs and hooked his boots one over the other.

"Do you know him?"

Adam stiffened slightly. "Yes. He's a friend of mine."

"Does he live here?"

"No." Adam was more reticent than usual. "I've told her about Cissy. She's going to ask Sendeyo to send out the warriors to look for her."

"Oh, please thank her for me!" A chill ran down Emma's spine at the thought of the files of strong young men combing the wilderness for Cissy. If anyone knew the land and could find her, it would be they!

Adam relayed the words of gratitude to Endebelai, who sat listening and nodding. Then she began a long, rambling speech. In the midst of it Adam leaned over and whispered to Emma.

"She's telling you a story. . . . When Le-eyo lived," he translated, "he wanted to bring his dead children back to life. Enkai, the Maasai god, told him the next time a child died, Le-eyo should lay the body outside and say, 'Man die and return. Moon die and stay away.' Soon a child died. Le-eyo was afraid the moon would never return. Since the child was not his own child, he said, 'Man die and stay away. Moon die and return.' Le-eyo went home and found that his own child had died. He took it out to the plain and said, 'Man die and return. Moon die and stay away.' But the child did not return to life. Then Enkai spoke to Le-eyo and told him, 'You have spoiled it for all mankind by not obeying me. Now no one will return from the dead—but the moon will come back each night.' "

Endebelai stopped and smiled into the darkness. Adam lifted his hat and ran his finger around the brim.

"But what is she telling me?" Emma asked urgently. "What does the story mean?"

Adam questioned Endebelai, who nodded and whispered a few more words. He leaned over to Emma. "She says to tell you that the story means this: Your sister is dead and will not return. But look outside tonight, and you will see the moon."

# Chapter Seven

❖❖❖❖

*Oh, a man there lives on the Western plains,*
*With a ton of fight and an ounce of brains,*
*Who herds the cows as he robs the trains*
*And goes by the name of cowboy.*

*He laughs at death and scoffs at life;*
*He feels unwell unless in some strife.*
*He fights with a pistol, a rifle, or knife.*
*This reckless, rollicking cowboy.*

—"The Cowboy"

*These two were rapid falcons in a snare,*
*Condemned to do the flitting of the bat . . .*
*Their hearts held cravings for the buried day.*
*Then each applied to each that fatal knife,*
*Deep questioning, which probes to endless dole.*

—George Meredith
"Modern Love"

"NO!" EMMA STARTED to rise in the old woman's hut. "Cissy is not dead! The soldier came for her—I'm certain I heard him!"

"Emma—" Adam stood and pulled Emma to his side. "It's just a story. These people explain their lives through stories. Endebelai has lost six children—babies. These people *live* with death, and their religion is all wrapped up in getting through it. It's a hard life out here—"

"But Cissy isn't dead." Emma shrugged out of his arms and looked down at Endebelai. The old woman rocked gently, her face a study in peace. "Tell her I am going to find my sister."

142

Adam transmitted the message in the singsong language, and the old woman whispered a reply without looking up. Adam relayed the words. "She says to tell you good-bye and to wish you the Maasai farewell: I pray to God that you meet nobody but blind people, who will not harm you."

Emma gazed down at the crouching old blind woman, her heart aching to touch those eyes with healing even though her mind was in tumult. "Tell her . . . thank her for the food. Tell her I shall return soon and examine her eyes. Perhaps there is something I can do."

Adam relayed Emma's sentiments, to which Endebelai responded in a low voice. "I told her what you said," he whispered as he guided Emma out of the hut, his hand resting lightly on the waves of her unbound hair. "Then I gave her the guest's farewell: May you lie down with honey and milk. She answered, 'So be it.' I reckon that means she'll be looking for you to come back and take care of her eyes. But you better try to round up some good medicine first . . . she won't come for help otherwise—and neither will anyone else. These people want potions and chants and charms. They won't even bother to try what you give them unless you add in all the extras. You might want to work up a little dance—maybe a waltz with some cancan thrown in. . . ."

Adam's words tapered off and he watched Emma's long hair as she moved through the doorway ahead of him. His efforts to lighten the situation were useless, he knew. She was too intensely driven to achieve her every goal. And things were only going to get harder for her.

Emerging into the bright sunshine, Emma

sucked in a deep breath of fresh air. "You certainly know a lot about the Maasai."

"This clan of Maasai. They came through for me when I needed help." Adam stuffed his hat onto the back of his head. He squared his shoulders, determined to detach himself from her. "They're my family."

Emma glanced up, startled, but he had already set off in the direction of the horses. She surveyed the circle of low huts and the children peering from their doors. Adam's *family*? But these people were savages.

Look at them—nothing of civilization to speak of. They hardly wore clothes; they had no transportation; they didn't even wash! But then she remembered other things . . . their religion, their betrothals and marriages, their formal greetings, their legends and tales, their homes and fires. Perhaps . . .

"Emma!" Adam's shout from outside the fence drew her attention, and she hurried across the clearing toward the horses. "Let's get a move on. The sooner we get back to the station and find out if anyone's seen your sister, the better."

Without looking back at the village, Emma climbed onto her mare. Every part of her body that rested against the horse and saddle instantly began to ache again; every muscle and every inch of tender skin remembered her long trek across the plains. Even her hands as she lifted the reins seemed to protest the ride she must make.

Adam scrutinized her, his blue eyes shadowed by his hat, while she attempted to adjust her skirt and petticoats into a more comfortable position.

"A lady in England normally rides sidesaddle, you know," she said by way of explanation. She realized she was not much of a rider at any rate, and stretching her legs across the horse's wide back made her feel awkward—even vulnerable somehow.

"At least you don't have that damned corset on."

Emma's eyes darted to Adam's, and she read the amusement twinkling in their depths. She followed his glance and saw her undergarment lying beneath the bush, a gathering crowd of curious children encircling it. One held a long stick and gingerly prodded the stiff corset. When it suddenly rolled onto one side, the children shrieked in horror and scurried backward as if it had been alive.

"I have several others in my trunks at Tsavo," Emma commented as she urged her horse alongside Adam's. "I suppose I shall have to put one on when I'm back in polite society."

The cowboy turned with a slow grin and raised one eyebrow, but he said nothing. Spurring his horse into a canter, he led Emma away from the village and toward the early sun.

They spent the morning riding through the trackless yellow grasslands potted with deep antbear holes and hidden scrub thorns. Dust rose with every step of their horses, filling the riders' nostrils and coating their clothing. Though Emma called for Cissy, and Adam regularly fired his gun into the air, they neither saw nor heard any sign of humans during the stretch of long hours.

They were not alone, however. Large herds of gazelle, antelope, zebra, and giraffe grazed contentedly, pausing now and then to stare at the strangers intruding on their domain. Truly aware of her surroundings for the first time, Emma gazed in awe at the huge creatures roaming the bush.

A rhino and her calf sauntered across the plains

to sniff blindly at them. And once a squealing warthog dashed in front of them, her six piglets running behind her, tails in the air. Adam pointed out a circle of vultures soaring over a lion's kill somewhere in the distance. Emma shuddered at the realization that it might be Cissy's body, and she insisted they inspect. But when they arrived at the kill, they saw it was a young hartebeest. A pack of hyenas, blearily sated from the feast, fed on the carcass.

Adam wanted to tell Emma how the hyenas took over a kill after the lions were finished—how hyenas and vultures picked the bones clean, leaving an almost tidy skeleton lying on the plains. But he held his tongue, knowing his words would make her think about Cissy and what might have happened. Still, he found himself wanting her to share with him in the mysteries of this land. It had always fascinated him how cleverly things worked together out here, almost as if according to a plan. He had never been a religious man. Probably just another way of fighting his parents' control. And he had fought them.

When he had chosen to follow his own path against their will that he stay and run the family businesses, they had turned away from him and angrily given him up to his stubbornness. Years had passed in which there had been no contact. He had written to his mother once . . . but his father had readdressed the envelope and sent it back unopened. Then one day he had learned it was too late ever to make amends.

Now he could see himself in Emma, the side of her that held back, that detached, that refused to give up the dream. Her father had died but Adam hoped she would not have to live forever with the unresolved pain of that broken bond.

"Is your mother back in England?" he asked as they rode away from the hyenas.

Emma looked up startled from her absorption in her surroundings. "My mother? No . . . she died some time ago. I thought you knew."

"No." Adam reached down and stroked his horse's neck. "Are you anything like her?"

"Not in appearance—" Emma's hand tightened on the reins. Why was he asking about her mother? Could he have guessed that in spirit she and her mother had been almost identical? They had loved the same things—needed the same things. In their walks through the countryside, her mother had taught Emma to notice the wounded animals. She had taken her elder daughter with her when she went to visit the workhouses where the little orphan children lived. And it was her fiery spirit of determination and independence that finally had led her into so much trouble. . . .

"I expect they'll have buried your father," Adam said, breaking into her thoughts. "There's not much you can do about funerals and such out here."

Emma nodded. "It's all right. I should think he'd be pleased to be buried near a railroad."

"Plant me out on the plains like this. Nobody around but the animals. Remember that, Emma."

"Why should I remember that?"

"Just remember." Adam's eyes were unreadable.

Emma turned away and gazed out at the open grasslands. He had become so remote with her now, and she couldn't understand it. Once they had spoken easily and freely. He had touched her and taken her in his arms as if the whole world might see and he wouldn't care. But now, out in the vast emptiness, he had withdrawn. His words were veiled and his touch almost awkward. Their lovemaking had changed him. He was afraid now. Afraid that she would want more of him than he could give.

Swallowing the lump in her throat, Emma set her jaw and looked up at the sapphire sky looming overhead, larger and more dominant than the earth upon which they rode. The sun beat down like a golden hammer, searing her skin and forcing rivulets of perspiration down her back. Adam rode in silence, and Emma could not bring herself to speak. How could she tell him he had broken through all the barriers in her heart—slipped into a place no man had been before?

"You're blistering." Adam's low voice sounded unnaturally loud in the silence of Emma's thoughts. She blinked in surprise as he took off his hat and set it on her head.

"Are we far from the station?" Emma wondered aloud, reaching up to straighten his hat. Its warm felt brushed against her fingertips, a part of him—the only part of him—she could touch.

Adam eyed the sun and glanced around at the trees and low hills. "I'd say another hour or so. You thirsty?"

Emma nodded. "And hungry. I feel as if I haven't eaten for days." .

"We'll find out what anyone knows about your sister, and then we'll eat and rest up on the trip back to the coast. You're going to need your strength for the search we're about to make."

"Do you think it will take long to get the money

transferred? I cannot bear to sit around waiting when Cissy's life is hanging in the balance."

"Emma . . ." Adam said her name softly, feeling a sudden urge to protect her. He fought it. "Emma, you know it's not very likely that Cissy—"

"I shall never believe she's not alive," Emma cut in. "Until I have searched every mile of the protectorate, I shall believe Cissy is alive somewhere."

"You might not ever find her, you know."

She knew he was trying to prepare her for the worst. But somehow the very thought of it made her shrink inside and caused a part of her to wither. "I believe I shall know when my sister dies."

"How will you know?"

"I shall . . . *feel* something. Something in me will respond to her. I know it sounds odd—"

"No. No, it makes sense." Adam's face was solemn as he rode a few paces ahead. "I think when somebody you love gets into trouble, you know somehow."

Emma gazed at his broad shoulders rimmed with sunlight. For what seemed like the hundredth time that morning, she lost herself to a feeling of giddiness at being with him. The exhaustion, the soreness, the shock of her sister's disappearance, and her father's death—everything receded for long moments at a time in his exhilarating presence. But he could only know what she was talking about if he had loved someone that much—and loved in a soul-binding way, as she loved Cissy. He must have meant his wife. Whom else could he have loved that much? And yet, the way he had held *her* in the night . . .

The rest of the way, they rode in silence. Emma found she could only focus on the immediate future: finding Cissy and sorting out her feelings for Adam. She knew she must never let him close to her again. If he touched her, she would only want him more. And he was too dangerous to her plans and her future. More important, he was too dangerous to her heart.

The sun had slipped over the zenith when Adam and Emma at last rode into Tsavo railhead camp. A cry arose instantly from the workers, and men poured out of the corrugated tin buildings to hail the arrivals.

"Emmaline!" Nicholas Bond, neatly dressed as usual, dashed through the main station doorway and down the steps. His dark coattails fluttered in the breeze as he ran toward her, top hat in hand and black spats shiny in the sunlight. "You're alive!"

Without responding, Emma slid down from her horse and forced her aching legs toward him. Her wrinkled skirt hung heavy with dust as it pulled around her mud-caked boots. She pushed her tangled hair back from her forehead as the dapper Bond rushed forward. "Cissy? Have you found her? Is she—"

"No. No one's found any trace of her." Nicholas caught Emma around the waist and drew her close against his chest. "Dear God, Emma, I thought I had lost you. You should never have—"

"I must find Cissy." Emma pulled away.

"But it's impossible that she could still be alive." Nicholas clutched Emma's shoulders, half shaking her. "One could never survive on the plains. There's no water . . . and the lions and cheetah—"

"Save it, Bond." Adam stepped beside Emma, and Nicholas immediately removed his hands from her shoulders. "Her sister *could* be alive. People do survive alone out there . . . I did, in case you've forgotten. And there's a chance she could be with this German soldier. The main thing now is to get Emma something to drink and eat. We've been riding all day."

Nicholas glared at Adam. "I shall see to her needs, Mr. King. Your services are appreciated by the Crown, but now Miss Pickworth is under my protection."

"Emma's name is now Mrs. King." Adam took a step forward. "And she's under *my* protection."

Nicholas's mouth dropped open. He turned wide-eyed to Emma, who brushed a hand across her forehead. "Adam, please. Don't bait him. Let me explain—"

"Adam! Adam, you ol' buzzard!" A laughing voice echoed across the heated air, and the three turned to see a short, compact young man striding toward them. His white hat waved high in one hand while his head of bright yellow hair bobbed happily. "Where you been? I been scoutin' this place high and low. You got my horse?"

"Soapy." Adam sidestepped Nicholas to greet the younger man. "Red's back, sound as ever. She's covered half the protectorate since you've seen her."

"Hey, gal." Soapy reached out to the horse Emma had ridden and stroked her neck. "You look as limp as a worn-out fiddle string, Red. Wha'd you run off on me for?"

"Soapy, this is Emma." Adam placed his hand on Emma's back and guided her toward the man she recognized from her traumatic first night at

Tsavo. "Emma, meet Soapy Potts. He's my right-hand man on the ranch."

"I'm the cook—you bet I've got my job locked in!" Soapy tossed back his head and let out a deep belly laugh. Emma could not help but smile as his mirth caught hold inside her and tickled the corners of her mouth. "You ever ate anything the boss here cooked? Meat so tough you got to sharpen your knife just to cut the gravy!"

Adam glanced at Emma, a wry grin creasing his face. "Don't listen to him. His coffee's thick enough to eat with a fork. Come on, Soapy. Get these horses fed and watered, will you? We're heading out as soon as we can get a train back to the coast."

"Now just a moment, Mr. King!" Nicholas burst in. "I should like to know what is going on here."

"Please, Mr. Bond." Emma laid her bare hand on Nicholas's taut arm. "I shall explain everything. It's all quite simple, really. But I must insist upon your escort to a room where I might sit down and relax before a pot of tea and some cake. I have very little time to spare and must make the most of every minute."

"But of course." Nicholas cupped his palm lightly around Emma's elbow. "We shall go into the station at once. I have an office where you will find everything you need."

As he started to lead her away, Emma turned back to Adam. "Will you come? There will be maps in the office, and we can chart our course—"

"No." Adam's gaze swept over her face, then locked briefly on her lips before coming to rest on her green eyes. "Tea's about the last thing I want to drink right now. Come on, Soapy. Let's see how the horses are looking. We need to get our hands on another nag for you to ride. Emma and old Red have hit it off pretty well."

"Now, wait a minute here, boss!" Soapy protested.

"I'll be back for you, Emma. You speak your piece to Bond and be done with him, because when I get on that train for Mombasa, he'd better not be anywhere in sight."

"I shall go when and where I please," Nicholas sputtered. "Especially if it involves Her Majesty's Railway. Miss Pickworth needs comfort and compassion right now, and whatever mad scheme you've pressed her into I shall make every effort to subvert."

"You do that." Adam glared at Nicholas for a moment, then turned to Emma. "I'll have our gear ready to go as quick as I can."

"Thank you." Emma wanted to say more—wanted to show him how much his loyalty meant to her, how she was relying on him even though she wanted to be strong. But he turned on his spurred heel and strode across the stationyard before she could say another word.

Soapy's wide gray eyes ran up and down her once before he hurried after Adam. Emma watched them go, strange replicas of one another in their boots and denims, their plaid shirts and neckerchiefs. Soapy rose only as tall as Adam's shoulder, but his hat—

Remembering suddenly, Emma reached up to touch Adam's hat on her head. She wondered how she must look with her hair astray and her skin ruddy from the sun.

"We must see that you have a proper helmet." Nicholas pulled his eyes to hers, and Emma realized he had been staring at her body. She glanced down to find her blouse unbuttoned almost to her breast—something she must have done unaware in the heat of the trip.

"This one worked quite well, actually." Emma drew Adam's hat from her head. "It has an excellent design. I suppose the Americans have spent a great deal of time in this sort of climate. Now"—she lifted her skirt—"do show me to your office."

Without answering, Nicholas led Emma up the stairs and into the whitewashed station building. The office workers, who had retreated to their desks after the initial excitement over Emma's return, looked up curiously. Nicholas spoke briefly with one of them to ask that tea be sent in. Then he escorted Emma into a small office with a scrubbed wooden floor, bare walls, and no ceiling. The silver tin roof radiated heat down into the room, and Nicholas hurried to open the one narrow window. Sparsely furnished with an old wooden desk, two rickety chairs, and a horsehair-covered settee, the office was stacked with crates and sacks of imported goods. It smelled of ink and burlap and rust.

"How lovely to sit on a cushion." Emma spread her skirts wide and gingerly settled her sore body on the settee. The last thing she wanted after her long ride was to confront Nicholas in this stuffy little room. Yet there was something about him— something so like her father in his mannerisms— that she felt little room for protest.

Nicholas grasped his hands behind his back as he walked toward her from the window. "I still cannot believe that cowboy brought you back so quickly," he began. "You must have been exhausted when he found you."

Emma looked at Nicholas intently. His words bespoke tenderness, concern, but his tone revealed his irritation. She suspected that a great deal of that annoyance somehow fell upon herself, as though she had done something highly untoward in running off to find her sister. Nicholas unclasped his hands and perched awkwardly on one of the chairs.

Emma cleared her throat, trying to think how she could make things right. "*I* insisted we come straight back to Tsavo station," she said carefully. "I wanted to leave immediately, but Mr. King would not hear of going before I had rested the night. But you see, I must begin to search in earnest for Cissy."

"Emmaline, you cannot be serious."

"But of course I am." She stopped speaking as a young man hurried into the room with a tray of tea and a loaf of thick bread. He set the tray on a small table, quickly poured two cups, and sliced the still-steaming bread. As he left the room, Emma gratefully lifted the sweet liquid to her lips.

"Emmaline, do you know . . . about your father?"

"Yes. Adam told me," she said in a low voice. Her fingers suddenly trembling, she set the cup on the saucer. "Is his grave near?"

"Just back of this office—with the other victims."

Emma's eyes darted to his face. Victims of the lions, he meant. Victims of Africa—the savage lands. A martyr for the empire. The London papers would give her father a glorious death: "Godfrey Pickworth—member of Parliament, Commissioner of the Queen's Railway—suffered a heart attack while on duty for the Crown. . . . Certain a marauding man-eating lion had killed his daughter—" Emma stopped her thoughts. She must come to terms with her father's death, with his passing, with the part she had played.

"I shall visit my father's grave before I leave," she said, fighting for control. "You must understand . . . my father would have insisted on finding Cissy. I *must* find her, Nicholas."

"Very well," Nicholas said. He set his cup on the tray. "We have already sent out search parties to comb this area for both of you. The men returned not long before you did. It appears that your sister is nowhere in the vicinity of the railhead. Now that you are back, I'll reorganize the men and use Tsavo station as the base. But I must warn you, the railway cannot afford to spare the workers for long. A week at the most—"

"A week is not long enough." Emma ran her finger over the brim of the hat in her lap. "*I* shall search for Cissy *until I find her*," she said without hesitation. "I'm planning to travel from here to Mombasa and to transfer a portion of my inheritance into the bank there. Using those funds, I'll outfit a large party, and Mr. King will be my guide. I intend to go to the border first and speak with the Germans to discover what has become of Cissy's soldier. From there, I simply shall comb the country until she is found. Adam has contacts with various tribes, and—"

"I daresay he has!" Nicholas Bond said in a wholly disapproving voice as he stood up from his chair. "Emmaline, have you any true knowledge of Mr. King? Do you know his background, his involvements?"

Emma frowned, disturbed at Nicholas's patronizing attitude. "I believe I know everything I need to know about Adam King. He understands the protectorate and its people, and he has agreed to do it."

"For a large fee, no doubt."

"Of course." Emma's voice was flat. "We were married in the Maasai village where we stayed the night. Having taken a husband, I now can collect my inheritance and pay for Adam's services."

A long silence hung in the room. Emma picked up her teacup and took a sip. She could not bring herself to look at Nicholas. His cautions about Adam were beginning to arouse hidden fears about the cowboy. Although his attitude bothered her, she knew it was important to convince him that she had gotten married. He must be thinking how preposterous the whole thing sounded—and indeed it was. Probably he even knew about Adam's wife, and he might use it to block her plan. At last she set her cup back on the tray and looked up.

Nicholas Bond's face was a study in marble. A thin rivulet of perspiration had trickled from his sandy-red sideburn down his jaw. Emma cleared her throat. "Nicholas, will you see that my baggage is transferred onto the train. I have to—"

"Emmaline!" His face suddenly flushed a deep crimson. "Are you serious? Have you actually married Adam King?"

"Yes." Emma drew back from his vehemence. "It is a business arrangement."

"Business? Have you any idea what sort of partner you've taken on?"

Emma got to her feet and walked to the window, wanting to escape, to get away from Nicholas—whether or not it ruined her chance of securing his help. "It doesn't matter to me—"

Nicholas's voice was steely. "Adam King is a money-grubbing agitator, whose sole aim is to stir up trouble." He stopped for a moment, as if searching for a thought. "He's a mercenary, Emma! He's working with the Germans to instill unrest. He regularly receives crates at the coast. Do you know what's in them?"

"No." Emma barely heard the word choke from her throat.

"Guns! Ammunition! Oh, he'll tell you they're farming implements. For his ranch, he'll say. But they're guns! His real name is not even Adam King, it's Adam Koenig. He's a German himself. Just ask him, Emma. And *if* Cissy was abducted by the Germans, you can be sure *he* knows something about it."

Emma gripped the felt hat, rolling its brim in her white-knuckled fingers as she stood beside the window. How could all this possibly be true? And yet what *did* she know about Adam?

"You're telling me—" She collected her thoughts. "You're telling me that Adam could find out where Cissy is?"

"Yes. If the German soldier did call her name— and if the Germans have your sister—then he knows where she is being hidden."

"Being *hidden* by the Germans? No . . . you're wrong, Nicholas. It was just Rolf, the soldier who loved her. Not the Germans."

"Perhaps." Bond let the word hover on the air for a moment. "Yet Adam King is not to be trusted."

"Nicholas, why would the Germans want to take Cissy? It makes no sense."

"It makes perfect sense. They've had no end of trouble building their railway to the Uganda territory. Right now they're lagging behind us in the race to finish. Since our relations with the kaiser are steadily deteriorating, if we accuse the Germans of causing a British citizen's disappearance, it will fuel their nationalism against us. Exactly what the kaiser wants and needs to motivate his forces!"

It did seem to make sense. Everything he said fit with what she knew about the political situation . . . and yet Rolf and Cissy had seemed so naturally in love. But then what did she know of political intrigue?

"Why would Adam King be importing guns?" she challenged. That part certainly made no sense.

"Ten years ago the Germans faced a native uprising. The Africans had been armed by the Arabs with breech-loading rifles. The Germans know that if they can get guns into the hands of natives in the British Protectorate, we will have a great deal of trouble from the African tribes. Adam King is an agitator. His job is to import those guns and get them into the hands of the people. He even knows the tribes and speaks their languages!"

Trying to mask her confusion, Emma straightened her shoulders and glared at Nicholas. "You told me Adam was a slaver."

"He is." The railman bent and lifted his cup to his mouth. Emma wanted to believe he was stalling—but he had told her everything with such conviction. He set the cup back on the tray. "Emma . . . I know this is all a blow to you. Your father and Cissy. Let me just make it very simple. King is no good. His relationship with the Germans originated from his work in the Uganda territory, from which he exports slaves. They are sent down the old slave trails to Bagamoyo and Dar es Salaam on the coast of the German territory. The Germans turn their heads and let him continue because of the work he is doing for them against us. It's all very simple . . . not much to tell except the story of a mercenary. The empire is laced with such men, Emma. We simply keep our eyes on him and try to thwart him when we can."

As he finished speaking, Emma turned back to the window and rested her forehead against the cool pane of glass. Adam . . . a traitor, a mercenary, a slaver? Could he really know where Cissy was right now—while leading her on just to get at her money? . . . She couldn't believe that of him . . . and yet he *had* been very resistant to her proposal until she'd mentioned her inheritance. She lifted her eyes to the window, and a movement by the track caught her attention. *Adam.*

Dressed in a clean blue plaid shirt and black leather vest and a new black felt hat, he was walking beside Soapy, speaking earnestly. His hands moved as he explained something, obviously serious. His black boots caught the sunlight, their silver spurs sparkling. As she watched, her heart aching inside her, he suddenly stopped and looked straight up to the window where she stood. Their eyes locked for a moment, then Emma stepped backward.

As she did, she felt Nicholas's arms encircle her. He turned her around to face him inside the protection of his embrace. "Forget him, Emma," he whispered. "Your agreement can be broken easily. The marriage was a sham anyway . . . you as much as said so yourself. Who peformed it—one of the Masai?"

Emma nodded.

"There. You see? They're savages, and the marriage has no significance whatsoever. Emma . . ." He drew back and lifted her chin so that she was forced to look into his light brown eyes. "I told you once how I felt about you. I'll do anything I can to help you find Cissy. Marry me, Emma. I love you and I'll be far more to you than a guide to find your sister. Our marriage will not be a bargain . . . a convenience. It will be a true union. A marriage to last forever."

Emma stood before him, stunned by his words. Her feelings . . . the tumult of emotion his indictment of Adam had evoked in her . . . was more than she could bear. She tried to sort through everything. She had to tell him something. But she didn't know what to think, or how to feel. Suddenly everything inside her was dying—all the warmth Adam had flamed in her seemed quenched in the flood of evils Nicholas had poured upon it. But instead of hating Adam as she knew she should, she felt herself angrily wanting to protect that flame. She couldn't let it die. Not just yet. Not until she had seen for herself . . .

"Nicholas." She looked up into his face. Even as she began to speak, she knew she was making a mistake. She should trust him and do as he said. Her father would have approved of him . . . even Cissy had liked him. "Nicholas, I've given my word to Adam. If you say he might know where Cissy is, that's all the more reason to use his help. Perhaps I can find her by watching his movements and listening to his conversations with Soapy. I might even learn enough about his treachery against the queen to help you put a stop to his work. Certainly the slavery—"

"Emmaline, you can't be serious!" Nicholas exploded. "You can't mean you're going to continue to associate with him after all I've told you!"

"I am." Emma stepped out of Nicholas's embrace and walked toward the door. She knew she was lying to him—she hoped she could prove nothing against Adam . . . but either way she had to know. She had to find out the truth. "I am going with him to the coast and then to find my sister. Please wire ahead to Government House and tell Lord Delamere we shall be arriving shortly."

"Emmaline." Nicholas strode toward her and shoved his hand against the door so she could not leave. "I love you. You must marry me. Stay clear of Adam King. He'll hurt you, Emma. Believe me!"

"I shall do as I think best," Emma whispered, her green eyes flashing. "I shall do what I choose to do. And I choose to go with Adam King."

She turned and jerked the door open, forcing Nicholas to step aside as she made her way out into the station. He raced to her side and caught her arm, spinning her to face him. "I swear I'll not let you go so easily, Emma. I love you—I'll come for you and find you."

Emma pulled her arm free and walked away without looking back. "You do as you think best, Mr. Bond. And so shall I."

# Chapter Eight

✦✦✦✦

*I did not like my fireside,*
*I did not like my home;*
*I had in view far rambling,*
*So far away did roam.*
*I had a feeble mother,*
*She oft would plead with me;*

*And the last word she gave me*
*Was to pray to God in need.*

—"Young Champions"

*We are not sure of sorrow,*
  *And joy was never sure;*
*Today will die tomorrow;*
  *Time stoops to no man's lure;*
*And love, grown faint and fretful,*
*With lips but half regretful*
*Sighs, and with eyes forgetful*
  *Weeps that no loves endure.*

—Algernon Charles Swinburne
"The Garden of Proserpine"

"I THINK IT would be a real good idea." Adam stood a few feet from the train, leaning over a small mustachioed Englishman whose wide brown eyes darted nervously. "You can make the trip back tomorrow morning and still take these fellows in time for their leave."

"But Mr. King—I have my orders," said the little man, his quaking voice barely a whisper.

Emma heard the hurried exchange between the men as she strode toward them, her arms folded across her chest. "What is the matter here, Adam?" She was in no mood for nonsense, and she knew that her weariness was beginning to affect her judgment.

"Seems the train isn't scheduled to leave Tsavo station until tomorrow morning, ma'am." Adam gestured with his chin at the man before him. "Mr. Perkins here is the engineer, and he says he won't run the train without permission."

"Permission from whom?"

"Mr. Bond usually makes out the schedule." Mr. Perkins edged toward Emma, away from Adam. "We've a trainload of men going on leave tomorrow."

"I cannot wait until tomorrow," Emma said firmly. "My father was a commissioner of this railway, and under his authority I insist that you start the train at once. Every hour could mean the difference between my sister's life or death."

"But madam, with all due respect, we do not run the train at night." The little man glanced at Adam uneasily, but stood his ground. "There are elephants and rhinos and such roaming about the track. And in the dark, it is quite impossible to spot a huge gray beast in time to stop the train—"

"I don't care about elephants." Emma brushed her hair back from her forehead and shoved Adam's hat onto her head. "I want you to start this train. Now."

"I cannot do it." The engineer faced Emma square on.

"You will either start the train or I shall start it myself."

"Listen to the lady, little fellow." Adam moved his tall frame a step closer to the engineer. "You get that train started. I'll clear it with Bond, if that's the trouble. Just get on with your business." He gently lifted Mr. Perkins and turned him to face the train engine. Setting him back on his feet, he patted him firmly on the shoulder. "Now get."

"Yes, Mr. King." Without looking back, the engineer hurried toward the locomotive.

Emma watched Adam's eyes follow the man up the steps of the locomotive. In the afternoon sun, the cowboy's skin was a golden tan. The light breeze ruffled the dark hair beneath his hat and blew his shirt against the hard curves of his arms and chest. He was wearing a confident smile, his eyes sparkling a brighter blue than the sky.

"I'll clear things up with Bond." Adam spoke suddenly, turning to Emma and catching her by surprise. He quickly read her eyes, and his smile faded. He realized at once what he had done— shoving the engineer about, controlling people as he usually did. She would hate that in him, he thought, even though she herself was fighting to gain control of the things surrounding her. Angry at himself for caring at all what Emma thought of him, Adam turned his head.

Emma knew he had turned away because of the look he had seen in her eyes. Cursing herself for letting him see what she knew was her hunger, her aching desire for him, she resolved to force every emotion from her face. "*I* shall speak with Nicholas Bond," she said in a hard voice. "We have an understanding."

"Oh, you do, do you?" Adam took her arm above the elbow and swung her around to face him. "Well, understand *this*. Bond is my enemy"— He tightened his grip on her arm until her eyes fluttered to his viselike hand,"—and any friend of Bond's is my enemy."

He glanced up to the verandah of the station building, and his expression told Emma who stood there. "Leave Bond to me," he spat, and abruptly released her arm.

Emma saw the slender man outlined in the late sunlight. His top hat sat stiffly on his head, and his light brown eyes bored into the two figures beside the train. She didn't want any more fighting. She'd had too much of it in her life . . . and she wanted

Adam to be different. "I just want to leave this place—"

"Get on the train." Adam locked eyes with her for a moment. Never mind what she thought of him. The only way to get things done was to grab the matter at hand like the horns of a stubborn steer. You wrestled it till it bent to your will. "Soapy's in the passenger car. Go there. I said I'd take you to the coast tonight, and I will." He started to walk toward the station building, then stopped and turned back. "It may take money."

"I'll pay it . . . any amount." Emma thrust her hands into her pockets and doggedly marched toward the train. She was too tired and hungry and sore to think. It was all too much to sort out. Yet as she gripped the iron bar beside the door and pulled herself up onto the first step, Nicholas's words came back to her.

*Adam's a mercenary. A money-grubbing agitator.* She looked back over her shoulder. *Money* . . . Adam said it might take money to get the train started. Was this the beginning, then? Would he ask for money at every turn . . . try to get as much from her as he could?

Her heart sinking, Emma hurried up the steps and into the cool darkness of the railcar where she had last sat with her father and Cissy. All the seats were empty now, save one. A white hat rose over the back of the berth. Clutching the seat rails for support even though the train was not moving, Emma made her way down the aisle.

"Mr. Potts?" She peered around the corner, and Soapy leapt to his feet.

"Howdy, ma'am!" He whisked his hat from his head, leaving his bright yellow hair standing on end. "Call me Soapy. Been my name since I was two days old and rolled into the washtub and nearly drowned."

His brilliant smile warmed the tired recesses of Emma's heart. "So you're Adam's cook?" She sat down on the opposite seat and placed the hat Adam had given her on her lap. Her eyes wandered to the window, and she hesitated a moment before reaching for the shade.

"Aw, I give it a shot when we're out on the range. . . ." Soapy's hand covered Emma's as she moved to raise the shade. "Let the boss handle him, ma'am. He can draw faster than you can spit and holler howdy."

"Draw?"

"His iron. Adam King was raised with a gun in one hand and a milk bottle in the other. He can take care of himself, sure enough. That ol' tenderfoot Bond ain't got a chance against the boss."

At this, Emma instantly pushed Soapy's hand aside and lifted the shade. Her eyes flew to the two men standing on the verandah of the station. For that instant, neither man moved. Nicholas's hat lay in the dust at the bottom of the stairs, and his coat hung over a chair. He was standing rigidly before Adam, his fists knotted at his sides and his chin jutting forward. His red-gold hair glimmered a burnished copper in the afternoon sunlight slanting across the verandah.

Adam stood not a foot in front of Nicholas. He had pushed back his new hat and rolled up the plaid sleeves of his shirt. Emma could see his gun in the holster at his side. His right hand hung over it, the fingers spread wide.

"Dear God, Soapy!" Emma cried, rising to her feet. "Are they going to kill one another?"

"Hardly. Like I said, ol' Bond don't stand a chance."

"But Nicholas hasn't even got a gun!" Emma gasped as Adam took a step forward and Nicholas took one backward. Suddenly Adam began talking —fast, yet quietly. Emma could see Nicholas nodding, then shaking his head. Adam jabbed the other man's chest with the finger of his left hand, just as he had done to the ship's purser. As Adam jabbed, he stepped—each thrust pushing Nicholas backward until he stood against the railing of the verandah. Then before Emma knew what was happening, Nicholas ducked under Adam's arm and spun around behind him. Instantly a revolver flashed in his hand as he held it pointed straight at Adam's heart.

"No!" Emma turned from the window and shoved past Soapy out into the aisle. Grabbing up her skirts, she ran between the seats toward the open door.

"Whoa there, Miss Pickworth!" Soapy thundered behind her, his boots pounding the metal floor of the car.

But Emma could think only of Adam, lying in a pool of blood. She would lose him, too. Just as she had lost Cissy . . . her mother . . . even—

"Emma!" Adam's huge dark form lunged through the open door, and Emma ran headlong into him. His scent, his hard warm body, engulfed her as he whirled her lightly upward and around away from the open door. His boot flew out and caught the door, slamming it shut behind him as the train suddenly lurched forward into motion.

"Adam . . ." The breath sighed out of Emma all at once. "I thought Nicholas—"

"Hell," Soapy chuckled from somewhere in the shadows. "She thought the ol' tenderfoot was gonna do you in! I couldn't have stopped her with a forty-foot rope and a snubbin' post."

"Emma?" Adam held her away from him and looked straight into her eyes. "You all right? The train's changing tracks, and we're on our way."

She nodded. He might have been killed, no matter what Soapy said. She had seen the gun herself. And Nicholas . . . Her blood suddenly ran cold. "Where's Nicholas?"

"He's out there." Adam reached out to flip back the shade from the door's window. Emma craned forward. As the train backed into position, she focused on the upright figure at the foot of the station steps. Nicholas had put his hat back on, and a cluster of men had gathered above him on the verandah. One held his coat.

"What happened?" she whispered.

"Ol' Bond knew he was near enough to hell to smell smoke!" Soapy laughed and shook his head as Emma turned to him. The two men stood in the aisle staring at her curiously. "Why, Miss Pickworth," Soapy said, "by the worryin' you been doin' over that little set-to, I do believe you think mighty highly of the boss here."

Emma's gaze darted from Soapy to Adam. "I think highly of *life*, Mr. Potts. It is my intention to preserve and extend it—not to see it ended in a blast of gunpowder. And Mr. King, if you cannot refrain from provoking people to the point of using weapons, then I shall disengage your services. Is that clear?"

Adam's eyes locked on Emma's. He pushed his hat back with the tip of one finger. "You don't want to see any more fighting."

"I don't want there to *be* any more fighting." Emma gripped the seat back beside her as the chugging train picked up speed. She needed to rest . . . to close her eyes and escape the fact that Cissy was missing and that her father had died and that here she was in the middle of Africa with two strange Americans—one accused of slaving and mercenary activities against the empire. And all she really wanted to do was curl into that very man's arms, rest her head on his shoulder, and fall asleep.

"Promise me, Adam," she said with an urgent note in her voice. "Promise you'll never use a weapon against Nicholas Bond again."

"What makes you think he used his gun?" Soapy protested.

"This goes for you, too, Soapy." Emma hardened her voice. "No guns . . . and no fists."

"Aw, you can't take away a man's right to use his guns—"

"It's okay, Soapy." Adam laid a hand on his friend's arm. He knew Emma was issuing a challenge. He looked into Soapy's doubting eyes. "There are a lot more effective ways to handle Bond anyhow. No guns, Emma—not while I'm working with you. Soapy neither."

Emma eyed them both. What had Adam meant about there being more effective ways to deal with Nicholas? Surely he *had* used his gun against the man—how else could he have gotten out of that situation? But now she had made him promise.

"Emma?" Adam was looking down at her when she glanced up. "You need to rest."

Emma nodded and walked ahead of him down the aisle to a middle seat. Soapy edged past them toward his original seat. As if he had read her mind, Adam drew Emma down beside him, placed one arm around her, and gently eased her head onto his shoulder. He propped his boots on the opposite seat and raised the window shade. As they sat in silence, Emma could feel the tension drain slowly out of his shoulder.

"Sunset in Africa. My favorite time of day." He spoke in a low voice, and Emma could not resist the lull of it. "Saddle up my horse and ride out to the corral. Cattle rounded up for the night. My men gathered around the fire. A lion roaring in the distance . . ."

Emma relaxed her body against Adam's and gazed out at the pink-and-golden sky. Thorn trees silhouetted in black spread their jagged branches across the fading horizon. A pair of giraffes slowly emerged in the dusk, their long necks swaying almost in rhythm with the train as it slipped along the track.

Adam stroked his finger up the side of Emma's neck, and she shut her eyes, a warm glow spreading through her at his touch. In a moment he began humming a deep and lilting melody, and as she drifted off to sleep she heard his song. "I have promised you, darling, that never will words from my lips cause you pain; and my life it will be yours forever, if you only will love me again. . . ."

Adam did not stop singing until the sun had gone and the train was shrouded in darkness. The words and melodies occupied his thoughts, and he needed that solace with Emma lying in his arms . . . so soft.

He looked down at her. Moonlight filtering

through the window gentled over her. Dark lashes spread across her cheeks, pink from the heat of the sun. The ridge of her nose was almost red. He shook his head slightly. He hadn't thought to give her his hat until it was nearly too late. But what did he know about handling a woman? She'd be tan before long. Ladies hated that, he knew. But he thought Emma would look fine with her skin a golden brown.

What was he to do with her! Here she was, all snuggled up next to him like they belonged together. Like they really were married. . . .

No, he couldn't think that way. He couldn't want her with him. She was trouble. Too strong-willed— too stubborn. And she didn't know a thing about real life. Just tea and corsets and fancy dancing. Couldn't even ride a horse, although she *had* done pretty well with Red.

He glanced down at Emma again. Her hand had slid across his leg and he could see the brass ring on her finger. She had said it was all business, and it was. She wanted to be a nurse. That suited him just fine. He needed a nurse.

Damn . . . he wanted more than a nurse—he wanted her! He thought of the way she had moved against him when he'd held her beneath the thorn tree. She'd been so ready, so hungry for him. And the way she had loved him. He'd halfway felt like a greenhorn himself . . . she seemed to know just what to do, just where to touch him. . . .

Shutting his eyes, he willed away the tumultuous thoughts that flooded over him. He couldn't feel this way. There was Clarissa and his future to think about. She'd probably be coming soon. Those pale blue eyes would look up at him, and she'd touch his arm with her thin fingers. He would take her to bed . . . and he'd think of Emma.

Emma's body. Slender and beautiful—but not frail. She wasn't frail anywhere. Her skin was so smooth, and her hair was so silky to touch. Reaching up, he stroked down the side of her head, letting his fingers trail through the golden strands. She stirred slightly, sighed, and eased closer against him.

Adam groaned inwardly. He wanted her again . . . badly. But there was something more than just her body. Her spirit. It matched his in its fiery stubbornness, its determination to follow a dream. He liked being with her, talking to her, dancing with her, making plans. He liked the way she tossed her head and shot looks of insolence at him. He even liked the way she had ordered him not to use his guns. It took guts to tell a cowboy he couldn't use his gun. Emma had guts. And she was beautiful. And he wanted her. And he was in trouble . . . deep trouble.

He clenched his jaw and looked out the window. It was going to be a long night.

The sudden cessation of rhythmic rocking brought Emma out of the depths of sleep—a sleep so heavy she felt unable to move or even to think, as if she lay beneath a stone that allowed her only to see and feel. Her opened eyes fell first on a pair of worn black boots, crossed one over the other and resting on the train seat in front of her. She gazed at them for a moment knowing whose they were yet unable to link herself with the reality before her. She had dreamed of those boots—and the man who wore them. He had walked in them through her sleep.

"Emma." His voice. Deep, lulling, hypnotic. She loved the sound of it. "Emma, are you awake?"

Stiffening as a jolt ran through her, she looked down at her body stretched out against Adam's. Her hand lay wantonly across his leg, her fingertips resting on the inside of his upper thigh. Her head rested on his shoulder, and her hair spread across his chest, covering his shirt with a golden fan.

"Emma?"

"Yes—" She sucked in her breath and sat up. "Yes, I'm awake."

"We're at the station. Mombasa."

She glanced out the window. The early sun had ruddied the whitewashed station buildings and bathed the porters' uniforms in a pink hue. There were only a few men standing on the platform, and all stared in confusion at the train as if it, too, were part of a dream.

Emma could feel the humidity pressing in on her, and the reality of her mission loomed suddenly larger than life. "I must see Lord Delamere at once." She started to rise. "I must get to the bank—"

"Emma." Adam caught her arm and pulled her back to his side. He touched her cheek and brought her face around to meet his. The confused tumult of thoughts that had tormented him for the past several hours demanded to be spoken. "Emma, I've held you all night, and I've been thinking—"

"Don't think." She looked into his eyes. Their sapphire depths were bottomless. His desire for her burned like the hottest of blue flames—but she knew it for what it really was. Desire. Hunger. It would burn her up, consume her, and in the end leave nothing but ashes. "I have business to attend."

She rose stiffly from the seat to find Soapy shuffling down the aisle toward them. He let out a huge yawn, then smiled sleepily at Emma.

"Mornin', ma'am. You look as limp as a neck-wrung rooster." He scratched his chin and held out the hat Adam had given her to wear. "Here—c'mon, let's go get some grub. You, too, boss."

Emma felt Adam rise beside her, but she did not turn. Instead she placed the hat on her head and slipped out into the aisle in front of Soapy. She would not think about Adam now, she told herself as she hurried toward the door. She would not look at him, she would not dwell on him. There were more important things in her life. She had allowed his passion to sidetrack her once, but not again. Forcing her thoughts to the day ahead, she lifted her chin and pushed open the door.

The heat hit her like a lead weight, but she grabbed the iron railing and made her way down onto the platform. The waves in her hair began to curl even tighter in the moist air, and she ran a hand around the back of her damp neck. A bath and a change of clothing would help—and a solid meal would be even better. Her stomach rumbled at the thought as she strode purposefully toward the gate. None of it mattered, though. Food must wait, rest must wait. Everything must wait until she had set her plans in motion.

She heard Adam and Soapy behind her, deep in conversation as they walked toward the baggage car—no doubt to collect their horses and the trunks. Never mind. They knew where she was going, and they could find her later.

Mombasa town was just coming to life as Emma hurried past the station to look for a trolley. She passed a fisherman making his way to the shore, a heavy net draped over one shoulder and a short spear in his hand. Two gray monkeys scampered across the road before her, no doubt searching for the cast-off remains of someone's breakfast. A shoe seller down the street was unboarding the wooden shutters at the front of his little shop, while his wife used a bundle of seagrass tied with twine to sweep the white sand from the sidewalk.

Spotting the cluster of trolley pullers at the other end of the station, Emma headed straight for the lounging young natives. Seeing her, they nudged one another and set aside the mangos that had been their breakfast. Their regulation attire—crisp white uniform shorts and epaulet-shouldered shirts—looked foreign and somehow out of place on sleek bodies that seemed meant for soft leather skins and ocher paint. Emma selected a trolley, and the young men helped her onto one of the small vehicles.

"Government House," she said, wishing she could speak their language as easily as Adam. One day she would. During the night she had made a decision—she would stay in this country, and nothing would deter her. "To Commissioner Eliot's house."

The young men nodded in understanding and pulled the trolley onto the street. How long had it been, she wondered, since she had ridden down this very path with Cissy and her father and Nicholas? So much had happened. She tried to think back. Had it really been only five days that had changed her whole life? . . . She hadn't even had time to visit her father's grave.

The palm trees lining the road blew gently in the ocean breeze just as she had remembered, their fronds drifting this way and that as if they rode on the sea currents. The same children skipped across the street, staring in curiosity at the trolley and its passenger. The same gate swung open as Emma descended to the ground. Everything was the same, and yet everything was different. *She* was different. How innocent she had been. . . . She motioned the gateman to pay the young men, and he nodded obediently as she lifted her skirts and half ran down the drive toward the two-story building.

"Lord Delamere?" she asked the middle-aged man on the verandah. She recognized him as the African servant who had carried the tray with Adam's note up to her bedroom suite. "I must speak with Lord Delamere at once. Where is he?"

"He is at his farm in Njoro, memsahib," the man said in a well-schooled voice. He eyed her curiously. "He is not here."

"Commissioner Eliot?"

"No. He has not returned from his leave."

Dismayed, Emma slowly drew her hat from her head. "Is anyone of the government here?"

The man shook his head. As she looked toward the house, she could see a gathering of servants peering through the glass door at her. "The house has no British today."

"But there must be someone! Who is running the government?"

The man thought for a moment. "The government is not running today, memsahib."

Emma ran a hand over her forehead, struggling to control her disappointment. "I must get to the bank. Can you call a trolley for me? Have you a messenger?"

"You could go with Bwana King."

Glancing up at the name, Emma saw the smile spreading across the servant's face. His eyes lit up, and his lips drew back to reveal his fine white teeth. Emma turned at once to follow his gaze. Adam's horse galloped down the path toward the house, then stopped short as its lanky rider pulled back on the reins.

"Nobody here?" Adam looked down at her, grinning. "Thought not. The Delameres are usually up at Njoro this time of year. Come on, Soapy's waiting for us at the bungalow."

"The bungalow?" Emma gripped the hat in her hands. "But I must get to the bank."

Adam leapt down from his horse and walked to her. "Emma," he said softly, "things are done different from the way they are in England. You hired me to help you. Let me do my job."

"But you don't understand—"

"Listen to me, Emma," he interrupted, his voice more commanding this time. He turned her to face him. He didn't want to have to talk to her straight like this, but she was stubborn. "It's about Cissy. Either she's with somebody right now—or she's dead." His voice sounded harsh even to him, but she had to deal with it now or *she* wouldn't survive. "Bond is right about that. A person can't live long in the bush alone. Now we sent the *Moran*— the warriors—out to look for her, and they're damned good trackers. But if she's not with *someone*, Emma, there's no way . . ."

His voice drifted off. She knew his eyes were on

her face, but she couldn't bring herself to look at him. She closed her eyes against his words and held them shut, not wanting to hear any of it—though she knew he spoke the truth.

"What I'm trying to tell you, Emma," he continued more softly, "is that waiting a day or two here at the coast isn't going to make much difference."

Emma looked directly at him, but there was a faint tremor in her voice. "We didn't see *anyone* . . . not one single human that whole day of riding—"

"But that doesn't mean they weren't around. The Masai are like the animals in some ways. They know how to hide and watch. They keep track of their territory. They know what goes on and who's in it. You couldn't expect them to come running out to say 'howdy' to us—two strangers shouting and firing guns, scaring off all the game."

Emma shook her head and forced herself to continue. "And if no one found her . . ."

"Emma." Adam reached out to her, then drew back his hands. Maybe it was better to stay distant from this resolute Englishwoman. In the end, she would have to face it alone anyway.

Emma looked away. She couldn't accept that her hopes amounted to nothing.

"C'mon, Emma," Adam said firmly. He took her hand and walked beside her to his horse. In a moment he had settled her on the saddle and climbed on behind her. He pulled her tightly against his chest and started riding down the drive.

Adam's horse wound its way expertly through the narrow cobblestone streets. A touch of a knee or a slight tug on the reins turned the stallion in the right direction. It was as if horse and rider were one. Emma felt the power surging through the two—Adam's legs taut along hers, the horse's muscles straining and rippling beneath.

Though conscious of everything, she rode as if in a dream. Her ability to feel had evaporated, and she could only absorb her surroundings in a detached, semiconscious state. The narrow alleys merged one upon the other as the whitewashed houses crowded through the town. Children played, old men lounged, young men sold coffee from gleaming brass pots, women hurried by in their black Muslim veils with only their kohl-lined eyes visible and staring curiously. There was a salty smell of fish and the sea and old baskets and leather. But most of all there was Adam.

His arms around her were warm, almost too warm in the sweltering morning air. The ends of his neckerchief brushed against her cheek, and her shoulder nestled in the curve of his arm. She rested her head against the hard plane of his chest, and despite all the sounds—the cries of the vendors, the laughter of children, the rattle of passing trolleys—the throb of his heartbeat filled her ears.

Before long the houses diminished in number and the cobblestone trickled away into a path of white sand. Adam led his horse through a gate and down a long straight road through a grove of coconut palms. The trees had been planted in straight rows, like an odd tropical orchard. Tufts of dried seagrass grew up around their bent trunks, but between them stretched wide expanses of sand.

"Is this yours?" Emma whispered, marveling at the magnitude of the grove.

Adam nodded. "Seastar—my plantation. I planted the trees about eight years ago, and we had our first crop of nuts last year."

"Coconuts?" Emma straightened up and looked

about her. There was something otherworldly about the rows of palm trees, whose trunks rose into the sky like curved ostrich necks. She had seen engravings of coconuts in books. They were brown and hairy and filled with a white liquid—but she could not imagine them being worth anything. She had never even tasted one.

"I sold the nuts on the local market. But in a few years I'll be exporting the copra—that's an oil that comes from the meat. They use it in Europe for soap and candles. I'll sell the dried leaves for thatch and the fiber around the nuts for ropemaking."

Her curosity piqued, Emma gazed into the branches of the tall trees as they rode along. A plantation . . . It conjured images of a two-story brick home with tall white columns, fields bursting with cotton, slaves. Slaves. The thought brought her quickly back to reality. She had a double mission. She had vowed not only to find Cissy, but also to unlock the secrets of Adam's activities. Here she would begin . . . at Seastar.

Just as she had taken a deep breath to clear her head, they rounded the edge of the grove and came out onto a wide expanse of cleared land. But instead of a brick mansion with white columns, they faced a rambling, thatch-roofed bungalow. A long verandah with blue-painted posts and blue doors circled the whitewashed building. It had wide windows that faced the grove on one side, and on the other—the sea.

After the long voyage to the protectorate, Emma had thought she never wanted to see the ocean again. But her mouth fell open in astonishment at the utter beauty of the seascape. As Adam slid off the horse and lifted her down, she could not draw her eyes from the endless stretch of turquoise-

and-purple water broken only by a line of white surf across the reef.

"I bought this land right after I got here." Adam led the horse around to the front of the house facing the ocean and tied it to the verandah railing. "Built the house a few years later when I had things going pretty well inland. I stay down here when I come to pick up my shipments."

"Shipments?" Emma's spine tingled.

"Farm machinery. Tools." Adam stepped onto the verandah. "Medicine sometimes. I expected some cattle dip to come in on the ship you were on, but the purser couldn't find it in the holds. Guess while we're here I'll have to run down and see if it's come in on another ship."

Emma's thoughts flew to the scene she had witnessed from the ship's railing. Had Adam been so angry with the purser over cattle dip? It hardly seemed likely. Only something very valuable could have caused that much emotion. She thought of Nicholas's assertion that Adam imported guns . . . of course, with English customs officials roaming about that day and with the Germans knowing about his every move, Adam would have been edgy. Angry that the shipment had not come in. Perhaps he thought it had been discovered.

"I'm planning to put in a railhead right along there." Adam broke into Emma's thoughts, and she realized he had been speaking while she had heard nothing. "We'll ship the nuts into town where they have a factory going up. I've invested in that, so the whole thing should be pretty profitable."

"You're very business-minded," Emma said evenly. She lifted her skirt and climbed onto the verandah beside him. Adam was gazing out to sea, as if staring into the future.

"I have a lot of plans." He turned to her, but his look was distant, unreadable. "This country is where I aim to make my dreams come true. All of them."

"And what of your family back in America?" Her mother would have been horrified at how forward she had become, but she had to be bold to learn what she needed to know.

"What about them?" Adam scowled at her.

"Do they know about your life here? Have they come to see you?"

Adam took off his hat and tossed it onto a gazelle horn hat rack that hung beside the door on the verandah. He walked over to a woven wicker chair and sat down. His family was the last thing he wanted to discuss with Emma, or anyone, for that matter. "They know where I am."

The frown on Adam's face told Emma there was a great deal in his background he'd like to forget— but she needed to press deeper. She walked to the chair beside Adam's and seated herself. "Will they come from Texas to see you one day?"

"Doubt it. My father wasn't too happy with me for leaving home when I did. My mother begged me not to go."

"But you went anyway."

"I always do what's right for *me*." The blue depths of his eyes lit a fire in her blood. "You know, we're alike in that, Emma."

Emma locked her gaze on the sea. "Was there no work for you in Texas?"

"The frontier is gone. Texas is crowded with ranches. Too crowded for me, anyway. Heard about Africa and the new colonies . . . and I decided to come here to start my empire."

"Your empire?"

"Ranching, farming, factories, the railway." Adam leaned back in his chair. "This land is raw and untamed. Lawless. A man can do what he wants. It's not like America or Europe."

"Has your family lived in Texas for generations?" She sensed he was tiring of the conversation.

"Nope. My great-grandfather was from Germany." Adam stood up suddenly as if to leave, and Emma leapt to his side.

"Germany?" Her voice had an almost eager edge.

Adam glanced at her curiously. "Germany. The family name is Koenig. Means King . . . you know, they changed names when they came over." He shrugged. "But I've got some Irish blood in me, too. Even a little Cherokee."

He started down the verandah, and Emma hurried after him. But just as he approached the main door, Soapy came running around the corner of the house.

"Boss!" His gray eyes were wide as his boots pounded along the wooden floor. "Boss, they just sent a message from headquarters."

"Yeah?"

"Your shipments are in!" Soapy stopped before Adam, his white hat in his hand and trickles of sweat streaming from his blond sideburns. "All five crates came in on a ship this morning. Everything made it safely past customs . . . nothing opened. They're all sealed up tight and stored at headquarters. We can go get 'em. Shall I round up some fellers?"

Adam's eyes shot across to Emma. "Why don't

you head on inside, and Miriam—she works for me—will show you your room. There's a bathtub, and Soapy brought your trunks. Just tell Miriam when you want to eat, and she'll fix something for you."

Adam turned back to Soapy as if Emma had suddenly evaporated. Tossing his arm over the shorter man's shoulder, he began to walk toward his horse. "I'd better go with you, Soapy. In case there's any trouble."

# Chapter Nine

✦✦✦✦

*His eyes are bright*
*And his heart as light*
*As the smoke of his cigarette;*
*There's never a care*
*For his soul to bear,*
*No trouble to make him fret. . . .*

*Saddle up, boys,*
*For the work is play*
*When love's in the cowboy's eyes—*
*When his heart is light*
*As the clouds of white*
*That swim in the summer skies.*

—"The Cowboy's Life"

*The skies seemed true above thee,*
    *The rose true on the tree;*
*The bird seemed true the summer through,*
    *But all proved false to me.*
*World, is there one good thing in you,*
    *Life, love, or death—or what?*
*Since lips that sang, I love thee,*
    *Have said, I love thee not?*

—Arthur William Edgar O'Shaughnessy
"Song"

EMMA STARTED DOWN the verandah after Adam and
Soapy. If they were going after the crates, then she
must follow. It might be her best chance. She
would hide and listen and watch. They would talk
about the crates, perhaps open them—and she
would see inside. Then she would know. . . .

"Memsahib!" A woman's voice rang out on the

186

verandah behind Emma. "Come in! Bwana King say breakfast for you . . . sleeping . . . bath."

Emma turned and took a step backward from the black-veiled figure, who suddenly began to circle her like the vultures she had seen in the open bush. "Who are you?"

"Miriam!" The figure edged around Emma, blocking her path to the two men. "You come inside, Memsahib Emma. I cook fish for you—"

"No, thank you." Emma tried to shoulder past. "I must go into Mombasa. The bank."

"The bank? No, you stay here. Bwana King say."

"When did you talk to Mr. King? He's been with me every moment—"

"Bwana King tell Bwana Potts," the woman said urgently, her voice almost strident. "You stay. You stay here!"

Emma sighed. Oh, what was the use of it, anyway? she thought, glancing out to the already empty road. She never could have followed the men unnoticed. At least not at this time of the day. Obviously Adam was determined that she remain at the house despite her intentions to the contrary. Prevented from going to the bank—which in turn blocked her search for Cissy—Emma felt trapped . . . and angry with the man who had trapped her.

She turned her attention to the black-veiled woman. Bright brown eyes sparkled at her through the rectangular eyehole. Two beefy bare feet poked out from beneath the hem of the heavy garment. Other than that, Emma had no idea what Miriam looked like.

"Are you a slave?" Emma asked suddenly.

The eyes blinked twice. "Slave?"

"Does Mr. King pay you a salary? Wages?"

"I live here, memsahib. Seastar my home."

"But are you paid for your work?"

Emma thought she heard a slight sniff from beneath the folds of fabric. "My home here. My children here. My husband die."

Emma took a step toward the woman. "Do you have money?"

"No money!" The voice became almost hysterical. "No money. I stay here with Bwana King."

Startled at the reaction she had provoked, Emma drew back uncertainly. If Miriam lived and worked at Seastar without pay, then what *could* she be but a slave? Yet why had she spoken of Adam and this place so fondly, called it her home?

"Miriam." Emma reached out to the robed woman. "I did not mean to upset you. I'm sorry. Please take me inside the house and show me my room."

"You come." A plump, heavily bangled arm shot out and grabbed Emma's wrist. Miriam marched her newfound ward through the open door. "Sitting room," she announced as they hurried through the house. Emma barely had time to scan the spacious room before they had moved on. "Parlor here, kitchen that way outside, bathroom, bedroom, bedroom, bedroom. Here you stay. Bwana King's bedroom."

Miriam dragged Emma into the room and thrust her onto a large armchair upholstered in white cotton. From it she surveyed the room, unable to move in the sheer brilliance of the setting. A huge four-poster bed occupied one wall, a wispy white mosquito net draped over it like a canopy. A sunbeam from the curtained window nearby crept across the bed's white linens, then fell onto the wooden floor. A tall mahogany wardrobe filled one corner and a cabinet lined with books loomed in another. Seashells of every shape and color imaginable marched across the window frames and shelves, and large chunks of lacy coral sat beside the wardrobe.

"You rest here, memsahib," Miriam said. Her voice was soft for the first time, and Emma startled from her reverie. "I bring food soon."

"I must go to the bank." Emma started up, but Miriam's plump hand signaled a halt like a London bobby amid a sea of carriages.

"When Bwana King comes back, you go to bank. Now you rest." She said the words with such finality that Emma could only slump back onto the chair and watch the woman waddle out of the room and shut the blue door behind her.

For a long time she simply stared out the window toward the turquoise sea with its line of white breakers. She was not in charge of her life at this moment, and she knew it. She had let Adam force her into this position. Even Miriam had taken control. Under normal circumstances, Emma knew, she would have risen defiantly to fight off the restrictions. But her body ached so painfully, her mouth tasted so dry and brackish, and her mind spun in such a tumult of confusion that she could not bring herself to resist.

Instead she drifted to the door along the wall and pushed it open. The bathroom's gleaming porcelain seemed to call out to her, and she went to the sink and laid a hand on the cool tap. Turning it, she let the warm water flow over her tired fingers, rinsing away dirt she had not even taken the time to notice.

But when she tilted her face to the mirror, she gasped in horror at the creature she faced. Her hair hung in tangled waves, stuck here and there with bits of grass and leaves, making her look like a half-blown dandelion pod. Once the proper shade of creamy ivory, her skin had burned to a ruddy glow that highlighted the sparkling green of her olive eyes. Her cheeks were flushed, and her delicate skin had darkened at least three shades.

Appalled, she let her eyes travel down her body, only to find it in even worse disorder. Her blouse hung halfway open across her breast, her skirt was torn and dusty about the hem, and her layers of crinoline had mysteriously collapsed. Without sparing a moment, Emma turned one of the taps in the porcelain bathtub, releasing a stream of scalding water. Then she raced out into the room, unbuckled her trunk and flung it open. She hastily located her brush and comb and scurried back into the bathroom with them.

The gleaming white lion-footed tub was filled nearly to the rim. A bar of lavender soap nestled in a ceramic dish to one side. Emma stepped into the steaming water and let it gently lap up her sore legs, tender breasts, sunburned arms—until only her head remained above it. Then she slid beneath the surface and felt the water seep into the roots of her hair.

Never had she enjoyed a bath so. After soaping herself twice, she scrubbed her hair three times. She even let all the water out of the tub and refilled it. Losing all track of time, she gazed up at the thatched roof and the slender poles supporting it. And all the while she plotted.

It didn't matter where Adam was, she decided as she climbed out of the tub and rubbed herself dry with a towel. She would dress in her finest clothing, place her most beautiful hat on her head, and set off to the bank. In fact, it probably would be better if Adam weren't with her to bungle her presentation by hesitating about the marriage. She would simply declare it to be so and sign the necessary papers. Then she would find an outfitter and order everything they would need for the trip.

She paused a moment while wrapping the towel around her damp body, then started for the door. Really she had no idea how much food to order for a two-month journey—nor did she know how many men they would need or how they would travel. Lifting her head, she turned the handle. It didn't matter. She would decide, Adam or not.

As she flung open the door and marched into the room, a tall figure eased out of the blinding light in front of the window. Seeing the familiar form, Emma gasped.

"It's me." Adam sauntered into the center of the room, his eyes raking up her towel-clad body from her long shapely legs to the tendrils of wet hair that had escaped from the towel on her head.

Emma froze for a moment, surprised by his presence in the room. "The crates—" she croaked at last. "You went after the crates."

"Got them and came back." He took off his hat and tossed it onto the bed, then ran his fingers through his slightly damp blue-black hair—all the while watching her.

"If you'll excuse me, I'll just get my dress from the trunk." Emma started forward then stopped again. Adam took a pace toward her, his eyes sealed to hers. Her heart was hammering, and she shivered in spite of the heat. She could smell his sun-warmed skin—a muskiness that mingled irresistibly with the lavender soap that had scented her own body.

"Emma—" Adam took another step until he loomed just in front of her. He reached out and ran his finger down her bare arm. It was silky . . . soft as down. "Emma, I—"

"Bwana King!" Miriam's shrill voice echoed through the room as her fist pounded the closed door. "*Chakula tayari, sasa hivi!* Food ready, Memsahib Emma!"

Adam didn't move, and Emma couldn't. His very presence seemed to diminish the strident voice at the door. To Emma, he seemed distilled to his very essence at this moment—his cotton shirt clinging to the muscles of his chest and arms, his eyes as blue as the ocean that framed him, his face as brown as the coconuts. Her irritation suddenly drained away; all she wanted was to touch the soft cotton of his plaid shirt, to stroke his hair, to feel his lips on hers.

"Bwana King! Bwana King!" Miriam knocked again.

Adam pulled Emma to him suddenly as though he, too, were deaf. His arms wrapped around her body, and his mouth found hers. Closing her eyes, her nostrils dilating with the quick intake of breath as he pressed hard against her, she ran her hands over his broad shoulders. Letting them slide beneath his black leather vest, she felt the ripple of his muscles while he loosed the towel that held her hair and let it fall to the floor.

As though their previous lovemaking had never been, Emma's hunger for the man in her arms soared and swelled inside her. His lips roved across her cheek, his tongue found her ear and caressed each curve of it, his breath warmed her neck.

"You smell so fresh," he whispered. She was different every time he was with her, he realized in amazement. No longer the tough, stubborn fighter, *this* Emma was soft in his arms—pliant, silken, all woman. Her skin tasted like rain, and her hair . . .

"Adam, I've wanted you to hold me again—" Emma bit off the words. No, she couldn't let him know how she felt, how vulnerable she was to him.

"There's nothing I've wanted more than I want you." He pressed her to him and could feel her breasts swell against his chest.

"Damn." He looked into Emma's eyes, then suddenly held her at arm's length. What could he tell her about his feelings? He didn't even know how he felt. "Emma . . ." Confusion crossed his face, like a cloud briefly blocking the sun.

Emma gazed into his blue eyes and noticed the furrow creasing his brow. It was as though words of emotion had never escaped his lips, she realized. To admit his feelings would be to admit weakness—and Adam King could never be weak. Emma stood riveted to the floor, somehow wanting him even more for revealing a hint of his own vulnerability. Yet she could not trust her own mind or her heart. As she waited in silence, he dropped his hands from her arms and looked away.

"Coming, Miriam," he hollered suddenly, and spun away from Emma. Striding across the room faster than she had ever seen him move, he threw open the door before an intently eavesdropping Miriam and barreled outside, shutting the door behind him.

As Emma whirled to the door, it opened again just a crack. "She says dinner's ready," Adam called out, though he kept his face from view.

The door shut again, and this time Emma flew into action. She would *not* let her heart be played with! Storming across the room, she flung open the trunk. She tossed her dresses aside one by one, then jerked out an emerald-green silk skirt and its matching jacket. Adam King would *not* take her into his arms one moment and run from her the next. She would *not* be toyed with!

She tore the towel from her body, pulled a chemise from the trunk, and slipped it over her head. With every garment, her determination to be in control grew fiercer. She clipped her newest corset around her waist and lifted her breasts into position. She would *not* succumb to him every time he touched her! She pushed her arms through her chemise and then her white silk blouse. She would *not* let him touch her at all! A clean crinoline fit neatly about her waist, and she elected to forgo the bustle. She would *not* look into his eyes anymore, and she would *not* respond to the hunger she saw in them!

Hurrying across the floor to the bathroom, Emma struggled into her skirt and jacket. She fastened the black toggles down her breast, then jerked a comb through her hair. Those impossible waves— and the whole mess of hair was wet anyway! Sighing in exasperation, she pinned up the offending tresses and returned to the bedroom. She slipped on her boots and buttoned them as quickly as her trembling fingers would allow.

Rummaging through her hatboxes, she at last discovered her green, ostrich-plumed flimsy and clamped it onto her head. Glancing back into the room as she made her way to the door, she saw Adam's hat lying on the bed. She was half-tempted to toss aside the ridiculous green bonnet in favor of his more practical one, but realized her real reason was far more personal. The hat was a part of him—and despite everything she wanted him close to her.

Frowning at the weakness of the thought, she flew out the door and down the hall. She must get to the bank. Striding through the sitting room, she realized she had no idea what time it was. What if the bank had closed? What if she had dawdled too long in the bath and missed her chance to put her plans into action today? Furious with herself, she pulled on her green kid gloves and set her jaw.

"Emma?" Adam bellowed from behind a door. "Emma—"

At the creak of the opening door Emma turned to find the rigidly still cowboy, his blue eyes depthless. Slowly they traveled the length of her body, taking in every detail of her green hat, her shining hair, her silken dress, her skintight gloves, her pointed emerald boots. Then his gaze rose back to her face, and she saw his desire for her—fiercer than the sun that beat down on the white-hot sand.

Emma jerked her eyes from his, half-afraid her own expression had mirrored his. "If you'll excuse me . . ." She halted for a moment, shoring herself up against the emotions that crashed like the sea waves within her. "I should like to take a carriage to the bank. A horse will do, if you have no other form of transportation."

"I have a carriage." Adam recovered quickly from his initial surprise at the physical change in her. He walked toward her through the doorway. Had he revealed his inner feelings in that one look when he first saw her? Dammit, the woman could paralyze him, sap his control. He had to keep his mind on what he really needed her for—her nursing skills. And the sooner he got her to his ranch, the better. He forced a smile to his lips and a light half-chuckle into his voice. "The bank is closed during the middle of the day, Emma. Sort of a tropical tradition. You might as well come on in and join us for some lunch."

"But I—"

"You'll like the fish Miriam's fried up for us." He took her elbow and propelled her past the open-mouthed Soapy into the dining room. "It's called tilapia. They catch it just off the coast here. And here's a slab of coconut right off my plantation. Have a seat."

Before she could protest, he had pulled out a chair and deposited her gently onto it. He motioned to Soapy, who scurried back into the room and sat down across from her.

"Dang, Miss Pickworth," Soapy said, reaching out for the salt and nearly knocking over his glass of beer, "you got all gussied up. You look mighty fine."

"Thank you, Soapy." Emma smiled inwardly at the wide gray eyes staring at her. "This is my normal sort of attire, actually. Cowboy hats and dusty stockings leave something to be desired."

"I liked how you looked in my hat." Adam stabbed his fork into a piece of white fish, then punctuated the air with it as he talked. "I won't argue with a few green ostrich feathers on a velvet hat. But you were a lot easier on the eyes without that corset. . . . I'll tell you, Soapy—we'll turn Emma here into a bush woman yet. We'll get her out on ol' Red and teach her to drink rye whiskey and before she knows what hit her, she'll be as good as any cowpoke on the range."

"Sure thing, boss." Soapy chuckled. "But you got a lot of layers to get through first."

"I think I can manage." Adam casually put the forkful of fish into his mouth, then looked up at her, grinned, and winked.

Emma silently stared at him and could read nothing. In her heart, she knew he remembered their time alone in the bush and those moments when he had held and kissed her in his bedroom—she knew their lovemaking had moved him. But now he had masked every emotion with lightheartedness. It was as if he were trying to tell her all that had passed between them meant nothing to him. She was just a game, an amusement.

Without speaking, Emma carefully ate her fish, which she thought delicious in spite of herself. She heard only the barest strains of conversation between the men, who picked up where they had left off when she'd entered the room. They laughed, told jokes, regaled each other with tales of their past adventures. Emma smiled wanly.

How had she let Adam matter to her? She stared down at the wedge of white coconut. Perhaps she had made a grave mistake in hiring him to guide her through the bush in search of Cissy. She would have to be near him constantly, and unless she could somehow barricade her heart against him, he would be able to send it reeling with just one look!

She lifted her eyes to him. His jaunty smile and twinkling eyes betrayed nothing of his heart. He leaned back in his chair suddenly and bellowed with laughter at something Soapy had said.

"Hey, Emma!" He turned to her, his face awash

with fun. "What's wrong, don't you like Soapy's stories?"

"I beg your pardon." She dabbed at her mouth with her napkin to hide the trembling of her lips. "I was not listening."

Adam shrugged. "Shall we tell her about the time when I first got here and was trying to find my ranch?"

Soapy smiled, his yellow hair spiked up above his merry face. "You'da thought he was a tenderfoot the way them British officials sent him off in the wrong direction without hardly nothin' to eat or drink." Soapy shook his head. "The boss was real young then. Just a kid off the ranch in Texas. Them fellers didn't want no Yankees fillin' up the land— even though he'd bought his piece fair and square."

"I was used to Texas scorpions and rattlers," Adam said, only halfway addressing Emma. "And I could handle a herd of stampeding steer no trouble. But when that rhino went after me—"

Both men burst into guffaws. Emma looked from one to the other, fighting off tears. Adam wanted her to be nothing more to him than another of the "fellers." Suddenly her silks and crinolines felt awkward, inelegant—only a curtain for the gangling cowgirl Adam wanted her to become. She was just a tenderfoot he had to break in. How could she harden herself against him? She clenched her jaw as she heard the men break into song, then glanced at the doorway to find Miriam standing in the shadows.

And suddenly Emma knew what she must do. She had to find out every horrible truth about Adam . . . about the slaving, about the gun smuggling, about the treachery with the Germans . . . about his wife. Everything. Not for Nicholas. Not even for her country and the queen. But for herself. Because, she realized with great clarity, once she knew all about him, her *mind* would never let her *heart* take control. She would be safe.

"The rattlesnake bites you, the scorpion stings," Adam sang loudly, his deep, melodic voice filled with hearty enthusiasm. "The mosquito delights you with buzzing wings; the sand burrs prevail and so do the ants, and those who sit down need half-soles on their pants!"

"Ah, the devil's country—good ol' Texas," Soapy sighed.

Adam nodded and went on singing. "The heat in the summer is a hundred and ten, too hot for the devil and too hot for men. The wild boar roams through the black chaparral—it's a hell of a place he has for a hell."

"And do you have slaves in Texas?" Emma asked quietly.

The room fell silent as both men turned to stare at her. Soapy coughed slightly and looked back at Adam, a frown creasing his brow.

"Slaves?" Adam asked. "Slavery was abolished a long time ago, Emma. After the War Between the States—you know that."

"Yes, I suppose so." Emma folded her napkin carefully. "England has forbidden the practice. I have heard, however, that some places in the world do trade in human flesh. Do you know anything about that?"

Adam scratched behind his ear. "Well, I've heard there are still slaves in a few countries. But I don't know who could get away with it for long these days."

"I suppose slave trading would be a lucrative business." Emma slid her chair back. "One could probably make a great deal of money in a very short time. Enough money to do what one wanted, I imagine. Of course one would need protection . . . weapons . . . and perhaps connections within the government. Possibly a headquarters within a major city—where one might receive shipments of supplies and so forth."

"I guess so." Adam looked at her strangely for a second, then shrugged and leaned back in his chair. "Well, I'm feeling mighty full. Miriam, thank you. That was a real good meal."

The black-shrouded figure hurried out of the shadows and swept up Adam's plate. "*Asante sana,* Bwana King," she said, her eyes soft.

"Miriam tells me she does not earn wages working for you." Emma said the words evenly and deliberately, all the while observing the reactions of the three people in the room. Miriam stopped still, her hands frozen on the plates. Soapy's mouth fell open. Adam stood up abruptly, his chair scuffing loudly across the wooden floor.

"Emma, come with me." He stepped the two paces to her chair and grasped her upper arm. Without giving her room to struggle, he lifted her from her chair, set her on her feet, and guided her toward the door.

"Release me, Adam King," she hissed as he propelled her out of the room toward his bedroom. "You release me at once, or I shall report you to the authorities. Nicholas was right! You are a—"

"Put a lid on it, Emma. Just be quiet." Adam kicked open the door to his bedroom and pushed her inside. "You don't know anything."

He plopped her down on the edge of the bed and suddenly began to strip off his shirt. At the sight of his bare bronzed chest, Emma sat stiff with

indignation and fear, watching him rip off his belt
and peel down his denim trousers until he was
pacing about the room in nothing but his drawers.
At first certain he would force himself upon her in
anger, she soon realized he was hardly aware he
had unclothed himself.

"You need to get your facts straight before you
go saying things people could take wrong, Emma."
Striding across the floor as if stalking some imaginary prey, Adam resembled a big sleek cat. He
flung open a trunk at the end of the bed and flipped
a pair of clean denim trousers onto a chair.

Emma watched in stunned silence as Adam angrily jerked out a soft flannel blue plaid shirt and
tossed it onto the chair with his trousers. Before
she could think what to say next, he had disappeared into the bathroom and she heard the water
running.

Now wasn't that just like a man, Emma thought
angrily. She had accused Adam of slave trading
. . . basically caught him at it with her insinuations
about Miriam . . . and all he could do was drag her
into his bedroom, undress in front of her as though
she had no more morals than a guttersnipe, and
then storm off to take a bath! And he hadn't even
defended himself. He had not even denied he was
a slaver!

Her eyes burning with rage, Emma rose from the
bed and marched across the room. "Then tell me
the facts! Explain to me why Miriam is working for
you with no wages." She flung open the bathroom
door and barged into the sunlit room. "If you
would *explain* it all, then I would listen—"

She stopped midstride and caught her breath.
Adam was reclining chest deep in clear water, his
huge frame filling every inch of the lion-footed

bathtub. Emma tore her gaze from his taut, firm body and focused on his face. He was grinning.

"Howdy." He shifted a little, and it was all she could do to keep her eyes on his. "Hand me the soap, would you?"

Emma clenched her teeth, grabbed the thick bar from the sink, and hurled it at him. He reached up and caught it deftly in midair.

"Thanks."

Emma knotted her fists. "If you *are* a slaver, then . . . then . . ." She blinked back the tears that suddenly filled her eyes. "You had better tell me the truth, Adam King! I shall not go off on a search for my sister with a man who—"

"Emma." His voice was low, soft, as he sat up and leaned forward. "Emma, listen—"

"You listen to *me* for once!" She glared at him, suddenly realizing the hopelessness of discussing anything at this moment—and aware that it was exactly as Adam wanted. "Despite what you may think, I am a proper woman, not a greenhorn cowpoke! Women find it very difficult to listen to irrational men who tear off their clothing in front of us and then think they can explain everything while sitting totally nude in a bathtub. When you're *decent*, we shall talk again."

Emma slammed the bathroom door and stormed out into the bedroom, her cheeks flaming. Behind the closed door, she heard a deep chuckle that quickly rumbled into hearty laughter.

Hurrying out of the bedroom through the back door, Emma grasped a blue verandah pole and leaned her forehead on it. The wash of the waves, the whisper of the palm trees overhead, the cry of the seagulls—all were lost to her deaf ears. Every sense within her was tuned to the throbbing in her head and the ache in her heart. *Adam King.* Why, with every effort she was making to take over the reins of her life, did Adam have to force his way in and turn everything upside down? She had not yet made it to the bank, she had not discovered anything about his past, she had not learned one thing about Cissy's disappearance . . . every single goal she had set, Adam had thwarted.

"Miss Pickworth?" The soft voice startled her, and as she looked up Emma realized she had been crying. "Miss Pickworth, you all right?"

Soapy waited beside her, his hat in his hands. He had cocked his head to one side, as though he had not seen a weeping woman in a very long time.

"I'm fine," she said vehemently. "It's just that I am quite angry with Mr. King's behavior. He is rude and boorish, not to mention the fact that he is participating in illegal—"

"Now just a cotton pickin' minute, thar." Soapy shoved his hat onto his head. "The boss ain't never done nothin' illegal to my way of thinkin'."

"To your way of thinking, perhaps not." She fastened her eyes on the unkempt ranchhand. Perhaps he was naive enough to reveal Adam's sins in an attempt to justify his boss's behavior. "To most of civilization, trading in human flesh is both illegal and immoral."

"Ma'am, I don't know what you're talkin' 'bout with that there tradin' in human flesh." Soapy shook his head gravely. "Mr. King has a high regard for most folks as can look you straight in the eye."

Emma wrapped her arm around the verandah

post and looked out toward the sea. The tide had come in, and waves were crashing just beyond the line of palm trees at the garden's edge. A movement caught her eye, and she turned to see Miriam wandering toward the beach with two children, one holding to each hand. She had a baby tied to her back.

"Why does Adam not pay Miriam?" Emma asked softly.

"She don't want him to." Soapy's voice was matter-of-fact. "Her dead husband was meaner'n a rattlesnake on a hot skillet, I'm tellin' you. And his family tree ain't much better. The boss had him workin' on the coconuts when some enemy come along and pulled his picket pin. Miriam found the boss right after she buried her husband and asked him if'n she and her young'uns could stay here and work. But she didn't want no pay. Said if'n she had money, her dead husband's kin would come after her fer it. All she wants is to stay right here and cook and clean for the boss. He said okay and took in all them folks like they was family. Been here for nigh onto two years, and—"

"Soapy, what lies are you telling now?" rumbled a familiar voice from behind them. "Don't pay any attention to him, Emma. He's always airing his lungs."

Emma swung around, and the sight of Adam made her draw in her breath. Though he was dressed no differently from the way she had seen him before—muted blue plaid flannel shirt, denims, black boots, and black leather vest—somehow the freshness from his bath radiated across his broad shoulders and down the lean lines of his legs. He had placed a silver band around his black Stetson and it glinted in the afternoon sun. A brilliant smile spread across his face, and his eyes mirrored the soft blue gray of his shirt.

"I was just tellin' her about Miriam, boss." Soapy stepped away from Emma in deference to Adam.

"Pack of lies, no doubt." Adam winked at Soapy. "The cook here always tries to make me out a hero. Wishes he'd lived in the days of Jesse Chisholm—"

"Aw, boss." Soapy hung his head for a moment. "Ye're gonna get Miss Pickworth all mixed up."

Adam chuckled, then turned to Emma and held out his elbow for her to take as a servant drove a carriage up to the side of the verandah. "Mrs. King, Soapy," he said, his eyes never leaving Emma's. "Her name is Mrs. King."

# Chapter Ten

❖ ❖ ❖ ❖

*He could talk on any subject*
*From the Bible down to Hoyle,*
*And his words flowed out so easy,*
*Just as smooth and slick as oil.*
*He was what they call a sceptic,*
*And he loved to sit and weave*
*Hifalutin words together*
*Tellin' what he didn't believe.*

—"Silver Jack"

*Go from me. Yet I feel that I shall stand*
*Henceforward in thy shadow. Nevermore*
*Alone upon the threshold of my door*

*Of individual life, I shall command
The uses of my soul, nor lift my hand
Serenely in the sunshine as before,
Without the sense of that which I forbore—
Thy touch upon the palm.*

—Elizabeth Barrett Browning
*Sonnets From The Portuguese*

EMMA SEATED HERSELF as far from Adam as possible on the narrow leather carriage seat. She clutched her green velvet chatelaine bag on her lap and kept her eyes focused on the long rows of palm trees as Adam set the carriage in motion. With a wave to Soapy, he began to whistle a light tune.

The afternoon sun beat down upon them despite the carriage top, and the humidity swiftly curled the tendrils of hair around Emma's neck. Velvet and silk, she realized, had not been a terribly practical choice for this outing. Khaki and cotton would have served her better. And a different hat. . . .

"What's on that hat, anyway?" Adam asked suddenly, almost as if he had been reading her thoughts.

Emma kept her eyes averted and spoke as she might have to a mere acquaintance. "Two ostrich feathers and three aigrettes. One rosette of purple taffeta and one of green velvetta . . . oh—and a rhinestone-and-jet buckle."

"Mighty fetching."

Emma glanced at Adam to find him grinning crookedly. She shifted on her seat. It was too bad if he didn't like her hat. She had bought it at the finest milliner's in London. Cissy had adored it . . .

though Aunt Prue had thought it dreadful. Perhaps she should have listened to her aunt.

"I just got this buggy in about three months ago." Adam kept his voice level, casual. He'd just talk to her like she was anybody, he decided. That would keep his mind from the tangle he'd nearly gotten into in the bedroom. And the sooner they got going after Cissy—and he got Emma to his ranch—the better. Then it would all be over, and she'd be gone.

Relief easing the tightness in his chest, Adam continued. "This is a damn fine buggy, if I do say so. It's a Stanhope—made in Ohio. It's got wrought-iron sill plates and full-length body loops. I ordered the Sarven's patent wheels, though the shell band hub wheels would have been just as good. You know, one of the things I like best about this particular buggy is that it's hung on a high-grade gear with elliptic end springs . . ."

Thinking of Aunt Prue was enough to warm Emma's troubled heart. What would the dauntless woman do in this circumstance? She tried to envision the stately, white-haired dowager as a young woman caught in the midst of turmoil and with no one for support.

"The reaches are made of double-bent hickory." Adam's explanation of his new carriage intruded on Emma's thoughts. "I picked the Brewster-green color. Thought it might fit better in the bush. Camouflage, you know. And I knew the full-spring cushion and back would help out on these rough roads."

"How lovely." Emma's vision blurred away from the Brewster-green carriage as her thoughts drifted back to England and her beloved aunt. There really was nothing to consider. Aunt Prue would go in search of Cissy without a second thought. And she would take any path to do so—the more adventurous, the better.

Of course, Prudence Pickworth had never had many opportunities for daring. Married at seventeen to Uncle Theodore, she had been forced into the role society had predestined for the beautiful daughter of a wealthy industrialist. Nevertheless, she had slaked her thirst for intrigue by reading countless books considered improper for females, by attending lectures of the African Association and the East India Tea Company . . . and by allowing herself minor flirtations with her husband's associates while he was away on business.

Yes, Aunt Prue would approve of Emma's actions.

"Well, I thought about getting a surrey, but you know they can be a lot harder to handle in rough terrain." Adam was leaning forward, elbows on knees, his hands gesturing animatedly as they rode into the city of Mombasa. "Probably should have gotten a mountain wagon. Costs about the same. I thought about it long and hard, but then—"

"We have a Stanhope in London." Emma forced her voice to lightness, just like his. She looked about her at the narrow whitewashed buildings, trying to imagine them leading toward Piccadilly instead of Arab markets lining the shores of the Indian Ocean. "I do adore a Stanhope for calling. One hasn't the energy to climb in and out of a surrey all afternoon. So tiring."

"Dreadfully tiring." He cocked his head at Emma and grinned. She grinned back.

It felt good, suddenly, to be casual with him. Friendly. They had shared so many intense moments, she hardly knew what he was like in normal life. Perhaps she would find him deadly dull, as were so many of the men she knew. Perhaps if they sat down to tea, he would speak only of carriages and the financial markets and the latest sporting events. Cricket. Emma glanced at Adam, half hoping she would indeed find him boring. It would make it so much easier to let go. But as she watched his face, she saw it suddenly go rigid. His eyebrows narrowed, and his lips hardened into a white line.

"Bond." He spat out the name. "I should have known."

Startled, Emma followed his scowl to the slender figure leaning against a pillar of the Bank of England, a small stone building with iron bars on all the windows. Nicholas straightened as his eyes met Emma's. He swept off his black top hat and descended the three whitewashed steps to the dusty street.

"Emmaline!" Nicholas halted beside the carriage, his face alight with joy. "How lovely to see you, my darling. You look ravishing!"

Emma surveyed the light brown eyes and carved features. "Why, Mr. Bond, such a surprise to find you here. I imagined you still at Tsavo. Any news of my sister?"

"None at all, I'm afraid." Nicholas dropped his eyes to the ground. "We've had another lion attack. Lost an Indian railworker. The situation is growing tense. . . . Do let me help you down."

"Step aside, Bond." Adam had somehow materialized at Nicholas's side, and before Emma could make up her own mind, the cowboy had lifted her to the ground. "The lady's with me, and we have business."

"Emmaline?" Nicholas pressed forward protectively.

"It's quite all right." Emma smiled, hoping it might somehow ease the tension. "Mr. King is being a gentleman. And have you business here at the bank, Nicholas? Perhaps we three can have tea afterward—"

"My business is to tend to your welfare, Emmaline," Nicholas said. "I told you I would find you, and I have. I cannot stand by and allow you to be duped of your money by this man."

Emma bristled. "Pardon me, but what I choose to do with my money is my own affair. Neither of you has any right to tell me what to do with it, where to go, or how to spend my time. I owe you nothing. Lest you forget—Mr. King is in my employ, and you, Mr. Bond, are but the briefest of acquaintances. Now, please allow me to conduct my business without any further interference."

Lifting her skirts, Emma pushed between the two men and hurried up the steps. She probably would never know why they despised one another so, and it was just as well. Let them fight out their problems without her. She opened the heavy wooden door and glided into the cool depths of the bank.

For all its presumptuous name, the Bank of England at Mombasa contained nothing more than three old oak desks, behind which sat three wearylooking men. Each was engrossed in a ledger, lit only by the green glow of a small lamp in the dimness of the room. No one looked up as Emma's heels clicked down the stone floor toward the first desk.

"Excuse me." She tapped her finger on the ledger before the first man. Slowly he lifted his pale blue eyes to stare at her. She might have been Marley's ghost talking to Scrooge for the openmouthed disbelief she received. "Excuse me," she began again. "My name is Emmaline Ann Pickworth . . . King."

"Yes?" The man's Adam's apple rose and fell as he spoke. "I've not seen you before."

"No, I only just arrived. May I speak with the manager? I have very important business to attend to."

"But of course. Do follow me." The clerk rose and led her back to the last desk. A portly man watched her approach, his eyes the same pale blue as his younger counterpart's.

"Father . . . er, Mr. Richards." The young man stammered for a moment, then forged bravely ahead. "May I present . . ."

"Mrs. Emmaline Pickworth King." Emma leaned forward and grasped the clammy hand. "Allow me to set forward my request in the simplest terms, Mr. Richards. I realize you are very busy, and my time is of the essence."

"But of course, Mrs. King. Please sit down." Mr. Richards shot a frown of dismissal at his son.

The younger man turned from Emma and shuffled back to his chair.

"As a new resident of the protectorate," Emma began, "I am in need of funds. I arrived not a fortnight ago and have, in the meantime, both lost my father and married a local rancher."

"Do accept both my condolences and my congratulations."

"Thank you." Emma began to hope Adam would stay outside with Nicholas. This man seemed totally responsive, but he was sure to become less so if he saw the American."I wish for you to telegraph the Bank of England in London and request a transfer of money into this bank. I shall certify that with my father's death and my recent marriage, I am the rightful heir to a considerable sum."

"I see." Mr. Richards shifted. "And how much do you wish to transfer?"

"For the present time, one hundred thousand pounds."

Mr. Richards's pale eyes bulged, and he rocked back in his chair, his lips sagging. "One . . . one hundred *thousand* pounds?"

"Of course. Have you a problem with that?"

"You want to transfer one hundred thousand pounds into *this* bank?"

"That is what I said. I need some of it to pay . . . an employee, and the rest to outfit myself—" Emma stopped speaking, her patience suddenly thin."It is not important why I need it. It is my money, and I intend to have it transferred. Surely you cannot object—it will be to this bank's benefit to act as agent and to have these funds in your vault. You *do* have a vault?"

"Well, yes . . . but it is quite small." He ran a finger around his collar. "I should not like anyone to know the sum involved."

"No one will know. Not even my husband."

"I'm not at all certain the London branch will transfer that amount. You'd find great difficulty even spending that much money here in the protectorate. But of course, I shall be delighted to handle the transaction for you—"

"Howdy, John!" Adam's voice echoed the length

of the stone room. Emma rotated to find the front door ajar and a bar of sunlight streaming in.

"What's the delay here? My wife giving you fits?"

"*Your* wife?" Mr. Richards gaped as Adam strolled toward his desk. Nicholas strode into the bank behind him, dusting off his top hat.

"Of course. Emma King—newlywed. Didn't she tell you that?"

Emma smiled sweetly at Adam. "I see you already know my husband, Mr. Richards."

"May I speak with you in private, Mr. Richards?" Nicholas's voice was hard. "Emmaline, have you lost your mind?"

Nicholas grabbed the banker's arm and started to pull him to one side. Adam's huge hand shot out and stopped them both cold.

"Let's talk this out right here, why don't we." Adam's tone was deceptively light, and he lowered his hand before Nicholas could knock it away. "Emma's my wife . . . married me of her own free will. And she needs her money. You have no choice but to get it for her, John."

"They are not legally married." Nicholas edged closer to the wide-eyed banker. "And besides that, Adam King already has a—"

"Give her the money, Richards. Now." Adam took a pad and pen from the desk and shoved it into the man's hands. "Write out the message to London and telegraph it right now."

By this time the other two men in the room had risen to their feet and were hovering by their desks with anxious faces.

Emma nodded. "Do as he says, please." She stared at Nicholas's flushed face as he watched the banker scribbling a quick note. Was Nicholas right? Was she being duped of her money by Adam? She glanced to where the cowboy stood towering over John Richards, watching every word the man wrote. He meant to see that she got his money . . . fair payment for services rendered. But how much more of her money did he intend to get his hands on?

And what could Nicholas's motives be? She examined the tall, straight engineer with a critical eye. *He* certainly was not after her money. He didn't even want her to have it sent from England. Perhaps he *did* love her truly, as he had said. Perhaps he was merely doing his best to protect her from Adam. Mr. Richards finished writing and tore the slip of paper from the pad.

"Good." Adam pronounced the word as God might have when He first observed His creation. "Now send it."

Emma could not help glaring at him. She stepped over to Mr. Richards and swept the telegram from his fingers. She read the words carefully, digesting every line.

Adam stared at her bent head. That ridiculous hat looked like it might topple off at any moment, he thought. And what was she so mad about? He'd done his best to get her damned money for her, hadn't he? If he hadn't been around, no doubt the banker would have turned yellow about carrying that much money for one person. Richards hadn't been long in the protectorate, and Adam knew he was too lily-livered to last. And of course Bond would have seen to it that Emma never got a cent until she was married off to *him*. Adam looked at her slender hands as she clutched the message . . . the bright brass ring, her trembling fingers . . .

"This will do," Emma said firmly. Her voice belied the emotion Adam knew she was feeling. But what was that emotion? What had he done this time to set her off? "Please send it at once. I shall expect to receive approval for transfer by tomorrow afternoon at the latest."

"But Mrs. King—" the banker began.

"Tomorrow afternoon. And tell Mr. Fitz-Lloyd, who is a close friend of my family, that I shall expect nothing but the finest service."

"Mr. Fitz-Lloyd . . ."

"The chairman of the board of directors of the Bank of England." Emma tipped her head. "Good day, Mr. Richards."

Before he could answer, she turned on her heel and strode out of the bank. The warmth of the sinking afternoon sun felt wonderful after the dankness inside the bank. Emma tore off her hat and marched down the steps. She tossed her hat onto the carriage seat, lifted her skirts, and climbed in. "Find your own way home, Adam King," she muttered to herself. "You've managed to take care of all *my* affairs as well as your own thus far."

Grabbing up the reins, she flicked them across the horse's back as she had seen Adam do earlier. The mare shied, then jerked the carriage into a fast roll. Before Emma knew what was happening, the horse had cantered blindly down a narrow alley and was thundering across an old stone bridge. Her heart beating wildly, Emma realized she had no idea how to control the animal. She let go of the reins and grabbed onto the carriage-top bows. Suddenly the carriage swayed into a wall, knocking off a chunk of plaster, then careened around a corner on two wheels. Ragged urchins shrieked in fear at the white-eyed horse and flung themselves into the shelter of arched doorways. Dogs barked from roof-tops. Someone threw a stone. The horse whinnied in fear and reared up as the pebble struck its flank.

"Stop!" Emma heard herself cry helplessly. She let go of the bows and grasped for the reins again just as a back wheel came loose. The wildly rocking carriage floundered past a long row of houses and out onto the beach, its gyrations growing more reckless by the second. The horse bucked every time the carriage swung to one side, and it was all Emma could do to stay on board as she threw herself at the flopping reins.

Just as her bone-white fingers closed over the leather reins and they began cutting through her palms, a strong hand closed over hers.

"Whoa there, Poker—" Adam leaned from the saddle of Nicholas's galloping stallion to grab the harness and pull the carriage to a skittering halt.

The carriage suddenly toppled over from the loss of its wheel, and Emma slid to the sand in a heap. Adam sprinted to her side, then stopped. He stood frozen over her, staring down at her immobile face and twisted limbs. Her golden hair spread out across the sand and curved around her bosom. One hand lay on her belly, the brass ring glinting pink in the sunset. Her green eyes were open, but glazed and dull . . .

Emma lay still, her senses aware only of the purple-pink sky overhead and the delicious lapping of waves nearby. Then, above her . . . Adam. His face was a picture of dread—his nostrils flared, his mouth open in a white-rimmed circle of fear, his eyes black, his hair whipping in the wind.

"Emma—" The word choked from his lips. "Dear God." Slowly he lifted his hat from his head.

Emma blinked and licked at her dry lips.

"Emma!" Adam hurled his hat to the sand and knelt at her side. "Don't move. . . . Here, let me—"

"No!" Emma rolled onto her knees and struggled to her feet, pushing his arms away. "Leave me alone, Adam King. I can take care of myself . . . I don't need your help."

She grabbed her skirts in her fists and stumbled away from him toward the waves. She didn't need him! She couldn't. Her mind suddenly leapt into a tumult of cascading thoughts . . . Adam tried to take over *everything*. Now he had rescued her again from her blundering attempts to be rid of him! Starting from the moment she had met him on the pier, he had always been around to take over . . . to see that things went his way.

"Emma!" Adam seized her arm in an iron grip and spun her around. "What's wrong with you? I thought you were dead back there, woman!"

Emma's green eyes blazed. "I am *not* dead! And stop interfering in my affairs. I can manage—"

"To lose control of my buggy and send it tearing all over Mombasa town!"

Pulling free, Emma set off down the beach again. She could hear Adam right beside her, but she set her eyes on a distant line of palm trees silhouetted against the pink sky. "You are my employee," she said firmly. "I am paying you to find my sister!"

"You haven't paid me a dime yet."

Emma ignored him. It was not his place to order her about. She would eat when she pleased and wear what she wanted and go wherever she needed to go without his permission! She fully intended to pay for her food and lodgings at Seastar, and therefore—

"What's got you so riled up, anyway?" Adam

took two paces ahead and stopped Emma in her tracks, his strong hands covering her shoulders. She was struck by the realization that she would be powerless should he choose to exert himself. "We aren't ever going to get the chance to look for your sister if we don't take care of things here first."

"The money! That's what you're talking about, isn't it?" Emma tried to look into his eyes, but the sun had set so swiftly she could see only deep shadows.

Adam paused silently for a long time. His hands slid from her shoulders down her arms to her hands. He held them gently, the fingers pressing into her palms and his thumbs running along the slender bones on top. At last he let out a sigh and shook his head.

"Damn it, Emma. Is that what you think?"

Emma averted her face. The faintly shining moon hung over the water like a silver teacup. She blinked at the sudden watery blurring in her eyes. "I have a great deal of money."

"I know that."

"You seem to like money."

"I like money." Adam laced his fingers through Emma's. "I don't know a man worth his whiskey who *doesn't* like money. I plan to make my fair share of it . . . and more, if I can, before they plant me in the ground. But not off you."

Emma blinked again. A tear threatened, and she tried to lift her hand to brush it away before it could spill over. But Adam held her hand firmly in his.

"I've ruined your Stanhope." Emma's voice quavered, and she fought to regain her poise. "I shall pay for it, of course."

"It'll need a new wheel." Adam's lips were close

to her ear. "I'll send some of the fellows out after it tonight. And the horses."

"The horses." Emma swallowed. She could feel his breath on her neck now. Her control was wavering again . . . she heard her mind telling her to fight him, not to let him take over. His lips moved from her ear to her neck. She shivered as he trailed moist kisses down to the hollow of her throat and back up to the curve of her jaw. His hair brushed her nose, and it smelled of sunshine and soap. Slowly she lowered her head into the thick silky strands and let her lips lightly caress his hair. But the sensation of melting deep within her was enough to make her draw back, startled.

"What are you doing?" She pulled away from him and stepped backward. "You must stop it, Adam. I . . . I'm paying you. You're my employee—"

"I'm not your damned employee." Adam walked forward and caught her in his arms. "I want you, Emma . . . as bad as you want me."

"You're wrong. I don't want you or need you or anything else. I'm perfectly fine without you." She kept her eyes on the moonlit waves. "I have my plans all made, and they do not include you."

"Plans don't have anything to do with what I'm talking about." He pulled her closer. "I'm talking about right now . . . about how beautiful you are in the moonlight. I'm talking about the way you feel against me, and the way you shudder when I kiss your neck."

He bent down and kissed her neck again. And she realized he was right. The curling bud in the pit of her stomach blossomed as his lips found hers, seeking hungrily for every response. She wanted him . . . desperately. He pulled back from her, and she fought to catch her breath.

"Why must you always be trying to control me?" she whispered, struggling to keep her mind engaged and her body detached. Perhaps they could discuss her feelings in a civilized manner. "You're always barging in on my affairs and taking over. I despise that. My father—"

"Okay, Emma . . . okay." He stroked his fingers down her cheek. Suddenly he understood what it was all about. Her anger, her frustration with him—the crazy things she did and said. It was all her father and the rules and the prohibitions. He had sensed it before, but he'd been too used to doing things his way to try to change.

He gazed down at her as she stood in his arms, shivering with the chill breeze. Her long hair blew across his arm, so soft. Her fine little nose sniffled every now and then, and her cheeks were wet. Hell . . . it hadn't been fifteen minutes since he was sure he'd lost her forever. When he'd seen her lying there beside that carriage, so still and pale . . .

"I'll back off," he said firmly, and he knew he could. He'd let her take over the way she wanted to. Having more pride than knowledge, she'd probably mess things up good. But he'd give her the chance. "I turned in my gun, didn't I?"

Emma smiled gamely. "Thank you." She squared her shoulders, determined to assert herself. "Now where is Seastar?"

Adam pointed to the nearest row of palm trees, and Emma realized they were but a short stroll from the clearing in front of his verandah. She lifted her skirts and set off toward her destination, her boot heels sinking into the sand with each step.

"So, what're you going to do now that you're in charge?" Adam folded his arms across his chest as he sauntered beside her.

Emma gazed at the moonlit sand. Tiny white crabs sidled across it down to the wavelets caressing the shore. What *would* she do if she truly were the overseer of her own life, with neither the benevolent assistance of Aunt Prue nor the harsh strictures of her father to guide her? Suddenly she felt as she had when she'd learned her father was dead—lost, hesitant, unsure which direction to take. She had never experienced the freedom she longed for so hungrily.

Glancing at Adam, Emma stepped up onto the unlit verandah. When had this man beside her learned to be so strong? Had it happened when he had left his family to come to Africa? She saw that his face—as usual—was a mask . . . he hid his emotions so very well. Even his casual humor often seemed to be another disguise. She could just make out the glimmer of blue in his eyes. His strong, sensual lips were barely parted, his jaw rigid.

And then suddenly she knew the answer to his question. What would she do now that she was in charge? Before her mind could raise a hundred objections, she took a step toward Adam, wrapped her hands behind his neck, and pulled his face to hers. His lips were warm, and he hesitated only a moment in surprise before he realized he had his answer. Responding eagerly, he drew her closer and let her sweet mouth trail kisses across his face and down his neck.

For once it was so easy to get what she wanted, Emma realized. No fighting at all. Adam stood still on the verandah, allowing every touch she had longed for, every caress she had dreamed of giving him. She ran her fingers through his hair, drank in the scent of his skin, kissed every inch of his face and neck.

It was such sweet torture to surrender the reins of his passion, Adam could barely control himself. Never had a woman lost herself so in his body. Her hands slipped down the length of his corded arms, each fingertip searing a path of fire along its course. He could feel her uneven breathing on his cheek as she fumbled with the buttons on his shirt. Freed at last, he felt her arms wind inside his shirt and around his back. She began to kiss his chest wantonly—nuzzling her lips in the hair that ran across it, running her tongue in circles around his dark, flat nipples.

"Emma—" He could barely speak her name, but his thoughts raced with wanting her. How could this innocent creature know just where to stroke him, just what her trembling shudders against his body did to him? Suddenly it was all more than he could take. He swept her, weightless, into his arms and carried her across the dark verandah to his room.

The door swung open easily, and the twin lamps beside the bed wavered slightly in the breeze. Adam strode to the bed and brushed aside the mosquito netting. But before he could lower her to the coverlet and give his body over to the throbbing drive that racked it, Emma twisted lightly out of his arms. She dropped to her feet and swiftly toppled *him* onto the bed with the touch of a forefinger.

"Emma, come here." Surprised again, he reached out to grasp her arm, but she leapt nimbly over an open valise on the floor and perched just out of his reach.

"I'm the boss, Adam King," she said, a smile curving her lips. Knowing instinctively it would please him to watch her body—heaven knew his gaze had raked down her more than once—Emma began to undress. Heady with her newfound power, she slowly slid her green jacket from her shoulders and then began to open the buttons of her blouse. Never taking her eyes from his face, she watched his blue gaze devour her creamy shoulders and the soft rounded flesh of her bosom. She lowered her skirt over her hips and turned from him slightly to ease away her crinolines. Before she could turn back, his hands had encircled her waist, and he was pulling her onto the bed beside him.

"You're making me crazy, Emma!" He groaned from the sheer joy of holding her in his arms. She tried to wriggle free, but he held her securely this time. "Every good cowboy needs to get the better of his boss once in a while, you know."

He bent to kiss her, and she was there instantly, meeting him with equal passion. Their bodies pressed and twisted against one another; their hands strove to cover every sought-after curve and hollow. Emma thought she had never been so near to losing all control. Every part of her ached for him. His fingers tore aside her chemise, and her nipples firmed beneath his touch. The hard, pulsing knot at the pit of her stomach dissolved as his moist lips wove a tapestry of passion across her writhing body.

Weak and panting, Emma found it all she could do to rise above him and tug at the leather belt on his denim trousers. As her fingers fumbled his trousers open, he unbuttoned her boots and worked at the clasps of her corset. Muttering curses between kisses, he freed her at last from all her encumbrances. He lowered himself back onto the bed, watching her high-pointed breasts rise and fall as she stripped away his trousers and boots and tossed them onto the piles of baggage beside the bed.

"I want you to lie very still," Emma whispered, certain only that she had to know every part of him. Even though she was racked with desire for him, she would take her time. She had made up her own mind to have him, and she would please herself this night. For once, she would have her way.

Looking down at him, she slid her naked buttocks onto the tops of his thighs, just below the part of him that she knew could satisfy her as no other. She leaned over his chest and let her hair caress him, let the tips of her breasts gently stroke circles over him, allowed her hips to sway sinuously to the rhythm of her own hunger.

Groaning, he cupped her breasts in his palms— and when he began to tantalize her with swift, teasing strokes, she turned her head in unmasked pleasure. She gazed down at the tumble of clothing and bags on the floor, and her numbed mind registered nothing but the ecstasy of the moment. She could only feel his hands on her hips, his breath along her neck . . . and then her eyes focused on something small and golden—something softly moonlit—lying on the rug beside his open saddlebag. It was a woman's locket.

# Chapter Eleven

✦✦✦✦

> I'm acquainted with high-flyin' orders
> And sometimes kiss some gals good night.
> But, Lord, they're all ruffles an' beadin',
> And drink fancy tea by the pail;
> I'm not used to that sort of stampedin'
> 'Longside of the Santa Fe Trail.
>
> —"The Santa Fe Trail"

> I must not think of thee; and, tired yet strong,
> I shun the thought that lurks in all delight—
> The thought of thee—and in the blue Heaven's height,
> And in the sweetest passage of a song.
> Oh, just beyond the fairest thoughts that throng
> This breast, the thought of thee waits, hidden yet bright;
> But it must never, never come in sight;
> I must stop short of thee the whole day long.
> But when sleep comes to close each difficult day,
> When night gives pause to the long watch I keep,
> And all my bonds I needs must loose apart,
> Must doff my will as raiment laid away—
> With the first dream that comes with the first sleep
> I run, I run, I am gathered to thy heart.
>
> —Alice Christiana Meynell
> "Renouncement"

EMMA LEANED FORWARD across Adam's naked chest and lifted the golden locket from the floor. Her breasts grazed his skin, and he clutched at her back, wanting to ease himself inside her . . . but when she straightened over him, she held the necklace dangling from her fingers. He grew instantly still, quiet, watching as Emma carefully pried open the locket.

The face of a beautiful woman gazed out from its small oval frame. She had deep-set clear eyes, curls that hung in ringlets to her shoulders, a full and pouting sensual mouth. She was not smiling.

Emma snapped the locket shut. Her body suddenly felt chilled. She dropped the locket onto Adam's chest, and the chain snaked across his belly. Then she sat back on his thighs and looked at him.

"Clarissa." He said the word softly, never taking his eyes from Emma's. "Someone I know back in America."

For a moment Emma could only sit frozen, staring at him. Then, very deliberately, she slid from his body and stepped off the bed. Clarissa was the name on the letter she had read. Adam's wife. Emma had been aggressively loving another woman's husband. She felt only emptiness—only a sense of his betrayal. Carefully she lifted her clothing from the floor. Adam loved another woman, not her. He had given himself to another woman . . . he would never belong to her. And he hadn't even had the strength of character to tell her.

Without looking back, she walked across the floor toward the door that led into the hall. She could hear the bed creak behind her as she opened the door.

"Emma!" Adam's whispered voice was urgent. "Emma—"

She drifted into the hall and shut the door behind her. Two paces away, she entered another bedroom. Numb, she let her clothes fall to the floor. She poured water into the basin. The night was hot despite her chilled skin, and she rubbed the cool, damp washtowel over her naked body.

Drying herself, she ambled to the bed and pulled off the white cotton bedspread. She drew the spread around her body, then sat down on the edge of the bed and regarded the sea through the open verandah windows. Adam had another woman in his life. She had known that all along . . . from the very start. He had never told her he loved her. He had never given her anything of himself except his body.

She got up and moved to the window. The moon had risen fully, casting a curling ribbon of white over the indigo ocean. On an impulse, Emma opened the verandah door and stepped outside, the ends of the cotton spread trailing behind her. The sea breeze blew her hair out around her shoulders and fanned the corners of the spread. Sighing, she leaned on the wooden rail and rested her head against a post.

"You all right?"

The voice came from the shadows, and Emma whirled, startled, to find Adam leaning against another post a few paces away. The cinder from his brown cheroot lit his face with an amber glow. Could she never escape the man? His blue plaid flannel shirt was open at his chest, and his denim trousers had no belt. He was barefoot.

Emma turned away from him and gazed out to sea. "I suppose one is allowed errors in judgment when one is boss."

"I've made my fair share of mistakes being boss." Adam shifted from one foot to the other. "But you didn't make a mistake with me tonight. If we'd been together, it would have been . . . right."

"You love another woman."

"I never told you I didn't." Adam took a pull on his smoke. He had to be careful with her. He didn't want to hurt her . . . but he couldn't let things get out of control. He needed her help—he couldn't let her leave him just yet, though he knew there would come a day . . . "There've been women I cared about."

"I don't even know how you feel about me." Emma kept her eyes glued to the ocean, not seeing it.

Adam blew smoke into the air, trying to appear collected. He didn't like to talk about feelings. He'd never been able to put his finger on them the way women could. Women were complicated, and he was basic. He turned and looked at Emma . . . and suddenly he didn't feel simple. Just the wave of her hair down her back, the curve of her cheek, made him feel uncomfortably tangled up, like a fly in a spider's web. He cleared his throat.

"Well, I think you're mighty nice to look at. I like your eyes a lot." He watched for her reaction, but she didn't move. He knew he had to say something more. "And you're a special kind of woman. You're . . . special."

Emma nodded. The empty words he spoke told her everything she needed to know. He felt nothing for her but sexual desire. And in the presence of that knowledge—in the despair it gave her—she knew suddenly, overwhelmingly, that she loved him. She loved him not just a little, but with her whole heart. She loved his smile, his voice, his gentle ways, his intelligent mind, his ambition . . . even his stubbornness. She loved him.

"I do believe I have behaved quite foolishly with you," she said softly at last.

"You have not behaved foolishly, Emma." Adam hurled his cheroot to the sandy ground below the verandah. "I think you're great, but . . ."

Emma listened to the silence behind that last word for a long time. Then she pulled the edges of the bedspread over her shoulders. "But what?" she whispered. As she turned to leave, her mind finished the sentence for him: *But I'm not in love with you. . . . But I'm promised to someone else. . . . But this won't last forever. . . . But don't fall in love with me.*

"Roll out there, Mrs. King!" Soapy's voice reverberated through Emma's sleep-fogged brain. "Wake up and bite a biscuit!"

The ranch hand kicked open the door to the room where Emma had slept. She struggled to her elbows within the cocoon of white bedspread in which she had fallen asleep the night before. Soapy barged in, lugging her heavy trunk. Behind him trundled Miriam, a breakfast tray loaded with food in her hands. In silence she set the tray beside Emma on the bed and gave a quick little nod, then hurried out of the room.

"The boss wants you to shake a leg so we can get going." Soapy set the trunk beside the bed as he spoke, then raised his head. His eyes traveled up and down her bare legs before he forced them to her face. "You're supposed to eat this grub as quick as you can and get dressed. He said to tell you to put on somethin' simple for travelin'—without all them doodads and fancy fluff . . . but the truth is, I think he really—"

Soapy stopped and scratched his head. "Well, it don't matter what I think. The boss wants to get to town and get all your supplies, so's when the money comes in at the bank we can head out. See, he got a message this mornin' from the ranch that Tolito—" He caught himself again and shook his head. "It don't matter about that right now. I ain't supposed to say nothin' to you about that in case you change your mind 'bout comin' to tend . . ."

"Tolito?" Emma sat up fully, her eyes wide.

"Aw, shucks, ma'am. They ought to hire me to keep the windmills goin'. I can talk the hide off'n a cow." His gray eyes clouded, and he hung his head for a moment. "The boss said nobody's supposed to give you no trouble from here on out. You're in charge of the whole outfit and *not* him. He told me just to come in here and get you goin' and then back out. And don't never say nothin' else. 'Specially 'bout Tolito."

Emma had to smile. "Don't worry, Soapy. I shall not let Mr. King know you did anything but wake me up . . . but the truth is, I should really like to know what you can tell me about this Tolito. Is this the ill person I'm to attend?"

"Yep, but I can't say nothin' else. If'n you knew what happened and how things come to be the way they is, you might not want to help Tolito." Soapy began backing toward the door. "And you got to help Tolito."

Emma rose to her knees. "I have never refused to assist anyone for any reason. And I never shall."

"That's what I done told the boss. I said I thought you was a real good woman and real kind, too." Soapy grabbed the door handle. "But he said you was ornerier'n a bay steer . . . and as hard to pin down as smoke in a bottle."

Soapy backed out into the hall and shut the door firmly behind him. Emma stared at the blue-painted wood for a moment, then rocked back on her heels. So Adam thought her ornery and hard to pin down? Good. Very good. Best of all, he had told Soapy she was in charge. And she would be.

The heartache that had nearly consumed Emma the night before now swiftly dissipated, and a surge of confidence shot through her. She had made a mistake in letting Adam into her heart—but she was a woman who had always risen above error and misjudgment. More important, she was a woman who had learned to put her heart on a shelf. She had learned to place people and feelings where she wanted them . . . to hold herself wisely detached. Her plans, her ambitions, were far more important and caused far less pain. And she always succeeded in getting what she wanted with her goals. Not so with people.

Therefore she would simply place Adam King on the back shelf of her life. He was her business employee. She would speak to him as such and treat him as such.

Without further pondering, she devoured the breakfast Miriam had brought and swiftly set about to dress herself. Adam did not want her to wear "fluff"? Emma pulled out her brilliant turquoise-blue *la pliante* gown—the one with the black-and-silver bows at the shoulders, the intricate sworls of black velvet across the skirt, and the deeply plunging neckline—and laid it across the bed. She hurried into her chemise and corset, choosing the tightest and most uplifting of her collection. After slipping on her stockings she stepped into a pair of high-heeled, turquoise kidskin walking shoes. Then she fastened the fluted frame around her waist to hold out the large back pleats of her fashionable gown, which she expertly donned and buttoned.

A trip to the mirror over the washbasin saw her

hair swiftly pinned and a sweeping, wide-brimmed hat with three blue ostrich feathers fastened atop the curls. She pinched her cheeks, pulled on her turquoise kidskin gloves, and marched out of the room.

"Good morning!" She sang out the words brightly as she paraded into the parlor. "I do hope the carriage is waiting."

Adam turned from his position by the door where he had been engaged in animated conversation with Soapy. His eyes widened, taking in the tossing feathers and swishing skirt as Emma strode across the room. Both men stepped aside to let her walk between them onto the front verandah.

"Do come along, gentlemen." Emma lifted her skirts and glided down the steps. "We haven't all day." She climbed into the carriage by herself—cringing within at this lack of decorum but determined to need *no* help whatsoever today. The carriage was the Stanhope, its wheel repaired and its seat newly polished. As usual, Adam had seen to things without delay. Never mind—she would equal or better his professionalism.

"Are you driving this morning?" Adam asked lightly, breaking into Emma's thoughts.

She turned to find him grinning at her disarmingly . . . and fought to keep from bristling at his obvious reference to the fact that she had nearly destroyed his carriage and herself along with it. She wasn't going to let him get the better of her! "Of course I am not driving. I have plans to make and a letter to write."

Adam nodded and climbed in beside her. "Well, you're going to have a rough time of letter writing on this road."

"I shall not be *writing* to my aunt—I shall plan

the letter. It must go out on the next ship." She boldly peered into Adam's blue eyes. "Do start the carriage. We have work to do."

"Who's your aunt?" Adam put the carriage in motion and lifted a hand of farewell to Soapy, who watched curiously from the top step of the verandah.

"Prudence Pickworth. She is married to my father's brother."

"You have any other relatives in England?" He pushed his hat back on his head, feeling the morning humidity beginning to intensify. It was hard enough to be sitting this close to Emma without the very *air* heating up around him. He knew he shouldn't be asking about her personal life; he shouldn't care. Yet she'd be going back to England soon. . . . "Do you have somebody to live with? Or a house or something?"

"My father owned two homes . . . one in London and one in the country. We lived in the city after my mother died." Emma fell silent. It was none of his business what happened to her. She shouldn't even want to tell him. "I requested the country home as part of my inheritance. . . . It's so beautiful. Near Wales and the sea. At any rate, I knew I should never have the home because of my father's will."

"That you get married before you could inherit."

Emma nodded. She didn't even know if this marriage with Adam would count back in England. So quickly begun . . . so quickly over. "Cissy wanted to stay in London." Emma covered with brightness the lump building in her throat.

"And you have your aunt."

Emma looked up, startled. How could he have known what Aunt Prue meant to her? "Yes, of course. My aunt cared for me . . . us . . . after our mother's death. And she saw that I went to St. Thomas's nursing school in spite of my father."

"How did your mother die, Emma?" Adam regretted the question as soon as it was out. They'd almost reached the city, and he had no right asking her anything personal, especially after the way he had treated her the night before.

"I don't know how she died." Emma's voice was quiet. "She withered away each day until finally she just died. Aunt Prue said it was caused by a broken heart. My mother had suffered a great loss, you see."

Adam nodded. He didn't see at all, and he wanted to know more. In fact, he realized, he wanted to know everything . . . all there was to know about Emma. Why she wore what she wore, where she had lived, how her house had looked, what she had done as a child, what books she loved, what had happened in her family to cause such grief and sorrow . . . everything. But he'd never know any of it. She wasn't his to open like a Christmas package and enjoy.

"Well, here we are." Stifling his thoughts, Adam pulled the carriage to the side of a rutted road. "This is the main business district of Mombasa. The bank is just down that street."

Emma clutched her bag and sat forward, fighting the tenderness for Adam she had allowed to creep into her heart. "Very well. I've hired you to use your knowledge in helping me find my sister. I want you to put together the finest equipment and men we can find for this endeavor. Make certain we have enough food, drink, tenting, animals . . . everything to sustain us until we find out who is holding Cissy."

"*Holding* her?" A note of skepticism crept into his voice.

"You told me she is with someone if she is still alive." Emma heard herself reaching out to him for reassurance. "You said she would be under someone's care."

"That would be my guess. But Emma—"

"I know what you think. I know what you and Nicholas and everyone thinks." Her voice quavered, and she fought to control it. "But I shall not rest until I *know* what has become of Cissy!"

"Okay . . . okay." Adam stretched out his hand and almost covered Emma's white knuckles, then caught himself. "I really think she's alive, too. I really do. We'll find her."

"Yes, we shall. Now begin at once to outfit us for the journey. I feel as if we've been at it for days."

"We have been at it for days." Adam jumped down from the carriage and hurried around to help Emma down. When he got to her side, he saw that she had already stepped to the ground and was disappearing into the nearest mercantile.

Adam and Emma spent the morning roaming from shop to shop. Adam spoke fluent and rapid Swahili to the local shopkeepers, some of whom were African and some Arab. Emma provided the stunning stamp of authenticity, wealth, and immediacy as she stood beside Adam in all her finery. Not a soul refused to deliver the enormous number of goods they ordered—solely on credit. Adam simply rattled off long lists of needs, while Emma nodded, looked haughty and wealthy, and it was done.

In the process Emma learned that Adam could have managed very well without her. In his years in the protectorate he had established quite a reputation for himself, and nearly everyone they traded with seemed more than eager to do business with him. If she hadn't thought the cordial treatment might stem from his involvement in illegal activities, she would have had to admire his acumen.

Adam, on the other hand, began to appreciate the quick thinking Emma had displayed in choosing to dress herself in such finery. It certainly garnered the attention and respect they needed to accomplish what they were after. Plus, she was a great hand at decision-making. If he had the slightest doubt about what to order, or a quantity or quality of an item, she stepped in and made a sound judgment. And it was final. She had the last say-so, and he found himself glad to give it to her. He had to admit that for a woman, she had a pretty good mind for business.

Their teamwork lifted Emma's spirits. She found herself laughing along with him or joking over some small victory as they walked down the narrow streets between rows of tiny, open-fronted dwellings with craftsmen calling to them.

A heady aroma of spices—cinnamon, cloves, incense, curry powder, red chilies, cardamom, cumin seed—wafted around them along one street. As they turned a corner, the smell of drying fish, roasting maize, and boiling Arab coffee rose up to drift along, clinging to their clothing and nestling in their hair. And this olfactory feast, mingled with the scent of seaweed, sand, and salt, was served on the sea air.

"I feel as if I'm in some sort of fairyland," Emma said, her voice hushed with the wonder of it all. They had just stepped out of the large whitewashed labor office building after hiring six African porters to accompany them on their trek. "It's all so different here."

"It's a strong land. The smells are strong, the people are strong, the animals are strong, the earth is strong. A man can do things here."

Emma glanced up at the strong face above her. She had seen that look of vision in his eyes before. It drew her. "A woman can do things here, as well. I intend to."

Adam turned to her for a moment, then tore his eyes away. "A woman could do a lot here . . . if she wanted to." He couldn't tell Emma about Clarissa, about how he had tried and tried to get her to come to this land. Clarissa was afraid, uncertain. She thought it would be dirty and frightening. And the people . . . "Are they all really so very black?" she had asked. No, she didn't understand at all. She didn't know Tolito and Endebelai and Sendeyo and Kiriswa. She probably never would. Maybe he was a fool to think any woman could.

"Oh, my goodness!" Emma's cry startled Adam from his thoughts. "Just look at this poor child."

Emma was kneeling on the rocky street beside a young boy whose leg was wrapped loosely in dirty rags that failed to hide a festering sore. Her turquoise gloves lay in the dust and she was gently probing the child's wound with her long fingers. She might have been in a London hospital the way she concentrated on her examination.

Adam shook his head. Here was the Emma he could not hide from. He crouched at her side and spoke quietly to the child, who answered haltingly. "He says he burned his leg on his father's coffeepot fire. His father sells coffee from one of those big brass urns we've seen on the street corners."

"It's a nasty burn. He's in a great deal of pain." Emma looked into the deep black eyes of the frightened boy. He had slid back against the brick wall as far as he could go and was acting as though he might bolt at any moment. "He burnt it some time ago, I should say. Perhaps a fortnight?"

Adam spoke to the boy again. "He says he can't remember when it happened. He wants us to go away."

Emma leaned closer to the youth. "Please tell him to have no fear. Tell him I want to help him. . . . Oh, Adam." Adam relayed the message and Emma began to remove the layers of bandage. The burn had grown septic, crusted with dried yellow pus and showing a bright fiery red around the edges. "Oh, you poor boy. Does it hurt dreadfully?"

As Emma talked quietly while she worked, Adam translated her words into the soothing rhythm of the boy's native Swahili. Totally unconscious of the growing crowd of curious onlookers, she could see only the boy, his large, tear-filled eyes gazing into hers. She could smell only the infection—the symbol of her mission to combat disease wherever she could. She could hear only the words of Miss Nightingale: "It is the excessive accumulation of filth that is the wellspring of infection. Clean the wound. Keep it clean until all sign of the disease is gone."

"Adam, we must have clean warm water. And clean cloths. Please see to it." Emma spoke quietly, but with an undeniable authority.

Adam laid a hand on her arm. Her eyes were veiled, glazed as though she had entered a place he could not go. "Emma, I don't think I'd better leave you here. These people aren't sure about what you're doing. The boy's father is right behind you."

Emma swiveled her head, surprised to see the throng. For an instant her determination wavered. What right did she have, after all? She had not even asked the child if he wanted her assistance. But it was obvious he was in pain . . . that he needed medical care. . . .

With a gesture Adam was fast coming to recognize, Emma squared her shoulders resolutely and turned back to the boy. "Then send someone for the water and cloths—surely they must see that he's suffering!" she said, her eyes never leaving those of the trembling child. She took his small brown hand. "If only I had access to medicine, I could help him."

Adam removed Emma's hand from the boy's and placed it on a round leather pouch that hung from the child's neck. "This is his medicine. It's an amulet, Emma. Inside are herbs, powders, maybe some hair and grass. They believe . . . *he* believes . . . that this is going to heal him. Even if you cleaned him up and even if you had medicine, his family wouldn't follow up on what you said to do."

"But why ever not?" Emma's wide green eyes blinked in dismay.

"The people don't understand yet. They haven't had the chance to learn about infections and diseases. They don't know all the scientific reasons for things. Nobody's taught them." Adam sighed, wondering how to continue. "See, they believe spirits cause illness. Evil spirits. That's why the boy has his amulet—it'll fight off the spirit that's making him sick."

" 'Are you telling me just to leave him here? Just to walk away and let this wound fester and perhaps grow gangrenous?" She stopped and looked away, her lower lip quivering. "This child is just like the one in the village, isn't he? He's just like all the other ill children in this land. No one is doing *anything* for them!"

"You—" Adam caught her arm and pulled her around to face him. "You, Emma. You can do something for the ill children in this land, teach their families about dirt and infection and healthy food and all the things your Miss . . . Miss—"

"Miss Nightingale."

"Miss Nightingale taught you. You can help change this country. But it's going to be slow. And you've got to find your sister first, Emma."

Dear God, Emma thought as she rose slowly to her feet. I feel torn in a hundred pieces.

"Just hold on, now." Adam turned to the man behind him. He rattled off a string of syllables, and the man nodded reluctantly and loped away. "The boy's father is going to get some cloth and water. I told him you bring special healing powers from England that will drive his son's evil spirits away."

"But I can't guarantee—"

"I thought I might find you in the midst of trouble, Adam King." Nicholas Bond's voice cut clearly through the unintelligible babble all around them. Adam and Emma broke off their conversation as the tall railman descended from a trolley. "I've been out to your place, King. Your cohort, Potts, told me you'd brought Miss Pickworth into town to spend her money. How much has he used up, Emmaline?"

Emma's spine prickled. "Good afternoon, Mr. Bond. You are looking well today."

"Good afternoon." The crowd parted before him as Nicholas made his way toward Emma. The railman removed his top hat, and his light brown eyes fell on the child. "Emmaline, what in heaven's name are you doing?"

"This child has a septic burn. I am tending it." For some odd reason, Emma found herself speaking exactly as she once had to her father. Even her heart was beating with the same irregular rhythm . . . and she found herself bracing her shoulders for the possibility of violence.

"Emmaline, you are a genteel woman." Nicholas shook his head as he spoke. "Kneeling in the dust and touching a raw infection is no place—"

"But it *is* my place." Emma held her head high, her green eyes blazing. "Nursing is my passion and profession. Do not presume to forbid it to me, Nicholas Bond. I shall never be refused."

"King, you're behind all this." Nicholas spun on the tall cowboy beside Emma, his voice harsh with repressed fury. "You're up to no good, and I warn you—"

"Don't warn me about anything, buckaroo. I've got enough dirt on you to—" Adam bit off his sentence. He looked into the railman's eyes and saw his enemy's face drain of color. "Just back off. My wife and I have been taking care of business. *Her* business."

"Your wife again! Good God, Emmaline . . ." Nicholas's face suffused with red, and he grabbed Emma's wrist. Before she could resist, he had pulled her into the crowd and over to the other side of the street.

"Release me at once!" Emma cried, struggling to free herself from his grip. "I shall not be treated as your property."

Nicholas stopped suddenly and whirled around, his hands on Emma's shoulders. "No, you are not my property—nor are you Adam King's!" His brown eyes ignited. "You've allowed this man to control your thoughts, and you're making mistake after mistake. Start to think again! Listen to me—"

"I'm listening." Emma shook his hands free of her shoulders and glanced across the street to Adam. He was gently placing the boy in his father's arms. As she tore her eyes away, he began to soak the cloth in the warm water. "I have listened to you, Nicholas. But to this point, I have been unable to prove one evil about Adam King!"

"We've just had word at the central office. He's received another shipment."

Emma caught her breath. "A shipment—"

"Of guns. Ammunition. Supplies for the rebellion he's helping to foster among the natives. Five crates arrived yesterday morning. He managed to get them past the customs officials unopened . . . as usual. We think he's got someone working for him on the inside. And he seems to have some sort of a headquarters where he stores the crates until they can be picked up and spirited off to his ranch for distribution."

Nicholas stopped speaking and scrutinized Emma. Her face had gone white, her breath barely escaped between her parted lips. Five crates . . . yesterday . . . What had Soapy said to Adam? "Everything made it safely past customs . . . nothing opened. They're all sealed up tight and stored at headquarters." Headquarters.

Emma cleared her throat and let her eyes drift back to Adam. He was leaning over the child, carefully stroking the wet rag over the burn. With eyes full of trust, the little boy stared at the tall man in his big black hat. Emma looked away, uncertainty tearing her heart in two.

"You are right about the crates," she said softly.

"He received five crates yesterday morning . . . but I have no idea what is inside them. He told me it was cattle dip, and I—"

"Cattle dip!" Nicholas threw back his head and laughed. "Now that is a jolly good one. Dear Emmaline . . . you can't believe him?"

"I shall not believe anything until I have seen for myself." She dropped her eyes to her hands. "I have hired him to find my sister, and that has nothing to do with his other occupations. I need his assistance."

"You need *my* assistance! Let me take you to the border, Emmaline." His brown eyes deepened with warmth. "After all, I am a representative of the British government. You'll get nothing out of the Germans without official assistance, I can assure you. Why should they divulge any information—let alone information of such potentially explosive nature—to an Englishwoman and an American cowboy off on a lark? And why would they tell the truth to you, anyway? Adam is in the Germans' employ. If the Germans *are* holding your sister, Adam King knows where she is at this very moment!"

"No!" Emma's hand flew to her trembling lips. "Nicholas, I cannot believe Adam is capable of such duplicity. Surely you are mistaken!"

"I tell you, he is deluding you, Emmaline." Nicholas grabbed her arm and shook it as he spoke. "Listen to your mind! Do what is right. Come with me to the border. I shall find your sister for you. And then we shall find a future of happiness together—"

"Stop. Stop speaking, Nicholas." Emma jerked her arm free. She stepped backward and rubbed her fingers across her brow. All her life she had

been told to do what was *right*. All her life she had
been ordered to obey her mind . . . to block out the
voice of her heart. But she had listened to her heart
anyway. Her heart had given her hope to go on
living after her mother's death; her heart had led
her to become a nurse; her heart had told her to
come to Africa and make a life here. Though she
had suffered greatly for listening to her heart, it
had never led her astray.

"Emma?" Adam's deep voice echoed into the
recesses of her troubled thoughts. "I'm trying to
steer clear and let you handle this, but—"

"No." Emma looked up into the clouded blue
eyes. Then she turned to Nicholas. "Thank you for
your information, Mr. Bond. I shall take it under
advisement, and I shall let you know the instant
*anything* develops to support your statements. In
the meantime, I must tend to this child. Do ask Dr.
McCulloch to give me a sampling of his medicines,
will you? I shall collect them the next time I see
you. Good day, Mr. Bond."

"Emmaline!" Nicholas tried to catch Emma's
wrist as she pushed past him, but she kept herself
at a distance. "Emmaline, I shall not let you do
this. I cannot let you make this mistake! I shall
follow you. Where are you going from here?"

Emma paused and gave a haughty toss of her
head to the two men behind her before starting
across the street.

"We're going to the bank," Adam told him, "to
get her money." He tipped his hat to Nicholas and
winked broadly.

# Chapter Twelve

+ + + + +

*Out on the prairie one bright starry night*
*They broke out the whisky and Betsy got tight;*
*She sang and she shouted and danced o'er the plain,*
*And made a great show for the whole wagon train.*

—"Sweet Betsy From Pike"

*I saw the different things you did,*
*But always you yourself you hid.*
*I felt you push, I heard you call,*
*I could not see yourself at all—*
*O wind, a-blowing all day long,*
*O wind, that sings so loud a song!*

*O you that are so strong and cold,*
*O blower, are you young or old?*
*Are you a beast of field and tree,*
*Or just a stronger child than me?*
*O wind, a-blowing all day long,*
*O wind, that sings so loud a song!*

—Robert Louis Stevenson
"The Wind"

"APPROVAL TO DISBURSE your funds has arrived from the Bank of England in London, madam." Mr. Richards looked up from the telegram he was holding, and his eyes locked with Emma's. "Of course we cannot make the amount you requested . . . er, one hundred thousand pounds . . . available to you at this time. It would deplete the bank's resources severely, as I'm certain you can understand."

"I need only one thing from you at this time, Mr. Richards." Emma took the telegram from his pudgy hand. "Your bank must cover all my accounts immediately. Do present Mr. Richards with the sum of my purchases, darling."

Adam pulled the wad of receipts from his back pocket and thrust it at the banker. "I'm sure these folks aren't expecting you to pay them back today, Emma. You could wait until your money arrives from England if you wanted to."

"I do not want to do that." Emma arched her eyebrows at Adam. Was there some ulterior motive in his desire to have her money remain at the bank? "I wish to establish myself as a reputable businesswoman in the protectorate. Mr. Richards, tend to this matter at once. And when my funds do arrive from England, you are to release them to no one but me." She glanced at Adam, wanting to trust him . . . yet Nicholas's accusations still rang in her ears. "Adam dear, please wait outside while I speak to Mr. Richards of other matters."

Adam scowled and squared his shoulders. He looked into Emma's eyes, his own darkened to indigo. She didn't trust him. He could hear it in the clipped tone of her voice and the veiled look in her eyes. What had Bond told her? Damn him. Adam glanced at Richards. Emma was wrong to count on the banker. He didn't have the stomach to protect her interests. Adam looked back at Emma. Hell. He'd have to let her do what she wanted . . . he'd promised to let her make her own choices.

"I'll be waiting in the carriage." He turned and strode out of the bank into the late afternoon sunlight.

"Now, Mr. Richards," Emma said with a sigh escaping her lips, "I need a check for five thousand pounds made out to Adam King."

The banker pursed his lips and swiftly wrote out the sum, tore off the check, and handed it to Emma.

"If by some chance I should need other funds," she continued, "or a portion of them . . . I shall expect you to send them at once."

"But where will you be?"

"Traveling. My husband and I are looking for my sister. She is missing."

"Missing? But—"

"We shall be traveling to the border and also to my husband's ranch. If I should need financial assistance, I shall send . . ." Emma glanced down at her hands. She pulled off her turquoise glove and gazed at the brass wedding ring on her finger. She slipped it off and held it out to the banker. "I shall send this ring. Do not entrust my money to anyone—not even my husband—unless that person has this ring. Do you understand?"

"Yes, yes. Of course, Mrs. King." Mr. Richards nodded several times for good measure, then took the ring in his round fingertips and held it to the light, examining it carefully. "It's brass," he said, glancing at Emma curiously.

"An heirloom," she replied haughtily.

"A brass ring. Slightly bent." The banker's voice was carefully neutral; only the merest sheen of perspiration across his brow revealed the effort it cost. He nodded. "I shall release nothing without this ring."

"Good. And now I shall be off. I intend to depart with the first light of dawn." Emma took back the ring and put it on. "I shall not return until I have found my sister."

\*   \*   \*

"Did you get all your business worked out, Mrs. King?" Adam was slouching back on the carriage seat, his black hat tipped low on his forehead so that Emma could barely see his eyes.

"Very nicely, thank you." She handed Adam the check for half the sum of his services. He gazed down at the slip of paper, then stuffed it into his shirt pocket. She waited for a moment, wondering if he would assist her into the carriage. He made no move, so she gripped the sides of the Stanhope and climbed in beside him. "You needn't be angry that I conduct my affairs in private, Adam. Secrecy is the hallmark of good business."

Adam sat up and grabbed the reins. "Who taught you that one—your father?"

Emma glanced at him. "*You* taught me that one, darling."

A grin tugged at the corner of Adam's mouth, but he said nothing. All the way back to the plantation, he thought about the woman at his side. At times she could be so tender and sensitive, so easily moved, so often close to tears. Yet she had a tough inner core of determination that led her beyond the mundane existence of daily life. She *would* make a difference here in the protectorate. She had helped that child on the street despite his cautions. . . .

He looked down at her hands lying across her lap. She had bathed the boy's wounds with her bare fingers, stroking his dark skin and binding his leg. She had examined his scalp for lice, his eyes for glaucoma, his teeth and mouth for signs of vitamin deficiency. Then she had turned to his father and given him a stern talking-to. He was to bring the child to Seastar as soon as she sent word. And he was to bathe the boy's burn daily in warm salty water. Adam had to smile as he remembered the boy's father nodding fearfully, as though the white woman spoke words from God himself. Indeed, Emma had told the man that God sent her to take care of the boy . . . and it had worked.

"Are you planning to use your money to set up a clinic or something?" Adam could see that his words had startled Emma from her thoughts. She was beyond tired . . . close to exhaustion, though she'd never admit it. "You told that boy's father to bring him to you. Are you planning to order medicine?"

Emma nodded. "Medicine . . . yes. I must do that. You told me you'd received shipments?"

"A few tonics and pills. I didn't have much notion what to order."

"A doctor is what we need most. And a hospital." Emma sank back on the seat, the humidity intensifying the drain on her body from the day's activities. "I must go back to England soon and speak to the Medical Society. I must locate willing doctors." She felt her eyes closing with the weight of the burdens she carried. "I must find Cissy . . . I've lost her. . . ."

Emma's lids drifted shut, and she sank into an uneasy sleep. Snatches of dreams tormented her: Cissy wandering alone on the plains, weeping for her . . . her father clutching his chest and calling her name . . . her mother gazing at her from dark-circled eyes . . . Miss Nightingale pointing a long finger in Emma's face—"Medical assistance is needed around the world" . . . Nicholas clutching her shoulders and shaking his head again and again . . . Adam . . . Adam . . . Adam . . .

\* \* \*

"Emma?" The deep voice in Emma's ear dragged her from the depths of unconsciousness. "Emma . . . it's time to go."

Emma forced her eyes open and found herself gazing into darkness. "Where am I? What time—"

"You're here, with me." Adam brushed a strand of hair from her cheek and rolled over on the bed. In a moment he had lit the small oil lamp on the bedside table. The room took on a golden glow, misted by the mosquito netting draped all around the bed.

Emma rose quickly to her elbows and looked down at her nightgown-clad body. "What has happened? Where is—"

"Calm down, Emma." Adam's hand gentled her back onto the stack of pillows under her head. "You fell asleep in the buggy, and you didn't wake up when we got to the house. I put you into bed, and you've slept all night."

"With you?" Emma's eyes darted to his naked body, half-covered by the white spread.

"I don't see anybody else." A slow grin spread across Adam's face. "Don't worry—I told you I'd let you decide what you wanted. Of course, a husband likes to take a good long look at his wife every now and then."

Emma sat up again and jerked the sheets to her neck. "How dare you? I am *not* your wife!" Her cheeks flushing, she watched Adam climb out of bed. His long nude body gleamed in the soft glow of the lamplight, and Emma could not resist letting her eyes rove across the planes of his back and down the taut curves of his buttocks. He walked toward the trunk where his clothing lay, and Emma watched him lean over to lift his hat from a chair. "Did you undress me?" she asked in a low voice.

"Of course." Adam turned suddenly, and Emma was faced with a full view of his body.

"Oh." She averted her gaze, startled at his raw masculinity.

"Couldn't leave a thing like that to Soapy, now could I?" Adam's voice was tinged with laughter. "Besides, I already knew what delights you've been trying to hide underneath all those damned corsets and petticoats."

"You had no right to undress me!" Emma scrambled across the bed and landed lightly on the floor. "You have no claims on me, Adam King. We've already established that."

"We've established a marriage—" Adam caught her by the waist as she tried to hurry past him. He'd tossed his hat to the floor. "We *did* do that, didn't we?"

Emma spun in his arms, her body suddenly tingling with the nearness of his presence. "It was a business arrangement. I should think we've been over that enough times!"

"And I should think we've been over this enough times. . . ." He leaned down and kissed her lips hungrily. "We've been prancing around each other like a stallion and a mare for days now. You wanted me—you said so yourself . . . and God knows I've been lying here beside you all night—"

"I didn't ask you to lie beside me." Emma met his eyes. Their blue had mixed with the golden lamplight, and they shone a catlike green. She could feel the hardness of his bare chest pressing against her breasts with only the thin cotton of her gown between them. "I didn't ask for any of this. . . ."

"You've asked for everything you've gotten, woman." Adam slipped his hand down her back and cupped the swell of her buttock. Pressing her hard against him, he began a sinuous swaying. "You *did* want to teach me how to dance that fancy waltz . . . and somehow we never got around to it. How about it? You want to take me for a spin?"

Holding her body tightly to his, he eased her through a complete revolution. Every line of his tall naked frame melded into hers, and her cheeks grew hot at the result their dance was having on him. But that thrust of his male sensuality accomplished far more than flushing her face. Her breasts ripened and the depths of her being melted into a luscious pool of myrrh.

"How does it go, now?" he asked in a gravelly murmur against her neck as he brushed her nightgown from her shoulder. "One-two-three . . . one-two-three . . ."

"Honestly, Adam." Her head swimming as he spun her slowly around, Emma fought to regain her elusive decorum. "Have you no scruples?"

"I've got whatever you want." He took her trembling hand and covered it with kisses as he continued the langorous dance around the room. Burying his face in her hair, he found the lobe of her ear and flicked it with his tongue.

Every last shred of righteous indignation evaporating in a burst of unbearable heat, Emma rose up and caught him tightly against her. Digging her fingers into his back, she moaned as his tongue caressed the shell of her ear. "Adam . . . oh, Adam."

Continuing to circle aimlessly around the room, he slipped the shoulders of her gown down her arms, easing the smocked white neckline over her breasts. When their full, rosy tips came into view, bathed in the pink of early sunrise, his breath caught in his throat. Slowing their rhythm, he bent his head to kiss and fondle each heavy globe.

Emma stood mesmerized in throbbing ecstasy, her head thrown back and her fingers twined in his hair. His legs, cocked to each side of hers, seared through her sheer gown. Parting her thighs, she stepped around one of his legs and pressed it between her own.

A groan escaping his lips, Adam lifted his head from her breasts and captured her eyes with his. "Take what you want from me," he murmured. "Your whole body is on fire . . . I can feel your hunger burning me up."

Her lips moist and parted, Emma let her eyes consume his face. Skin glowing with golden heat, eyes as blue as the hottest flame, hair as dark as her desire. Barely breathing, she tried to fight the conflagration she knew would destroy her in the end. Ashes . . . it would all turn to ashes.

"Adam." The word choked from her mouth. Every sense screamed to have him . . . to take what she needed . . . to fill herself with him.

"Come." Fettering her to him, pressing her hips against his thigh to heighten her pleasure, he began to ease her toward the bed. Around in sinuous circles he moved, each movement of his leg stirring the pool of passion flowing inside her. "I want you, Emma," he whispered, his fingers trailing molten lava down her back. "And I know you want me."

"I do—" Emma gasped out the words. "I do . . . but dear God it can't happen. You're going to destroy me . . ."

"Destroy you?" Adam halted suddenly and caught her up hard. "Is that what you think?"

"You'll try." He was a man, wasn't he? And

hadn't she learned by now that men were controllers—and destroyers? He had such power over her that she feared he might consume her. "No . . . I don't want to want you."

"Oh, but you do."

"No." Emma pulled out of his arms and ran across the room to the door. All she could see before her was the face in the locket. The curls, the unsmiling mouth, the staring eyes. Clarissa. She flung open the door and raced across the hall into the bedroom where she had slept the night before.

Her trunks lay neatly stacked along the wall, and she pulled out a khaki traveling skirt and jacket. Within moments, driven by her urgency to be free of this silent house containing Adam in all his unleashed power, Emma had washed and dressed. As she started across the room toward the verandah door, she saw the hat Adam had given her on a chair beside the bed. Clenching her teeth, she marched over to it and shoved it onto her head. She needed its wide-brimmed protection from the sun, she told herself. Of course, Adam would probably mistake her intent and think she worn it just because he had given it to her. . . .

"Howdy, howdy!" Soapy barged out of the outdoor kitchen, carrying a lantern in one hand and a steaming platter in the other. He skipped up onto the verandah and into the dining room, which Emma had just entered. "Eggs—bright-eyed and bushy-tailed! Bacon fresh from the hog. Coffee strong enough to haul a wagon. C'mon, ma'am!"

Miriam followed behind Soapy like a wispy black ghost in the dim light of early morning. Emma watched them scurry around the room, lighting lamps, setting plates and silver for three on the long table, filling glasses with fresh milk.

"All your men are here, ma'am. They're out by the stables gettin' the wagons hitched up to the oxen, puttin' everything in order. Looks like a good crew of Africans to work with." Soapy was even livelier than usual, his wide smile lighting the room. "This is the first real wagon train I been on since seventy-eight when my pa took all of us young'uns out west to the new territory. We didn't have no ma 'cause she'd died of the fever right after I was borned—and then Pa up and died right after we had barely got settled. Didn't even have the cabin finished. If'n the King family hadn't took us in, don't know what would've happened."

Emma raised her eyebrows with interest. Soapy was a wealth of information about Adam and his private affairs . . . his past. "You lived with Adam's family?"

"With their ranch hands. All nine of us kids." Soapy shut his mouth and looked out the window with a faraway gaze. "Adam was sort of a second father to me. He ain't that much older, but he jest acted kinder fatherly in his way of takin' care of me. 'Course he always kept himself apart. Never lets nobody know what he's really thinking, Adam. He's a real loner—he don't let you know he cares." Soapy turned back to Emma. "I know him well enough to see it now. When Adam King cares about a thing . . . or a person . . . ain't nobody gonna stop him from doin' what he thinks is right. He never apologizes. Never does a thing he hasn't thought out real careful. He's his own man, but he does care. That I know."

Emma walked to the window. The sun was rising out of the sea, a great ball of flame dripping with golds and oranges and pinks that spread out across the sky and into the water. Soapy had gone back out with Miriam, and Emma closed her eyes in the silence of the room. There was only the smell of eggs and bacon and hot coffee, only the sound of the waves crashing on the beach, only the early morning damp chill on her cheeks—only the darkness behind her eyelids.

"Emma . . ."

Adam's voice covered all the other sounds. Emma turned to him, and his presence erased the smells of breakfast, the vision of darkness, even the coolness on her skin. He walked toward her, his hat in his hands.

"I'm sorry. . . ." He looked away from her for a moment, then turned back. "About what I said in the bedroom. You made it clear how you felt about things, and then I just barged in and did what I wanted to anyway. I'm sorry."

Emma held her breath and gazed into the deep blue eyes above her. This man . . . this enigmatic man! Even his friend from childhood didn't *really* know him. Hadn't Soapy just told her that Adam never apologized?

She shook her head and let out her breath in a rush. "Oh, Adam. It's all right. I don't know what to do about you any more than you know what to do about me. The best thing is just to find my sister—"

"Hot sausage! Fresh mango juice—whoa. Excuse me, boss." Soapy stopped in his tracks, his eyes darting back and forth between Adam and Emma.

"Looks great, Soapy." Adam broke from his stance before Emma and walked across the room to his chair. "Let's eat . . . if that's okay with you, Emma."

Emma smiled with resignation. "Yes, let's eat."

"Good thing," Adam said, seating himself. "This is our last decent meal till we find that sister of yours. Miriam's had a hand in this breakfast. You ought to taste what our camp cook thinks are eggs. And the coffee . . . thick enough to plow—"

"Now just a dad-burned minute there, boss!"

The wagon train set out down the road between the rows of palm trees just as the sun climbed into the pale blue sky. Adam had spoken to the six native men they had hired through the labor office. Emma, he had told the men, was the "wagonmistress," and they were to answer to her and no one else. The three wagons laden with supplies were pulled by teams of oxen, and a string of horses followed at the rear. One wagon held the five crates Adam had received. Emma noted it carefully—noted that the crates were strapped with steel bands, nailed, and locked with padlocks. Red dust rose as they made their way around Mombasa and out onto the open plains. It was not long before they had left the sea to follow a narrow, rutted trail leading south toward the German-British territorial border.

For many days they traveled. Emma rode Soapy's horse, and her legs and stomach tightened with the exercise. Her skill at handling the mare grew daily, until even when she closed her eyes at night she felt Red's swaying stride beneath her. She reined the surefooted horse around antbear holes, beneath thorn trees, over narrow gullies, down steep ravines, and back up again. Soapy labeled her "gritty . . . downright gritty, for a woman."

They slept under the starlight. Emma rolled herself in a thick layer of blankets to ward off the chill of the night air. She slept—or tried to sleep—between Adam and Soapy, with her head toward the fire. Adam suggested they each keep a rifle beside them at night, though he promised to put his away at the first sign of Nicholas Bond . . . who, he said, was no doubt on their trail.

They ate Soapy's cooking, which was as awful as Adam had claimed. Usually he created some sort of a stew from the Thompson's gazelles or impalas Adam shot each day to feed the men. They drank water from their reserves. And they rode.

Never had Emma seen so much open land. They rode toward the towering purple Mt. Kilimanjaro with its snow-capped peak. Herd after herd of giraffes, gazelles, elephants, and Cape buffaloes observed the travelers. Bands of curious baboons swung down from the trees to watch the three wagons pass. Prides of lions sprawled in the shade of acacia trees. There were soaring vultures and marabou storks, families of rhinos, packs of stalking cheetahs. But the land was void of humans save for the occasional band of wandering Maasai warriors or the rare village the troupe happened to pass.

At each place they asked about Cissy, but no one had seen her. With each disappointment Emma grew more despondent over the fate of her sister. These were the tribes who would be caring for her if anyone were, she realized. If they had seen no one, nor heard any rumor of the young woman from other tribes, then Emma's hopes looked dim indeed. Yet she buried her sorrow and fear and concentrated on the task at hand, managing the wagon train.

Adam spent the days riding at Emma's side. He took it upon himself to "educate" her. He taught her the habits of each of the animal species they passed. He taught her about all the different tribes living in the protectorate—the Maasai, the Samburu, the Kikuyu, the Luo, the Wakamba, and on and on. There seemed to be hundreds of different tribes, each with its own unique customs and language.

But all the tribal names and lore were not nearly as overwhelming as another aspect of Emma's "education." Adam began to teach her Swahili. Hour after hour they rode, Adam pointing out objects and telling her the words. The grammar seemed impossible—everything divided into classes—until finally he told her just to start speaking with him and it would begin to sound right.

This they did . . . hour after hour, day after day. Emma's skin became burnished from the sun, though during the day she never took Adam's hat from her head for a moment. The hat was uncomfortable atop her piles of curls, so she left her long hair hanging down her back, where it bleached a light silver gold. Her muscles firmed, her mind sharpened with mental exercise, her riding improved, her management of the wagon train proved competent, and eventually no one questioned her decisions.

Adam thought he had never known a greater pleasure. His horse's back was his home, the fresh air his tonic, the grass his bed and floor and table. And to have this fine strong woman riding at his side . . . he would hardly have believed anyone, man or woman, could meld so quickly into his way of life. It was as though she had been born on a horse, she had taken to it so well. She knew instinctively how to handle the animal, just as she handled the sick children. Gentle words, gentle hands, firm control. There she was, her back straight as an arrow . . . and beautiful. He'd never seen any woman look so incredibly desirable.

"We've been riding for days now," she said suddenly, catching his unabashed stare with her olive-green eyes. "I think the border station should be just a short distance to the west, by this map."

Adam cleared his throat. "Let me see." He took the rumpled paper and studied it carefully. They had ridden almost to the base of Kilimanjaro. The two peaks—one smaller and jagged, the other rounded and snow-capped—rose majestically into the azure sky. Adam scanned the surrounding low foothills. "Just over that rise, I'd imagine."

Emma nodded and slipped her compass back into the saddlebag behind her. "I wonder if they will have a bathtub I could use."

He knew she was speaking meaningless words to keep her thoughts from the reality facing her. But she had to make decisions now, real decisions. "Emma, how are you going to feel if the soldier boy is still in the ranks. If he hasn't deserted?"

"I don't know how I shall feel about anything until it happens." Emma pushed her hat back on her head. "I only hope they tell me the truth. The truth. If they lie, then . . . Adam, do you know any of these Germans?"

"Not that I can recall." He spoke up quickly . . . too quickly, Emma thought. "We don't have many Germans hanging around Mombasa. And hardly any of them venture into the interior. Things are getting pretty hostile between the kaiser and your queen, you know."

"Yes, I know." Suddenly Nicholas's warnings echoed in Emma's mind, and all she could think of was his condemnation of Adam. Her fears erased the man who had sung ballads by the campfire, the man who had taught her everything he had learned in his years in this land, the man who had held her and kissed her and loved her. Instead she saw riding beside her the man Nicholas had painted— a man who traded in slaves, who supplied ammunition and guns to previously unsullied natives, who worked with enemy Germans while living in English territory.

"Look, there it is!" Adam's excited voice broke into Emma's thoughts, and she looked up. Her eyes focused suddenly on a compound of long whitewashed buildings at the foot of Kilimanjaro. The compound was bordered by a barbed-wire fence, and guard dogs at the gates set up a fierce barking at the approach of the wagon train.

Emma's heart sped up to a frantic pace at the sight of the bastion. Could Cissy be inside, hidden away until the English government got involved and turned her disappearance into a political scandal? Did Adam know where she was, as Nicholas had said? She looked at the cowboy beside her. His narrowed eyes were focused on the approaching border guards, his strong jaw rigid.

"Good afternoon," he said as four mounted men reined their horses before him.

"Good afternoon to you, Herr Koenig," the blond German in the foreground said with a smile. "What are you seeking so far from your home?"

Emma had frozen at the name the German had used, but she forced herself forward. "We wish to speak to your commander, sir," she said. "We shall leave our wagons and men beneath those trees in the distance, and you may direct Mr. King and myself into your compound."

"Commandant Doersch is occupied today, madam. We are training a new battalion."

"But we have come all the way from Mombasa to speak with Commandant Doersch." Emma felt a bilious panic rising in her throat. "My father was a member of the English Parliament, and it is on his behalf that we come to speak to the commandant."

"Have you papers—documents?"

Adam sighed and took off his hat. "Be reasonable, Lieutenant Burkstaller." With that, Adam launched into a string of German words, of which Emma—who had studied French in finishing school—could make very little. The blond German nodded twice, shook his head, then looked back at his companions.

"*Ja, ja.*" he said at last. "Okay, you come inside. I shall try to find the commandant."

Emma gave Adam a riveting stare, but he just shrugged and spurred his horse into a trot behind the Germans. She turned to Soapy, who shook his head in wonderment.

"I ain't never seen the end of what the boss can pull out of his bag of tricks, ma'am." Soapy grinned sheepishly. "Next thing you know, he'll be talkin' Chinese. I'll get the wagons rounded up for the night."

Emma let out a sigh of exasperation and followed Adam through the gates into the compound. A moment later they dismounted and strolled past the main office building of the complex. Beyond it lay a huge training ground with soldiers marching in rigid formation, shooting at targets, lifting weights, and doing exercises. All had on the same uniform Rolf had worn on board the ship, and Emma found her eyes scanning the ranks of faces for his. Every man, it seemed, had fixed his stare on her—even the trainers—and all movement in the training yard ceased as she walked across it.

"Commandant Doersch!" the soldier barked at a tall slender man with graying temples. "Herr Koenig of the British Protectorate, with his wife, Frau Emmaline Koenig. Frau Koenig brings a message from the English Parliament."

"Frau King," Emma corrected. Panic fluttered in her breast at the introduction she had been given. Hadn't Nicholas warned her that the very thing the Germans wanted was to involve the British government in Cissy's disappearance? And she had inadvertently played right into their hands by mentioning her father. Trying to calm herself, she smiled and held out her hand. "Commandant Doersch, how good of you to see us."

"What message do you bring from the English Parliament, Frau Koenig?" The man's steely gray eyes allowed no room for wavering.

"On behalf of my late father," she said carefully, "who was a member of Parliament, I am in search of a missing person. May I speak with you in private?"

The man nodded curtly and turned on his heel toward the verandah of a small building. Adam started to follow, but Emma gestured for him to remain behind. No secret messages *this* time, she thought. Nothing spoken in languages she could not understand.

"Commandant Doersch," she said when they stood in the shade of the verandah and the men had begun to resume their activities, "may I speak frankly with you?"

"Please do." The man's mouth was a stiff line, and Emma could hardly see how his words made their way out.

"Have you here in your quarters a young soldier—a new arrival—by the name of Rolf . . . Rolf Ulric?"

A flicker of recognition sparked in the gray eyes. "What information do you have for me about a German soldier named Rolf Ulric?"

"First I must know if he is here."

The man hesitated for a moment. "Rolf Ulric is not here. Why is he of interest to you?"

"Where is he? Did he ever come here?"

"Frau Koenig. Tell me what you know of Rolf Ulric."

Emma pursed her lips and glanced at Adam. He was deep in conversation with the man he had called Burkstaller. How had he known the man's name? And why had she been so foolish as to leave Adam by himself?'

"Commandant, I do not know anything of Rolf Ulric. That is why I have come!" Emma knotted her fingers together. "You must tell me—"

"I must tell you nothing. You are wasting my time unless you can give me information about Ulric."

"I didn't come to give you information, sir. I came to ask information from you."

"You expect the commandant of the German border patrol to give you—an Englishwoman with no diplomatic standing—information about my battalion?" One corner of the man's mouth turned up, and Emma knew it was all the smile she would ever see on this face. "Go now to your husband, Frau Koenig. I have work!"

He gave her a curt nod of dismissal, then disappeared through the door on the verandah and shut it firmly behind him. Emma stared at the empty verandah in horror . . . all this way to learn nothing! No! She ran after him and pounded on the door. "Commandant! My sister is missing—you must tell me about Rolf! Where has he—"

"Emma." Adam's hand clamped over Emma's

arm, and he turned her around. "We've worn out our welcome. Come on."

"But he's told me nothing!" Emma exclaimed as Adam steered her off the verandah and across the training ground, to the amusement of the troops. "Adam, let me go! I don't know anything about Rolf! I've got to—"

"Be quiet, Emma." Adam hurried her to their horses and practically threw her onto Red. "Let's just get the hell out of here."

Adam grabbed Red's reins and pulled the horse along behind his, out through the gates and across the plain toward the three wagons. The late afternoon sunlight threw long shadows over the grass as the sky deepened toward darkness, shrouding the looming mountain in deep purple. Emma's head sagged onto her breast, tears of disappointment and frustration falling freely down her cheeks. Adam said nothing but merely led her into the wagon camp and helped her down from her horse.

"Soapy!" he called. "Bring out the whiskey."

The little cook sped around the front of a wagon, bottle in hand. "Good news, boss?"

Adam picked up a cup from beside the fire and poured it half-full. "Had a little run-in with the commandant." He took Emma's hands and set the mug in the curve of her palms. Then he lifted the bottle and took a drink.

Emma stared down at the tin mug through tear-blurred eyes. It was almost dark, and the fire in the center of the circle of wagons glittered brightly. What difference did anything make now? It was over, all over, and she had failed . . . she had no idea where her sister was or even if she was still alive. Emma put the mug to her lips and let the fiery liquor pour down her throat and burn its way into her stomach. Without stopping to catch her breath, she drained the remainder of its contents.

"Emma?" Adam took a step toward her, his voice full of concern. She grabbed the bottle from him and carried it with her as she circled the fire.

She could see the eyes of her hired men as they observed her from a distance. Never mind what they thought. It was almost fully dark anyway. She took another swig directly from the bottle. For some reason she could not block the tears that had begun to fall, and now they streamed down her cheeks without ceasing. Cissy was dead. Suddenly she was certain of it. She had failed to protect her sister, failed to find her . . . and now she would never see her again. Never even know what had happened to her. She took another drink. Her head felt light, but she didn't care. Nothing mattered.

"Emma?" Adam squatted on his heels beside her. In his hand he held a handkerchief. "Emma, come here."

Unable to resist, Emma was drawn into the cradle of Adam's arms. He tilted her head and wiped her cheeks with the soft cotton handkerchief . . . and suddenly it was as though she were a little girl again—a little girl cradled in another man's arms while he dried her tears with his big white hankie.

"My . . . my father used to—" Emma bit off the sentence and convulsed into sobs.

"Tell me about your father," Adam's voice was low but firm.

"It was different before . . ." Emma's shoulders heaved with the suppressed memories that now flooded her. "We were a family before . . . before my mother died. Before the count. My mother met the count when she went on a holiday to the Continent with her sister. They met at a spa in Bavaria, and . . ."

Adam dabbed the handkerchief across Emma's cheeks again. "And your mother fell in love with the count."

"Yes"—Emma sniffled—"though she swore she never *meant* to care for him at all. She asked my father to release her, but he refused. And then she ran away."

"Where were you and Cissy during all this?"

"We stayed with Aunt Prue. And then my father went to find my mother, and he . . . he shot the count in a horrible duel and brought my mother home." The words poured out, their release easing her pent-up emotion. Somehow it felt right to tell Adam. The months of pain over her mother's death had nearly killed her—but this man who now held her made her feel so alive again. She had never told anyone the whole story before . . . she could not bear to relive it. Now she sensed it would drain away at last and leave her whole. "After that my mother grew ill, very ill. She lay in her bed at our country home until finally she died."

"And from then on, your father was—"

"He was very angry, you see." Emma took another drink from the bottle. "He thought we—Cissy and I—would do what our mother had done. And you see, men adore Cissy. She *was* always thinking of running off with one or the other of them because Father was so angry all the time and she longed to escape. We were unhappy. I was meant to keep watch over Cissy . . . but I never did it very well. And *now* look!"

Emma burst into a fresh round of tears. Adam took the bottle from her trembling fingers and set it

on the ground. He wrapped his arms around her
and kissed her cheek. "Your father was angry at
himself for not treating your mother right . . . for
not keeping a close enough watch over her love for
him." His voice was lulling. "That's why he hurt
you, Emma. He wanted you to protect Cissy, and
when you failed, he saw himself failing all over
again. He was angry with himself, not with you."

Emma swallowed. She had never seen it that
way before. All she had known was the brunt of
her father's fury; and she had been unable to see
beyond it. Even now she could barely reason out
Adam's words. Her mind felt fogged and befud-
dled. Cissy's face kept emerging in the flickering
flames of the campfire.

"I've lost Cissy," she whispered. "It's all over,
you know."

"I talked to Burkstaller." Adam's words sent a
warm stirring through the hair around Emma's ear.
"Rolf Ulric deserted his battalion the night after
they landed in Mombasa. The men said he was
unhappy, got into a brawl with the captain of the
troop. No one saw him go, but Burkstaller told me
everyone thinks he left to find the woman he had
been seen with on the ship . . . the Englishwoman."

Emma sat rigid in Adam's arms. "How—how
did you find out?"

"I paid Burkstaller to tell me," he answered
matter-of-factly. "With your money."

# Chapter Thirteen

❖❖❖❖❖

The bawl of a steer,
To a cowboy's ear,
Is music of sweetest strain;
And the yelping notes
Of the gray coyotes
To him are a glad refrain. . . .

The rapid beat
Of his bronco's feet
On the sod as he speeds along,
Keeps living time
To the ringing rhyme
Of his rollicking cowboy song. . . .

The winds may blow
And the thunder growl
Or the breezes may safely moan;
A cowboy's life
Is a royal life,
His saddle his kingly throne.

—"The Cowboy's Life"

Take up the White Man's burden—
   The savage wars of peace—
Fill full the mouth of Famine
   And bid the sickness cease.

—Rudyard Kipling
   "The White Man's Burden"

"YOU PAID . . . YOU paid Burkstaller with *my* money?" Emma jolted upright, incredulous. Her head swam with the movement. "But where did you get it?"

"From that little bag you carry around." Adam frowned. "Where else would I have gotten it?"

"From my bag? But that's my property . . . you've stolen my money!" She pushed her way out of Adam's lap and struggled to stand. "You've robbed me! Nicholas said you would, and you have—I never believed him, but—"

"Emma!" Adam wrestled the stumbling figure back into his arms. "Emma, did you hear what I told you? Rolf Ulric deserted the German army— he left the battalion. *He never made it to the border.*"

"The border? Rolf was never here?" The words didn't make sense in the fog of her brain.

"No. He bailed out right after the troop set off."

Emma leaned her head against Adam's chest and tried to think. Oh, why had she drunk so much whiskey?

"Listen to me, Emma." Adam's breath was warm, and instinctively she lifted her face toward his. "Rolf Ulric deserted the night before Cissy thought she heard him calling her. The battalion was traveling down the coast on foot—"

"Could he have gotten to Tsavo by the next night?" Things were beginning to make sense. Emma could hear her heart beating louder, throbbing faster in her temples.

"If he were on horseback, I bet he could've made it." Evening his voice, Adam pushed the warm surge of feeling for her away. He couldn't get caught in that trap of emotion. Her tears, their moments of tenderness had almost gotten to him. Stick to the matter at hand, he reminded himself. "The battalion was on the coast. There are lots of villages down there . . . he could have found a horse."

Emma held her breath and closed her eyes. Rolf could have found a horse. He could have ridden to Tsavo by the next night. He could have been calling Cissy's name outside the railcar . . . Cissy.

"Cissy!" Emma threw her arms around Adam's neck. "Cissy! Oh, Adam, she's alive! Rolf's got her . . . I knew it. I *knew* it!"

"Now Emma—"

"Cissy!" Emma picked up her skirts and whirled out of Adam's arms. Cissy was alive, and they'd be together soon! Emma began a wild reel around the embers of the campfire, her hat falling to the ground and her long hair floating around her shoulders. "Cissy, Cissy," she began to sing to the tune of an old English folksong. Suddenly everything looked bright and filled with hope. She would find her sister, and they'd be together. Cissy would be at her side again, talking and laughing . . . they'd share their dreams and their ambitions, just as they had before. And Emma would not be alone anymore.

"Emma, you're going to fall in that fire—" Adam lunged for her as she kicked her foot over the coals and spun around crazily.

"Boss?" Soapy emerged from the shadows to stare openmouthed at the dancing woman. "She gonna be all right?"

"Emma . . . Emma, come here!" Adam tried to catch her, but she darted away at the last instant, caught Soapy by his arms, and jerked him into the dance.

"New moon! New moon, I pray to thee," Emma sang, sailing past Adam with an astonished Soapy in her embrace. "Tell me who my true love shall be; whether he's dark, or whether fair; and what the color of his hair . . ."

"Ma'am . . . ma'am—" Soapy blurted.

"La la la la la," Emma sang out. "Tra la la la la la!"

"Ma'am, we ain't found your sister yet." Soapy caught at his own hat as it began to slip from his head. "We still got all of Africa to look for her in, remember."

The words slowly penetrated Emma's consciousness, and suddenly she stopped dancing. It was true. They hadn't found Cissy . . . they had no idea where to look. Her shoulders sagged, and she dropped her head. Perhaps it wasn't even true about Rolf. Nicholas's words echoed in her mind: "If the Germans have your sister, then Adam knows where she is being hidden . . ." She could almost hear him add, "The German army will tell you this Rolf Ulric deserted. It's all a ruse. He's probably at the border now. . . ."

Emma stared across the plain toward the border patrol compound. Was Rolf there after all? Was Cissy there—or being hidden somewhere else? She turned to Adam, who stood beside Soapy. He jutted his chin in the direction of the chuck wagon, and the shorter man shuffled away, knowing he had been dismissed. Did Adam know where Cissy was? Hadn't he taken her money out of the bag and given it to that . . . that German?

"Adam." Her voice tinkled like a thin, broken bell.

"You've got too much liquor in you, woman." Adam caught her arm and pulled her against him. "Singing, dancing, crying—you need something to take the edge off."

Emma's eyes darted to his. "What do you mean?"

Crushing her mouth with a kiss, he lowered her to his pallet. "You just need to get things in the right order, Emma. You'll do better if you stop trying to think. And quit *feeling* so much."

"But you—oh!" She gasped as his hand slipped inside her blouse and cupped her breast.

Tossing a blanket over them, he drew her to his full length and cocked one leg over hers. He tormented her lips open with his tongue, then forced his way inside. Pulling up her blouse, he lifted her chemise over her breasts to release them into his hands.

"Adam!" She sucked in her breath as he began to roll her nipples between thumb and forefinger. Fear mingled with a sudden flood of desire inside her. Trying to push him away, she felt the solid rock of his chest against her hands.

"That's it," he muttered, pressing her hips to his and starting to slide her skirt up her legs. "We've both been wanting this."

She could see his face in the darkness, and she read finality in his eyes. Holding her breath, she tried to squirm backward, but he caught her bare thigh and eased it over him. Her body pulsing with unbidden heat at his touch, she bit her lower lip to try to quell the surge of passion.

Sliding his fingers up the inside of her leg, he let his other hand continue to play with her breast. He could feel her wavering against him, the woman within demanding release. Searching out the key to unlock her, he eased her silken drawers down, and she gasped and writhed against him as he caressed her hidden flower, stroking the hot moist petals.

"Adam, stop . . . I can't—" She caught her breath again as his fingers slipped inside her. Her head reeling, she felt helpless beneath the masterful hands that were lifting her into realms of blind ecstasy.

"Stop?" Ceasing the rhythmic motion, he felt her body blossom even more hungrily against him.

"No! Don't stop—"

As he began to stroke her again, she fumbled for his buckle. Her fingers blundered into the hard rod of his desire and she moaned aloud. But her liquor-befuddled body was helpless. Unable to part the buttons on his trousers, she gave in to the dance he had willed her body to play. Higher and higher she swirled through the mists of passion. When his lips drove against hers and his chest pressed her aching breasts, she could bear it no longer as a flood of passion swept through her to wash away every vestige of control. Digging her fingers into his shoulders, she shuddered wildly against him until she was completely spent.

"Dear God, Emma . . ." His voice was ragged against her ear.

She sagged into him, bereft of all but the essence of her soul. Swirls of color and patterns of exhaustion played before her eyes. His large hands stroked her hair as she buried her face in the folds of his cotton shirt and gave herself to a contented sleep.

"Have you ever drunk hard liquor before, Emma?" Adam murmured, shifting her body so that she nestled even closer.

"Wine." Emma's words muffled into his neck. "Wine at dinner sometimes . . . I had sherry once."

"Damn." He was silent for a long time, pondering the realization that with her he was unable to bury his feelings in a game of passion. "Damn," he muttered again.

Emma stirred a little from the depths of sleep, then purred and curled closer into Adam's embrace.

The sun's rays had just slipped over the horizon to cast a pink tinge on the snow of Kilimanjaro when Emma woke to the sound of low voices speaking at a distance. She raised herself on one elbow and squinted toward the two figures standing behind a wagon. Adam . . . she recognized the deep timbre of his voice. She sat up and craned to see who the other man was—the German, Burkstaller!

A shiver raced through Emma as she rose to a crouch and gathered her skirts around her hips. Running across the dewy grass, she felt her head begin to throb painfully. When she reached the side of the wagon, she dropped to her knees and gripped the wooden wheel.

"And what did they say?" Adam asked.

"Nothing." Burkstaller was smoking a small cigar that smelled dreadful. Emma's stomach turned over, and she thought she might be ill. "They said they had discovered nothing. No sign of the woman."

"And the soldier—Ulric?"

"The same. They know nothing of him."

Emma swallowed. They must be speaking of the British government! But how would Burkstaller know that the English had no idea where Cissy had been hidden? Spies, perhaps? Tensing, she leaned toward the voices.

"Anything else?" Adam asked.

"You are followed."

"Nicholas Bond?"

The German nodded. "The foreman of the railway. He left Mombasa two days ago."

"Great." Adam muttered something under his breath, then reached into his back pocket. "Here's the rest of the money. Keep it under wraps for a while, will you?"

"Of course, my friend." The German smiled and dropped his cigar onto the ground. "Good luck with your search—"

"Ma'am?" The word was spoken loudly behind Emma. Gasping, she whirled to find Soapy standing with a lantern. Before she could look back, Adam was beside him and the German had vanished.

"Emma?" Adam's voice was harsh. "Damn it, woman—what are you doing out here in the cold?"

"What are *you* doing?" she nearly screamed. She jerked her skirts up and struggled to her feet. "I heard every word you said to that German, Adam King! I heard it all—"

"Good." Adam bristled. "That's good, Emma. Then I don't have to tell you anything."

He started to walk away, but Emma leapt forward and caught his arm. "You stop right there and tell me what you were talking about."

"I thought you heard it all."

"You tell me—"

"I had him telegraph Delamere in Mombasa."

"Lord Delamere's not there! He's at his farm—"

"He came back. He was due in yesterday." Adam looked from Emma to Soapy and back again. Then he shrugged and shook his head. "I'd left a message for Delamere to keep tabs on the search for your sister."

"You're trying to get the government involved so you can stir up trouble for the protectorate, aren't you?" Emma heard the note of stridency in her voice and knew she was repeating Nicholas's accusations.

"What in hell are you talking about?" Adam stared at her for a long moment. "Burkstaller came to tell me about the telegraphed answer from Delamere. He said the British haven't found any sign of Cissy. Nothing. I took that as good news . . . at least she might still be alive. Delamere said no one has seen anything of Rolf Ulric, either. To me, that means we've got two missing people who just might be together."

Emma dropped her grip on Adam's arm. The sunlight was brightening, and suddenly she felt sicker than ever. "You paid him . . . Burkstaller."

"Of course. You don't get a high-ranking German officer to tell you secrets about his battalion and telegraph the British government in the middle of the night for free!" Adam jammed his hands into his pockets and glared at her in obvious exasperation.

Emma looked away, her fingertips at her throbbing temples. Perhaps she could massage the pain away.

"You shore did put it away last night, ma'am," Soapy spoke up brightly. "I never seen nothin' like it!"

Flinching from such inescapable good cheer, Emma turned back to Adam. "What about Nicholas?"

"You heard what Burkstaller told me. Bond is following you."

"Why would he do that?"

Adam's lips curled back. "Because he wants you. Hasn't he told you that enough times himself? He thinks I'm a rotten bastard who's out to steal you blind, and he wants to save your poor little helpless—"

"Boss." Soapy stepped forward and laid a hand on Adam's arm. "We. ain't gonna profit none by stirrin' things up with Nick Bond. You told me that yourself."

Adam let out a disgusted sigh. "What else, Emma? Have I told it right, or do you want to know more?"

Emma stared at him in silence. The rising sun had lit his blue eyes with a fiery glow that seemed to mirror the anger in his heart. What had passed between him and Nicholas? she wondered for the hundredth time. Who was the man to trust? She knew she could not rely on both.

"Burkstaller," she said at last. "How do you know him?"

"I met him at a bar in Mombasa five years ago." Adam pulled a cheroot from his shirt pocket and lit it. "He'd just gotten here from Germany. He'd left a woman behind—his wife, I think. He was drunk and got kind of rowdy."

"The boss took him back to Seastar and—"

"That's enough, Soapy," Adam cut in. "We got to know each other."

"And?"

"And what?"

Emma glowered at Adam. She wanted to ask him all the questions in her heart. Did Burkstaller pay Adam for favors just as Adam had paid him? Or was any of it even true? Had she misread the conversation as badly as Adam would have her think? She opened her mouth to speak, then shut it again. Would she believe Adam even if he told her the truth?

"Never mind," she said softly. The truth would come out only with time. Either they would find Cissy and Rolf, or they would not. Either the British government would step forward and accuse the Germans of duplicity, or it would not. Nothing could be certain until it happened.

Emma turned and started back to her pallet. The camp had begun to rouse, and she could see the men loading oxcarts for the journey. Soapy wandered over to the fire, stirred it, and began to pull out his pots and pans. Kneeling, Emma rolled up her blankets.

"I thought we'd head for my ranch."

Emma squinted into the sun to find Adam standing behind her. She could not read his face. "I told you I would go with you," she said softly.

"We'll look for your sister along the way. There'll be new tribes we haven't talked to. New country."

Emma nodded. What else could they do? If he were telling her the truth, there was no point in returning to Tsavo or to Mombasa. Delamere had reported no news of Cissy or Rolf. And they would learn nothing else from the Germans. They had no choice but to search the trackless plains. They might as well begin with Adam's ranch.


The days and nights repeated themselves endlessly as the wagon train journeyed away from Kilimanjaro across the burning plains of the protectorate. Adam and Emma spoke with any scattered tribes and warrior clans they happened to meet. No one had seen or heard of a white woman in the area.

Soapy told Emma the whole story of his arrival in Africa—how happy he had been when Adam had written for him to come, how seasick he had been on the trip, how good it had been to sit by the campfire with his old friend. He talked about his family in Texas and told her again the story of Adam taking in all the brothers and sisters when their father died. He talked and talked. Emma listened, and Adam whistled.

Emma lost track of the days. The tension between her and Adam crackled, but their deliberate distance kept it from bursting into flame. With every passing hour she struggled to sever him from the place he had taken in her heart. Her inability to do so—her certainty she could never do so—caused a palpable ache she could not dissipate.

Every evening Soapy would stretch out by the fire, shake his head sadly, and say, "I'm 'fraid we're almost back home to civilization." Adam would nod with a faraway smile and answer, "Nearly."

Finally one morning Adam looked down at his compass and pointed toward a small knobbed hill in the distance. Emma scanned the grove of acacias growing just beyond it at the base of another low rise. Through the shimmering sunlight she could just make out a faint area of glistening white.

"King Farms," Adam said quietly. "My ranch."

At midafternoon they rode up to the fence enclosing the cluster of whitewashed buildings. Soapy swung down from his horse and lifted the wire that secured the gate, and one by one the wagons filed onto the farm.

"She stretches north and south," Adam explained, his eyes on the rambling white cottage just atop the rise. "Twenty-one thousand acres of prime grassland. Water's a little slim down here, but I've brought in two pumps, and I'm collecting rainwater in my tanks. I'm planning to build a dairy when the railway comes through here and they get Nairobi started."

Emma watched the fine lines of his jaw as he spoke. His eyes were trancelike, as if he were seeing into the future. She thought of Seastar and the way he had talked of his palm trees.

"I drive the cattle down to the coast now, but one day we'll have a rail station right down there." He pointed to a level spot in the distance. "Everything will go by train. I'm counting on that railway."

He looked at Emma. His eyes, blue as the sky, pierced hers. She knew at once what they were telling her. Why would he stir up trouble for the protectorate when his very existence depended on the British railway? Why would he work with the Germans against the English, when his own properties sat on English soil? She could almost hear what Nicholas would say. "He wants all this land to be German someday, of course. And everything he possesses is financed by his illegal activities anyway, not by profits from his farming and ranching, as he'd have you believe."

"This is my home." Adam's words cut into Emma's thoughts, and she focused her eyes on the low building they were approaching.

Like all the other homes she had seen in this land, Adam's had a wide verandah. But this one was stone—built to last forever. The plastered walls had been whitewashed, and she saw that a shiny tin roof was the source of the light she had seen at a distance.

"Just got my roof," he said, his eyes following her gaze. "I plan to get tile shingles later, but this is better than thatch. Keeps the bugs down."

Adam dismounted and lifted his hands to Emma. Keeping her eyes on the verandah, she slid into his arms. For one moment they stood together . . . their eyes caressing the lines of the home, their bodies aligned, their arms woven.

Then suddenly around the corner of the verandah flew two huge Irish wolfhounds, their feet nearly sliding out from under them as they raced happily toward their master. Barking excitedly, they bounded down the steps and pounced on Adam, who quickly drew Emma to one side and then embraced the dogs.

"Hey! Whoa, there, Theseus!" Adam stumbled backward, laughing. The larger of the dogs jumped up to lick his cheek, and his hat tumbled onto the ground. "Emma! Meet Theseus . . . and this one's Hercules."

"We just call 'em Seus and Herc, ma'am," Soapy confided. " 'Nother one of them foreign languages the boss picked up somewheres. Like I told you, the boss'll surprise you with the dad-blamedest stuff. Named his dogs some heathen tongue. . . ." The little cowboy ambled away, leading the horses toward the stables just above and behind the house.

Emma looked back to the verandah to find Adam deeply engrossed in conversation with two Africans. One wore a floor-length white cotton caftan and a red fez on his head. He stood sedately to one side, nodding. The other was dressed in skins. His hair was plaited and ochered, and he carried a long, leaf-bladed spear in his right hand. He spoke rapidly, and Adam replied in the same language. Struggling to make sense of the Swahili, Emma strained in frustration. Something about lions . . . cattle . . . a raid. She recognized most of the individual words, but flowing together as they did in this conversation, she soon had to abandon her efforts.

Stepping onto the porch, Emma reached down and patted the fawning wolfhounds, who nuzzled her open palm. She walked past an old chair, her mind unconsciously filling the verandah with white wicker furniture, stuffed yellow cushions, huge potted philodendron plants . . . perhaps roses—

"Emma." Adam turned and drew her into the circle.

She fought the blush that rose from her proprietary thoughts. What right had *she* to mentally furnish and decorate Clarissa's home?

"Emma, I want you to meet my top men." Adam gestured toward the skin-clad warrior. "This is Lenana, the ranch foreman. He's a Samburu . . . a close relative of the Maasai tribe. Most of the tribes around here are Wakamba." Adam nodded to the other man. "Jackson here's a Wakamba."

"Jackson?"

"He worked for some missionaries in the interior for a while. He took on that name when he was baptized, he says. Jackson runs the house, takes care of the cooking and all that."

"*Jambo*," Emma said proudly. It felt more than wonderful to be able to express herself in a native language.

Jackson smiled. "*Jambo*, memsahib. Welcome to King Farms."

"He learned English from the missionaries," Adam explained. He winked at Emma—pleased that she was using Swahili. "If you want to wash up, Jackson will show you your room. And then there's someone I want you to take a look at."

"Tolito?"

Adam nodded, wondering briefly how she learned the name. Before Emma could speak again, he signaled to Lenana, and the two men strode down the verandah steps toward the wagons at the base of the hill to settle the men and unload the gear.

"Please come," Jackson said quietly. He turned and pushed open a heavy wooden door.

Emma followed the sweeping white caftan into the house. As she entered, a soft gasp escaped her lips. The design of the home was spectacular—a flagstone entryway, smooth wooden floors, soft white walls, windows from ceilings to floors, huge spacious rooms, fireplaces in the sitting room and dining room. Nearly every room seemed to open out onto a verandah, and each verandah opened onto a magnificent view of Africa at its most vibrant. Every detail of the home had been thought out carefully and executed to perfection . . . yet, unlike Adam's house at Seastar, this one had almost no furnishings.

The rooms were nearly bare save for a few rickety wooden chairs, an old table or two on spindly legs, a straw mat, an old lamp. The bedrooms Emma passed as she followed Jackson down the long hallway stood completely empty. But when they came to a large room near the back of the house, Jackson slowly pushed open the door as if showing Emma an inner temple.

"The room of Bwana King," he said in a hushed voice.

Emma peered around the door to find a huge wooden bed against one wall. It was covered in a simple yellow plaid coverlet with white linens. A writing desk stood beside the door with an old rattan chair against it. Scattered about on the floor were boxes and boxes of books. Several books were piled on the desk along with a stack of writing paper.

Pulling her head back into the hall, Emma looked at Jackson. "Why has Mr. King not furnished this house?"

"He is waiting, memsahib."

"Waiting for what?"

"He is waiting for Memsahib Clarissa to come and bring with her the chairs and tables."

Emma lowered her eyes for a moment. Of course, Clarissa would bring her own things. She raised her head. "Has she not come to this house before?" she asked evenly.

"No, memsahib." Jackson shook his head gravely as he spoke. "Bwana King says she will come soon. But we on the farm believe she will not come."

"And why is that?"

"Bwana King has waited many years to bring the memsahib. She does not come. We think she will not come ever."

Emma frowned. Adam's wife had never been to this wonderful land? Never seen the home Adam had built for her? Never known his world . . . his whole life? How could that be a marriage?

"You will sleep in this room, memsahib." Jackson led her to the door beside Adam's room. "It is for our guests."

"And who are Mr. King's guests?" Emma asked, walking ahead of Jackson into the dimly lit chamber.

"We do not have many guests here. Bwana and Bibi Delamere come to visit. Others of the English government also. Bwana Burkstaller—"

"Burkstaller?"

"Yes, memsahib. He has come to visit." Jackson hurried across the room and drew aside the thin cotton curtains to let in the late sunlight. Before Emma could ask anything else, the African men who had traveled so many miles with her came into the room with her baggage. She confidently ordered them in Swahili to place the trunks and hatboxes along one wall, then watched in silence as Jackson followed the men leaving her alone at last.

Slowly she wandered across the room. She took off her dusty black hat and set it on the windowsill as she gazed out across the darkening plains. The thorn trees dotting the grasslands threw long purple shadows. Two giraffes wandered up to the distant wire fence, then bent their long, graceful necks to examine the foreign obstacle. Obviously disdainful, they lifted their legs casually over the fence and sauntered across the grass toward a leafy acacia.

Emma sighed. Adam was married—she had to stop dismissing it so easily. It didn't matter that his wife was far away in America and that she had never bothered to join him in Africa. What did matter was that Clarissa was his wife; he had built this house for her, left it unfurnished for her things . . . he carried her picture in his bags. . . .

Memories of laughter as she and Adam rode side

by side across the plains would have to die. She would have to forget his touch, his smile, the little phrases he used, the way his spurs spun when he walked . . . she would have to let him go in order to get on with her own life.

Blinking back tears, Emma lifted her chin to the challenge. She strode across the room, quickly washed her face and hands in the basin beside her bed, and set off down the hall toward the sitting room.

The moment she entered the bare room, she saw a figure huddled over an open chest. Bottles clinked, and an occasional low curse rose from the depths of the chest.

"Adam?" Emma asked, edging toward the figure.

"There you are." Adam lifted his head and turned to her, his gaze narrowed. "This is all I've got . . . dug it out from the stables. I haven't had much use for it, and I don't know if it's worth anything."

Emma frowned at the serious tone of his voice. Stepping beside him, she knelt to the floor and peered into the chest. Dark brown bottles lay scattered among rolls of dusty bandages, paper-covered boxes, and foul-smelling jars. Emma reached down and lifted one of the bottles.

"Dr. John's Asthma Cure," she read. "Guaranteed permanent cure. Asthma, hay fever, influenza, catarrh, cramps. Ordinary colds in the head."

"No, you won't need that." Adam took the bottle from her hand and replaced it. "How's this? Dr. Baker's Blood Builder . . . and here's one. Famous Swiss Headache Cure. Maybe this pain reliever."

Emma's fingers rested lightly on Adam's leg while she searched through the bottles, quietly reading their labels. Adam sensed she was ready to help, to do anything, even though she knew nothing about Tolito. His heart warmed to her for that . . . but he caught himself and tried to think of something else.

Adam stifled the feeling that anyone could matter to him. If you let people get close, they would tie you up and control your life. His father had always told him that. A man had to be free. It was almost the only thing his father had ever told him . . . they had never really talked. And when Adam had chosen not to take over the family ranch but to start his own life, his father had held his mother back. "Let him go, Ma," Adam heard him say. "Just let the good-for-nothing go. Don't ever let anybody get ahold of your heart, I've always said. They'll always fail you . . . even your own damned son."

"Adam?" Emma's words jolted him back to the present. "Adam, what are these for?" She put the bottles back in the chest and turned to the man at her side. "What's wrong, Adam? . . . Take me to Tolito."

He scowled as he stared intently into Emma's eyes, wondering if she would be able to understand without knowing everything.

Adam gestured down at the chest. "Do you want any of these bottles for him?"

"Him? No." Emma started for the door. Somehow with all of Soapy's innuendos and Adam's strange behavior, she had decided this Tolito was a woman. But it didn't really matter. The thing to do was to see what was wrong . . .

"This way." Adam took her elbow and led her down the verandah steps. They hurried over the darkening road toward the cluster of whitewashed buildings below, the two wolfhounds close at their heels. The first building they came to was a small house, its door painted green, red curtains hanging in the windows. It was a stone house with a thatched roof, and Adam opened the door gently.

Stepping inside, he let Emma precede him into the lamplit room. She could see at once that the house contained a small sitting room and two back bedrooms. At the sound of their entrance, Soapy walked out of one of the bedrooms, hat in hand.

"Looks bad." He sighed and shook his head. "He's sufferin', boss. I think it's gone putrid."

Adam dropped his hat onto a chair and stood frozen for a moment. Then he turned and strode quickly out of the house. Emma glanced at Soapy. The little cowboy shrugged.

"Adam and Tolito is like brothers, only Adam don't like to admit it." He picked up Adam's hat and sat down on the chair. "Like I told you, Adam's a strange feller all in all," he continued quietly, his fingers stroking the hat brim. "He'd give his life for you . . . but he'd never let you know he cares a lick about you."

Emma barely heard the little man's words. She didn't want to think about Adam now. She had a job to do. "Take me to Tolito. I want to see him."

Soapy nodded and motioned for her to follow. They walked into a tiny room, lit brightly by three lamps. A low wooden bed stretched against one wall, and beside it squatted a small three-legged stool. Emma's eyes were drawn instantly to the African man lying in the bed. He looked at her, his face a silent mask of pain.

"Can you speak to him, Soapy?" she asked, her voice unconsciously taking on the crisp tones she had adopted so often at St. Thomas's Hospital. She rolled up her sleeves and marched across the room to the bed.

"He can talk English, ma'am." The cowboy followed her and leaned over Tolito. "This here's Miss Emma. She's gonna help you get better."

"I am called Tolito." The man spoke clearly, but each word was an obvious effort.

"Think I'll head out and see 'bout the boss," Soapy said. "He don't like to be around nobody when he gets like this. But I always check up on him anyhows."

Emma nodded absently and settled on the stool. Nothing Soapy said had registered; her mind was absorbed in the patient before her. "Now, Tolito," she said softly, "tell me what has happened to you."

"Lion," he answered. His deep eyes darted away from her face and he struggled to still his trembling lips.

Emma swallowed. Would she now have to see firsthand the ravages these beasts could wreak on a human body? Must she see a living form of what might have befallen Cissy?

"A lion attacked you . . ." she said tentatively.

Tolito nodded. "I was foreman of the farm . . . now Lenana's job. I do not go to guard the cattle. One night lions attack cattle by the pumphouse. They take two calves. You understand?"

Emma nodded.

"I do not go down for three nights. Each night more calves killed. Bwana King say I do not go down. But I go. Four lions come. One jump on me. I cannot lift my shield—" He stopped and closed his eyes.

Emma reached out and stroked the man's furrowed brow. He stiffened momentarily at her touch, then relaxed. As she ran her fingers over his skin she saw ancient scars—not tribal markings, but scars from very old wounds . . . perhaps a knife.

"Why could you not lift your shield?" she asked, her voice gentle, soothing.

The brown lids slid back. "Bwana King say I cannot tell you about old trouble. Just lion."

Emma's brows drew together in consternation. Adam King certainly had many secrets to keep. Well, if she ever meant to resolve her feelings for him, she would just have to uncover these secrets and find out what lay behind his enigmatic exterior. Focusing back on Tolito, she lifted her palm from his forehead and took his hand.

"Now, you must let me see these lion wounds, Tolito." She began to pull back the blanket, uncertain how this warrior would feel about a woman seeing his body. "I am called a nurse . . . a healer of sorts. I shall just take a look at what the lion has done and see if I can't help to ease your pain."

She continued to speak in a low voice as she carefully ran her long fingers down Tolito's limbs. Trying to control the expression of horror that threatened to contort her face, she surveyed the lion's ravages. It was clear at once that the beast had landed on Tolito's shoulder and raked his claws down the man's body, so that the least of the wounds were lower. Again, however, she was surprised to see the markings of old wounds—raised and puckered scars tracing their way down his dark brown skin. Had he been attacked by some other beast as a child? she wondered.

Emma touched the long gashes that ran down his left leg; each of the jagged tears should have had countless stitches in order to heal with minimal scarring. But they *were* healing. The leg would bear the lion's marks for the rest of Tolito's life, but she saw at once that he would eventually regain full use of it.

"We must bathe this," she explained. "Each day, we must soak it in healing waters. Perhaps I can make a tincture from those bottles Bwana King has collected. Now let me see your back."

Tolito rolled slightly to his side, and Emma leaned over him. Here the lion had done much worse damage. She pulled aside the layers of crude bandages and gazed at the still-raw wound. Clearly at least one rib was broken, and the claws had penetrated deeply into his back.

"Can you pass water?" she asked. Tolito nodded. This was a relief to Emma. Perhaps the internal organs—the liver especially—were unaffected. "I shall bind you tightly here to heal the rib. And we must find a way to make stitches. Your leg has healed too much to stitch, but this wound must be closed to heal properly. Do you understand?"

Tolito nodded.

"And now your shoulder." Emma peeled away the blood-soaked dressings and drew back in disbelief. Tolito's arm had been nearly severed. The wounds lay open, filled with pus and looking almost gangrenous. Though someone had obviously been tending the shoulder, infection had begun to set in. A doctor needed to care for this, Emma realized immediately, or Tolito would lose all use of his arm, if not the arm itself.

"You must see a doctor," she said gently. "Why has Adam not taken you to the railway doctors? Dr. McCulloch—"

"No!" Tolito half rose from his bed, then fell back in agony. "No! Not railway doctor . . . no, no."

Emma sat still for a moment. Why would he refuse to be tended by Dr. McCulloch or Dr. Brock? Surely they were professional. Did he prefer a witch doctor? But no, he had let her examine him.

"Then you must go to Mombasa," she said, straightening. "I will care for this infection and for the other wounds, but I cannot put your arm right. You *must* see a doctor."

"I die." The words escaped the man's lips as if with his last breath. "I am cursed. Evil spirits—"

"You shall not die!" Emma's voice was firm, sharp. Filled with the conviction of her chosen profession, her words cut through the native's terrified babbling. "You do not have evil spirits, and for that matter I cannot imagine who would want to curse you, Tolito."

"Yes, yes. I am cursed."

"You are not cursed, and you shall not die. But we must get you to a doctor. I shall speak to Adam about it at once. First, however, I shall bathe these wounds." She turned toward the door between the two bedrooms. "Now where is your water supply?"

"No!" Tolito's half-shouted word fell on deaf ears as Emma pushed through the door into the other bedroom. It was shrouded in semidarkness, but a figure rose swiftly from the bed when Emma entered. Both gasped simultaneously.

"Who are you?" Emma peered through the gloom at the approaching silhouette. The robed and veiled figure stopped just before her and slowly lowered the concealing folds of fabric. Emma's mouth fell open in astonishment. She was staring at the most beautiful woman she had ever seen.

# Chapter Fourteen

✦✦✦✦

*In the east the great daylight is breaking*
*And into my saddle I spring;*
*The cattle from sleep are awaking,*
*The heaven-thoughts from me take wing,*
*The eyes of my bronco are flashing,*
*Impatient he pulls at the reins,*
*And off round the herd I go dashing,*
*A reckless cowboy of the plains.*

—"The Cowboy's Meditation"

*Love took up the glass of Time, and turned it in*
*    his glowing hands;*
*Every moment, lightly shaken, ran itself in*
*    golden sands.*

—Alfred, Lord Tennyson
"Locksley Hall"

EMMA BLINKED AND took a step backward. "Who are you?" she asked again in a low whisper.

The woman removed the red-patterned cloth from her head. Her skin was dark—she must have some African blood, Emma realized—yet it glowed with a beautiful golden sheen, heightened in the dim lamplight. Her deep brown almond-shaped eyes were heavily rimmed in kohl. Her nose was thin and shapely, her lips full, her cheekbones high, her neck long and slender. Her hair, black and as shiny as onyx, hung to her waist in tight, rippling waves.

"Linde!" Tolito called weakly from the other room, and the almond eyes turned their mesmerizing gaze from Emma's face. "Linde!"

The woman slipped around Emma and flew into Tolito's bedroom. For a moment Emma stood rooted to the stone floor. She had never been face to face with such exotic and mysterious beauty. She had always considered the height of female attractiveness to be someone like Cissy—long golden hair, fair skin, blue eyes, an hourglass figure. Yet this woman was fully robed and as dark as King Solomon's beloved queen of Sheba. And Tolito had not wanted Emma to see her . . . Why?

Whirling, Emma rushed back into Tolito's bedroom. The woman was crouching on the low stool and she had rewrapped her face in the red cloth.

"Who is this, Tolito?" Emma asked.

Two pairs of dark eyes turned on her. Tolito ran his tongue over dry lips.

"She's his half sister." Adam's voice came from the doorway behind Emma, and she turned in surprise. "Her name's Linde."

"Half sister?"

"Tolito's a Masai." Adam entered the room, his hat in his hand. "He's from the tribe we stayed with out on the plain. Remember Endebelai? She's their mother. Linde is half Somali."

Emma paused a moment, recalling the old blind woman who had served her breakfast in the Maasai village. And there were her children.

"Tolito's Masai clan roamed north several years ago in search of grass," Adam continued. "Their cattle were raided by a band of Somali warriors, and some of the women were taken."

Emma stared into Adam's eyes. He had veiled them again, she noticed. Not letting anyone see into his heart . . . not wanting her to sense any vulnerability there. Yet somehow everything about him was becoming clearer and clearer. She could see past the veil; she must reassure him.

"Tolito is going to be all right," she said quickly. "I'll need to make a tincture to bathe his wounds. I should like to suture the lacerations on his back and side if we can find proper materials. But he must see a doctor about his shoulder—"

"No," Adam cut in. "No doctors."

"He needs a surgeon if he's ever to have use of his arm again."

"He didn't have use of it before."

"Why not?" Emma looked deeply into Adam's eyes, but he averted his gaze.

"Old wounds. He's a Masai warrior, Emma." He reached down and straightened the edge of Tolito's blanket. "Anyway, he won't see a doctor."

"He's told me that, but I don't understand. Surely Dr. McCulloch would tend him, Adam!"

Adam turned and stared at her. "No, he wouldn't. I've talked to McCulloch, and he refuses to take Tolito in. He said Tolito doesn't work for the railway, so he's ineligible for care."

"But that's preposterous! This man needs immediate medical attention, and Dr. McCulloch has no ethical right to refuse him. I shall just speak to that man. My father—"

"Your father is dead, Emma," Adam snapped. "And you'd better stop relying on his name to get you things." The silence hung heavy as his words sank in. Then he shrugged and looked down at his hat. "Just take my word for it—they're not going to treat him."

Emma stared at him for a long moment before shaking her head in exasperation. "It's simply preposterous," she muttered, striving to keep the tremor from her voice. "I shall speak to Lord Delamere as soon as I return to Mombasa. Is there a doctor at Mombasa?"

"They're all connected with the government," Adam replied gruffly.

"And have you some sort of trouble with the government as well as with the railway?"

"No, it's just that . . ." He wasn't about to reveal anything but the stubborn woman was doing her damnedest to pry it all out. "Look, can he be moved or can't he?"

"Yes." Emma's green eyes flashed. "But I must stabilize his broken ribs first, and try to stitch him up. When did this happen?"

"Just before I left for Mombasa. I was going to try to get a doctor to come back here with me, but then . . ."

"But then you found me."

Adam nodded. "We made a deal, and this is your part. Do you want to work on him tonight?"

"Of course. Why should I let him suffer any longer?" Emma unbuttoned her sleeves and began rolling them up. "I shall need assistance."

"I'll help," Adam said quietly, his tone suddenly softening.

"What about Linde?" Emma lifted her eyebrows at the woman huddled in the shadows. Her long thin fingers reminded Emma of Miss Nightingale's —gentle, yet strong.

"She can't speak much English."

"That's all right." Emma gave a perfunctory smile to the dark figure. Somehow this enigmatic woman had played an important role in Adam's life. He had wanted her hidden, kept a secret. Why? Could she be his lover? An arrow of panic shot through

Emma's heart, and she glanced up at the woman again. The beautiful, mysterious almond eyes gazed back. Who *was* she? Emma had to find out.

"Do you need anything from the main house? Medicine? Cloth?" Adam turned up the lamps in the small bedroom as he spoke. "This is Soapy's house, but he doesn't keep it too well supplied."

"Soapy's? But where do *they* live?"

"Tolito lives down in the village," Adam explained. "He's got a wife and some kids. Three, I think."

Emma nodded. Adam had not said Linde lived in the village. Was she Soapy's mistress? Or Adam's? Or perhaps . . . a slave? "I shall need that chest of medicines and some boiling water," Emma said briskly. "And bring me a clean sheet. I shall teach Linde to make bandages."

Adam started for the door.

"And a needle," Emma called. "Find me a needle and some thread."

Adam looked back, his brow furrowed. "A needle? Why would I have a needle?"

"I have." Linde rose from the shadows. Her voice was low and husky. "I have needle."

Adam's eyes shot to Linde's face in a silent, unreadable message. Emma looked from one to the other, hoping for a clue to the past between them. But she could find nothing. It was as though Adam were repeating an invisible vow with the dusky woman—reminding her of a promise—yet saying nothing. Then he was gone, slamming the door behind him.

For the remainder of the evening, Emma forced herself to concentrate on Tolito. Adam and Soapy brought down the chest. Emma boiled up a tincture of various medicines, hoping to create a healing and anesthetic soak for Tolito's wounds. She put Linde to work tearing the sheet into strips for bandages. Soapy quickly elected to spend his time in the stables. "I reckon I'm 'bout as helpless as a froze bullsnake 'round here," he said. "Hope you don't mind if'n I make myself scarce."

Emma was relieved to see him go. She feared there would be too many people already just with Adam and Linde at hand. Yet she wanted to watch those two interact as best she could.

As Emma began to work, Adam sat beside Tolito and held his hand, gripping tightly as the pain grew, stroking his forehead when it subsided. He bent over and murmured words in Tolito's language, words to which the African nodded and sometimes even smiled. And finally Adam began to sing.

Emma had heard his voice occasionally crooning an old tune as they rode across the plains, but he had kept the words mostly to himself. Now, in the lamplight, his voice echoed soft and melodic. "I've been thinking today, as my thoughts began to stray, of your memory to me worth more than gold. As you ride across the plain, 'mid the sunshine and rain . . ."

Linde hummed along, tearing the sheet methodically. But when Emma finished cleansing Tolito's leg and began to suture his back, Linde glided to her side. Adam held the African's head, giving him sip after sip of whiskey while Linde helped to hold his torn, writhing body. Emma was astonished at the way the young woman worked beside her, never flinching at the tedious and bloody suturing of skin. Instead, she seemed to anticipate Emma's every need and was always ready with a sponge, a length of thread, or a fresh bandage.

"This, you see, has started to heal," Emma explained as if Linde could understand. "It will make a scar, but your brother will not have pain here after a few weeks. He already has many scars. . . ."

Linde nodded, her eyes intent on Emma's face. "Arm?"

"We shall clean it, but we can do nothing more tonight. I do not know how to repair or set this bone. And the muscle is badly torn." She gave Adam a significant look. He *must* see that guarding his secrets could cost this man his life. "Skin is not so difficult to suture, but muscle . . . I simply cannot do it. He must go to a doctor in Mombasa."

Adam gave a tense nod of consent. "I'll get him there."

Satisfied, Emma bent again to her work. It seemed only minutes as she wrapped tight bandages around Tolito's broken ribs and cleansed and treated the infection around his shoulder. Yet she heard song after song rise from Adam's lips, and Linde hovered about, each minute making herself more and more indispensable.

"There," Emma announced at last, lifting her tired shoulders and trying to straighten her back. Adam stopped singing and looked up in surprise from his trancelike fixation on the wall. Tolito had drifted into an inebriated sleep in his arms, no longer feeling the pain while Emma worked to repair his ravaged body.

Linde rose from her crouch and smiled. "There," she said.

Emma glanced at her. The red cloth had fallen to her waist, baring full, shapely breasts barely contained in a tight, silken blouse. Her raven hair fell around her shoulders like a madonna's. Yet as

Emma gazed at the woman, she realized Linde was totally unconscious of her sensuality. She was childlike . . . innocent. Vulnerable.

"You have done well, Linde," Emma said quietly. "Now Tolito can begin to heal properly. Do you understand?"

Linde inclined her dusky head. "I like."

Emma looked at her with a puzzled expression. "You like what?"

Linde smiled, her full lips parting over perfect white teeth. "I like *you*."

Emma glanced at Adam, then cleared her throat. "Well, thank you. Thank you very much."

Linde took two steps forward and grasped Emma's hands in hers. "Thank you. Thank you," she crooned, pressing her forehead to the backs of Emma's hands.

"She's been very worried about him," Adam explained quietly. "She hasn't left his side for a minute. Not even when his wife comes."

"But when I came, you made her hide in the next room." Emma found her voice harsh. She was tired . . . and tired of the mystery. Why couldn't Adam tell her his secrets? Why must he build walls around himself?

"Let's go up to the house." Adam took her arm. "Thank you, Linde. Call me if he wakes up and needs anything."

Linde nodded, but Adam had already propelled Emma out of the room. He walked swiftly through the chill night air, as if wanting to forget where he had been, as if anxious now to dismiss it all.

"Why did you hide Linde from me?" Emma demanded when she had caught her breath. Adam was marching her through the main house toward the dining room.

"I did *not* hide her from you." He threw open the dining room door to reveal a table spread with cold meats, crackers, fresh sliced bread, fruits, and hot tea. "She was right in the next room, wasn't she? If I'd wanted to hide her, I could have done a better job than that."

"You didn't want me to see her—" Emma suddenly thought of Cissy, and Nicholas's accusations that Adam knew where she had been hidden away.

"Be quiet, and eat this, Emma." He half tossed Emma onto a chair and started piling a plate with food. Before she could speak, he had thrust it before her with the command, "Eat!"

The protest died in Emma's throat, and she began to eat. She wanted to be angry with him, to insist that he stop forcing her away. But now she felt too drained, too emotionally and physically spent to rail against him. Gradually her empty, knotted stomach groaned and relaxed, and she began to feel stronger. She had no idea what time it was, but the moon shone brightly through the open windows. Adam slouched across from her, his own plate empty. He was staring down at the table, his face rigid and his blue eyes deeply shadowed.

Emma could sense his uneasiness, and a part of her wanted to reach out to him. Yet her anger resurfaced, too. Did he believe she hadn't the fortitude to hear the truth? She fumed over his refusal to tell her his true feelings for her. And most of all to admit that he loved another woman. Why? Why did it have to be that way? He must feel something for Clarissa, even if it were just the memory of a flaming passion. Or perhaps Emma herself was just the flaming passion, and Clarissa the true love.

"I'm going to bathe." Emma stood up suddenly. "Good night."

Adam looked at her, his eyes misted and drawn. "Thank you, Emma . . . for Tolito. You were good in there."

Forcing herself from the urge to go to him, Emma nodded and turned away. She found her tired feet running down the hall, and when she burst into her bedroom, she slammed the door shut and leaned against it, breathless. Suddenly tears were streaming down her cheeks, and she crumpled in exhaustion to the floor.

Adam . . . oh, Adam. Was she any better than he? Had she told him of her love—a love so strong she could never deny it to herself? She loved him. And though her inner voices told her it was wrong . . . impossible . . . she could not suppress it.

Struggling to rouse herself, Emma wandered across the empty bedroom and into the bath. She turned on the brass tap and watched the steamy water slowly fill the porcelain tub. What difference did anything make? she thought as she undressed. What good was life without him? She might find Cissy . . . she might start her nursing work . . . she might even bring doctors to the protectorate and help to found a hospital. But how meaningless her life would be without love! Without Adam.

Sliding under the water, Emma soaked off the layers of grime from days of riding across the plains. Her skin had turned an undeniable brown from the sun, but she stared at it blankly. What was the point of lily-white skin? What was the point of anything! With the realization of her despair, Emma felt a surge of determination flow through her. No—she would not live a life of hopelessness and uncertainty.

With renewed purpose, Emma scrubbed her skin and washed the dust from her hair. This very night, she promised herself, she would confront Adam, insist that he tell her everything . . . Nicholas, Tolito, Linde, the crates, the railway, the government, Burkstaller—

Rising from the bath, she toweled herself dry and strode into the bedroom. She turned up the lamps, tore open her trunk, and jerked out a long white robe. Never mind her damp hair. Never mind her bare skin. She would have it out with Adam now. She fumbled the rows of ribbons into semblances of bows and half-ran out into the hall.

Now, Adam King. Now, she chanted to herself as she marched toward the dining room. The door was shut and she drew it open, the words she had planned for him at the ready.

The room was empty. Undaunted, Emma strode back down the hall to his bedroom. Without knocking, she pushed open the door and walked in.

Clad only in his denim trousers, Adam was standing by the window gazing out into the moonlit night. The room was dark save for the silver beam that fell through the window and covered him with light. His back was pearled with beads of water, and his hair shone blue black with dampness. He turned and looked at Emma, his eyes aflame.

"Adam King." Emma marched toward him determinedly. "I want the truth and I want it now."

"You want the truth?" Adam surged forward like a cat. Emma stopped midpace, her heart suddenly in her throat. "You want the truth, Emma?"

Emma held her breath as he circled her. She caught his scent, wild and raw. His paces were silent, the only sound was his breath . . . heavy.

Swallowing, Emma lifted her chin. "Yes, I do. I want the truth from you. No more lies."

Adam watched her as he prowled. Her strong shoulders held so stiffly high. Her stubborn little chin jutting foward. But as her eyes followed him, he saw her tremble ever so slightly . . . just enough that three droplets of water fell from the ends of her hair to land on the rounded curve of her buttocks. She wanted the truth? Then he'd give it to her.

Coming up from behind, he grabbed her upper arm and whirled her around to face him. "The truth, Emma? Here's the truth—" He pulled her beside him toward the window. Jerking aside the curtain, he forced her body against the sill. "Look . . . there's the truth."

Emma stared into the darkness, confusion and fear blinding her eyes. What had she thought, coming to him like this? What— Suddenly, in the trees just outside the window, she saw a movement. She focused on the long, sweeping branch of a gray baobab tree. Leopards! Two spotted cats crept along the branch, their thick tails tossing gracefully from side to side. And then she saw something else . . . a hulking shape, an animal hanging in the forked branch. The leopards pawed at the dead antelope, its horns hanging wildly askew toward the ground. And then they tore into their meal, ripping at the flesh and grunting with pleasure as they feasted.

Emma gaped for a moment in silence at the raw carnal pleasure of the two creatures. Then, half-sickened and half-mesmerized, she stepped backward to leave. But as she did so she felt the rock-hard body of Adam solid as a wall behind her.

"The truth," he growled. He caught her shoulders and turned her around.

"Adam . . ." Her breathing was shallow. "I don'
understand."

"The truth is that we are no different from
those leopards. They schemed to catch that gazelle, and they caught her. Then they dragged
her up into the tree where no other animal could
have her and went away. Then they came back
tonight and . . ."

"And what? What are you trying to tell me?"

"Every man is out to get the most he can for
himself. He'll plot and scheme and stake out his
claim. Then he'll move in for the kill. And once
he's got what he was after, he'll hide it away where
no one else can have it so that he can enjoy it for
himself."

Adam searched Emma's eyes as he spoke. Confusion had tormented them to a mossy green, and
they darted across his face from his eyes to his
mouth like a scared animal's.

"And that's what you're like?" Emma whispered.

"That's what everyone's like," he said savagely.
"That's what you're like. You want to find your
sister, don't you? And to hell with everything
else—"

"No! I came here to help you . . . to help Tolito.'

"I made you come here. You didn't want to. And
you want to be a nurse, right? Never mind how
anyone else feels about it. Never mind that someone might want you to—"

He paused and looked away. His pulse roared,
and he clenched his jaw against the throbbing in
his temples. Why was he hurting her like this?

What had she done to deserve his wrath? It wasn't Emma he was angry with . . . it was himself.

"And you've done everything you could to make all your dreams come true, too." Emma's voice was trembling. "Haven't you?"

Adam whirled back to her. "Not everything." Again he stopped himself. No, he couldn't tell her. He couldn't bring it out again; he'd hidden it so well. But damn her—*she* had brought it out! And now he'd been forced to look at it again, that ancient longing, that hunger to share his life with someone.

"What is it, Adam? What is your dream?"

He dropped his hands from her arms and walked away. No, he wouldn't tell her. He didn't need to add another heartache to his life. He had angered his parents, turned them against him. And Clarissa —look what he'd done to her. And he'd allowed Tolito's life to be ruined. . . . So many mistakes.

"Adam, tell me!" Emma ran across the room and caught his wrist. "I only want what's best for you. Don't be mistaken about me . . . I love you—" She caught her breath and froze, her green eyes wide with dismay. "I shouldn't have—"

"No!" Adam whirled and gripped her shoulders again. "No, you were right to have said it." He looked away, anxious as a big caged cat. "Damn it, Emma—I've messed up so many times—so many lives. But this time . . . this time I'm not going to go wrong. Not with you. I love you, Emma."

His eyes locked on hers, the knowledge between them almost too stunning, too ponderous to bear. And then the insatiable hunger that had threatened to tear them apart hurled them together, more powerfully together than they had ever imagined possible. Like the leopards devouring their feast, the two inside the moonlit room fell upon one another.

Lips, hands, bodies roving, they clung and sought to slake their thirst for one another. Adam had never known his body to pulse with such passion. As his hands possessed Emma's shoulders and reveled in the slender slope of her back, he came alive to every nuance of her flesh. Her skin sang with tenderness, with a heady scent of lavender and spice, with silky honey that melted on his tongue. The gentle curve of her stomach singed the hair of his own belly, and the firm lines of her legs pressing against his set his loins on fire.

"Adam, I've longed for you so," she whispered. Her breath on his neck sent ripples of desire through him. "I've wanted you every day. . . ."

"I'm all yours, Emma. Every day . . . every hour . . . every second." He wanted her to know it all. He wanted to hold nothing back now, nothing. "I love you, Emma. I love you."

She caught her breath at his words, and the sharp uplift of her breasts against his chest sent him nearly mad. Unable to restrain himself, he snatched at her robe with its damned little bows. His large fingers fought for a moment with the tiny ribbons, and then he could wait no longer. Tearing aside the frail white fabric, he gazed down at her breasts. Her long hair half covered them, but the uptilted rose-hued nipples peeked between the tresses to flaunt themselves at him.

Groaning, he brushed aside her hair and ran his thumbs in stroking circles over the tips of her breasts. Emma gasped and lifted herself into him, the ecstasy of his caress turning her body into a warm pool of liquid desire. She ran her fingers across the steel planes of his chest as he stroked her, then followed the path of her fingers with her lips and tongue. Moist, aroused beyond her wildest imaginings, she slid against him as her hips began to dance uncontrollably.

"Emma . . ." Her name escaped his lips in a ragged sigh. She drove him to such a frenzy that even now, still half-clothed, his body was in agony for her. He tore the robe from her shoulders and let it fall to the floor as she leaned into him and began to slide his trousers down his legs. Innocent . . . he knew she was so innocent, so untaught . . . and yet she instinctively loved him better than he'd ever been loved. She was like an animal, a she-cat.

He sucked in his breath as her lips caught him, as her arms wove around his legs and her breasts pressed against his knees. Her warm tongue caressed . . . her mouth drew him in . . . her hands kneaded the hard flesh of his buttocks. And then she looked up at him, her green eyes glowing with love.

"Emma." He said her name again, and it was all he could seem to draw out of himself. He knelt beside her, his lips roving over her face and neck. "You drain everything out of me until I'm weak."

She gazed down at his hardened body and smiled. "So weak," she whispered, stroking her fingertips up his thigh.

Letting out a throaty cry, he lowered her to the rug beneath them and reached to part her legs. But as his hand found the silky skin of her inner thigh, she twined her legs around his body and locked her ankles behind his back. Gazing down at her, open and throbbing for him, he began to stroke her, caressing and teasing, and playing with her until she begged him to fill her.

He slipped inside then, and she drew her legs

around him. Her heels pressed into his back as they rose and fell together, the delicious surge and ebb of passion pushing them onward and upward. Adam felt as though he had somehow melted into Emma. His body was one with hers, and his mind and heart and soul had been given over freely. Her arms held him, her fingers gripped his back, her legs slid to twine with his, her breasts rolled against his chest.

"Adam, I—" She fought to speak the words. "I want to feel you more, somehow to become you . . ."

Knowing what she needed better than she knew herself, he pulled her closer and rolled onto his back. Sighing with pleasure, Emma rose over him. Her long hair cascaded onto his chest, its silken strands tumbling over him as she began a weaving, sinuous dance upon him. She moaned, lost in a world of aching, pulsing heat, as his fingers stroked her to the rhythm of her movement. He devoured her with his eyes . . . her breasts swaying above him, her hair falling down her back, her head raised, and her eyes closed in ecstasy.

He slid his hands over the swell of her hips and across her back, lowering her over him until her breasts waltzed in the tumult of her hair as it teased his chest. Never, never had he known such pleasure. He was so full, so rigid and thrumming within her, that he had to fight for control as she rose to the peak of her own need. Struggling to hold back—mounting with desire every moment— he somehow found himself wanting only to please her. Yet every touch of his hands on her and every movement he made to satisfy her only brought him more intense stimulation.

Emma was wanton upon him. Lost in a vision of lights and colors, in which every sense was tuned only to the joy of her body united with his, she felt as though her breasts had taken on a life of their own and that her sweet inner core had become everything that she was. She was nothing but this, and she wanted to be nothing but this—the full cup, the molten volcano, the dancing nymph, the throbbing violin of passionate love.

And then, when her head reeled with dizziness and her body had climbed to the peak of tension, he cupped her waist in his palms and lowered her more deeply onto him. With that movement the floodgates broke within, yielding wave upon wave of vibrating release. Adam held back for one last moment, savoring the uncontrolled massage of her inner tunnel upon him . . . and then he joined her in the throes of shuddering ecstasy.

For long moments afterward, neither could move. Emma lay with her head on his chest and her legs stretching down over his. His hands began to caress the tangle of her hair as it fanned out across her naked back. He let his fingers trail over her round buttocks and back up across the curve of her hips. He had never known anything like this feeling of lying here with her. It was all so right . . . so good.

"Are we on the floor?" she asked softly.

Adam grinned. "Feels that way from my angle."

Emma nestled her head back onto his chest. His body was the perfect bed—every angle and plane of it made just for her. "I feel . . . complete."

"Emma . . ." Adam tried to focus his thoughts. It was so hard. He'd never had to reach deep inside himself. "Emma, I want you to stay."

She looked up again, and he propped the crook of one arm behind his head to gaze into her green eyes. "Stay? But I must find—"

"Cissy, I know. I want you find her, and I'm going to help you find her. But after that . . ."

Emma stared at him. What was he asking? That she stay and be his mistress? That she never go on to become a nurse? And what if his wife heard of it, or decided to come? Did he want her to give up her life for him . . . to be nothing more than a kept woman?

"After that," she said softly, "I have my mission to fulfill. I suppose I am like the leopards. Being a nurse here in Africa is my dream, and I intend to make it come true."

"I don't want you to give up your dream, Emma. You can—" She stopped his words with a touch of her fingertips.

"Shh, Adam." Slowly she slid from his body and rolled him into her arms. "Let's not talk about tomorrow. It's impossible."

"But it's not impossible." Adam rose to his knees. "I don't believe anything you really want is impossible. Every dream I've had, I've made come true. I've forced it to come true, even against the odds."

"This is different." Emma stood and walked over to his bed. "You cannot force this dream . . . you cannot force me." She slid into bed and pulled the covers over her body. It felt warm and cozy beneath the puffed spread, and she stretched with the languorous satisfaction of a contented cat.

Adam stood with his gaze fixed on the window. For the first time in his life, he'd found what he had been seeking . . . and she would not come to

im. She refused to belong. He couldn't have her.
He watched her eyes closing in peacefulness.

He'd go to her and tell her everything. That was
what held her back . . . the secrets he'd kept. He'd
tell her the whole damned story. But no, he *couldn't*
do that. And there was something else keeping her
from him even more powerfully. Clarissa? Cissy?
Emma's own determination never to belong to any
man? Her dead mother's past? What was it?

"Adam," Emma called out to him sleepily.
"Adam, please come to me, my love."

Sighing with resignation, he padded over to the
bed and eased his large frame beside her. She drew
him into her arms and nestled her head against his
shoulder. Never mind about tomorrow, she
thought. Never mind that she knew almost nothing about this man who held her. Never mind that
life promised only emptiness without him. For now
. . . for this moment, she knew he loved her
and wanted her. And that was enough.

## Chapter Fifteen

✦ ✦ ✦ ✦

*Sky is his ceiling, grass is his bed,*
*Saddle is the pillow for the cowboy's head;*
*Way out West where the antelope roam,*
*And the coyotes howl round the cowboy's home;*
*Where the miner digs for the golden veins,*
*And the cowboy rides o'er the silent plains;*
*Where the prairies are covered with chaparral frail,*

*And the valleys are checkered with cattle trails;*
*Where the eagles scream and the catamounts squall,*
*The cowboy's home is the best of all.*

— "Speaking of Cowboy's Home"

*When I was one-and-twenty*
*I heard a wise man say,*
*"Give crowns and pounds and guineas,*
*But not your heart, away;*
*Give pearls away and rubies,*
*But keep your fancy free."*
*But I was one-and-twenty—*
*No use to talk to me.*

*When I was one-and-twenty*
*I heard him say again,*
*"The heart out of the bosom*
*Was never given in vain;*
*'Tis paid with sighs a plenty*
*And sold for endless rue."*
*And I am two-and-twenty,*
*And oh, 'tis true, 'tis true.*

— A. E. Housman
"A Shropshire Lad"

"LIONS. WE HAVE a lot of trouble with lions." Adam buttered a thick slice of toast as he spoke. Emma observed him across the table, her eyes following his every movement. "They get old, you see, and their teeth and claws start to fall out. Then they can't hunt as well, and they start to search for easy prey. That's when they go after my cattle."

"They could decimate your profits, I imagine." Emma lifted her teacup to her lips.

"Exactly. I supply a lot of beef to Mombasa. And when the rail line comes through my land, I'll be able to increase my herds because the transportation will be so much simpler."

Emma nodded. The dreamer was speaking, and she warmed to this part of Adam that merged with the dreamer in her. It felt so odd, and so good, to be here breakfasting with him. The sun had barely risen over the acacia trees behind the house. A warm pink glow dyed the white tablecloth and lit up the pitcher of water. They had risen together—she and Adam—in the semidarkness of dawn. Together they had bathed and dressed, she in a soft blue muslin dress, he in his denims and shirt. They had spoken little but touched often, the gentle, intimate caresses of people who know one another well, the soft kisses of fulfilled lovers . . . the secret gazes of those who share body and soul.

"We talked before about the town to be built inland—Nairobi," Adam said quietly. "It will be built in the highlands, where the good farming land is to be found. That ought to bring an even higher demand for my beef, and I can upgrade my ranch . . . if I can keep the lions down."

"Yes, I've heard of the city." Emma thought back to Nicholas's excited panoply of dreams. Somehow those dreams sounded so different from Adam's; somehow Nicholas's voice had betrayed greed, gain for gain's sake. Adam spoke lovingly of his plans, as though striving for his dreams were more important than achieving them.

"Everyone's talking about the town." Adam drank the last of his coffee. "Frankly, I'm not too crazy about the idea. Civilization has ruined the American West, and it'll destroy this land too if someone doesn't set out to take care of it—starting right now."

"But there's so much empty land . . . and so many animals."

"Uncountable herds of bison used to range across the West. Now you have trouble finding any, thanks to wholesale slaughter. And it'll happen here, too. Sometimes I see a herd of elephants walking toward a waterhole, and the line of them stretches out so far that I start to doubt myself. But then I walk down on the harbor and see the rows of hundreds of tusks piled up, and I see it all so clearly again. For every dainty little earring, an elephant dies. For every damned dagger hilt, a rhino dies."

"Adam . . ." Emma wanted to reach out to him, to erase the dark side of his vision into the future.

"I have a lot of trouble with people who don't respect the land. And cityfolk don't know anything but hunting for fun—the future of the animals be damned." Adam set his cup on the table and looked away. His jaw was rigid, the tiny muscle in the corner twitching.

"You won't let it happen," Emma murmured. Adam turned to her, a question mark furrowing his brow. "You won't let them destroy the land and the animals. You'll work through the government somehow. You'll be named to some post, some ministry of wildlife—"

"I'm an American, Emma. And the British have their grip on this country so tight it'll be years before the Africans can get it back."

"Get it back?"

"Do you think the Africans are going to sit around and let you tell them what to do forever?" He glowered out the window at the wakening farm. "They have their own government, their own way of managing. Their own *civilization*—no mat-

ter how savage your government thinks they are.
. . . The white man's burden. Now that's a laugh."

Emma listened, her breathing shallow. Was
Adam speaking treason? Or was he only speaking
from his impassioned vision into the future? Would
his fury lead him to try to defeat the English? Did
he think the Germans would be better for the land
and the people of Africa than the English?

"Well, enough of politics and the future." Adam
broke into her thoughts before Emma could sort
through them. "But if you plan to stay in the protectorate, Emma, you'd better know what's going
on. One of these days things are going to get . . .
troublesome. And if you're smart, you'll know
where you stand. . . . Now, how about a ride?"

"On a horse?"

Adam grinned. "I don't have a Stanhope out
here. Not enough roads. But if you're too
sore . . ."

"I am *not* sore," Emma said, bristling slightly. "I
am quite a good rider now, if I do say so myself."

"Damned good."

"It's just that all my riding clothes are dirty from
the trip . . . and there's Tolito."

"I expect Tolito's still sleeping from his ordeal
last night. We'll drop by on our way out. Linde's
there with him, and she takes good care of him.
Besides—" Adam stopped himself, unsure. Then
he gazed into Emma's green eyes and he knew.
"Besides . . . I want you to see my ranch. I want
you to know where I live and what I do."

Emma nodded. She wanted to share it with him
. . . more than almost anything.

"We'll visit the villages and ask if anyone's heard
of your sister. And we'll be back here by noon to
check up on Tolito again. I have an English saddle

out at the stable. You can ride sidesaddle, and you won't need to change clothes."

For an instant Emma bent her head and studied the sunlit brass ring on her finger. It would be Clarissa's saddle she'd use. Clarissa's saddle . . . and this was her house, and her husband. She looked up, ready to refuse Adam's request. But then she saw his blue eyes, filled with the frank desire for her company.

"A ride would be lovely," she said softly. "I should like to see your ranch very much."

Together they returned to Adam's room and slipped on jackets and overcoats against the chill morning air. Emma set Adam's hat upon her head, and he straightened it for her. Hand in hand, fingers entwined, they left the house and walked briskly to the long row of stables behind it.

"Wait in the barn. It's warmer there, and I'll bring the horses in to saddle them." Adam gazed down at Emma, this fiercely independent woman, as he spoke. He felt an urge—unfamiliarly strong and insistent—to protect her. He reached out and fastened the top button of her wool jacket. "Get inside before you freeze. Soapy's probably still asleep in the loft."

Emma's eyes traced Adam for a moment, his buckskin coat tight across his broad shoulders as he turned toward the horses. Framed in the light of dawn, he seemed almost to glow. His dark hair and black hat, tan coat, indigo trousers, black boots . . . all set up a vibrant contrast with the emerald and pink of the landscape behind him. He was onyx on a field of rubies and sapphires, more brilliant because of his darkness.

Thrusting her hands into her jacket pockets, Emma hurried into the barn adjoining the stables.

No different from the barns she had meandered through as a dreaming child on the family's country estate in England, Adam's was filled with the aroma of sweet hay and well-used leather. Rows of saddles rested on a long beam supported by sawhorses. Bridles and other tack hung from bent nails on the wall. Bales of hay had been stacked in one corner, and a pile of loose hay lay beside the door.

Listening to the sounds of Adam releasing the horses, Emma ran her fingers along bright red-and-green-and-gray wool saddle blankets as she strolled through the barn toward the dim recesses at the back beneath the loft. Her heart felt light, somehow . . . airy.

All the confusion in her mind seemed to have settled into nice packages with little bows. Cissy was with Rolf, and soon enough Emma would find her. Tolito would get well after a trip to Mombasa to see a doctor. But Emma knew she had made a difference, and before long she would find a missionary doctor to join. Or perhaps she would start a clinic herself, here, on Adam's ranch. She would live in a little house like Soapy's, and she would sew curtains and learn to speak the native tongues as well as Adam . . . and sometimes she and Adam would ride out on the ranch—

Emma's thoughts halted abruptly. Her eyes, dimmed by golden dreams, had failed to focus, and she had bumped her knee on something hard and unmovable. Reaching down into the darkness, she felt along a rough wooden edge and realized with a start that it was one of the five crates Adam had brought from Mombasa. They were here, hidden, unopened. She touched their icy padlocks and metal bindings. Cattle dip . . . Nicholas's laughter echoed in her mind as she traced her fingers over stamped black letters she could barely read: King Farms Ltd., Mombasa, British Protectorate of East Africa.

"Who's there?" The click of a gun followed the harshly muttered words, and Emma froze. "I said who's there?"

"I . . ." She swallowed and turned her head a little to one side. "Emmaline Pickworth."

"Well, damn." Soapy's voice registered relief. "What're you doing pokin' around back here in the barn, ma'am? Ain't you got no sense? You coulda got yoreself killed."

Emma turned slowly and tried to smile. "Do forgive me, Soapy. I didn't mean to frighten you. I was just waiting for Adam."

"Mornin', partner!" Adam's hearty voice boomed through the lofty barn. "You're up just in time. Come help me saddle up this worthless old mare of yours."

"Shoot, boss." Soapy gave Emma one last sideways glance, then turned and shuffled toward the light. "Ol' Red cain't rightly be called mine no more. Yore little woman's took her over so's I ain't never gonna get her back."

Emma stared down at the crates. She had ridden with them all the way to the border and back to the ranch, and now here they sat. She'd hardly given them a thought, so intent had she been on finding Cissy. But now she realized this might be her last chance to know—to *really know*—about Adam. Inside these crates were guns and ammunition . . . or cattle dip. And inside them lay the proof of Adam's guilt or innocence.

She reached out and lifted one of the padlocks,

turning it this way and that in her hand. Then she squinted back at the wall full of tack and tools. Letting the lock fall against the crate, she closed her eyes for a moment and made her decision. She must open a crate.

"Emma!" Adam called to her. She could hear the horses stamping impatiently. "Are you coming?"

Taking a deep breath, she turned and found her way toward him. "I used to sit in our barn in England," she said, replacing the turmoil she felt inside with a pleasant memory. "I'd sit and read for hours and hours in the hay, and no one knew where I was. Father said I was wasting my time, but Mama said I was just dreaming . . . and without dreams life was worth nothing."

She slid her boot into the stirrup and started to pull herself up when she felt Adam's lifting hands at her waist. Silently he adjusted her reins and straightened the saddle blanket. He pictured Emma stretched out across the hay, reading a book of poetry or something. He could see her father, purple veins throbbing at his temples as he criticized her. And he could almost see her mother. . . .

"Once I run off—took a apple pie, too, right off'n the kitchen winder—and stayed gone three days." Soapy was settling his hat on his head. "Slept in a ol' ditch and got rained on. When I finally decided to go home, Pa took one look at me and tol' me to go milk the dad-burned cows. He'd never know'd I'd been gone."

"We'd miss you around here, Soap." Adam grinned lightly as he followed Emma out of the barn. "Stick around, old partner."

"I ain't goin' nowheres . . . 'cep' down to the house for some grub. That trail cook you got is plain terrible."

Tolito was sleeping peacefully when they looked in, and Emma chose not to wake him. Linde had bathed his wounds twice in the night, and Emma knew the woman had hardly slept. Even so, her dark eyes sparkled with life, and her smile seemed to warm the very corners of the room. Telling Linde to get some rest, Emma and Adam left the little house.

To Emma, the morning ride was glorious. The horses pranced through the dewy grass, shaking their heads and snorting happily in the crisp air. Dozens of Thompson's gazelles, their black-and-white tails flicking briskly, glanced up at the riders, then took flight with springing leaps. Hartebeests—Adam called them *kongoni*—watched sedately, their ears and horns sticking from their heads in perfect parallels. A mother rhino lifted her double-curved gray horns into the air as a warning to the intruders, then returned to grazing beside her baby.

Adam took Emma to his pumphouse and showed her the inner workings of the priceless machine he had imported. Drawing water from a borehole set deeply into the ground, the pump supplied a lifeline for the cattle during the dry seasons. Afterward they rode along his fences, and Adam stretched his arm across the land as far as Emma could see to show her the boundaries of his ranch—endless acres, unfenced and unmarked.

He took her to his three large ponds and pointed out the lion pugmarks—which looked like Aunt

Prue's kitten's pawprints only many sizes larger—sunk into the muddy shoreline. A hippo Adam called Jojo lived in the ponds. He said it had wandered away from its family during an exceptionally rainy year and had found his ponds. Adam and Emma dismounted and sat on a warm rock, watching Jojo surface to blow streams of mist into the blue sky.

Later in the morning, Adam guided them to two villages, one Wakamba and the other Samburu. Neither had seen or heard of a white woman or a white man wandering across the plains. In fact, they had never seen a white woman at all, and Emma found herself again subjected to the curious, half-frightened inspection of the African children. And again, she surveyed them carefully, and her conviction was reaffirmed. These people needed medical care badly, and she meant to be the one to supply it.

When they rode back into the farm complex, Emma went straight to Tolito. He had awakened and was staring lifelessly at the ceiling. Adam hunkered down on the stool and took his friend's hand. Leaning over, he spoke quietly and intently to the African.

Emma took in the little scene, Adam talking and Tolito nodding wordlessly. Then her gaze traveled to Linde. The woman had dressed in a brilliant green gown and peacock-blue headwrap. She had let it fall away from her face and the rippling waterfall of her black hair. Her eyes were locked on the two figures before her, and she followed every movement of Adam's lips. For a moment Emma's heart faltered as she imagined this gorgeous creature in Adam's arms . . . his secret lover. How understandable it would be.

She, the most beautiful woman for countless miles; he, the wealthy landowner taking her to his empty bed.

But then she began to see clearly. Linde's look of utter devotion was focused not on Adam but on Tolito, and whenever their eyes met, her gaze softened, melted. Was she really Tolito's sister . . . or was she his lover?

"Linde," Emma spoke softly, not wanting to interrupt Adam, "where are the bandages? We must rebind Tolito's ribs."

The young woman hurried into the adjoining room and returned with a small basket filled with torn sheets. Linde had poured the tincture Emma had made the day before into small clean bottles, and they, too, lay in the basket. Marveling at the woman's instinctive sense of order and cleanliness, Emma took the basket.

"You must rest, Linde," she said softly. "I shall sit with Tolito for a few hours. You must be very tired."

Linde shook her head adamantly. "I not rest."

"But you've been awake most of the night. Please—"

"No, memsahib." Linde looked away as her lower lip started to tremble. "I will not leave Tolito. My brother . . . saved me, and I—"

"Linde." Adam stood up abruptly, knocking over the stool as he rose. "Linde, we'll be back this afternoon. Send word if you need help."

The young woman nodded, her black eyes wide. Adam took Emma's arm and started to lead her out of the room.

"I beg your pardon." Emma jerked free and glared at him. "Linde was speaking to me when you interrupted, Adam. And I am staying right here with Tolito so that she can rest. Besides, I have to change the dressing on his back."

Adam looked from one woman to the other. Linde's eyes were those of a cornered animal, and he was glad. She'd said too much already. If Emma stayed here with her . . . He turned back, determined to force Emma to leave. But then he saw the flash of green in her eyes. She had made her choice, the choice he knew she would always make: she'd chosen her work over him.

"I'll be up at the house," he said under his breath, before walking out of the room and shutting the door behind him.

Emma checked Linde and saw that for the first time her golden skin had gone wan. Fingers trembling, Linde smoothed out her skirts and fluttered to Tolito's side. They spoke rapidly in earnest tones, and Linde's voice wavered to the point of breaking. Finally Tolito reached out and touched her arm softly. She nodded and sniffled, then stood up.

"Linde wants to help you." Tolito spoke slowly but confidently to Emma. "She will not leave me because she is my sister. We are one family. She says you are a powerful *laibon* from a magical land, and she wants to be your servant."

"A *laibon*?" Emma repeated, surprised. "Isn't that a witch doctor? Oh no, my dear Linde. I am not a *laibon*. I am a nurse. I have received special training to teach me how to care for sick people and to heal them. I do not need a servant."

Linde lowered her eyes sadly. "I am not anybody."

For a moment Emma frowned in confusion. "But of course you are somebody. You are Linde. You are Tolito's sister. You are—"

"No." Tolito broke into Emma's speech. "Linde is not anybody. She is half-blood. Not Masai. Not Somali. Not marry. Not wife. Not children. Not home."

Emma picked up the stool Adam had knocked over and sat down. For some reason she understood perfectly what Tolito was telling her. She knew what it was to feel as if you didn't belong . . . as if you were worth nothing to anybody. A movement caught her eye, and she turned to watch Linde begin removing the dressing on Tolito's back. Her careful fingers gently eased away the bandages, and her low voice spoke words of comfort all the while. And suddenly Emma saw it all.

"You shall work with me, Linde," she announced briskly. The young woman's dark eyes flashed in surprise. "After I have found my sister, I am going to start a clinic. My own clinic, here with the Masai and the Samburu and the Wakamba. And you shall be my assistant, my helper. I shall train you, though Lord knows you have more natural skill than most of the women at St. Thomas's. One day we shall bring a doctor from England, and we shall build a small hospital. And—"

Emma looked up and saw that Linde was weeping. Huge crystal drops welled in the depths of her ebony eyes and rolled down her cheeks into the soft folds of peacock-blue cotton at her neck.

For the remainder of the day, Emma labored with Tolito and Linde. She forced her thoughts away from Adam. The warmth in her heart from their loving had not grown cold, but she knew she could never be his. She must look in the crates to prove him innocent and clear his name with Nicholas Bond and the British government. And she must prepare her *own* future in this land. This was where it lay—here beside the ill and needy; here with the woman she would train to be a nurse. Her future did not lie with Adam in the big ranch house at the top of the hill. That would never be her destiny.

"Emma?" Adam pushed open the front door of the house and stopped in amazement. Soapy's living room had been transformed. His rough wooden table was spread with neat rolls of clean white bandages. All of the bottles from the crate had been removed and most of them emptied. He could hear them rattling in the huge vat of boiling water on Soapy's little cookstove. Two chairs and an old board had been fashioned into another table and covered with a white cloth. Across it lay knives, needles, spools of thread, scissors, spoons, and gleaming tin cups.

"Adam!" Emma bustled out of Tolito's room at the sound of Adam's voice. She had rolled her sleeves to her elbows and was wearing a brilliant white apron over her blue dress. Her hair had been pulled into a tight knot at the top of her head. Adam had never seen her smile so radiant.

"What are you doing in here?" He walked tentatively across the room, whose unfamiliarly scrubbed floorboards squeaked beneath his boots. The glass in the windowpanes shone golden pink with the setting sun, and the newly washed walls reflected the light.

"Oh, Adam. You should just see!" Emma threw her arms around his neck and kissed him on the cheek. "We've begun everything! Linde and I have started to prepare the clinic. She's going to be my assistant, you see, and I'm going to train her. I'm going to teach her everything I know. Oh, Adam, it's such a lovely idea, you can't imagine. She's perfect!" As the stream of excited words poured forth, Emma pulled Adam into Tolito's room. "She's so intelligent, and she has a wonderfully natural skill. We get along marvelously. She brought me lunch, and we ate together as though we might have been sisters. We've cleaned everything up . . . just look at this room. And we've boiled all the bandages now to reduce the chance of infection. We've thrown away almost all of those old medicines of yours and combined what we could into useful tinctures and washes. And we're boiling the rest of the bottles to use for future medicines. Which I am going to order—"

"Emma." Adam stopped the rush of words by kissing her hard on the lips. She caught her breath and looked up at him, her olive eyes sparkling with happiness. "I love you, Emma."

Glancing at Linde and Tolito, Emma saw that they could barely hide the smiles that tickled about their lips. She faced Adam again. "I'm very happy," she whispered.

His eyes lingered on hers, then traveled down to caress the line of her nose and lips and chin. He'd wanted her here on his ranch—he'd brought her. And by God, he'd find a way to keep her.

"Emma, I've gotten a message from the corral on my western border." He stroked the side of her face with a fingertip. "They think they've got lion trouble. I'm heading over there, and I won't be back until late. Soapy's going with me, but you'll be okay here. There's nothing to be afraid of. Go n up to the house when you're ready. I've ordered you some supper."

"Thank you." Emma took his big hand in hers and wove her fingers through his. How it could all work out, she could not foresee, but that it would, she suddenly had no doubt.

"I've arranged to have Tolito go by train to Mombasa when you think he's feeling well enough. And I've sent out a party to contact all the villages on my ranch for any sign of your sister."

Emma smiled up at him. This man was good. His heart was honest and clean. How could she have doubted him? He cared for people, and for his land and the animals. He was just and fair. She had seen nothing—*nothing*—to condemn him, and she would tell Nicholas Bond that very thing.

Adam led Emma out onto the small verandah of the house. Then he took her in his arms and lifted her against him, his lips full and warm on hers. She was so soft, he thought, so feminine with her gentle curves and silky skin. He ran his hands down her back and over the swell of her hips, and she rose into him with returning kisses. Her arms twined around his back, her fingers stroking up and down the valleys and hills. He could hear her breath growing short as her breasts pressed against his chest. Cupping her head in his palms, he drew her face away and gazed into her eyes.

"Emma King." He said the name caressingly. "I'm coming back for you tonight."

"I'll be waiting." Emma's voice was husky, and Adam almost abandoned the call to hunt lions in favor of a much headier prey. She slipped her hand down the front of his chest, her fingers trailing fire.

"Be careful out there," she whispered. "I want you with me tonight."

Before he lost all self-control, Adam tore himsel away and ran down the steps to his horse. When he looked back, she had vanished.

The moon hung high in the sky when Emma finally left the little house and walked old Red back up to the stables. She had eaten with Linde again, and her heart warmed to the feeling of having a new friend. It was as if she had found a soulmate in Linde, so closely did their movements and ideas mesh. They spoke a rambling mixture of English and Swahili and Masai, enough that few messages went astray. Linde learned quickly, and Emma found herself eagerly anticipating the day when they would open their clinic and begin to work together. With Linde translating at her side, Emma could even teach classes in nutrition and child care.

Sighing contentedly, Emma led the horse into the stable and filled the manger with new hay. Then she removed the saddle and hoisted it into her tired arms. Tramping into the barn, she found a lamp hanging from the door and set the saddle down to light it. She did feel perfectly safe here— the soft call of the night birds, the gentle chirp of crickets, and the occasional grunt of a hunting beast were all as familiar now as the squeaking of her brass bed had been in London.

She set the saddle on a beam and leaned back against it, looking up at the rows of pitchforks and rakes, brands and reins, hanging on the wall. Her heart was light and full and brimming with hope.

There remained one task at hand, she reminded

herself. She must open a crate. It would be full of cattle dip, and she would take some of it to Nicholas and laugh in his face, just as he had laughed in hers.

Straightening, she walked to the wall, lifted an iron crowbar, and set it on the floor. Then she found a pair of tongs and a small wire cutter. Tucking the tools under one arm, she carried the lantern with her free hand as she walked past the ladder to where the crates were stacked beneath the loft. She dropped the tools to the floor, and they clanged hollowly on the bare wooden planks. Hanging the lantern on a nail, she surveyed the chests.

They stood in two piles—three crates in one, two in the other. The top chest of the smaller stack was just at waist level. Emma picked up the crowbar and inserted it between the hasp and the padlock. Pulling with all her strength, she jerked and jerked and jerked—but nothing moved. She tried to place the bar under the lid but could find no leverage. Tossing down the crowbar, she picked up the tongs, worked them into the hook of the padlock, and twisted, leaning her whole body into the effort. Again, nothing moved.

Disgusted, Emma stood back and glared at the chest. Then she picked up the wire cutters. The padlock was far too heavy for them to be of any use, but perhaps if she could cut the iron bands across the chest, the lid would open far enough for her to slip in the crowbar. Climbing onto the top of the crate, she hoisted her skirts around her knees and began to snip at the iron bands. It was tedious, backbreaking work with the tiny cutters, and Emma almost threw them down and gave up. Adam was innocent, after all. She thought back on all the ridiculous things Nicholas had told her. That he was a slaver. . . . Across her mind floated images of Miriam, Tolito, Linde. Could these loyal workers be slaves? That he worked with the Germans and knew exactly what had become of Cissy. . . . She thought of Burkstaller and Adam muttering together behind the wagon and Adam paying the German with her money.

Growing uncomfortable with this last picture, Emma threw herself into her labor. Nicholas had accused Adam of working with the Africans to incite them against the British . . . and didn't Adam know all the native languages, have contact with many of the villages, employ members of at least three different tribes?

"Damn!" Emma sat down hard and tossed the cutters onto the crate. Adam couldn't be like that! He had to be the sort of man she'd dreamed he was, the sort of man whose gentle nature and kindness and fun he had shown her again and again. But was she being childishly romantic and naive? People could play many roles, especially if they had a great deal to gain by them. Money. Power. Land. These were the stakes for which men played their games.

Her heart weakening, Emma slid from the crate. She'd have to find another tool, something better. As she leaned against the wooden box and rolled her head around to loosen her stiff neck, her eyes fell on a moonlit shape above her in the loft. Its dark rectangular sides glinted with soft silver light. Curious . . . half-afraid for the first time, Emma raised her skirts and padded softly to the ladder.

Lifting the lamp from its nail, she began to ascend into the loft. It was not easy climbing through the tangle of her skirts, but when she finally reached the top, she knew the climb had been well worth her efforts.

Instead of a hay-filled space with pitchforks and horseshoes, as she had expected, Emma found herself walking into a tiny but neatly kept office. A small wooden desk, its rolling desk chair, and a heavy bookshelf lined one sloping wall. Along the other rested a small iron bed with a brightly pat-terned yellow-and-blue quilt. Soapy's sleeping quarters while Tolito was in his house, no doubt. But this desk? Surely Soapy did not keep Adam's books.

Emma slipped onto the chair and ran her hands over the top of the desk, fumbling with fountain pens, inkwells, and papers. Then she clicked open the side drawer. File folders! Perhaps this was what she needed more than an opened crate. She lifted the first folder she found and leaned back in the squeaky chair. It was a record of cattle transporta-tion, sales, credits, and charges. The next held neat copies of invoices, nothing untoward as far as Emma could see.

Leaning forward, she ran her eyes along the carefully lettered folders, stopping at the one labeled *Guns*. Pulling it out, Emma opened it with shaking hands. Did she want to see? Did she really want to know? The first pages were lists of shipping orders, crates arriving in Momba a. She read them as quickly as she could, wanting to believe there were no more ship-ments than a normal rancher might have or-dered. Then she came to a long list of African names, and beside each was listed a weapon. Some were shotguns, some were revolvers, most were rifles.

Emma blinked back the tears that stung her eyes, and wiped her palms on her skirt. Shoving the folder to one side, she continued her search along the file drawer. *Headquarters.* She pulled out the folder and spread it open. There was a property deed for a building in Mombasa. There was a small blueprint showing rooms labeled "Office" and "Storage."

Emma pushed it away, her stomach rolling in pain, and pulled out another file. *Burkstaller, Dietrich.* She peered at the sheet of paper through blurred eyes: "Payment for Services Rendered." The first column of figures was labeled "Transportation of Guns."

Feeling faint, Emma grabbed the files and tried to stuff them back into the drawer. Unable to make her fingers cooperate, she stood up, shaking. What could she do? She must escape! She must find Cissy and leave. Nothing was as it seemed here. . . .

Stumbling across the floor, she grabbed the lantern and swung around for one last look at the damning files spread across the desk and floor. As she whirled, the light fell on a long, gleaming shape in the corner beside the bed. A rifle! Unthinking, she ran over and picked it up, cradling it in her arm. She would shoot open the crate, and then Adam could never deny his treachery. . . . No, she would take the rifle and a horse and run away . . . No, she would—

"Emma?" At the sound of his booming voice, her blood ran cold. She spun around, the gun at her shoulder. "Emma, is that you up there?"

Emma stared down at Adam. His tall form loomed in the moonlit doorway of the barn. Slowly and carefully, she cocked the rifle.

"Stay away from me, Adam King," she said icily. "If you come one step closer, I shall shoot you."

# Chapter Sixteen

✦ ✦ ✦ ✦

*I have promised you, darling, that never*
*Will words from my lips cause you pain;*
*And my life it will be yours forever,*
*If you only will love me again.*
*Must the past with its joys all be blighted*
*By the future of sorrow and pain?*
*Must the vows that were spoken be slighted?*
*Don't you think you could love me again?*

—"Red River Valley"

*What have I done for you,*
    *England, my England?*
*What is there I would not do,*
    *England, my own?*
*With your glorious eyes austere,*
*As the Lord were walking near,*
*Whispering terrible things and dear*
    *As the Song on your bugles blown,*
        *England—*
    *Round the world on your bugles blown! . . .*

*They call you proud and hard,*
    *England, my England—*
*You with worlds to watch and ward,*
    *England, my own!*
*You whose mailed hand keeps the keys*
*Of such teeming destinies,*

*You could know nor dread nor ease*
  *Were the Song on your bugles blown,*
    *England—*
  *Round the Pit on your bugles blown!*

—William Ernest Henley
"England, My England"

"PUT THAT GUN DOWN, woman!" Adam took a step forward into the moonlit barn. "What's gotten into you?"

"You're not who I thought you were." Emma left the lantern on the floor of the loft and began to descend the ladder, the cocked rifle at her shoulder. "Just . . . just move out of the way and let me pass. I'm releasing you from your contract, but I shall take a horse. Send my clothing to Delamere at Mombasa—"

"Emma, what happened?" Adam started toward her, but he stopped when she leapt down from the ladder and lifted the rifle sight to her eye. He wasn't afraid of the gun—she didn't have a clue how to aim the thing, and it probably was unloaded anyway. But it was *Emma*. . . . What had happened to send her off half-loco like this? He'd seen her unhappy before; he'd seen her drunk; he'd seen her mad as hell. But never this.

She sidled toward him, and he could tell her arms were trembling as she struggled to maintain the heavy weapon at shoulder level. He watched her edging past while she tried to keep one eye on him, one eye on the gunsight, and see her way to the door at the same time. If she hadn't been so upset, he'd have wanted to laugh and sweep her up in his arms.

"I've seen your files," she whispered, walking slowly into the rectangle of moonlight on the floor. "I know everything. The guns. Burkstaller. Your headquarters in Mombasa—"

Adam's arm shot out in a cobra-quick move and jerked the rifle from her hands before she had time to react. Emma froze, her head light with the sudden realization of her predicament. And then the anger flooded in.

"Shoot me, then, Adam King," she shouted, throwing out her chest and taking a deep breath. "Shoot me right now—because I am going to tell Nicholas everything! I am English, and my country comes above everything else! I shall reveal how you've betrayed my government . . . how you've imported guns and ammunition into the protectorate and—"

"And assigned one rifle to each of my herdsmen, whose names are carefully listed beside the make and numbers of their weapons." Adam flicked open the Winchester's chamber and nodded in satisfaction. Empty. "I supply rifles and shotguns to my foremen and hunters, revolvers to my nightwatchmen. Delamere and every other landowner in the protectorate does the same. Bond knows that as well as he knows anything. I'm sure he would act fascinated to learn about the headquarters of my business operations in downtown Mombasa. But you might as well know, Emma, that my office sits right beside the main railway offices—"

"You're lying!" Emma stood rigid, fighting for control. "You always have the perfect answer. Nicholas told me you have a secret headquarters from which you carry out your operations."

"My office building is hardly a secret to Bond.

He walks past my place every time he's on his way to see his boss. I usually tip my hat at him when I'm in town, but—"

"Stop it. Just stop it, Adam." Emma buried her face in her hands, fingers pressed against her eyes. Dear God—how she wanted to believe Adam! It was all too much, too difficult. And suddenly she was so tired. All her dreams had risen to a peak this day with her hours visualizing the clinic with Linde . . . and then they had come crashing around her ears when she'd opened Adam's files. Now he was trying to build them up again. Trusting him would be so easy, but . . .

"Emma, please. Just tell me what made you go looking through my files. What did you want to know about me?" He knew he should be angry with her, but she looked so forlorn standing alone in his barn, crying into her bare hands and stiff with the cold night air.

"I was not prying." She sniffled. "I was . . . searching for something. A—a tool."

"What kind of a tool? Why didn't you just ask Jackson?"

"I just . . ." Emma faltered. Lying to him was no good. She hadn't the mental strength for it now. And her lies on top of his could only be doubly wrong. "I know all about Burkstaller. He brings you weapons, Adam! I read your file!"

"Of course he does. So does Delamere and anyone else coming up from the coast for a visit. It's kind of a tradition among the settlers. One of those crates back under the loft is for Delamere, in fact. I'll take it to him next time I visit at Njoro. See, I don't get down to Mombasa that often, and I have shipments coming in all the time. Burkstaller sometimes spends his leaves on the ranch here. We kind of keep it under wraps. The Germans probably wouldn't take too kindly to the idea . . . Emma, what do you think I am, anyway? What kind of dirt has Bond been filling your head with?"

Emma's shoulders sagged. If she told him, he'd only deny it. Adam had all the answers. Nicholas would assure her Adam had his "story"—his alibi—worked out to perfection. No holes. Every track covered.

She looked up at the man she loved. His blue eyes shone in the silver light. He was frowning, but even the downturn of his mouth was beloved to her. His soft shirt molded against the powerful lines of his chest, and his neckerchief rippled gently in the night breeze. All she wanted was for him to take her in his arms. To tell her he loved her. To take her to the big house and slowly undress her under the light of the stars . . .

"If you don't want to talk about it, that's all right by me." Adam shifted the rifle into his left hand. "I'm not a man to make a person talk if he doesn't want to. Words usually just cause trouble anyhow. You look at my actions if you want to know what kind of man I am, Emma. If you want to know me, don't go poking around in my business files or talking to some rattlesnake of a man who'd just as soon put a bullet through my head. If you want to know me—watch me."

With that, Adam leaned the rifle against a bale of hay and grabbed Emma's arm, drawing her roughly against him. She moved rigidly, despairing confusion still dominating her thoughts.

"I take what I want—clear and open." His eyes were hooded, their blue now deepened into indigo. Kissing her brusquely, he crushed her breasts against his chest, then pulled back and stared at her with a taunting smile playing about his lips. "You still haven't figured me out, have you?"

Emma tilted backward in his bruising embrace, wanting to be free. "No, I—" The words caught in her parched throat. "You're always different . . . I—I can't count on you. I can't trust you!"

He threw back his head and laughed. "Me? One minute you're spouting words of love, the next you're pulling a gun on me. I'll be damned if I can keep up with *you*. Let me tell you something, Emma." He traced her lips with a burning finger. "Nothing's sure in this world . . . nothing but the heat between a man and a woman. You want something to count on? Count on that."

Before she could respond, he lifted her into his arms and lowered her onto a pile of hay. Crouching over her, one knee resting beside each of her hips and his hands on either side of her head, he stared boldly down at her.

"I shall not allow you to trap me like this, Adam King," she hissed, grabbing his wrists. "I'll not be another of your victims!" Hurling her body against his, she writhed against him until he tumbled to one side in the hay. But as she pummeled his chest, struggling to free herself from the steel bonds that pinned her, she realized he was chuckling.

"You'll never be a victim," he said with a laugh. "You're too much of a hellion—and, unfortunately, I like that."

Emma glared at him. "At least you know what I'm like."

Adam nodded. But *she* would rather shoot him than believe what he had told her about himself. The thought fanned the flicker of anger inside him. She had been ready to pull the trigger on him— would have accepted his death before accepting his innocence. His mouth hardening, he searched her face as she lay stiff and haughty in his arms.

"What do you want me to be?" he growled.

She shot him a look of insolence and tossed her golden head. "You can't seem to be anything but what you are—a rough cad! A conniving rake—"

He crushed the words from her mouth with an angry kiss. Her stubbornness was hard enough to stomach . . . but this defiance! An urge to dominate her, to control even her thoughts swept through him. Subconsciously aware that the only card he had to play was her physical hunger for him, he pulled her hard against his chest and began kissing her. He would weaken her, make her helpless in his arms with wanting him.

Catching her breath at the sudden onslaught of passion, Emma instinctively sensed his attack. The thought of gaining the upper hand became foremost in her mind. Without considering the consequences, she hurled herself into battle.

"Oh no, Adam King," she said with a husky laugh. "You'll not beat me at this game!" Catching his hands that had already begun to fumble at her breast, she hoisted herself atop him and curled her bare thighs around his hips. Stretching his arms over his head and pinning them with one hand, she leaned across him and began to kiss his forehead. Her heavy breasts weaving before his face, she ran the tip of her tongue down his nose, across his eyelids, over his cheeks. Finally she began a slow and teasing kiss upon his lips.

He stiffened beneath her as her hips swayed heavily on his loins. Caught off balance by her actions, he could do nothing but gaze up into her green eyes, wanting her. A groan drifted from his mouth as she began to run her fingers down his long arms and across his chest. Could she feel his heart raging, his body the victim of her animal sensuality?

"Emma." He drew her against him, no longer caring about anything but this woman. *His* woman. Easing her face to his, he began to kiss her again, this time slowly, languorously, the way he knew she liked. Her sigh of pleasure warm on his lips, she eased softly over him and slid her legs down his thighs.

"Oh, Adam." What was happening? The battle had suddenly dissipated, leaving only a searing hunger in its wake. All she could think of was his long body so hard against hers, his lips coaxing her into arousal with every kiss. She rolled back into the hay, eager for the unfolding of their passion— but her head fell against something hard and cold. The butt of the rifle.

A flood of reality washed over her. The rifle. She had read his files; she had found out everything; she had almost shot him for it. And now—she had fallen into his trap again! Biting her lip, she suddenly covered her face with her hands and curled into a tight ball.

"Dear God!" she moaned. "You have to stop . . ."

"To stop what?" His voice was edged with bitterness. "Stop what, Emma? Wanting you? Needing you?" Pulling away from her he rose to his feet and put his hat on his head. "You want me to stop loving you, Emma?"

Her heart nearly breaking with anguish, she buried her face in the fragrant hay. Hearing his words echo again and again, it was all she could do to keep from spilling out her own avowals of love.

"What shall I do? What shall I do?" she whispered into the hay, clutching handfuls of it tightly in her hands.

As though he had heard her, Adam spoke softly as he walked to the barn door. "You do what you think best, Emma. If you want to leave, you can take old Red. She's yours. But if you want to come back down to the house, you're welcome. I'll light a fire in your fireplace."

Adam turned and strode from the barn. Emma rolled to her knees and watched him stop and confer with Soapy, who had been coming up the path. The shorter man nodded, then scratched his head in the familiar sign of bemusement he often used in her presence. Clearly there was nothing odder to Soapy than this woman who was always creeping about, pulling guns on Adam, losing the carriage to runaway horses, and otherwise making a total idiot of herself. After a moment, the two men lit cheroots and ambled slowly down to the house.

Emma glanced around her at the scene of her latest ineptitude. The rifle leaned against a haybale. The crates stood sealed as tightly as ever, the useless crowbar beside them. The tiny lamp in the loft flickered and went out.

Sighing, Emma wandered to the barn door and leaned against the rough frame, feeling a surge of now-familiar despair. Cissy was lost and she had no idea where to look. Her parents were dead. She was no closer to achieving her dream of nursing in Africa than she had been when fantasizing about it at Aunt Prue's house. She had trusted her quest to a man who was probably a criminal . . . or at the very least, one who put his own interests ahead of the law. The only proof of his innocence that would satisfy her was locked inside impenetrable crates.

Worst of all, she had lost her heart to a man with whom she had no hope of a future. And she could think of no way to retrieve her heart before it was irreparably broken.

As she lifted her face to the shining moon, praying for an answer, she realized she could see no smiling Aunt Prue with words of wisdom. She could not hear her mother's gentle voice. Even Cissy failed to admonish, with those sapphire eyes sparkling. No answers.

In the end Emma sighed, lifted her skirts, and started down the path. No, this time there were no answers—no simple way out. This time she must simply go forward . . . following her heart as she always had.

She pushed open the back door to the house and headed slowly down the hall. Adam's door was open, but she slipped past it into the room Jackson had shown her the day before. Oh, she was tired . . . so tired. Her heart was aching and her mind a tumult of unrest. A fire blazed brightly in the bedroom fireplace, and Emma sat down on the hard wooden chair before it. She stretched out her legs and rested her stiff boots on the iron grate. Then she leaned her head back on the rough slat and closed her eyes.

Emma awoke to the vision of a snowy pillow stretching out before her eyes. It smelled of fresh strong soap and sunshine and morning air. She breathed deeply, then lifted her eyes to the long beam of sunlight slanting across the bare wooden floor, creeping over her blue dress and petticoats that hung from the chair before the fire. A pile of gray ashes rested somberly on the stone floor of the fireplace. Emma knew at once that she was wearing her long white gown . . . and she knew how she had come to be wearing it.

Adam. She closed her eyes, imagining him finding her asleep the night before, quietly undressing her . . . caressing her body with his gaze . . . then carrying her to bed and carefully tucking the sheets beneath her chin. Twice now he had done this thing. How strange that she should feel so comfortable with a man's touch. She had never planned to allow any man to come that close to her heart and soul and body.

But now the day was passing—she could see by the sun it was well onto noon. First she must check Tolito, then tell her men to prepare the wagons. She would leave the following morning at dawn.

Adam had already gone by the time Emma dressed and went into the dining room. Jackson told her the bwana was on rounds, a routine he performed each morning after breakfast. He would not return until lunchtime. She ate quickly, then hurried down the path toward the little house, anxious to make certain Tolito had stabilized before she left him. Adam had promised to send him to Mombasa, and Emma planned to make him as comfortable as possible for the trip.

When she entered the house, Linde rushed out of Tolito's bedroom. She had not dressed in her usual colorful cottons but was wearing a thin white gown. Her hair flew about her shoulders as she grabbed Emma's hands and pressed them to her forehead.

"Linde!" Emma cupped the young woman's chin in her palm and lifted her face. "What's the matter? Has something happened?"

"Tolito has great pain!" The large brown eyes were wide with fear.

"Linde, why did you not come for me?" Emma pulled away and ran into the room. She could see at once that Tolito's condition had worsened. He was curled into a trembling ball, and though he tried to keep quiet, he groaned piteously whenever the pain became too great.

Emma swept to his side and turned him away from the wall where he had hidden his face. "Tolito, it is Memsahib Emma." She tried to calm her voice, knowing the anxiety in it would only frighten him more. "You are having pain this morning. Where is your pain, Tolito?"

At that, the man burst forth with a stream of loud, half-weeping explanation in a language Emma did not know. She gripped his hand and turned to Linde.

"His shoulder!" Linde translated. "He says it is his shoulder, and that the evil spirit of Bwana Bond was in the lion that attacked him—and now he surely will die!"

"The evil spirit of Bwana Bond? Nicholas Bond?" Emma frowned in confusion. Whatever could he be talking about? She decided he must be raving and the only solution was to sedate him as quickly as possible. "Tolito, you are *not* going to die unless you make up your mind to. Linde, fetch the whiskey that Bwana King brought in."

Linde ran into the sitting room and returned at once with a half-empty bottle of whiskey under one arm. "I gave the rest to him last night," she whispered. "Much pain. Very bad spirit of Bwana Bond."

Emma grabbed the bottle and poured a tin mug

full of the liquor, then sat on the little stool and lifted Tolito's head. He drained the mug at once.

"First of all, you must stop this nonsense about spirits if you ever want to be a nurse, Linde," Emma said fiercely. She held her palm over Tolito's forehead and knew at once he had a dangerously high fever. "Your brother was wounded by a lion, and Bwana Bond could not possibly have any reason to wish evil upon Tolito. Just because he and Bwana King do not like each other is no reason to blame these wounds on him."

Linde nodded, her eyes wide. Clearly she had had a long and difficult night, and Emma knew she should be gentler with the girl. But honestly—such nonsense! "Now tell me why you did not send for me at once. Tolito has been like this all night, hasn't he?"

Linde nodded again. "Bwana Soapy tell me you go away." Her lip trembled. "You are angry with Bwana King and will not come back."

"Oh, for goodness' sake." Emma rose from the stool, sighing in exasperation. "Just keep ladling this whiskey down him while I tend his shoulder. I shall have to do something at once. How I wish I had a doctor here."

Frustrated at her own lack of training—and even more so with this ridiculous notion about spirits—Emma stamped into the sitting room. She surveyed the table filled with medicines and the other covered with clean instruments. But what could *she* do? In fact, she'd been reluctant to do more to Tolito's shoulder than clean it. The thought of working with bone and deeply torn tissue was almost more than she could bear. Yet something had to be done, or the man might not survive the trip to the coast.

Rolling up her sleeves, she filled a tin pot with tools and bottles of medicine. Then she carried it back into the bedroom and spread everything out on the small table beside the bed. She had watched countless operations, and she had provided the primary nursing assistance during many of them. But to work on living human flesh herself . . .

She swallowed, breathed up a prayer, and turned to Linde. "You shall assist me whilst I operate. Turn up all the lamps, open the window, and shut the door. Your job is to give me the instruments I ask for, and to keep Tolito as comfortable as you can. Do you understand?"

"Yes, Memsahib Emma." Linde smiled gamely. "You are going to make Tolito well."

What seemed like hours later, Emma rose stiffly from her position over Tolito's prone body and turned to look out the window. A wild commotion of barking dogs and scurrying children had erupted in the houses just below the office buildings. Emma listened numbly to the noises, then turned back to her patient.

He was lying on his back, looking up at her with glazed eyes. His dark face sagged, and his mouth hung open at an angle. He was alive. He was awake. And she had done it.

With Linde at her side, Emma somehow had managed to find the two ends of Tolito's dislocated shoulder. She had slipped them back together with the help of her patient's stoic, deathlike silence. Then she had cleaned the festering wound again, noting that the infection was dissipating under constant cleansing, and had stitched up the layers of loose, torn muscle and skin.

"You are going to get well now, Tolito. You are going to feel better soon. But you must know that you will not have complete use of this arm ever again," she said softly. It was better for the patient to know the truth at once. She had done the best she could, and even that might not be good enough. "You must go to Mombasa as soon as you feel well enough to travel."

"Tolito's arm not good before lion attack, Memsahib Emma." Linde gazed down at her brother as she spoke. "Tolito nearly die many years ago. His arm die then."

Emma wiped her patient's forehead with a damp cloth. "Well, it's certainly not going to be any better now. But I do think he will start to heal much more swiftly now that we've put everything back together and closed it up. You must see that he keeps drinking the whiskey, Linde. He must stay in this stupor for another day or two. Otherwise the pain will be too great."

"Whiskey gone, memsahib." Linde gestured to the empty bottle.

"Very well. I shall go up to the house and send down some more. I expect Adam will be home soon, and he'll—" She stopped her thoughts. She could not think of Adam in this trusting, comfortable way. She could not allow herself to rely on him. She was strong and able without him—and that was what she must *never* forget. "I shall send Jackson down with the whiskey."

"Thank you, memsahib." Linde touched her bloodstained hands to Emma's. The two women gazed at one another, comrades in their passion for this work. Emma knew she had found a true ally . . . someone who thought as she did, cared as she did, and would stand beside her no matter what.

"You are my friend, Linde," Emma whispered in wonderment.

"My sister." Linde smiled and touched her forehead to Emma's palms. Emma leaned forward and did the same, then she pulled away and hurried out of the room.

The dazzling sunshine blinded her for a moment when she stepped out onto the small verandah. She groped for the post and leaned against it, breathing in the fresh air and letting her eyes focus on the red dirt road and the whitewashed buildings. Fighting off the intense feeling that this farm was a place she loved, a place she could so easily call home, she walked down the steps.

Just then the sound of thundering hooves pounded into her consciousness, and a heaving stallion bolted around the corner of the little house, nearly knocking her down. She leapt backward as the horse skittered to a pawing halt.

"Emmaline!" Nicholas Bond's voice called across the yard. "Emmaline, I've found you!"

Shading her eyes with her hand, Emma squinted up at the tall figure on the prancing horse. Nicholas looked fine indeed. Clad in proper English riding clothes—a white shirt, khaki trousers, knee-high brown leather boots, brown riding jacket, and red cravat—he swept his hat from his tousled golden-red hair and smiled at her triumphantly as if he'd found a lost treasure.

"Good afternoon, Nicholas." Emma tipped her head politely. With that movement, her eyes fell on the streaks and splatters of blood covering her dress and ungloved arms and hands. " 'Welcome to King Farms. You've been riding all day?"

"And half the night." Dismounting, he strode toward her. "I have exciting news!"

"Cissy!" Emma ran to Nicholas and took hold of his wrists. "Oh, you've found her! Where is she?"

"Now just a moment, Emmaline." Nicholas detached Emma's hands and stepped back, laughing. "What in heaven's name have you been doing, slaughtering cattle? I knew you'd fallen in with King, but I didn't think he'd have you—"

"*Nicholas!* Where is my sister?"

"Calm down, my dear." Nicholas led his horse to the porch rail and carefully tied the reins. Then he stepped back and smiled warmly at Emma. "We've had a message."

"From Cissy? Oh, where is she?"

Nicholas pulled open his jacket and extracted a sealed envelope. "I do not know what the message says, my love. It was addressed to you, so I delivered it. I thought perhaps you'd like to read it yourself."

Emma grabbed the envelope and ripped it open with trembling fingers. "To Emmaline Pickworth," she read aloud. The message had been carefully printed. "Your sister is alive and well. We are holding her prisoner. She is hidden well. You will never find her. If you want your sister released, deliver a chest containing seventy-five thousand pounds in gold to the base of the large waterfall in the Aberdare mountain range one week from this date. Place the chest in the cave beside the falls, then go back to the pool. Your sister will come out of the forest there. Do not attempt to find us or to retrieve the gold. Do not involve the government in any way. If you do not follow these instructions, your sister will die."

Emma looked up at Nicholas, then glanced back at the letter. "But this was written two days ago! How shall we ever get there in time with the gold?

Oh, they've got her, and I shall never see her again!"

"We can make it in four days easily—and that allows five days for transporting the gold."

Emma's eyes sparked with sudden determination. "I shall start out for the waterfall and join up with the gold when it arrives with Adam's men," she said excitedly, her thoughts wavering between delirious joy and shattering anxiety as she paced back and forth. "But if it's not there in time, perhaps I can speak to the kidnappers and delay them until it comes. Oh, dear God, who could they be? Who would have stolen Cissy away?"

"The Germans, no doubt. Just look at this. 'Do not involve the government in any way.' Of course that is just what they want you to do."

"But I shan't! I shall never tell anyone—and you mustn't either. We shall follow all their instructions to the letter."

Nicholas smiled down at Emma. "My darling, you are so strong and beautiful." His voice was low, hypnotic. "I knew you would do everything in your power to save your sister. And I shall be with you every step of the way. But Emmaline, I beg you not to follow these instructions. Do not give over this ransom! I firmly believe Adam King and his bloody German conspirators are behind this. They plan to use the gold against the British government. Come away with me. Let me find your sister for you, and you can keep your gold! I love you so, my darling. Leave Adam King—break your pact with him—and be my wife. I'm asking you to marry me, Emmaline. Will you do it?"

Emma caught her breath. "Nicholas . . . I cannot disregard this letter! And I cannot think beyond it to any future, with you or anyone. I must find my sister before anything else."

Nicholas cast his eyes downward for a moment, then squared his shoulders resolutely. "Very well. I shall take you to the Aberdares. I've brought my most trusted men with me. We shall send them back to Tsavo to telegraph for your gold to be sent. Will you have any trouble obtaining the gold? Seventy-five thousand pounds is a great deal of money."

"I have it. And if I didn't, I should simply find a way to get it. There's nothing I shan't do to get Cissy away from those horrible men. Oh, I do hope she has been treated well. If they are brutish—if they've hurt her, or abused her . . ."

Emma fought to control the trembling in her limbs that had suddenly overtaken her, and Nicholas instantly took her in his arms. "There, there, Emmaline my love. I'm quite sure the Germans want only the gold. You must believe your sister is all right. Come now. Stop your crying and let's make our plans. I shall take you with me to the Aberdares and find the waterfall the letter mentions. I've been up there on a survey and know my way about. And we must send my men after the gold—"

"What in the hell is going on here?"

Surprised, Emma looked up to find Adam glaring at her from his horse. In an instant he had jumped down and was striding over.

"What are you doing on my land, Bond?" He jerked Emma out of Nicholas's arms and grabbed her shoulders, gazing at her bloodstained clothing with alarm.

"Oh, no, Adam. It's not what you think. I've been working in there." Emma gestured at the little house. "I—I've had to operate . . ." Her shoulders sagged as she tried to sort through all that she needed to tell him. "The most important thing is that we've had a message from Cissy! Not really from Cissy—from her kidnappers!"

"Kidnappers? Give me that." Adam tore the letter from Nicholas's hand and scanned it quickly. "You believe this, Emma?"

"Of course I do! Who would make up such a terrible lie?"

"I don't know, but it sounds like something out of some damn mystery book to me. This protectorate may be full of men working hard to make a buck, but they're not criminals. Nobody's ever been *kidnapped*, for crying out loud. If you want money, you go and rob the bank or borrow it from your neighbor, more likely. You don't go kidnapping some girl—nobody even knew your sister was going to be here. And this thing took some scheming."

Emma stared at Adam in disbelief. Was he, too, trying to dissuade her from going after Cissy? How could he expect her to do anything but obey the letter—even if it were a hoax, even if he himself were behind it?

"I don't care what you think." Emma mouthed the words carefully. She knotted her fists against the mounting barriers. "I'm going to get the gold and take it to that waterfall. And if my sister comes out of the forest, then I'll know it was real."

"And if she doesn't?"

"Then I shall have lost my money. But that's a chance I must take." Her nostrils flared and she trembled with determination.

Adam stared at the ground for a moment. Then

he turned on Nicholas. "Where did you get this letter, Bond?"

"An African brought it to the station at Tsavo yesterday evening. I came at once."

"I'm sure you did. What kind of an African was he?"

"What do you mean?" Nicholas scowled, genuine confusion puckering his brow. Emma sympathized. She knew what Adam's grilling could do to one's fortitude.

"What tribe?" Adam barked.

"How should I know? They all look the same to me."

"Adam, what difference can it make?" Emma snatched the letter from him and shoved it into her pocket.

"The tribe might give us a clue where these bastards are from." Adam jerked off his hat and wiped his forehead. "Emma, come here and let me talk to you alone."

"You talk to her right here!" Nicholas said sharply. "I shall not be spoken about in private, King. I don't trust you."

"Well, I don't trust you either, buckaroo." Adam spun back to Emma. "You're right—you've got to do what the letter says. I don't believe anyone's holding your sister, but you don't have a choice. What we'll do is this: you and I will ride up to the Aberdares. I don't know where the hell that waterfall is—but I'll ask around and see which one is supposed to be the biggest. And which one has a cave. We'll send Soapy for the gold and start out right away. When we get there, we'll leave the chest in the cave, and when these kidnappers come out to get it, we'll surround them. Meanwhile you can wait down by the pool for your sister—"

"No, Adam!" Emma caught his arm, panic threatening to choke her. "We must do exactly as they say! We cannot try to capture them—they might kill Cissy. Just let them have the gold . . . I have enough to live on without it. I'm just going to be a nurse here in the protectorate. I shall need nothing more than a small house and enough money to buy food. I *must* give them the gold! And you mustn't try to stop me."

"She's right, King." Nicholas bristled. "Don't try to use your cowboy heroics to interfere. You'll only get people killed. Just let me handle this. Emmaline is coming with me to the Aberdares. I'm sending my men after the gold, and we'll meet them in the mountains. You're not needed, so you can keep your nose out of Emmaline's affairs from now on. Just stay here with your cows where you belong."

"Get the hell off my property, Bond." Adam reached for the rifle on his saddle, but before Emma could stop him she saw Nicholas suddenly go completely white. The blood rushed from his face, and his eyelids flew open in horror as if he'd seen a ghost.

"Nicholas, what—?" Emma started toward him, afraid that he was having an attack much like her father's. But Adam caught her arm and pulled her away. She turned, following the direction of Nicholas's shocked stare.

There, silhouetted in the sunlit doorway, stood what easily might have been a ghost. Tolito leaned against the frame, his clothing spattered with blood, his body wrapped in red-stained bandages, his face thin and wasted with pain. But most astonishing was the look of utter hatred in his eyes. Alert, intense, his dark eyes flashed at the man before him.

"Go," said Tolito. The word was spoken like the muted *crump* of an underground dynamite blast, and Emma took a half step backward from its physical force. But the word was not spoken to her. She pulled her eyes from Tolito's face and stared at Nicholas.

He was clutching his chest. "Who . . . who are you?"

"You know me." The man in the doorway straightened. "I am Tolito."

"No. It can't be," Nicholas whispered. He stood rigid, gaping at the African.

"Do you know Tolito, Nicholas?" Emma asked, glancing from one man to the other.

"They've met," Adam replied laconically. He walked to Nicholas's horse and untied it.

"Come with me, Emmaline." Nicholas turned his wan face to Emma and gestured weakly. "Come with me. Don't stay here any longer. I'll take you to find your sister."

Emma hesitated for only a moment, listening to the whispered voices of her heart. "I shall go to the Aberdares with Adam," she said quietly but firmly. "I hired him to find my sister, and he will stay with me until he does. We have a contract. But when I have found Cissy, I shall return to Mombasa and discuss your proposal—"

"No!" Nicholas lurched forward, his face suffusing with blood. "No, Emmaline—don't make the wrong choice. . . . Oh, God . . ."

This time when Nicholas looked up, Emma did start toward him. His eyes, glued to the doorway of the small house, were wide with shock; his lips were two thin, purple lines. Emma stared at the vision that had sent him into such a state.

Beside Tolito stood Linde. She had put on a vibrant purple dress and a flaming-red wrap. Her hair stood out around her shoulders like a thick cape of lustrous silk, and her dark eyes sparkled. Her gaze never left Nicholas's face as she walked past Tolito onto the verandah.

Slowly, with a queenlike air, she lifted her bronzed arm and pointed her finger down the road toward the open plains. "Go, evil spirit," she said haughtily. "Leave us or be cursed forever!"

Nicholas stood woodenly for a long time, then pulled away from Emma and straightened. He looked carefully at Adam. "I shall do everything within my power to bring about your downfall," he said in a voice edged with steel. *"Everything."*

Adam pointed at the horse with his chin. "Get out of here, bastard. And if I catch you on my land again, I'll kill you."

"Adam!" Emma whirled to the cowboy, but the look of murder in his eyes stopped her cold.

"You've had my offer, Emmaline." Nicholas mounted his horse and searched her face, eyes hard. "It is I or he. The truth or lies. England or treason. Security or uncertainty. Make your choice."

Emma stared up at him, then squared her shoulders, chin jutting out defiantly. "Or I can follow my *own* path," she said, her green eyes snapping. "The path I chose from the beginning and the path I intend to follow. Good day, Mr. Bond."

With that she turned and rushed up the hill toward the big house. But with each step she took, she realized ever more clearly that she had already chosen a path different from her original one. She had chosen to follow her heart—and now her heart was held captive in the strong brown hands of a man with eyes the color of the African sky. A man she still wasn't sure she could trust.

# Chapter Seventeen

✦✦✦✦✦

*No rest for the sinner, no breakfast or dinner,*
*But he lies in a supperless bed in the mud.*
*No corn nor potatoes, no bread nor tomatoes,*
*But jerked beef as dry as the sole of your shoe;*
*All day without drinking, all night without winking,*
*I'll tell you, kind stranger, this never will do.*

—"The Disheartened Ranger"

*We are the music makers,*
*And we are the dreamers of dreams,*
*Wandering by lone sea-breakers,*
*And sitting by desolate streams—*
*World-losers and world-forsakers,*
*On whom the pale moon gleams—*
*Yet we are the movers and shakers*
*Of the world forever, it seems.*

*With wonderful deathless ditties*
*We build up the world's great cities,*
*And out of a fabulous story*
*We fashion an empire's glory.*
*One man with a dream, at pleasure,*
*Shall go forth and conquer a crown;*
*And three with a new song's measure*
*Can trample a kingdom down.*

—Arthur William Edgar O'Shaughnessy
"Ode"

"I'M SENDING SOAPY to Tsavo." Adam's large frame blocked the sunlight from the verandah door. Emma straightened from the trunk she was packing in her room and turned to face him. "I'm not sending anyone with him," he continued. "He'll

359

do better and ride faster alone. He's an excellent shot, and I've given him instructions to guard your gold with his life. But Emma, I've got to tell you, I don't think you should—"

"Where is he?" Emma ran to the door, her heart racing. She had to catch Soapy before he left.

"Up at the stables."

Emma pushed past Adam, gathered her skirts, and tore up the hill. Soapy had just ridden out of the barn, an extra horse tethered to his roan, when she stopped breathless before him.

"Richards won't give you the gold unless you have a sign from me." She glanced down at the bright brass wedding ring glinting in the afternoon sunlight. "You must telegraph this message, Soapy: 'Send seventy-five thousand pounds in gold immediately to Tsavo station by order of Emmaline King. The brass ring will arrive on the next train. Do not wait for it to send the gold.' You must tell him it's urgent, Soapy. He mustn't wait for the ring!"

"What ring you talkin' 'bout, ma'am?"

Emma twisted her brass wedding ring from the finger of her left hand and held it up to him. "This. Send it on the first train to the coast."

Soapy leaned over and took the ring. "Well, there's only one train, ma'am. And if'n it's followin' its regular schedule, it'll be down at Mombasa by the time I ride into Tsavo. If'n I make it in time, they'll get your gold onto that train just before it heads back up country. But if'n I miss it—you ain't gonna get your gold in time to save your sister."

Adam came up behind Emma. His blue eyes flashed with enthusiasm. "Ride like hell, Soapy, and don't stop for anything. Get that telegram sent before the train leaves the coast, you hear me?"

"Yes, sir." Soapy held up the ring. "But what about this? Should I wait around and make sure it gets sent off to the coast?"

Adam looked at the ring, then turned to Emma. She had promised Richards her wedding ring for insurance? . . . "Hell no, Soapy. Just send the message, get the gold, and head for the Aberdares. Give the ring to somebody else to send to the bank. That ring isn't worth a damn to anybody anyway."

"Whatever you say, boss." Soapy tucked the ring into the breast pocket of his dirty checkered shirt and smiled down at Emma. "Don't you worry your pretty little head none about that gold, ma'am. I'll get it to you if'n it near kills me. And my word is as good as a hangman's knot."

With that, Soapy spurred his horse into a gallop down the hill toward the plains. Emma watched him beneath the shade of her open hand until he was no more than a speck riding across a sea of golden grass. Adam waited beside her, and she could feel the tension emanating from his body.

"Are you ready to go?" he snapped. He started down the hill toward the house, his spurs spinning as he walked.

Emma scampered after him. "What about Tolito?"

"My foreman's got orders to get him down to Tsavo as soon as he's fit. Linde's going with him to Mombasa."

"Thank you, Adam." She slipped past him as he held open the door to the house. But as she started for her room, Adam took hold of her wrist. Surprised, she turned to face him.

"Why didn't you go with Bond?"

Emma looked up into the piercing blue eyes. She

could never tell Adam her true reasons for choosing to travel with him rather than with Nicholas. Instead, she would ask the question she longed to have answered. "How does Nicholas know Tolito?"

"You don't need to know that, Emma. It's past history."

Emma lifted her chin. "And you don't need to know my motivations. We each have our secrets, haven't we, Adam? That's what keeps us safely apart."

"You don't trust me—that's what keeps us apart."

"Should I trust you?" Emma carefully freed her wrist from Adam's grip. She met his eyes, knowing that no matter what he told her about himself she would need more proof. But even if she could trust him, what future could there ever be for Adam King and Emma Pickworth?

"You should trust what I told you the other night." His voice dropped, suddenly low and gentle. "You should trust that I love you, Emma."

Emma turned her head. Not now, she told herself. If she heard those words now, she would soften inside, and she would want him. "If you love me," she said quietly, "help me find my sister."

They rode alone. No wagon train to slow them down this time . . . no heavy supplies, no plodding oxen, no broken wheels. Adam rode his black stallion, and Emma rode the red mare. They took just what they could carry in their saddlebags.

For three days they journeyed toward the fertile highlands of the protectorate. The land evolved slowly from dry, shimmering grasslands covered with roaming animals to verdant green hills dotted with tall trees and layered with rich red soil.

"Coffee and tea country," Adam told Emma. "You just wait and see. Already colonists are crowding into these hills, running off the animals and pushing the Africans into reserves. The English will make a profit, I'm sure, but at the expense of the land and the people."

"And the city you've talked about—Nairobi? Will it be near here?" They had stopped to drink at a cold, clear stream. Emma dipped her hands into the bracing water and ran her fingers over her face to ease her exhaustion.

"Right about here, I'd imagine." Adam could almost see the future city with its carriages and shops and hotels. The vision tore him in two—one half knowing the colonists would pour life into the country, and the other certain they would also destroy it. Uneasiness flooding him, he turned to watch Emma from a mossy bank. Wild passion fruit vines tumbled over the ground, and brilliant bird of paradise flowers bloomed in profusion. He shook his head, the persistent vision replacing lush foliage with a bustling town—gray stone buildings, proper streets with policemen, courts of law, shops, restaurants, little rows of houses. And bursting onto the scene, the hissing steam locomotive of the British East African Railway.

"It would be a lovely place for a home," Emma said, rising and brushing moss from her skirt. She was wearing Adam's black hat, but she hardly needed it. Mounds of snow-white clouds floated across the pale blue sky. The air in the highlands was crisp, sweet, and invigorating. "I could imagine building a house just there—on that little knoll. One could walk down to this stream and sit for hours in the silence of the morning . . . but a city? No, I don't think so, Adam. I just can't see it."

Adam had to smile. Always the dreamer, Emma was. He looked at her now, her long hair hanging golden and shining down her back. The wisped ends of it swept and danced along the curve of her bottom . . . and he imagined his hands on her soft skin. Caressing her with his thoughts, he struggled to quell the image of her body writhing against his, her full breasts ripe in his palms, her mouth wet on his. She was happy. Going to find her sister at last. It was all she'd ever really wanted, and he'd managed to do nothing but confuse her.

Look at her now—standing on tiptoe to smell the frangipani blossoms. Her face was full of light, beautiful and sun-kissed. Her green eyes shone like emeralds in a golden brooch. Damn. He was even starting to feel poetic about her.

Watching her pluck a single pink-tinged white blossom and lift it to her nose, he realized she'd brought a sort of magic to his life. He was looking at things . . . and people . . . in a new way. The future presented itself not just in terms of cattle, fences, and palm tree growth.

There was something else now to the vision. A warmth, a hope for companionship, a fulfillment . . . Hell, what was he thinking about? Adam turned to his horse and straightened the saddle blanket. Emma didn't trust him, for one thing. For another, she had never said one word about wanting to be around him after she found her sister. And even more important, she'd made it damned clear she was determined to be a nurse at some godforsaken outpost mission.

He took off his hat and stared at the band. *Let her go, Adam.* He could almost hear his father's voice.

Hold close to your heart. It'll only cause trouble in the end. Let her go.

"Adam, what is this flower?" Emma drifted toward him, her green eyes shining with wonder. She held the thick-petaled blossom cupped in her palms. "I've never smelled anything quite so wonderful. It's like a rich perfume!"

Adam stared at her. Her pink lips were moist. Her bosom rose and fell beneath the thin white ruffled blouse she wore. She was so alive, so beautiful.

"It's called a frangipani," he said quickly, stuffing his hat on his head to keep his hands occupied. "They come in yellow, too. Well, are you ready to head out? We ought to get there by nightfall."

Emma nodded slowly, her eyes still on Adam's face. "Adam, I—" She caught herself. She wanted to talk with him, but she had to be so careful. "Adam, I want to thank you for . . . for helping me. I didn't realize at the time I asked you, that you had so much to do—your ranch and Seastar and everything. I've taken up a great deal of your time, and—"

"I was glad to do it. And if we don't find Cissy here, I'll keep helping you until my contract runs out." He turned to mount, but Emma caught his arm.

"I . . . thank you also for teaching me about this country. The language and the animals and the tribes." She could feel the steel of his arm hot beneath her fingers. "I shall never forget what you've done for me."

Adam nodded, his gaze level. "No trouble. I'd have done it for anyone."

"Yes, well then. Thank you." Emma turned toward her own horse. Of course he would have done it for anyone. They had shared moments of passion, words of love—but in the end it all meant nothing. She grasped the leather reins and leaned her cheek against the red mare's neck.

"Emma." Adam's voice behind her was low, and Emma turned. He was standing close, so close she could feel his breath stirring her hair. He stroked away a strand of hair that had blown across her cheek. "You'll always be welcome at my ranch . . . or at the beach house. You know that."

Emma nodded. Her breath quickened as she gazed up at him. "I should like to visit. You'll be getting back to normal quite soon, I imagine." She glanced down at his corded body, the cotton shirt and indigo trousers. Her throat tightened against the tears that threatened. "You'll be wearing your gun again, I suppose. And I'm sure it won't be long before Clarissa—"

Adam cut short her words with a bruising kiss. His large hands found her arms and drew her to him, her breasts pressing hard against his chest and his taut thighs molding to hers. His mouth sought hers hungrily, like a man half-crazed from lack of sustenance. Blossoming instantly, Emma arched up into him, her arms twining around his neck, her hands weaving through his hair. How she had longed for him! It seemed an eternity since they had last held each other and feasted on love like two ravenous beasts.

And now she believed they would again—and she wanted this last loving more than she had ever thought she could want anything. Adam's lips blazed a trail down her neck, and his fingers teased her nipples to life beneath her blouse. His ragged breath seared her temple and cheek; his very touch drew fire in a promise of what might follow. Slowly he caressed his way up from her thigh toward the hidden mound between her legs. Her dress rose in gathers with the movement of his hand, and she felt the gentle breeze sweep her skirt around her knees.

Moaning with pleasure, Emma could do nothing but sway against Adam as his fingers began a rhythmic stroking. She kissed his lips, teasing them open with her tongue to explore the pleasures within. As she slid her hands to the front of his shirt, her mind swam with cautions, but her heart overruled them all. What difference could their loving make now? She wanted Adam . . . wanted his sensual dance, wanted his hands fondling every part of her. He could do what he willed—she wanted everything. "I can't think about anything but this, Adam," she murmured. "There's no future, no past. Only now—" Emma caught her breath at the tinkling sound behind her. Adam stiffened in her arms and rose sharply.

Emma whirled, drawing her blouse over her shoulders. For a moment she saw nothing. But then it came again . . . a merry, tinkling laugh— and then a second overlapping the first.

"*Okahaha.*" Adam said the word quietly, and it was followed by a deathly silence.

Then, very slowly, three young African girls emerged from a thicket of vines and trees. Each carried an enormous bundle of sticks hanging by a leather strap designed to go over the head so that the load rested on the bearer's back. Altogether different-looking from the Masai, these girls had round faces, flat noses, and chocolate-colored skin, and they were much plumper than the nomads of the plains. They smiled shyly at Emma and Adam, their black eyes sparkling.

"They're Kikuyu," Adam said, stepping away from Emma. With a sigh of frustration, he took off his hat, raked his fingers through his hair, then put his hat back on. Damn, he thought. Well, he'd better make the best of this. "I don't know much of their language, but maybe we can get them to tell us where the waterfall with the cave is."

He spoke haltingly, using his hands to signal his meaning. The three girls giggled behind their fingers until Emma was certain they had comprehended nothing of Adam's request.

Then, just as she thought surely the girls were leaving, one of them turned back with a sweet smile and gave a rather lengthy dissertation. She pointed toward the sky and then down. Emma turned and focused on the distant horizon. There, barely visible and shrouded in cloud, rose two towering, jagged peaks.

"Batian and Nelian." Adam's gaze was fixed on the shimmering vision. He couldn't look at Emma. The taste of her on his tongue was still so sweet it was all he could do to try to still his hammering pulse. "The twin peaks of Kenya Mountain."

"Is the waterfall near there?" Emma forced her voice to sound casual. Her legs trembling from the waning force of passion, she shivered over the lost moment.

"If we travel toward the mountain, we will come to the Aberdares." Adam watched the three Kikuyu girls as they vanished into the undergrowth. He would repeat their directions and maybe the knot of frustration and anger in his stomach would go away. "If we keep our eyes on the mountain, the girl told me, we will find the waterfall. She said there's a deep gorge nearly hidden by bushes and trees. A huge fig tree stands at the base of the gorge, and a stream flows out of the gorge. If we go up the ravine, we'll come to the pool of water. And if we follow that upward, we'll find the big waterfall and the cave." Adam finally turned to Emma. "She told me evil spirits live in the cave and we should not go near the gorge."

Emma met his blue eyes uncomfortably. The old closed-off Adam had returned and she knew nothing would be spoken of their unfulfilled desire. "I see. Well, Tolito thought Nicholas Bond had cast an evil spirit on him, and we both know how ridiculous that notion was."

Adam turned to his horse. "If the moon isn't shadowed by clouds, we can ride most of the night. We ought to get there by midmorning tomorrow."

"Adam . . ." Emma set her hands on her hips, willing her concentration to matters at hand. "You don't believe in this evil spirit nonsense, do you?"

"I don't believe in much of anything I can't see and touch." He stepped into the stirrup and mounted his stallion. "We'd better go find your sister."

After hours of travel through thick bush, Adam and Emma finally had to dismount and lead their horses. They were forced to slosh through ankle-deep mud and guide their mounts down steep ravines that melted into icy streams. Emma began to wonder if this whole land weren't cursed by an evil spirit. Adam told her it was a rain forest—a far cry from the savannah grasslands of his ranch.

In the afternoon the forest was generally quiet. But as evening lowered its dusky head, everything came to life at once. The forest supported a whole new sort of wildlife, hiding and creeping and

watching. There were leopards, slinking and eye
ing the intruders from the branches of huge trees
Bush babies stared at them with huge glowing
brown eyes. Birds shrieked, and bats fluttered by
overhead. Shy dik-dik—the tiniest of the antelope
—peered out at them with minuscule faces and
horns smaller than a fountain pen. Most startling
of all was the small furry hyrax, whose wild shril
cry sounded like the screaming wail of an aban
doned child.

At midnight Adam insisted they stop. They hud
dled into the curved roots of a huge tree, and
Emma slept on his shoulder. They did not speak o
their moments by the stream. Once Emma begar
to talk of it, but Adam silenced her. "It's not mean
to be," he said quietly, and she understood.

Early in the morning, when tendrils of mis
curled over the rocks and between the ferr
fronds, Adam and Emma began the last leg o
their trek to the waterfall. Weary, her legs stif
and sore, Emma dragged her mud-laden boots
uphill after Adam. The horses were no use, and
she could not imagine how Soapy would ever
make it up with the gold.

The sun had burned away the mist—though i
was still so cool Emma could hardly believe they
were nearly at the equator—when Adam suddenly
stopped beside a deep river.

"Here we are." He turned to Emma with a tired
smile.

She raised her eyes to the towering fig tree cov
ered with green creepers. Then she gazed down a
the swift stream. From a distance she could hea
the soft rush of a waterfall. A chill ran through her
and she took hold of Adam's hand. "We *are* here."

"Come on, then." He pulled her forward. "We'd

better try to take the horses with us . . . leopards, you know. Let's find the falls and the cave and set up camp. It's the right day to make the trade for Cissy, but there's not a damned thing we çan do until Soapy gets here. I'm sure if there *is* anybody up here, they've already seen us."

Emma nodded. "I think we would do well with a bit of rest."

Did Adam still doubt the letter Nicholas had brought? she wondered. Or was it a ruse to cover the plot he had worked out with the Germans?

Had Rolf been part of the plan? Had Cissy been with him all these days, dismayed at her lover's treachery? As Emma walked, she looked about her at the dense foliage. Was Cissy nearby? Could she be waiting just out of sight—perhaps watching them right now? Restraining herself from calling out to her sister, Emma waded across the chill waters of the stream and up the bank on the other side.

Sliding along in the mud, she struggled into the depths of the lush green bush. She knew she was deep in the heart of a gorge. The vine-covered tree limbs arched overhead like the lace-gloved fingers of an old woman. The sky above was only a ragged ribbon of deep blue that soon clouded to gray as it began to drizzle. But as they pushed farther and farther inward, all sound became muffled by the growing intensity of rushing water.

Adam and Emma found their way around a bend in the ravine and without warning came upon a small clearing. They stopped in surprise, and both gazed upward at the torrent of gray water rushing over the lip of a rock at the end of the gorge. The plummeting water bubbled and spun wildly down a profusion of smooth black stones until it calmed at last in a deep pool not far from where they stood. From there it slipped into the narrow but deep stream they had followed up from the fig tree.

"Do you see a cave?" Emma whispered. Though the raging water blocked every other noise, somehow her words seemed loud in the deathly depths of the ravine.

Adam pointed toward the cascade, and Emma followed the line of his finger until she spotted a deep black maw halfway up the side of the ravine. It would require a skilled climber to reach the cave, but she knew she was equal to the task if need be.

"Come on, Emma." Adam had not released her hand, and now he urged her forward into the clearing. "The wood around here's probably wet, and we don't have much to eat, but let's try to get a fire going anyway. Damn, I hope Soapy gets here before dark. I don't like the thought of camping out all night."

It was later than they had planned to arrive—midafternoon—and Emma sat down in the long damp grass with great relief. Her boots were caked with mud, and her tan riding skirt had been splattered almost to her waist. She wiggled her toes and felt small, swirling pools of water inside her stockings. Chilled to the bone, she wrapped her hands around her crossed arms.

When Adam started gathering firewood she attempted to rise and help him, but he gestured for her to stay where she was. All her thoughts had turned to Cissy. She wondered whether her fragile sister had been forced to live in this damp jungle all these days. What had she eaten? Who had protected her? Had she been able to stay warm? Emma could envision Cissy shivering by a smoky fire much like the one Adam was building at the side of the pool. Her sister was so tender, so pampered, so weak . . .

"Emma?" Adam touched Emma's arm. "You okay?"

Smiling bravely, Emma gazed at the waterfall.

Adam knelt on the ground beside Emma and warmed his hands for a moment before the flickering fire. Then he gently drew her into his arms and sat with her in silence.

Emma hardly knew when night fell, she was so tired. Adam spread their blankets beneath a tree, and they slept until well into the next day. They rose, hardly speaking . . . only waiting. They ate a little; Adam explored around the waterfall and devised a plan to climb to the cave; Emma mentally composed letters to Aunt Prue. Time crept slowly. In the late afternoon, Adam suggested they rest again to regain their strength for the journey home. Emma curled up beside him as he sat smoking.

When she opened her eyes, the clearing had deepened to emerald. The sky was a dark rose, and the water of the falls had turned black. She could feel Adam's arms around her, but a sudden sound jerked her fully awake.

Adam leapt to his feet at the noise and started for the rifle hanging on his saddle. Then he stopped, threw back his head, and chuckled heartily. "Ho, I am a jolly cowboy, from Texas now I hail," he began to sing loudly. "Give me my quirt and pony, I'm ready for the trail—"

Emma struggled to stand on her half-frozen legs. Her eyes settled on the rustling bushes down the length of the gorge, and at last she made out the welcome sight of bright yellow hair and two weaving, stumbling horses—one pulling a small cart.

"I love the rolling prairies, they're free from care and strife," Soapy sang at the top of his lungs. His gray eyes sparkled. "Behind a herd of longhorns I'll journey all my life."

"Soapy!" Adam strode across the clearing. "You're a sight for sore eyes, old partner."

"Just 'bout didn't think I could do it, boss." Soapy dismounted and led the horses onto the mossy stone. "I stopped off back at the ranch to pick us up a cart—that gold is danged heavy. Them horses nearly tuckered out bringin' it up from Tsavo. But then we had a hell of a time trekkin' up these mountains with the ol' cart. If'n you two hadn't gone trompin' down the bushes in this gorge, we'da never made it. Anyways, here she be!"

Emma hurried toward the heavily laden horse. She saw at once that the cart carried two chests, a small, heavily nailed wooden box—and . . . Emma stared in confusion. The other chest was none other than the crate she had tried to open at Adam's ranch. All the locks and iron bands had been removed, no doubt to lessen the weight.

"What do you have there, Soap?" Adam walked around the wagon. "Did you bring the crate, too?"

"I shore did." Soapy was grinning from ear to ear. "Fer once I done some smart thinkin'. I reckoned you'd head over to Delamere's place from here, bein's it's so close—and I knew he'd been waitin' fer this shipment. So I brung it."

Emma walked up next to Adam and gingerly touched the crate. Then she turned and stared at the smaller chest. Her father's gold . . . her gold now. She would give it all away to have Cissy back, and gladly. Nothing else really mattered now but that. The thought of clasping her sister tightly to her breast—

"Adam, we must hurry." She grasped the corner of the chest and struggled to move it from the cart. "It's almost dark, and I want to keep Cissy from one more night of torture. Let's take this gold to the cave."

Adam let his eyes linger on her. Her green eyes were the color of the forest; she was aching now, aching to have her sister, aching for some sense of normalcy, aching to be free of worry . . .

"Soapy, let's head up to the cave." Adam pointed out the black hole. "We'll carry the gold on two poles between us. It's going to take both of us to get it up those slippery rocks. You'd better bring your lariat."

Emma backed away from the cart as the men closed around the chest. They slid two slender tree limbs beneath it for support, then lifted it into the air like a palanquin, Adam at the front and Soapy at the rear.

As they started forward, Adam turned to Emma. "Stay here," he called. "If this thing is real, they might let your sister go while we're up at the cave. Just lie low with her until we get back down. There's the rifle if you need it."

Emma nodded, her heart in her throat as she watched the two men slowly winding their way past the pool toward the base of the waterfall. Trembling, she scanned the darkening forest for any sign of human life. She chafed her arms and glanced at Adam's rifle hanging in its leather scabbard.

A moment later Adam and Soapy had reached the waterfall and were shifting the chest onto the rope to haul it up. Slowly Emma walked to the cart and settled on one end. She leaned against the crate and took a deep breath, trying to calm herself. Then she looked over at the black lettering on the wooden crate.

She could open the crate now, simply lift the lid and learn everything she had longed to know about Adam. Either there would be long, shining steel rifles inside the crate, or there would be cattle dip. Emma ran her fingers along the rim of the lid. One swift movement and she would know whether Adam were innocent of Nicholas's charges . . . or guilty. But if he were innocent, she would only want him more, and she knew she could never have him. If he were guilty, she could ruin his life. But most important, she would have *proof*—one way or the other.

Emma stared into the gathering gloom. She could see Adam up on a wet stone, carefully easing up the chest of gold inch by inch. His hat lay discarded on a mound of moss at the base of the falls, and he had rolled up the sleeves of his white shirt. Emma thought back to the first time she had seen him—when he had lifted the small boy out of the path of the tumbling crate and saved his life. She could see him in her mind's eye, cradling the small dark child in his massive arms. How strange and wonderful he had seemed with his soft rippling shirt and taut denim trousers! She could see his boots even now, their silver spurs glinting. With an almost imperceptible shake of her head, she looked back at the crate and touched it, then stood up and walked away.

No, she thought, wandering to the edge of the little pool, she would make one unselfish decision in her life. Her mother's face seemed to float toward her as she peered into the cobalt depths of the pool. Her mother had made one right choice—and one choice of the heart. The second had caused everyone so much suffering. It had even led her mother to an early grave.

Emma gazed at her own reflection and knew she must not walk in her mother's footsteps any longer. She thought of Nicholas storming about so hotheadedly—declaring his love, proposing marriage, avowing his undying devotion to England and all that was honorable. And when she thought of Nicholas, she saw a man—upright, secure, proper—just like her father.

Sighing, Emma straightened from the pool. Once she had Cissy safe, she would marry Nicholas. Her money could see the fulfillment of his dreams of buying into the railway and being a part of the building of Nairobi. He did not love her—she knew that. She had loved, and she had been loved. She would never know that again. But in the end, what did love matter? For once, she would listen to her mind instead of her heart.

Strengthened by her resolve, Emma lifted her chin and watched the men climbing to the cave. But as she did so, a sudden movement in the forest caught her eye. Whirling, she saw the bushes part a few paces away.

"Good evening, Fräulein Pickworth." Rolf Ulric stepped into view, a wide smile across his face. And behind him—

"Cissy!" Emma's voice rang joyously through the air. Unable to contain herself, she tore across the clearing and threw her arms around her sister.

"Emma—oh, Emma!" Cissy's golden head bobbed against Emma's shoulder. The two clutched at one another, trembling with happiness.

"You were with Rolf all along," Emma sobbed. She wound her fingers through Cissy's hair and tilted up her sister's head. The tear-filled blue eyes she loved so well gazed back in rapture. "Oh, Cissy, you can't imagine—"

"Save your happy tidings, ladies." The harsh voice startled Emma. Just as she turned to find Rolf drawing a pistol, she saw Nicholas Bond jab the barrel of his rifle into the German's stomach. "Throw it down, Kaiser."

"Nicholas, whatever are you doing?" Emma gaped at him in astonishment.

Rolf hesitated a moment, then pitched his gun onto the moss. Nicholas picked up the weapon and thrust it under his belt. Emma turned her head in time to see Adam and Soapy racing down from the waterfall toward them. *"Adam!"* she screamed.

Nicholas grabbed Emma and pulled her to him, shoving the rifle barrel into her side. "I want the gold. Tell them to bring it back down or I'll shoot."

"Oh, God, *no!*" Cissy screamed in horror. "He's going to shoot Emma!"

"Emma!" Adam's voice thundered through the clearing. He ran ahead of Soapy but stopped short when he saw Nicholas. Suddenly the pressure was off Emma's side as Nicholas turned the gun on Adam.

"What do you want, Bond?" Adam called. "The gold? It's up there by the falls. Just let her go."

"What's goin' on, boss? . . . Damn!" Soapy barged ahead of Adam, his eyes wide and his pistol drawn.

"Out of the way, Potts!"

A deafening blast exploded in Emma's ear, and she sagged for a moment in Nicholas's grip. But as she straightened, she saw Soapy lying on the ground, his leg a tattered, bloody mass.

Before she could react, Nicholas drew back his fist and slammed it against her head, knocking her sideways to the ground. Then he leapt forward, ramming another cartridge in the chamber of his lever-action rifle. "You've told her," he barked at Adam. "You've told everything. You've ruined me."

Struggling against the blackness that threatened, Emma shook her head to clear her blurred vision. A heavy silence hung over the clearing, and everyone seemed suspended in time beneath the death sentence of Nicholas's words. Emma could see Soapy huddled on the ground, his revolver lying many steps away in the brush. Adam crouched behind him, one hand resting uselessly on his unarmed thigh. Emma lowered her head, cursing herself for her blindness—she should never have insisted he part with his gun.

"Nicholas." Her voice croaked from her dry throat, and she fought with her tangled skirts to rise from the mud. "Nicholas—"

"No!" He stepped out, trapping her dress beneath his muddy heel. And suddenly rage flooded through Emma. She had been pinned before—held back, held down, cowering beneath another man's wrath. But no longer!

"Stop it, Nicholas!" She jerked her skirt out from beneath his foot. But as she straightened, she saw him kneel and take aim at Adam's heart. Without thinking, she lunged between the two men and threw herself in front of Adam.

"Don't shoot him!" she cried. "I love him, Nicholas. Don't do it! You'll have to kill me first—"

She saw Nicholas's face go white as he stumbled

to his feet, the rifle swaying dangerously. "Emmaline. Get out of the way—"

"Emma!" Adam's arms shot out and he swept Emma behind him, holding her in place with hands of steel. "Soapy!" he roared. "Damn it, Soapy—get her the hell out of here!"

Emma wrestled to free herself from Adam's grip, cringing as she saw Nicholas lift the rifle a second time. She heard herself pleading with Nicholas to stop his madness. And then somehow Soapy was grabbing her arm and dragging her away.

"*Adam!*" she screamed as she bumped and slipped along the mossy rock toward the safety of the brush. Through the tangle of shrubbery she lost sight of the two men. Soapy scrambled down the ravine, and Emma suddenly felt hands trying to grasp her thrashing arms and legs—voices, desperate voices. Cissy's voice. But Emma could only continue to fight against the dark prison encumbering her. She must help Adam. She must get to him before . . .

Emma glanced up into the jade canopy of leaves and saw a large stone descending toward her head. Who held it, she could not tell. Before the flash of pain that preceded unconsciousness, she heard from the clearing the thunder of a gunshot.

# Chapter Eighteen

**✦ ✦ ✦ ✦**

*At night in the bright stars up yonder*
*Do the cowboys lie down to their rest?*
*Do they gaze at this old world and wonder*
*If rough riders dash over its breast?*
*Do they list to the wolves in the canyons?*
*Do they watch the night owl in its flight,*
*With their horse their only companion*
*While guarding the herd through the night?*

—"The Cowboy's Meditation"

*Dear as remembered kisses after death,*
*As sweet as those by hopeless fancy feigned*
*On lips that are for others; deep as love,*
*Deep as first love, and wild with all regret;*
*O Death in Life, the days that are no more!*

—Alfred, Lord Tennyson
"The Princess"

EMMA SHUT HER eyes against the invading light. No, she did not want to see. She did not want to feel. And all she could hear was the rifle firing, again and again.

"Dear Emma." Cissy . . . A cool hand stroked Emma's forehead. She wondered if she were dreaming. Everything was so confused, so jumbled. "Emma, we're at Tsavo station. You must wake up."

The olive-green eyes flickered open, and Emma gazed into her sister's face. Cissy looked pale and drawn from her ordeal. "Where is Adam?" Emma asked faintly.

Cissy shook her head. "They've sent a contingent up to the Aberdares. Delamere ordered it. We've heard nothing yet, of course. They only left a few hours ago."

Emma struggled to sit up. Her head felt as if it had been split open. "We're at Tsavo station?'"

Cissy nodded. "We've been here two days. Dr. McCulloch insisted on drugging you." She hesitated. "They've told me about Father. His grave is just outside. I've waited until we could go together."

Emma looked out the small window above the horsehair settee on which she lay. An azure sky reassured her the world went on. This was the office where once she had talked to Nicholas. She had seen Adam walking just outside . . . by the track.

Rising slowly to ward off the knifing pain in her head, she peered out again. The train was in the station, and workers swarmed about. But Adam was not there.

"Yes." Emma took her sister's small hand and held it tightly. "Let us go and visit the grave."

There was no headstone yet—no doubt a large, impressive marker had already been ordered—only a small cross stuck into the ground where their father had been laid to rest. Emma and Cissy stood together contemplating the barren mound, each sorting out her private thoughts. Emma knew only that she was free—free of her father's domination at last . . . and free to love him again as she once had.

"The train is just leaving." The gentle voice behind Emma drew her attention. She turned to find the strong blond soldier, Rolf. "Herr Potts refuses to have anyone but you to care for his leg, Fräulein

Pickworth. He says the rail doctors worked for his enemy—that madman Bond. Perhaps I may escort you?"

Still uncertain as to this man's role—unclear even now what *really* had happened in the mountains— Emma tentatively accepted Rolf's arm. He took Cissy's hand in his and led both women to the train.

Dazed, her head throbbing, Emma walked unsteadily down the aisle until she came to a central berth. The seat had been made up into a bed, and Soapy lay still and pale upon it.

"The bullet went clean through and I've damn near lost all my blood." He looked up at Emma. "Think you could patch me up, ma'am?"

Emma and Cissy took the seat opposite the cowboy. "Why did you take me away from Adam?" Emma whispered, gazing at him dully.

"Well, I'll tell you." Soapy groaned a little and tried to shift his body into a more comfortable position. "The boss told me to take you out of there— and you know how I always do what he tells me. I'll be damned if I didn't think I was nearly a goner, but I raised up and hauled you down the gorge anyway like he said to, and I brung you back to civilization. Me and that there German feller. I knowed none of us was worth a barrel of shucks up there on that damned cold mountain with that loco Bond and his rifle. If'n I hadn't a drug you off, Bond woulda shot you dead. He thought Adam had told you, see—"

"Told me what, Soapy?" Emma touched the cowboy's arm. "I don't know anything."

Soapy sighed and stared at the ceiling. The train jerked to life, its whistle sending a mournful cry into the afternoon air. Cissy wrapped her arm around Emma's shoulders and drew her sister back against the seat.

"Emma darling, you've had a nasty bump." Cissy stroked the hair from Emma's shoulder. "You should—"

"No!" Emma stiffened. "I need to know what happened at the waterfall. I don't understand it."

"If'n you'll patch up that damned bullet hole in my leg," Soapy said, "I'll try to tell you ever-'thing I know—though it ain't much more'n you know yoreself."

It startled Emma to realize how seriously he was wounded. Her hand stretched of its own accord toward his torn and bloody pant leg.

"I'm jiggered if I can pull it all together," Soapy continued. "Y'all know I ain't got nothin' under my hat but hair. Anyways, it ain't gonna make no difference if you know now. That bastard Bond give hisself away by acting like a dad-blamed fool." He glanced sheepishly at Cissy. "Beggin' yore pardon, ma'am."

Cissy looked at Emma, her blue eyes questioning. "Can you understand what he's saying?"

Emma smiled wanly. "I've learned to. Come on, then, Soapy. Let's take a look at that leg of yours."

Soapy took off his hat and put it over his face as Emma peeled back the sheet and began to probe at the bloody wound. "Ma'am, you know I ain't got the brains of a grasshopper . . . but did you also know I'm as yeller as mustard without the bite?"

Emma straightened Soapy's leg carefully and began to probe the wound. "If that means you think you're a coward, Soapy, I shall have to disagree. You went after Nicholas very bravely, and you rescued me as well."

"It's the pain," Soapy groaned. "Oh, the pain."

"I'm not even touching you right now, Soapy. Please be still. Cissy, I shall need some hot water." Emma turned to her sister. "Could you please—"

"Will this help, fräulein?" Rolf was striding down the swaying aisle, his long fingers wrapped around the handle of a steaming kettle. "I got it from the kitchen car, and they are heating more."

Emma nodded in surprise. "Yes, thank you."

"I shall try to be of service, fräulein." Though his accent contorted the words, his voice carried a soothing, comforting tone. "May I offer my sincere apologies for the bump upon your head? It was I who caused your suffering."

Emma shook her head and looked at Cissy. The light of love shone in her sister's eyes, and there was nothing Emma could do but take the kettle. "It's all right, Mr. Ulric. I suppose I needed to be calmed."

"Oh, Emma," Cissy murmured, her eyes tracing anxiously over her sister's wan face. She knotted her fingers as Emma began to clean and examine Soapy's leg. "You simply cannot imagine how worried Rolf and I have been about you. We've been everywhere looking for you, and we could hardly believe it when we realized it was you climbing up into those mountains. Whatever were you doing there?"

Emma sat up from her work on the injured Soapy, who lay rigidly silent. "You've been following me?"

Cissy nodded, her face intense. "It *was* Rolf calling me that first night when we were in the railcar. He had deserted the German army and come to find me. I had no idea he was going to do it, but once we were together . . ." She looked at the man beside her, and he drew her into his arms. "Rolf's in a great deal of trouble, Emma. The Germans are looking for him. We've got to get to Mombasa and ask for sanctuary from the British government. We're going to be married."

Emma once again straightened from her work to gaze at her sister. Never had she seen such beatific peace in Cissy's eyes. And there was a certain maturity that had not been there before . . . her face bore the stamp of hardship, struggle, growth. Somehow Cissy had become a woman.

"Are you certain, Cissy?" Emma searched her sister's blue eyes for assurance. Her aching head spun with confusion. "You've been through a great deal in the past weeks. Perhaps you should rest—"

"No, Emma." Cissy shook her head firmly. "Rolf is to be my husband. I have no doubt. We've been through hell and back together since I left you. We've talked it all out. We've made all our plans, and we know it's right."

"I brought with me a sum of money," the soldier added quietly. "I will buy a small farm here in the British Protectorate—"

"Here?" Emma's eyes darted to Cissy's face.

"I love this country, Emma. . . . Oh, I know it's hard to believe. Me, with all my parties and teas and new dresses." Cissy smiled at Rolf. "I really cannot explain it. Walking through the wilds, bathing in streams, eating smoky antelope meat . . . it's changed me, Emma. Somehow—here in Africa— I've found what I've been looking for all my life. While we were following you into the mountains, we found a lovely place for our home. It was rather high up, I thought, but Rolf says he wants to try growing tea there."

Emma leaned over Soapy's stiff form again and dabbed gently at his wound. Tea. She could hear

Adam's words even now as he predicted the future of the protectorate. "I'm very happy for you both," she whispered, lifting her eyes to her sister for a moment. "And I'm quite certain your tea farm will be a great success."

"I couldn't wait to tell you all about it," Cissy continued. "Rolf wanted to go straight to Mombasa, but I knew you would be horribly worried about me, so I insisted we go back for you. We've been trying to find you ever since. In fact, we arrived at Mr. King's ranch only hours after you had gone. His man Jackson sent us in the right direction. But you can imagine our surprise when we found ourselves under the barrel of Mr. Bond's rifle only moments after we'd found you. What in heaven's name was that all about?"

Emma sighed and shook her head; she hardly understood it herself. "Soapy? Are you there under that hat?"

The buckskin cowboy hat slowly slipped from Soapy's eyes. "I'm here. Am I gonna live to see tomorrow?"

"The bullet passed cleanly through the muscle of your leg. I've mopped you up, and once I have you bandaged, you shall be fine until a doctor at Mombasa can look at you. I'm sure he'll want to stitch your wound."

"Stitch it? Oh, hell!"

Emma turned to Cissy. "I'm not at all sure what happened with Mr. Bond. Perhaps Soapy can tell us something. But first, if you'll excuse me for a moment, I shall just go looking for some bandage material."

Rolf leapt to his feet. "I shall go for you, fräulein!"

"No, no. Please sit down." The pain in Emma's

head increased as she rose and started toward the door of the car. "I need to be alone."

She gripped the leather seat backs to make her way down the aisle. It was growing dark and she could see the conductor ahead of her moving through the car lighting the lamps. Nearly paralyzed by her sense of loss, Emma had all she could do to keep from crying. Where was Adam? Had Nicholas killed him? Why—oh, God, why?

From the things Cissy had told her, Emma realized that Nicholas must have written the ransom note, planning to take the gold for himself. It was obvious he had been even more surprised than Emma to see Cissy and Rolf emerge into the clearing. But what had made him do it? What had driven him to such blood lust that he would kill Adam?

Her vision blurred from the onslaught of tears, Emma was startled when she laid her hand on a seat back and warm fingers closed over hers. She tried to draw her hand away, but it was held firmly.

"Memsahib!" Linde floated up from the seat and pressed her forehead to Emma's palms.

"Linde—but what are you doing here?" As Emma stepped from the aisle to let the conductor pass, she saw that Tolito lay awake and smiling at her from his berth.

"My arm is better, memsahib." The African's eyes were warm. "Thank you. You have driven the evil spirit away, and now we are going to Mombasa as you wished."

Emma lowered herself gingerly onto the seat and drew Linde down beside her. "Has anyone told you about Bwana King?" she asked softly.

Tolito shook his head. "He is here with you?"

"No, Tolito. We had a great deal of trouble in the Aberdares. Bwana Bond came—"

"Bwana Bond?" Tolito jerked upward from his bed, then fell back in pain.

"What has happened, memsahib?" Linde asked, her face alight with compassion.

Emma recounted the story briefly. Linde and Tolito listened, their focus glazed in the distance. "The last we know is that the gun went off. And we came to Tsavo." She considered in silence for a moment, remembering words Adam had spoken to her long ago. "He wants to be buried on the open plains," she murmured almost to herself. "He told me not to forget."

Tolito's eyes were fathomless pools of night. "Why did you not stay in the Aberdares to help Bwana King?"

"I had been hit on the head and was unconscious. Bwana Potts had been wounded, and he and Bwana Ulric decided to bring us all to Tsavo instead of staying in the forest."

Tolito nodded. "The forest is very bad." He closed his eyes, and Emma thought he was drifting into sleep. But then he began to speak.

"Adam King came to my country many years ago." His voice, low and somnolent, lulled Emma into the embrace of Linde's arms, and she listened without comment. "He was not of the British, and at first they did not want him here. He bought his land from the land office, but they sent him away from Mombasa with a bad map. Nobody was with him, and he became lost. Those were the days when I was the *olaigwenani*—the spokesman—of my clan's age-set. The young men of my age-set were hunting a lioness, and we saw that she too was stalking her prey. It was Bwana King. He was near to death, and the vultures had come to the trees to wait."

Emma swallowed and gazed sightlessly out the window. The sun had slipped below the horizon, and the black skeletons of thorn trees rose into the orange sky.

"We took Bwana King to our *manyatta*, and he grew strong again," Tolito continued. "He became a member of our age-set. He learned our language. When he was able, I went with him to his land. I became his foreman. We worked very hard, and two years passed. Bwana Potts came from America, and he worked with us also."

"I came to stay with my brother and his wife." Linde spoke up, her voice a murmur. "He wanted many of us to come, but only a few would leave the village."

"One day Bwana King told Linde and me to go to Mombasa." Tolito paused for a long time, his brow furrowed as if he could not bear to bring the memory back to life. At last he began again. "We were to pick up his crates from America and also the woman called Clarissa—that is why Linde should go with me. The woman did not come, but we put the crates on the train. While we were riding on the train, Bwana Bond also was going. He went with his men to plan the railway line. That day, Bwana Bond saw Linde, and . . ."

"And Bwana Bond wanted me." Linde laid a gentle hand on her brother's chest to silence his labored speech. The words came with difficulty and her eyes sparked as she relived the painful event. "I am not wanting this thing to happen with Bwana Bond—I am telling him no, no. But he is trying to . . . force. We come to the station, and it is nighttime. Bwana Bond is chasing me, and I am running and shouting. Tolito comes to fight with him. Bwana Bond has a knife, and every part of Tolito is blood. I am crying and screaming, but Bwana Bond is cutting Tolito to kill him—his arm is very bad. Then comes Bwana King to meet us at the station. I cry to him what is happening, that Bwana Bond is wanting me and that Tolito is dying. Bwana King fights with Bwana Bond. Then Bwana Bond runs away."

As Linde's words faded, so did the last of the light. Emma sat beneath the dim lamp and stared out at the darkness. So Nicholas had tried to kill Tolito for the sake of his desire to bed Linde. Adam knew it all; Nicholas must have lived in dread that he would tell everything one day. The story, related to a railway investor such as Godfrey Pickworth— or, for that matter, to any of Nicholas's superiors— could destroy his ambitions and career.

And when Emma had come to the protectorate— an heiress and, after her father's death, a wealthy woman in her own right—Nicholas had seen the chance to make his dreams come true. But he knew Adam could easily tell Emma the story and ruin everything. No wonder he hated Adam.

"Emma?" Cissy's surprised voice pierced the darkness, and Emma glanced up. Her sister was staring down at her—and trying *not* to stare at Tolito and Linde. "What are you doing?"

"Cissy, this is Adam's brother Tolito," Emma replied, touching the African's blanket. "And this is Linde. She is going to nurse with me when I set up my clinic. If I set up my clinic . . ."

Cissy gazed wonderingly at the two in silence for a moment—a smile of acceptance spreading over her face—then took her sister's hand. "Then perhaps Miss Linde could bandage Mr. Potts's leg. I've never heard such groaning in my life. He does believe he's going to pass on."

Linde rose at once, and the three women made their way down the aisle. Emma saw nothing of the rest of the procedure, for Cissy settled her into a sleeping berth and drew the shade over the window.

"Sleep, my poor love," she whispered as Emma closed her eyes. "You shall have a hot bath at Government House, and you'll feel much better." Cissy stopped speaking, as if considering the significance of her words. Then she placed a cool hand on Emma's forehead. "We shall find your Adam and bring him to you. I promise."

# Chaper Nineteen
✦✦✦✦

*He could ride a blame streak o' lightnin', was a cracker-jack at a dance;*

*He loved poker better'n eatin', and he'd hob you if airy a chance;*

*He could cuss the worl' by sections when you had him halfway mad;*

*He'd drink an' shoot up the city when the whisky was extra bad.*

*His wealth was his horse an' saddle, pair o' spurs an' the clothes he wore,*

*An' a dollar or two in his pocket, but oftener less than more . . .*

*But for all he was rough on the outside an' didn't live by rule,*

He'd a heart in his breast as big, sir, as the biggest kind of
    a mule.
If he met a pard in a tight he'd divide up all he had
An' to help out a woman (you know it!) he'd shoot himself
    an' be glad.
He hadn't got no religion; but top o' the golden stair
There'll be heap o' church members missin', but [the cow-
    boy] you bet'll be there.

                  —"Panhandle Cob"

> *I hold it true, whate'er befall;*
>   *I feel it, when I sorrow most;*
>   *'Tis better to have loved and lost*
> *Than never to have loved at all.*

         —Alfred, Lord Tennyson
         "In Memoriam A.H.H.XXVII"

EMMA HARDLY KNEW that the train had stopped. She felt the sunshine and humidity of the coastal port, but she sat still and dazed in the trolley as it rolled along to Government House. Lord and Lady Delamere hurried down the steps to meet the returning women, eager to hear their stories, eager to calm them . . . and more than eager to insure that they left the protectorate with good feelings to take back to England and its prospective colonists. Emma vaguely heard Lady Delamere exclaim with joy over the news of Cissy's impending marriage and settlement in the highlands. Lord Delamere called Rolf's desire for sanctuary a "bit of a sticky wicket" but assured the couple all would fall into place.

No, they had had no news from the Aberdares. Emma heard these words and left the crowd to wander slowly toward the house. As she started up the steps, she heard Soapy's voice.

"I toted this dang thing all the way up the Aberdares halfway to Kenya Mountain, I'll swear, and I'm right glad to give it over to you." He was still seated in the trolley, but Emma turned to see him pointing at the crate that somehow had followed her across the miles.

Lord Delamere chuckled and bent over the crate. "I'm sorry for your trouble, Mr. Potts." He lifted the lid and peered down at the neat rows of green-and-white packets labeled "Bartlett's Finest Cattle Dip: Medicated Powder." "I say, this should get me through the year. Well done, Mr. Potts. I shall have to thank—" He stopped speaking and glanced at Emma, but she turned and went inside.

Emma was not aware of the passing hours as she sat beside the window Adam once had entered. He had wanted to take her away then, but she would not go. And now he was gone. Somehow it seemed she was always losing those she loved most . . . and just when she had found one, she must lose another. The emptiness—the terrible, aching, black emptiness of life without Adam—was more than she could bear, and tears of mourning streamed unchecked down her cheeks.

Then, just when it seemed she could go on no longer, Emma looked out the window into the moonlit night. Trolleys and carriages had begun to arrive. There was to be a dance that night, a dance in honor of Cissy and Rolf. A dance to the future. Emma watched the finely dressed men and women promenading into the hall below. Sounds of laughter floated up to her in the darkened room. And at that moment she realized she had no choice but to go on without Adam.

Though her heart would hold him always, she must learn to let go. She must live. She must carry on with her plans. The clinic would open, and

Linde would be at her side. Cissy and Rolf would marry and have children. Emma would visit. She would go to England and convince a doctor to return with her . . . and perhaps there would be a hospital.

"Emma?" Cissy burst into the room, all eager excitement, then stopped short at the sight of Emma seated by the window in the evening gloom. "Oh, dear, dear Emma! You're here all alone, and I've been so cruel to stay away. How heartless of me!"

She lit the lamp beside the door and turned up the flame. Emma watched her butterfly sister for a moment. The sheer joy of seeing Cissy alive was enough to warm her shattered heart.

"I've needed to be alone, Cissy." Emma turned from the light to gaze out the window. "I loved Adam, you know."

Cissy studied her hands for a moment, then ran across the room and threw her arms around her sister. "Oh, I *know* you loved him . . . and he loved you, Emma! I knew it from the moment I saw you together. He was wonderful, wasn't he? And oh, Emma—"

"It's all right, Cissy." Emma straightened up and patted her sister's hand reassuringly. "I must go on. I had made up my mind not to be like Mama . . . not to go on following my heart. Well, I found out that's quite impossible for me. I shall always go where my passions lead me. But I shall not be ruled by them. Unlike Mama I shall not pine away for my loss, and I shall not die of this."

Cissy smiled. "Lady Delamere is so thrilled about the wedding," she said softly. "We've set it for tomorrow afternoon. And once Rolf and I are married, Lord Delamere says he'll have no trouble getting Rolf a permit from the British government."

"I'm very happy for you, Cissy." Emma took her sister's hand. "Truly I am."

"Will you come down? You won't have to dance or talk to anyone, but it would mean so much to me."

"Of course, Cissy." Emma walked with her sister to Cissy's trunks against the wall. As they had for many years, the two sisters bathed and washed their hair. Then they began to lace and tie and buckle and button one another into their dresses. Emma had to laugh as Cissy whirled about the room in a bright yellow gown with long feathers sweeping from the velvet sash. Cissy had insisted on putting Emma into a soft blue-green silk. It gathered into a high bustle with deep ruffles at the back, and Emma could not help thinking of Adam's amusement at her female trappings. A warmth grew in her breast as she pinned her sun-streaked hair into coils atop her head and slipped on her matching blue-green gloves. The ache of losing Adam would never leave her . . . but she would have her memories, and she would have her future.

The two young women swept down the stairs to a chorus of ahs and the gentle clapping of the assembly. It seemed Emma and Cissy were now viewed as heroines of a sort, having endured the hardships of the wild and come through impossible adventures unscathed.

Cissy quickly vanished into the sea of celebrants. Emma spoke quietly to the few who chose to address her, then she followed everyone into the ballroom. Leaning against the cool plaster of a back wall, she sipped at a glass of sherry and watched the dancers whirl about the room to a lively waltz. Cissy and Rolf, enraptured in one another's arms, did not even see her as they swept past.

"Well, howdy, ma'am." Soapy's voice startled her, and she turned in surprise to find the little cowboy standing close beside her. His yellow hair, parted in the middle, had been slicked back on either side. Even more astounding, he had washed his face, and for the first time Emma realized that he had freckles.

"Soapy, how lovely to see you," she said, bewildered that the man did not seem more despondent. "You're looking well."

"They got a purty good doc down at the government clinic. I reckon he stitched me up jes' fine." Leaning on a cane, Soapy pulled out one of his black suspenders and snapped it against his chest. "You might jes' want to know that I was right there when he took a look at yore handiwork on Tolito. I never heerd such fine talkin'. He said you done damned good . . . damned good. He was purt' near happy as a flea in a doghouse. Says he wants to meet you—" Soapy stopped speaking and scratched his head. "What the hell's goin' on?"

Emma looked up to find that the music had faltered and stopped. The dancers were rooted to the floor, and all had turned toward the door. Voices, arguing, growing louder, suddenly filled the ballroom. In came three of the African doorkeepers surrounding a figure who rose head and shoulders above them.

Standing on tiptoe, Emma felt the blood rush from her head as Adam King took off his tall black cowboy hat and strode across the room toward her. She caught her breath at the massive man she hardly recognized in his clean white shirt, black coat and trousers, and shiny boots. His sunbronzed face wore a wide, healthy grin and his eyes shone like blue diamonds. Even his hair, shiny black in the lamplight, bounced with life as he strode through the awestruck dancers.

"My lord," one of the servants protested, "this man insists on entering the consulate without invitation."

"Mr. King!" Lord Delamere called out, his voice high and nasal.

"I'm back." Adam never took his eyes from Emma's. "Mind if I join you?"

"Not at all. Welcome!" Lord Delamere turned to the military band. "Carry on, carry on."

As the music started up, the dancers swung back into the waltz. But no one could refrain from watching as Emma suddenly tore through the crowd and Adam swept her up in his arms.

"Adam!" She hurled her arms around his neck, unable to believe that he was really here—holding her, kissing her lips, spinning her around and around. She wove her fingers through his hair and buried her face in his neck. "Adam, you're alive."

Adam stopped whirling and pulled Emma away so he could look down at her face. "You didn't really think Bond could get the best of me, did you?"

"That ol' tenderfoot weren't no match for a cowboy!" Soapy shouted gleefully, and Emma turned to find him smiling at her. "Coulda told you that, ma'am. Fact is, I think I *did* tell you once that there was no way ol' yellerbelly could whup the boss."

Adam shook his head at the thought that Emma had been so worried. He gazed down at her lithe body, so soft and slender in his arms. The dress had made her eyes look almost blue, or had she been crying? He led her out onto the verandah where once they had strolled together.

"Nicholas is lying up at the ranch right now," he said quietly. "He's got a couple of bullets in him, if you'd like to practice your nursing a little more. Couldn't help but wing him—he was pretty determined, if you'll recall. Oh, and I took your gold back to the bank. Richards sure was glad to see it."

Emma shook her head. She still couldn't believe he was here . . . and yet she could feel his arm around her shoulders, she could rest her head on his chest, she could hear his heart beating loud and strong.

"I wanted to bring you this." He stopped and turned Emma to face him. Slowly he reached into his shirt pocket and pulled out the shiny brass ring. It rested on the tip of his right index finger, and he looked down at it as he spoke. "When I first met you, Emma, I knew right away there was something different . . . special . . . about you. You proposed that ridiculous business arrangement, and I went along with it for the adventure, and because I needed a nurse for Tolito. I sure didn't need your money. My father left me a little shipping business when he died last year. Your father was right when he thought he recognized my name. Anyway, my pa said he wouldn't leave me the ranch in Texas—I was too unreliable. But he gave the ships to his son who had wandered away and never come home."

Emma listened in silence, her eyes on Adam's face. He had not told her his father was dead, and now she knew the pain he must live with for his failure to reconcile.

"I didn't need your money," Adam went on. "I thought—" He broke off, sighing. Damn, he hated trying to explain things! But Emma needed to know it all, and she had never failed to listen. Somehow she made the talking easier. "I thought I had everything. The ranch, the plantation by the ocean . . . I figured that would fill up what I was missing in my life. The empty feeling that I pushed away and tried to ignore. But it didn't go away . . . until you came along. At first I just thought I wanted you, just a man wanting a woman. But then I had to face it, Emma. I don't want to live without you in my life. Will you come back to the ranch with me? Will you be my wife?"

Emma looked up into the clear blue eyes above her. "But Adam, what about Clarissa? You already have a wife." Emma lowered her gaze to the squares of yellow light from the French door. "That first day on the pier when you tore up Clarissa's letter—I read it. Half of it blew across my path, and I could not resist. She signed it, 'your wife.' "

Adam shook his head, a slow grin forming at the corners of his mouth. "You read half the letter, Emma. *Half.* The whole message read, 'Your wife-to-be.' I was engaged to Clarissa for a long time. She was the woman my father chose for me. But I've never been one to do the thing I was supposed to do. I tore up the letter, remember? And I wrote back to her the day after you found the locket. I don't even know why I kept it—a tie to home, I guess. It's over, Emma. It had been for a long time."

"I've never been one to do the thing I was supposed to do, either," Emma whispered. "But I know one thing I must do—and that is to spend my life with you."

Adam took her into his arms and kissed her open lips. It was a lingering kiss, one that erased the bewildered ache in her heart and sealed the vow in his. Then he took her left hand in his and gently slipped the brass ring onto her finger.

"Care to dance, Mrs. King?" He drew her even closer than she had thought he could. "I'm not much of a high-toned dancer, to tell you the truth. But it sounds like our song in there."

Emma barely heard the strains of the *Blue Danube Waltz* as Adam led her back into the ballroom and whirled her around the room. The other couples drifted into corners to watch the lovers. Emma threw back her head in joy as she swayed close against Adam. Her curls tumbled to her waist, and her skirts billowed around her ankles. But all she knew was Adam's chest against her cheek, his hand burning at her waist, his body and hers moving as one.

> *I may pray different from other men*
> *But I've had my say, and now, Amen.*
>
> —"The Cowman's Prayer"

> *Ask me no more: thy fate and mine are sealed;*
> *I strove against the stream and all in vain;*
> *Let the great river take me to the main.*
> *No more, dear love, for at a touch I yield;*
> *Ask me no more.*
>
> —Alfred, Lord Tennyson
> "The Princess"

# The End?

The end of a book is never really *the end* for a person who reads. He or she can always open another. And another.

Every page holds possibilities.

But millions of kids don't see them. Don't know they're there. Millions of kids can't read, or won't.

That's why there's RIF. Reading is Fundamental (RIF) is a national nonprofit program that works with thousands of community organizations to help young people discover the fun—and the importance—of reading.

RIF motivates kids so that they *want* to read. And RIF works directly with parents to help them encourage their children's reading. RIF gets books to children and children into books, so they grow up reading and become adults who can read. Adults like you.

For more information on how to start a RIF program in your neighborhood, or help your own child grow up reading, write to:

**RIF**
Dept. BK-1
Box 23444
Washington, D.C.
20026

**Founded in 1966, RIF is a national non-profit organization with local projects run by volunteers in every state of the union.**

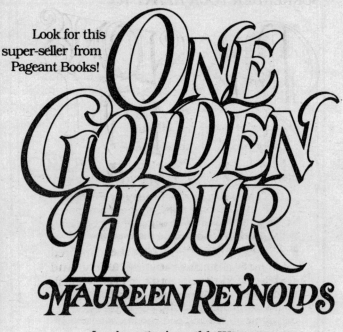